MEMORIES FROM THE JUNGLE

Memories from the Jungle

Mémoires de la Jungle

TRISTAN GARCIA

Translated by CHRISTOPHER BEACH

UNIVERSITY OF NEBRASKA PRESS

LINCOLN

The University of Nebraska Press is part of a land-grant
institution with campuses and programs on the past, present,
and future homelands of the Pawnee, Ponca, Otoe-Missouria,
Omaha, Dakota, Lakota, Kaw, Cheyenne, and Arapaho Peoples,
as well as those of the relocated Ho-Chunk, Sac and Fox, and
Iowa Peoples.

Library of Congress Cataloging-in-Publication Data

Names: Garcia, Tristan, 1981–author | Beach, Christopher,
1959–translator
Title: Memories from the jungle = Mémoires de la jungle / Tristan Garcia;
translated by Christopher Beach.
Other titles: Mémoires de la jungle. English | Mémoires de la jungle
Description: Lincoln: University of Nebraska Press, 2025. |
Includes translation or is translation
Identifiers: LCCN 2024048201
ISBN 9781496238535 paperback
ISBN 9781496242884 epub
ISBN 9781496242891 pdf
Subjects: LCGFT: Animal fiction | Novels
Classification: LCC PQ2707.A75 M4613 2025 | DDC 843/.92—dc23/
eng/20241210
LC record available at https://lccn.loc.gov/2024048201

Designed and set in Scala OT by Lacey Losh.

All the characters in this narrative were lovingly created
with and for Agnès Gayraud. I owe her this book,
and this book owes everything to her.

One can take the ape out of the jungle,
but not the jungle out of the ape.

FRANS DE WAAL, *OUR INNER APE*

Translator's Note

What would the language of a superintelligent chimpanzee who was raised in a human household and educated as a human child sound like? Tristan Garcia's novel *Memories from the Jungle*, which is narrated by a chimpanzee named Doogie, sets out to provide a speculative answer. In doing so, it presents unusual challenges for the translator. The task of translating one language into another is always a challenge, but the difficulty is compounded in the case of this novel by the fact that the language used by Doogie is not that of a human speaker. We find a clue to the nature of Doogie's language in the opening pages of the book, when an as-yet-unnamed human speaker characterizes it as "an idiomatic mix of his rudimentary language, enlivened by the pretentious forms that he so often attempted and sometimes combined with a makeshift pidgin . . . the language of an entirely other species."

While this characterization is in large part accurate as a general description of Doogie's speech, it is not particularly helpful to the translator, who must attempt to capture the idiosyncratic qualities of Doogie's use of the French language. These idiosyncrasies include unmotivated shifts in verb tenses (from present to past or past to present); shifts from first-person narration to second or third person (sometimes within the same sentence); the reversal of parts of speech (for example, using a noun in place of an adjective); departures from normative grammar; and a generally wonky syntax. Rendering these same "errors" in English, or finding their equivalents, requires a balancing act in which the language retains its strangeness while at the same time remaining legible to readers. Word order and syntax can be stretched only so far before they take a sentence over the border into nonsense. The language of Doogie's interior monologue cannot become so arcane or unintelligible that the reader is no longer able to follow his story or identify with him as a protagonist.

Garcia has described *Memories from the Jungle* as a novel of de-education ("*un roman de déformation*"). Doogie has been raised within a human environment and educated as a human child. By the time he reaches adulthood,

Doogie has acquired an extensive vocabulary and a basic grasp of the rules of grammar; he can express his thoughts to some degree by signing with his hands, but he communicates more effectively by using a tactile computer screen. Forced to make a long and arduous journey across the African continent, Doogie becomes increasingly alienated from his human education, and his language correspondingly devolves. In the final pages of his narration, he speaks to us in a series of short and barely coherent phrases: although he continues to use words that are recognizably French, his language is no longer contained within coherent semantic and syntactic structures.

Doogie's language also reflects the ways in which he, as a chimpanzee, sees the world differently from humans. Remarkably sensitive to his physical environment, Doogie describes objects in highly evocative and poetic ways, but he has difficulty understanding concepts such as death, God, and time: he speaks, for example, about hours "falling from the watch" and days "falling from the calendar." Garcia's simian creation uses assonance, homonyms, and rhythmic play to convey his complex emotions, communicating to us a feeling for how an ape might sense the world differently, what he might notice and appreciate, and what might fill him with love, jealousy, shame, anger, confusion, or fear. While there are moments in the novel when the wordplay of Doogie's speech resists translation into English, it is my hope that readers will be able to discern in Doogie's articulate disarray the subtlety of the mind that created him.

MEMORIES FROM THE JUNGLE

In a not-too-distant future, the African continent of planet Earth has been left in an experimentally fallow state for at least a century after having been devastated by wars, famines, and a wave of chemical pollution, and exhausted by its colonization by the human species, which now lives almost entirely in cities on other continents or inside vast and fully equipped orbital stations.

At an immense zoo near Lake Victoria, scientists and students are invited to observe the fauna that is still preserved there, whether in freedom or in the laboratory, with a particular focus on the great apes, marine mammals, dolphins, parrots, and ants.

All around the zoo, as far as the eye can see, the jungle of earlier times has reclaimed its rights, and now it is only the jungle's memory that preserves the traces of what is happening there . . .

It is here in Africa, on the western shores of the Gulf of Guinea, in the equatorial forest at the foot of Mount Cameroon, that this strange adventure begins. We will follow it to the extreme eastern point of the former Ethiopia.

THE CHARACTERS:

DOOGIE: educated male chimpanzee; the narrator (*Pan troglodytes troglodytes*)

JANET EVANS: female ethologue at the Victoria Zoo (*Homo sapiens sapiens*)

DONALD EVANS: brother of Janet (*Homo sapiens sapiens*)

GARDNER EVANS: father of Janet and Donald; in charge of the Victoria Zoo (*Homo sapiens sapiens*)

DIANE EVANS: mother of Janet and Donald; ethologue at the Victoria Zoo (*Homo sapiens sapiens*)

MR. PAYNE: male ethologue specializing in dolphins at Pointe du Bec (*Homo sapiens sapiens*)

MR. MCVEY: male ethologue specializing in whales at Pointe du Bec (*Homo sapiens sapiens*)

JACK: educated male chimpanzee (*Pan troglodytes troglodytes*)

ELLIOTT: educated male chimpanzee in captivity (*Pan troglodytes troglodytes*)

EMMA: educated female chimpanzee in captivity (*Pan troglodytes troglodytes*)

PONGO: educated male orangutan (*Pongo pygmaeus*)

JOHN: male common short-nosed dolphin (*Delphinus delphis capensis*)

LILLY: female common short-nosed dolphin (*Delphinus delphis capensis*)

CARUSO: male gray whale (*Eschrichtius robustus*)

BOB BEAMON: male gray whale (*Eschrichtius robustus*)

CAPTAIN ZIPPER: female gray whale (*Eschrichtius robustus*)

FENG PO-PO: female gray whale; daughter of Beamon and Zipper (*Eschrichtius robustus*)

MICHAEL: male student at the Zoo; Janet's fiancé (*Homo sapiens sapiens*)

MR. PETER: resident ethologue and linguist; Michael's father (*Homo sapiens sapiens*)

SINDHU: female student at the Zoo (*Homo sapiens sapiens*)

NAOKI: male student at the Zoo (*Homo sapiens sapiens*)

MEHDI: male student at the Zoo (*Homo sapiens sapiens*)

LI YANG: male student at the Zoo (*Homo sapiens sapiens*)

FAITHFUL: male mongrel dog (*Canis lupus familiaris*)

THOUSAND COLORS: male gray parrot from Gabon (*Psittacus erithacus*)

THE GARDENER OF THE ZOO (*Homo sapiens sapiens*)

AN ANT (*Petalomyrmex phylax*)

ANTS (*Tetraponera*)

KING: male lion (*Panthera leo*)

MACACAS: multiple Barbary macaques (*Macacae sylvani*)

SHE-SHEE: female bonobo (*Pan paniscus*)

BOBBY: male bonobo (*Pan paniscus*)

OLD BOB: old male bonobo (*Pan paniscus*)

BOBETTE: dominant female bonobo (*Pan paniscus*)

THE ADMINISTRATOR: male investor in the Zoo, from an
orbital station (*Homo sapiens sapiens*)

SILVERBACK: male gorilla in captivity (*Gorilla beringei graueri*)

DINAH: female chimpanzee educated by Diane Evans;
Doogie's mother (*Pan troglodytes troglodytes*)

LEONARD: male genetically modified chimpanzee; Doogie's
father (*Pan troglodytes troglodytes*)

THE ANIMAL: leader of the animal revolts (?)

A Human Being Speaks . . .

Sadly, it's my nature. No matter what happens, I still think about myself and others from the point of view of an ethologist.

That's why I think I can understand my behavior, even though it's why I also know the degree to which that understanding seldom affects my behavior and rarely changes it. But what this ape was for me, and what I was for him, I can't explain to myself. I was the last inheritor of a meandering movement through which we, as humans, placed ourselves in opposition to other animals, only to arrive at the paradoxical point where we realized why and how we nonetheless belonged to them. It was only very belatedly that it became permissible for us to understand ourselves as animals among other animals, and to understand the animality within us. At the twilight of our history, we discovered that we were also a species and that they were also individuals, even if they did not always become persons. Animals . . . We have detested them, and we have loved them; we have domesticated, tortured, and caressed them; we have given them Latin names; we have described and thoroughly explained their behavior, without any hope that they would ever show us what *we* are, and without any hope that they would one day forgive us. Too late, we grasped the differences that exist within a single species, the correct or incorrect way of approaching each one of them, the culture that a group of them could produce, and the singular genius of a few among them.

And at times we felt, too strongly, the desire to make them evolve, the desire to finally hear them speak to us. Because we are all alone, we big talkers of Creation.

Who knows why we wanted to make them into our children.

In part, it was because in modeling them in our image we wished to become the gods that we imagined they thought of as theirs. But it was also because we dreamed that, by understanding them, we would be able to rediscover to what degree and in what way we, like them, were animals.

We are something in between.

I suppose that in the past it was between God and animal, and today it is between animal and machine . . . I think that in his own eyes the human being is never anything other than something in between, and that he will always remain in that situation.

Inhabited as I was by the floating consciousness—which had now come to the surface—of our amphibious status of being plunged into the foul water of what we *are* while breathing the gamey air of what we *do*, what was it that motivated me to take care of this creature from a species other than my own, as if I had the opportunity to hoist him up toward me? And as if he had the same opportunity to pull me out from my mildewed humanity to show me what we humans, seen from the outside, really are.

Was it a debt contracted at the point in our evolution when we had to deny them, to oppose our nature to theirs? Will we, sooner or later, repay the debt that exists only in the accounts that *we* keep, since it certainly doesn't exist in accounts kept between animals? How would we even do this? By guiding them toward us? By going back toward *them*? By leaving them without us so that they can be themselves? By giving them rights that they will not take and to which they are indifferent? By assuming all obligations, ours as well as theirs? I don't know what animality will be for my children, or for the children to come. Will it be a vague memory from a museum, or will it once again be something alive?

I'm getting lost in all this.

The more I study and spend time with *the animal*, the less I think that I know what it is, where it came from, and where it is going.

These are nothing more than confused notes jotted down on paper, on the last page of my last notebook, before this little book goes back into the old wooden chest in the museum where I keep my unfinished work, no longer believing that it will ever interest my daughters or the children of my daughters. Because it's too late for that.

Now, like an image or a mirage, the animal is disappearing, and what he is, what he was, I don't think I know anymore. Everything is evaporating.

In my role as an ethologist, I have failed.

It seems to me that I will never again see my humanity from the exterior, through the eyes of another, a chimpanzee. That is finished.

I still think about it today, but I no longer reflect on it.

It is only his baroque chimpanzee language, so close to ours and yet so distant from it, a bit more or a bit less than human language, that regularly comes back to me. It was a primitive or, who knows, perhaps a futuristic language. It was conveyed through cries, through hand signs, and through the tactile screen of the computer he had at the time. It was jumbled sentences, with an idiomatic mix of his rudimentary language, enlivened by the pretentious turns of phrase that he so often attempted and sometimes combined with a makeshift pidgin. It was the unhoped-for fruit of fanatic learning. Because we took him for a genius, the poor thing. It was the language of an entirely other species, perhaps our last chance to hear strangeness in its complete form. That is what I believed at the time. We are much too familiar to ourselves. Look at how stiff, heavy, and conventional my own language is. Forgive me, and take all of this as an experiment that a short while ago gave meaning to the monochordal voice of our tired human existence, a voice that had nothing new to offer my blasé ears. Perhaps this experiment, *my* experiment, will in time also become yours. To perceive our words, almost identical but in a mouth that is so different from the one that constantly houses our ridiculous human chatter. I would so much like for his bric-a-brac dialect to resonate once again between the bulging folds of my civilized, polite, evolved, tired, and obsolete human brain.

And even if he is mute today, I can still hear and will always hear him grunt, laugh, and reason. If I could enter his little head one last time, oh, if only . . .

Doogie

*—The ape introduces himself.—After a long voyage in Earth's orbit,
he is returning to Earth.—He remembers his childhood
and his education at the Gardner family's zoo.—Brother,
mother, father, and sister.—A speech.*

I'm just a Doogie, I'm just a monkey. Poor Doogie, poor monkey. I'm so small, and everything is very big.

I'm a great ape, a chimpanzee, and not a little macaque, but Janet always calls me her monkey. And when Janet says—"Doogie, you're a good ape . . . Come, Doogie, come and cuddle, my little ape"—then I'm happy. Doogie is very smart.

Alas, when I see myself, Doogie, in the mirror, I say to myself: "You're an ape, you're a monkey. You're never a human, and you never will be. Be faithful to the human, Doogie." I make a face. I'm close to the mirror and I say, "Haouh!" What do I see when I see me? I see sadness in the mirror, I see joy on my eye. I have a big hand. Put your hand under your chin, Doogie. The hand is big, brown on one side and pink on the other. It is placed on the mirror, and I draw a smile without showing my teeth. How big your chin is, Doogie! How little your pushed-in nose is, and how black! How hairy your pelt is! Haouh! Haouh! You must not laugh at apes, Doogie. I make the menacing look, the stare, eyebrows high, ears forward, mouth open, nostrils flaring. You must not make fun of monkeys, Doogie. What do they know? What can they do? Being born and living in the Jungle! Eating fruits, eating leaves and ants, kissing, picking lice, fighting, hugging, being little, having children. But never knowing, never speaking, never building anything more than leaves, fruits, branches, nests, trees, and stones. Humans can know and speak.

You have big ears on either side of your skull, Doogie. The skull is the brain. "No, Doogie, the brain is *in* the skull." It was a joke, a joke, a joke! Oh, a monkey's brain is too small of a brain . . .

But Doogie's brain is more big than little. "Doogie, you're a genius!" Then I know, I smile. The stare, hair standing up, tongue stuck out, upper lip pulled in. Hin-hin. When Janet says, "Doogie, you're a genius like no one else, come on, Doogie, I love you very much," oh, Doogie is like a heaven! How small your eyes are, monkey. Humans don't know what you have behind your head, knock, knock, knock. But from behind my pupils, I can see you. I sniff and I close my shirt with the big fingers of my big hand. It has five gold buttons with a cross pressed into them. I know, I breathe, and I don't suffocate. I'm not handsome. I'm not very very handsome. When Janet says, "Doogie, you are a handsome and a very good monkey," I know that with her green eyes she doesn't see a human behind my big eyes. I'm only a Doogie. This isn't human hair on my skull, on the skull on my brain: this is animal hair, hair, hair.

I'm ready. There are still a few minutes that come out of the big watch Janet gave to Doogie—tick-tock, never lose it—still a few minutes on the ground and then it will be the beginning. Today and tomorrow I must be very handsome, comb my hairs, wash my hands and the glands on my neck, on my chest, under my arms, inside my bottom. "It's a very big adventure that awaits you, Doogie." I don't know. You must be very faithful to the human, the human must know, and everything, everything that is big belongs to him. Language belongs to the human, and the stars, the Earth, knowledge, power. Everything belongs to the human. I know it. I know it, but Doogie can't do it. Nothing belongs to the monkey except the Jungle. I walk around in the ironed white shirt, the black vest, the five gold buttons engraved with the cross, and the gray canvas trousers with two pleats. Are you handsome, Doogie? No, no, no! But I speak like a human, and if you loosen the waistline and zip up the zipper you are worthy. I have fewer hairs when I'm wearing more clothes. Sometimes happy, sometimes sad, that's my life. It's monkey.

Please excuse my speech. I say a lot of little words, too little for a lot of brain but too big in my skull. I hope to understand and learn. I hope to say things. I hope that one day everything that is big will be little in the words that come out of my mouth which I pull out with my big hand. You will look in Doogie's skull, and inside you will see everything that is big coming out of my mouth: yesterday, today, tomorrow, the world.

I jump onto the chair. I'm happy, everyone loves Doogie, and I'm so small in the mirror. Everything is big outside, and everything is big inside my head.

It's time for my speech. Clear the decks!

Ladies, gentlemen, young ladies: dear very dear respect.

As you can see, I'm not like you, but I almost behave like you. I'm a member of the species pan troglodytes troglodytes, here to serve you. My name is Doogie, and my nature is common chimpanzee, but I have a human culture. Hmm, hmm. You humans who live far from planet Earth, on one of the big stations in the beautiful middle of the bright stars, you will ask yourself: "Who is this very famous ape genius to whom it was taught to dress myself, to write, to read and to speak?" Far in the deep of the Jungle, excuse my speech, in the very deep of the very big forests of the planet Earth and of the continent, which you other humans have allowed to return to fallow land, I was born a chimpanzee, an ape and to serve you. But misery of sadness: woodcutters roam in the forests of the tropics between the banana trees, poachers. They walk in the forest, their beards long, with a lot of guns. They kill Doogies. One day they kill my father, dead. One day they kill my mother, dead. Doogie is sad, he is young. Doogie cries. He is only a Doogie, a poor monkey. Alone for one day, alone for two days. He has only himself to hold in his arms. He puts his fingers in his mouth, and his feet, like an animal. He tries to reassure the little monkey who you are. He screams, he moves his arms, and he falls down, very simply all alone. His heart slowly goes tick-tock, the cold is everywhere in his body, sleep has gone away. He is empty and it is over. He is too little to ever grow big.

Then Mr. Director Gardner, the very big director of the zoo of the Earth with a mustache, passed by close to me in the company of scientific men who were nice, and they said, "The woodcutters and the poachers are bad, and poor Doogie is a very little monkey," and they took me in. Mr. Gardner the director is a human man. He's a scientific man with a mustache who studies a lot every day and who thinks. He had a wife, Mrs. Diane, and he also had a daughter, Janet.

But Mrs. Diane gave birth to a very handsome very handsome little human baby by the name of Donald, Janet's brother. Mr. Gardner the director said, "We will have to give an education to Donald and Doogie, exactly the same, and it will be a human education." That is the experiment. I was like their baby. When Donald ate, Doogie ate. If Donald uses a spoon, Doogie uses a spoon. When Donald played, Doogie played with him, and Janet was always our friend. But when Donald said words that came out of his mouth, Doogie didn't say anything; he stayed mute. I'm only a monkey, I can't speak words that come out of my mouth, and Doogie was extremely sad. Mr. Gardner thought a lot, with the mustache, with science. He came into Donald and Doogie's big white room and he sat down next to the big bed on the checkered blanket. "It doesn't matter. It's not important, Doogie. You can say words with your hands. Look, your very big hand! And I have taught you how to take the words out of your poor mouth with your hands." When I speak to you, to you who are present here among us, I can only say "Haounh" with my mouth, and "Hiii Hiii" and "Hon," but there are so many words in Doogie's skull that can come down into my hands.

First, I learned to sort a thousand colored pieces of plastic for every word: the noun, the verb, and the adjective. Then, for Doogie's birthday, I found in the paper gift from Mr. Gardner the screen and the keyboard and thousands of thousands of symbols, and then grammar in the big book from Janet, and I pulled out the signs of words and of letters, the ones in the others, with hand movements, like those among you humans who only have silence and *shhh*.

Doogie was happy. Mr. Gardner, Mrs. Diane, and Janet too. "It's historical, Doogie, you're a genius," they said. "The experiment is a big success. It worked, and we must announce it." I like making the signs of speaking words so much, and I learned, always learning, always knowing. Doogie worked hard, very hard, always working hard, standing up, making pee and poo with toilet paper—excuse my speech lady gentleman—in the pot, playing with cubes, eating your soup, and standing up straight. That is education, and I got an education in order to serve you, lady gentleman.

Doogie is not just a chimpanzee, an ordinary chimp. He is smart, smarter than the others. Donald is not doing well. Donald is jealous, and he hits Doogie with the cubes. He sets traps. He says that Doogie peed on the rug. He says bad words, and he doesn't get good grades. But he is the human. Doogie is just an animal. Unfortunately, when he is five years that fell out of the calendar, Donald has a sickness. He's pale and he has red spots. Maybe Doogie gave him the sickness. We don't recognize this sickness.

Donald left. Way up there, he's in Heaven, higher than the stars I think. Mrs. Diane thinks that Doogie is responsible, and she is angry. Mr. Gardner the director of science defends Doogie, and Janet does too.

Much sad grief. Mrs. Diane doesn't put food in her mouth from her plate anymore, and she stays in bed with red eyes. She refuses to see Doogie. He is responsible, a bad monkey, and in the end it will be Heaven for her also.

So I grew up at the Zoo, with poor Mr. Gardner and his mustache pale with grief, and my friend Janet. When twenty years had fallen from the calendar, Mr. Gardner was sad and stiff. He had old age on his skull, and Janet sent Doogie here for an international tour in the stars, to all the orbital stations, on the Moon and in the suspended human cities, as well as with you, this evening, lady gentleman, in order to demonstrate the education by Mr. Gardner Evans that was an achieved success of the science of the Zoo in the vast Jungle of the Earth, on your former planet gone fallow, in order to raise money from the very rich supporters of the project, if you please.

Lady, gentleman, before you is the educated ape, marvel of marvels. I am a chimpanzee, but always faithful to the human. Nature makes, and man remakes, as Mr. Gardner Evans says, and I thank you for your attention with the expression of the salutations of my respect, my very dear respect, in wishing pleasure and happiness to the beautiful adventure and perhaps going to Heaven at the end. Give money as it pleases you to want to at the exit of the entrance, for the project and for the idea, and then you will see.

Lady and gentleman too, may my words offer a good entertainment. I am quite simply Mr. Doogie.

Earth

—After the speech, sadness.—The ape, accompanied by Michael, prepares to land.—An accident occurs.—He remembers the first time he saw Janet, his teacher.

How many times a hundred times I had given speeches in front of dressed-up humans sitting in velvet armchairs who applauded me. Mr. Doogie! All the humans lived in the air in very big orbital stations like the main greenhouse at the Zoo, in colonies on the Moon, after they diminished their what is called population. I saw the New York station, the Delhi station, and Tokyo, London, and Paris. Each time, always Doogie. In the evening, alone, when the big shiny receptions were over—cakes with cream eaten, champagne with bubbles drunk—Doogie gets undressed without help, and he turns off the bedside lamp like Janet taught him, saying "Good night" with his hand. "No, Doogie, you must not say 'houn houn' with your mouth in the dark to express yourself." Do I do that? Be faithful to the human, Doogie. Not without melancholy, I gaze at the black universe through the big shimmering round window. Janet stayed down at the Zoo on the old Earth. She's waiting for me. When I go back with Michael, Sindhu, and Naoki, with the money in the locked safe in my hands, smiling, I will descend from the ship on the steel bridge, the very big metal ship in the shape of a turtle that is taking me back to the Zoo. I will fall right into her arms, and she will say: "Oh, Doogie, what a good monkey you are. I've missed you so much, little ape." She has long hands, skin the color of an apricot when it's ripe, and a very thin very round ring which turns and shines. She caresses Doogie's neck while she speaks, she scratches his hair, and she looks for lice while laughing, but there are none thanks to the shampoo. She holds him in her arms like when I was afraid, and then I cry.

Soon, the Charles Bigleux will land. Through the blue porthole I see the water and the ocean, the wind that makes the waves zigzag, the light that draws crosses, and the planet Earth. How big, fast, and human is the technological Charles Bigleux that flies from the stars to the planet of Nature! On the inside of my brain, I can still see the large shape of the Charles Bigleux like a turtle, the ship that is huge like a thousand times Doogie lying on the ground, covered with a green reinforced shell to protect it when there was a war. "It's a military vessel, Doogie." The war of violence is over, and now humans are in the stars. Naoki, who is driving, is a tall thin boy from the Zoo, a yellow student of Mr. Gardner who is piloting the Charles Bigleux with his helmet and the control levers. Sindhu is a nurse who takes care of Doogie, but Doogie doesn't need anything. She has short hands without fingernails, and a bracelet, and she doesn't have breasts. Janet has breasts. No girl is beautiful like she is.

Michael is Janet's fiancé. Oh, no! Doogie doesn't really like Michael. He is a handsome, a very very handsome Mickey. He's nice. He's the favorite student of my father, Mr. Gardner. Doogie would like to be able to break his teeth with a stone, and then he wouldn't smile brilliant white anymore. We need to cut off his sex with the scissors, snip. "Doogie, please! Be nice to him! Stop that, you're a bad monkey." Then Doogie shows his teeth, he pulls up his underpants, and he gives his hand to Michael who strokes my skull. Doogie hates the top of his skull. Janet needs to give me the neck cuddle to look for lice that aren't there thanks to the shampoo. Michael doesn't do that. "What's the point of looking for lice if the ape is clean?" he says. Michael doesn't understand. But Doogie is so little. You would have to cut off half of an ape and put it on my skull to be tall like white Michael with blue eyes.

Michael is calling me. "Doogie, come here! We'll be landing soon; we need to get ready. Buckle your seat belt. Come up to the cockpit and buckle your seat belt." Buckle your mouth, buckle your mouth. Doogie doesn't want to buckle. I run toward the double-you-see at the end of the neon corridor. Come and get me, ha-ha. I pout, staring, eyebrows raised, nostrils puffed out, head lifted, eyelids blinking. Oh, my shirt is stained with a stain! Two stains. Three. I put my finger on the oil stain, yuck, and I know that I hear Michael who is looking for me with patience in the bedrooms, while Naoki and Sindhu fly the Charles Bigleux, under the noise of the motor that is screaming, toward the fat planet of Africa.

Doogie, lift your head. The honey liquid from the motors is falling down, dripping from above me, going drip-drip. "What's . . . ? It's the . . . compartment," says Michael very loudly with his mouth at the other end of the corridor from the double-you-see. And then, *boom*, everything explodes around Doogie, poor ape. You didn't know understand anything, and already the black of skull closes your too small eyes.

Memories

When I opened my eyes, a big little chestnut-redhead girl with pigtails caught me in her arms. I don't remember the words of that moment, but I'm sure I've remembered it at least once a day ever since.

"Oh, he's so cute! He's a monkey!"

"No, Janet, he's what we call an 'ape.' He's a great ape, an Old-World ape. The little apes, monkeys, are from the New World, like Ouistiti and Atele in the cages at the Zoo. Small monkeys have tails, but big monkeys—apes—don't have them."

"But he's so little. Daddy, look . . . he's so little . . . He's a monkey."

Her legs are covered by a warm cover like a coat of fur with red and blue checks. She's wearing a perfectly white shirt. She let go of her big black stuffed panda animal for me to have, and she strokes my skull, but I'm very scared. I don't know her; I don't know that she's Janet. For a few hours, I haven't had a father or a mother. Trembling, I see the big bed made from the wood of the trunks of pine trees from the forest, placed on the completely round brown rug that covers the floor that squeaks under the feet in the leather shoes of Mr. Gardner the mustache. It's dark; outside it's dark.

"He's not a toy, sweetheart. He's a little ape, a poor little pan troglodytes troglodytes two times. I'll take him to the lab tomorrow with the guys. We'll take care of him just like we take care of Jack, Elliott, and the others. It's too late to go down the hill this evening. We're exhausted from the hunt."

"Oh daddy! I'm begging you!" Janet almost cried while getting up slowly onto her two knees, her hands together. She spoke, whispering in a low voice.

"He's so scared. He's my monkey, daddy! Can I keep him? I want to take care of him! Can I? Oh, he needs me so much!"

The father Mr. Gardner didn't turn on the light, standing in the frame of the door made from the trunk of an oak. He looked at the stars far behind the venetian blinds of the window divided into four squares, just above the birch desk in the shadow, so carefully placed there by Janet the little girl, on which there is a bouquet of white flowers picked in the fields of the hill. He blew his nose and said:

"All right, sweetheart, just for tonight."

She held me so tightly in her arms under the shirt with the collar decorated with drawn violet flowers. I trembled, and she stroked my neck with the skin of her hand that smelled like fruit. She looked for lice as if in a fur coat. "You have to wash. You have to be clean, clean, clean like a stuffed animal, monkey," she said into my little pink ear. "Shh, monkey! You're a nice ape, a good very good ape. You're *my* ape. I want you to be happy in my arms."

I blinked my big black eyes under the eyebrows of my forehead. She murmured: "You have to feel good, like a baby. I'm going to get you one of his diapers, and that way you won't pee in the bed." She got up onto her tiptoes to open the big black oak door next to the library of picture books.

That was when he woke up and he yelled, and I saw him.

Crash

*—The ape wakes up.—The ship has crashed
on a deserted coast of the African continent.*

From the Jungle

When I opened my eyes, my white shirt was all stained. I thought: "Oh no, no, no, Janet is very angry." "Doogie, you don't know how to take care of yourself." I put my big hand on my skull, and I said, "Ouch, ouch, ouch," because Doogie's neck, stomach, very big feet and two knees all hurt.

"Doogie," I said to yourself, "you're completely trapped inside this little cabin." The shiny metal wall is sliced open as if by the can-opener for preserves. A girder the color of Janet's eyes when it is sunny has fallen through the ceiling. It fell two fingers away from Doogie, from my legs. Oh, how lucky very lucky that Doogie has such short legs! I have so much fear. Haoooooounh! I pound myself against the dented pharmacy box with the green cross made of sheet metal and silver which heals me. I cry out once, twice: "Michael!" But the word "Michael" doesn't come out of Doogie's wounded mouth. My tooth is in my lip, and my brain never comes out all alone through my tongue. You have to lift up your two buttocks. If you catch the girder above your head, after that you can climb up to the door that is cut in two. But my hand to the left of the right is caught under the white enamel water reservoir that is covered with dust and that has collapsed to the right of the left of Doogie. Oooouuh, Doogie hurts very badly all the way to his brain! He lifts his other hand, and he rolls up the sleeve of his shirt covered with stains of reddish oil, like you're supposed to, but now it's too short, hin hin hin. Then Doogie moves all of his fingers one after the other in the void. It's not worth the effort. Doogie alone, Doogie all alone, Doogie abandoned will go to the Heaven that doesn't exist.

Janet.

On Janet's chest, when it's hot, when the sun is very high, not as high as the stars of the night but higher than the Moon or the orbital stations, there are one, two, three, a thousand freckles on Janet's skin. She puts a clean handkerchief with red checks on her hair, she spreads cream on her skin, and she says: "Not for you, Doogie. You're too hairy." Doogie tried to remove his hairs. "Doogie, what are you doing, you stupid little ape? My shaving cream, my wax, and my razor! You are punished, you bad monkey! Oh, my poor, poor Doogie, I love you with all your hair. Come and cuddle."

Be smart, monkey! How many tests, how many experiments Doogie has passed! Always the best grade, the best Doogie. And afterward, Doogie, you always earned a cuddle.

I held the girder with my foot, my big toe placed on the opposite side from the other toes. The iron is so cold under the sole of Doogie's foot. Hin hin. "Doogie, I'm not happy with you," Janet says when she frowns, and when it's cold out or when it's cold in Janet's heart there aren't any zero freckles on her white skin. "I'm very angry. Don't use your feet when you have hands! If you keep doing that, we'll have to cut off your feet, you understand. Eat with your hands; your feet are for walking." And Doogie lowers his head. Not with my feet.

I look to my left, and I look to the right of my left. Janet isn't there. I place my second foot and I grunt. Hmmm, Doogie. Janet said . . . what did she say? "Oh, it's nothing, monkey. It's just that if I'm not there, maybe I'm transparent, maybe I'm in the air, just like that! No one can see me, and you certainly can't, but I can see *you*, my clever little one. If you do something naughty because I'm not there, if you use your feet, I just turn my ring—Doogie, look at my ring—and I turn into the invisible woman." Haounh. I closed my mouth, I let my hair fall back down, and I flattened myself down like a toad to apologize. "Oh, my poor little ape. I don't want to hurt you. Come and kiss my hand." Then, Doogie is a Heaven. Later, Janet laughed. "Doogie, I need to explain good behavior to you. When I'm not there and I can still see you, it's because there's a camera. Good behavior is a camera; everyone knows that."

Camera here, camera there. Doogie makes sure there isn't one in the toilet. But there's always one. The good behavior camera never goes away. He apologizes to Janet in his brain, and then I grab the big bar above me with my two feet, I plummet, the plaster crumbles under my buttocks, and I'm suspended with my head hanging down. Houh! Houh! Doogie isn't *trying* to act like a monkey. I pull myself up with my hands because the feet of an ape are not used to this. It hurts them to hold on too tightly. They're made for walking.

Hanging from one arm, then hanging from the other arm, I was able to touch the door. Knock knock knock. "You have to knock, Doogie." I push, and everything broke. Doogie, you ache all over. I put my big hand on my neck, and when I see my hand there's a drop of blood.

Oh, oh, oh, Doogie doesn't like blood! He's afraid, and he's crawling. It's hard for him to breathe in the completely dark corridor of the big Charles Bigleux ship. And what about Michael? Where's Michael? And where's Sindhu? Where's Naoki?

Doogie cowers, and he shows his teeth. That's mean. He's not afraid, but he's so little, and where is everyone?

Crack! A long and very large yellow tube comes loose. It hits him in the back, Doogie startles, on all fours, I stand up and I slide on the skin of my butt, and the long very long corridor without any light falls slowly while creaking. I roll like on the slide in the park on the hill at the Zoo, from one end to the other. I hurt myself on a multitude of little triangles of glass planted in a padded armchair for landing which is torn up and covered with moss. Doogie puts his foot down and he startles. His two buttocks have been pricked like by the cactus at the Zoo in the pit with the big and small lizards. Now his feet are warm, but he's still groping with the ends of his hands in the soft warm sand. It feels so good. Mmm, Doogie loves the sand of beaches and in boxes for playing. It's like a mommy. From under the black wall with severed wires hanging down, I can see light. Contorted, Doogie crawls and he cries "Hiouh!" because the glass is hurting my back, it's pricking like a fork and the vest is ripped once, twice. But when Doogie emerges, the sun is so big, round, yellow and white that I can't see a thing.

I put a finger over each eye against my nose, like when the ape playing blind-man's-buff with Janet hides his head under the leaf of a banana tree. And when I looked, blinking my eyelids, I saw the thousand-colors bird in a sky without any clouds. The big rays of the sun were like the wheel of a bicycle that has fallen down. It rolls, rolls, rolls over the desert and then over the forest that is thick green and that rustles, and gray smoke like a cigarette in Mr. Gardner's ashtray was rising from the sliced-in-two Charles Bigleux, the airship and spaceship in the shape of a turtle, smashed and broken like Donald's toy on the floor. Ten of Doogie's running steps away, there's a fire that is burning black smoke.

Michael is screaming.

Michael

—*The ape saves Michael from the flames.*—*The man is doing badly.*—*The ape finds a map.*—*Summing up the situation.*—*Nostalgia, alone at the water's edge.*

From the Jungle

I ran toward him on two legs, crying, "Distress, distress, fear, danger, serves you right, disaster, disaster." I gave him a hand because he was Michael, and Michael has authority over Doogie, as Janet and Mr. Gardner himself have said. I dragged the human along the beach of the crash.

Michael slides his pink tongue over his two lips that are swelling. He tried to make one or two words fall out.

"Doogie, great ape . . ."

But when the word falls out the sound is already broken, and Doogie can't understand anything. I have excitement in my hands so that I can pull him, then his shoulders, his shirt in tatters, and he cries out. He's suffering, suffering. I have to take care of him.

"Doogie," he says. "You must not go . . . to the Zoo. We shouldn't go to the Zoo, it's . . ."

Sighing, I put my big hand on his forehead, smack, like a slap but not mean. Doogie, be faithful to the human. But the blood from inside him was falling onto the ground. If this continues, Michael will be empty like a flask.

"You must not go to the Zoo. You don't know what . . ."

Not knowing and not understanding. Bad chimp. Oh, close your mouth and shut up, and I'll take care of your head. I put my big hand on his dry mouth. Speaking tires out the speaker, too much fatigue; any more fatigue and it will be Heaven if it still exists. Michael, you're going to sleep.

"Listen to me, Doogie. Leave me here. I beg you. Don't worry about me. There's . . ."

He lifted his head, pushing his chin in the direction of Doogie who is squatting down and stroking his cheek.

"Go, be careful and watch out for . . . them . . . for them . . ."

He repeated it, while I was looking behind me at the big trees decorated with tufts and plumes, the birds circling in the great silence, and the smoke.

"For them . . . for . . ."

And he went to sleep.

Not go to the Zoo?! Nonsense, nonsense! Michael doesn't want Doogie to get Janet back, that's what it is! Bad Michael! But . . . what if Doogie abandons Michael, if Doogie walks and calmly enters the Zoo. Janet says: "Doogie, monkey, I've missed you so much." She caresses Doogie and it's Heaven. But then what if Janet frowns and asks: "Where is Michael, Doogie?" Oh, no . . . Haounhn! Janet can see you. "Doogie, what's going on? You must be faithful to the human." I must find the Zoo, and I must take Michael and the others.

I looked all around me. Fire, ashes, smoke, metal, and the Charles Bigleux cut in two. There's neither Naoki nor Sindhu nor anyone. Michael is sleeping in a really strange way. Doogie pulled up the bottoms of his pants and he spit into the palms of his two hands before hitting the little fire with the dusty blanket and picking up the armchairs with armrests, the girders, and the doors, like in a game of pick-up-sticks.

And then I pushed Michael far away from there, pulling, my cheeks sucked in, han han, on the sand, with the sun going down. The forest made noises and the fire is out, slowly, *fizz*. I wait for help while counting the round pebbles: one, two, three, five, ten.

I wait for one day, and Michael sleeps. I eat the provisions, I hold Michael's neck and I put water on his lips in his mouth, and his stomach says *glup-glup*. I put clothes on Michael that have been soaked in the basin under the broken pipe, and he says words that don't come from his brain. A sick sickness.

I wait for two hours. I'm hungry.

I wait for three hours.

I wait for five, but I don't wait for ten.

Where are the rescues? Doogie's tired. I look fumble around in Michael's leather bag and I found it. Into my hand, squeezing tightly, I took a fistful of drawn and written papers, and I put them on the sand of the ground.

I turned over a postcard of the Zoo and turned it back again. It's a picture of the cages in summer under the sun, repainted white when Mrs. Diane wanted the Zoo to be beautiful. The counter at the entrance was decorated, and King the lion was watching from behind the bars at the far end of the huts at the entrance. On the other side of the postcard, I could make out words that had fallen from Michael's hand. I sniffed the blue ink and, groaning, I stroked the word that I recognized like a face that was always the same: *Janet*. Sadly, I don't have reading, even if I know the word for the name "Janet." I couldn't understand, poor Doogie, poor monkey. The words on the paper couldn't climb up to the eyes of the chimp with the too small brain.

I took out a rumpled map that was like a drawing of a photo taken from above, from the Charles Bigleux vessel, folded four times four into sixteen torn parts. I unfolded it with a lot of the care that maps need. Be smart, Doogie: it's a map like the one on Janet's big desk in spring when the sun is coming through the venetian blinds. "Pay attention, Doogie: I'm going to teach you about the map."

You have to work at it with a lot of concentration. I didn't smell bad, because I had washed Doogie with the soap from the broken pharmacy box that fell out of the Charles Bigleux. Good vanilla soap. Janet likes it when the ape doesn't smell like an ape: "that's civilization, Doogie." Smells are not always civilization, but vanilla sometimes is.

At ten steps away from Doogie, a big pool of clear water is in the shade of the green trees. I wash in the morning, the water from the pool in Doogie's palms on his face with the vanilla. "What a good ape you are, my boy." I pull on the vest that's over the shirt with holes in it. A hole is not civilization, but sometimes rolling up your sleeves is, yes, for working. Get to work, Doogie! You look at Janet's watch: eight hours have fallen from the top of the dial of the show-me watch. I smell the air around me. My chin that smells of vanilla is placed in my big hand that scratches it, and with my finger I follow the contour of the form of the big continent drawn on the card of the map of the planet. It's the Earth. It's the continent, and the Zoo is in the center. In the middle of the middle, a red circle traced in faded magic marker indicates the Zoo of Mr. Gardner Evans, Janet's father. I study it. Janet taught Doogie the scale of things, the correlation between the map and the ground. If I make two bars with two fingers at the scale of a thousand kilometers, Doogie, remember the evening walk from the entrance gate of the Zoo to the Evans' house on the hill. Then the Zoo, Doogie, in the middle of the middle of the continent, is four times a thousand times the length of the evening walk to the left of the great ocean to the right which is blue, and four times a thousand times the length of the evening walk to the right of the great ocean which is to the left. And it's six times to the top and five times to the bottom. And Doogie and Michael are on the Earth, somewhere on the map next to the Zoo in the forest of the Jungle. But where?

Figure it out, Doogie.

I look at Michael. He's carrying a nightmare everywhere on his skin which is sweating, and he's not very very handsome. Hmm, it's a problem. Too sick and you end up in the Earth, the body in Heaven and the brain also. There will be no more words. Hmmm.

I must take Michael to the Zoo now, Doogie. Be faithful to the human. I walked beyond the beach onto a rock, and the infinite is the ocean. It's just shit. I watched. Nothing.

Above the water, under the sad palm leaves like endives cooked in Mrs. Diane's oven, Doogie lets his big and very ugly feet fall into the void void void. Bad feet! He sniffles while looking for the handkerchief, and in front of him, on the white colorless smoke of the water, is a big gray rock like the back of whales next to a big island that is twice the size of Doogie lying down. The earth is holding up a very old mossy tree which is the color of the frost on the four Christmas windows when Janet and Mr. Gardner celebrate the father of Christmas. We don't know if he exists. The needles of the tree indicate the direction of the wind, which is turning, flick-flick, and birds with big beaks are perching under the branches and singing over the water. Sing, sing, sing . . . The music of the birds in the air, falling onto the water. Doogie closes the doors of the eyes of his brain, and in the black very dark room, in the winters at the Zoo of his skull, he keeps memories of Christmas, of when it was Christmas with the family.

Christmas

—Memories of happy times.—Christmas at the zoo.—Time passing.—Trips to Pointe du Bec.—Whales and dolphins from former times.

Memories

When Christmas finally fell from the calendar, the Zoo empties out and the students, the guards, and the employees go home to the colonies and the orbital stations to celebrate an old memory of humans. Those who don't have this memory, like Naoki, Sindhu, and Mehdi, stay at the Zoo.

So, at the Zoo and in the big house of Gardner and Diane Evans on the hill made of grass and gravel, you hear silence and the animal beasts who are making their sounds in slow motion. Even the Lion King is yawning. There are no visitors at the Zoo anymore, so they must sleep. The geese are sleeping, the seals are sleeping, and the giraffe is sleeping.

One Christmas, Doogie wakes up in his room in the form of a rectangle, in his very small bed protected by pine bars, in his pajamas. He scratches his underarms, he kicks the stuffed-animal koala and panda, and I climb over the edge of the bed to run and knock very quietly on Janet's big door. A peony flower is stuck into the iron keyhole.

The door groans, and I cringe as I enter the room, slipping on the white wool rug. Outside, the sun is falling up from the Earth with its head upside down. The light is flying around and chasing mosquitoes between the blinds on the windows. "Doogie!" Janet has woken up, her hair snarled in a crown like a twine or a stick, her hair dark red. She's wearing a perfectly white shirt with no stains, and she runs toward me barefoot on the floor. Her freckles are lit up. She's happy. It's Christmas! "We have to pack your bags, little ape!"

She took me in her arms and gave me a kiss on my neck.

"We're going to Pointe du Bec, monkey!"

I tickled her and she laughed, but we have to hurry. Donald screamed and ran into the room on all fours, viciously pinching Janet's calves, and I quickly jumped up onto the iron shelf, trembling, so that Donald wouldn't hurt Doogie. He was holding Mr. Gardner's big razor in his hand.

"Crr . . . ut your hair, br . . . astard!" he said. Donald stuttered. He had difficulty in his mouth with speaking, and before he had finished, Mr. Gardner, angrily, with white foam on his mustache and his two cheeks, wearing a shirt that was badly tucked into his pants, grabbed him by the shoulders, yelling:

"*Now* what are you doing?!"

Leaving for a trip is such an exciting feeling. I remember it well. Mrs. Diane, wearing hose and a scarf, was wise and calm and smiling. She helped the three best students of her and Mr. Gardner to close the bags of black leather suitcases, drop off the big locked trunks one by one in the hall at the foot of the big marble winding staircases, and then drive the little car with the fabric roof for when it rains and fill the open hold of the Charles Bigleux. But the sun is climbing the sky, and the animals are already awake: the big cats, the vivarium, and the birds in the main aviary. They feel the excitement that is rising with the sweat and the words all the way to the white cages at the foot of the hill, and soon there's an enormous cry, ever bigger, that continually floats on the air.

It's hot.

I have to play with Donald and help him, because he has troubles. Donald limps on his leg of course, and he speaks more slowly than I do. Donald is already six years on the calendar, and so is Doogie. During the day, Donald is in the school that he doesn't like on the hill, and Doogie is in the lab on the tile floor with Jack, Elliott, Emma, and Pong. Elliott and Emma from lab two are going to have a baby. They're already much bigger than Doogie, but they have less speech and less faithfulness to the human. Pong is the Kong, wise and wise and wise, a red-haired Pongo Pong Orangutan who will soon be old and who doesn't say anything anymore. Maybe he's the most intelligent of us since he has understood beyond words, or maybe he's the dumbest, ha-ha, because he hasn't understood anything underneath the words. We don't know. That's why there are experiments. Doogie always gets very very good grades. They say, "Doogie, you're the favorite," but it's jealousy. "Doogie," says Janet, "you're just sweet."

Doogie looks at Pong on his straw mattress behind the windowpane. Pong asks for a piece of wood, and Doogie obeys. That's just how things are.

Jack has a little more calendar than Doogie, and he's also a chimp. For a long time, Jack was the favorite ape of Mrs. Diane and Mr. Gardner. Jack knows how to speak several times ten times ten words, and he passes the experiments. He always finds the banana hidden under the crate, and he likes to throw and catch baseballs.

But Doogie is smarter than Jack. Jack isn't jealous, he's sad. Mrs. Diane says: "He only knows how to do a few tricks. He says the same words— banana, ball—and he can find them under the crate and throw them into your hand." Poor Jack: he's like a circus animal who doesn't astonish people anymore.

Well, everyone has his own circus. Now, Doogie is doing the circus act for humans with speech. And he knows it.

And I knew it.

At the last moment, in the hold of the Charles Bigleux, Mr. Gardner gets annoyed with his favorite student. He has the two aquariums of the dolphins John and Lilly made of smoky greenish glass transferred to the hold.

When the sun is at the top of the sky, it's time to leave. Janet is wearing the red dress, Mrs. Diane, in a pair of pirate pants, is reassuring John and Lilly, and two students are keeping Elliott and Jack busy with colored cubes and transparent sheets. You have to do up their seatbelts gently around their waists while calming them down. But since Doogie is good as gold, when the motors make the noise that moves and makes smoke, he has the right to slide under Janet's seat belt in the cockpit. It isn't hot anymore. It's a nice temperature inside, and a student helps Gardner with the takeoff, in the cockpit, with maps seen from above and with guidance from the satellite that is way up high—turn your head and you will see it as it blinks around the Earth.

The Charles Bigleux can cross the sky to the orbital stations that reflect the light of the Moon, or it can fly like an airplane to Pointe du Bec, very far to the right of the Zoo on the big relief map.

"This is where we're going, Doogie!"

Pointe du Bec is vacation. It's pretty there: the warm sand of the earth makes zigzags of dunes, and then it goes out into the salt water of the very blue very green ocean. A big house made of white tiles and rosewood palisades, it's the annex of the Zoo at Pointe du Bec, where Payne and McVey live, the two friends of Mr. Gardner Evans, specialists in the high science of whales. The vacation whales! When the bags have come out of the Charles Bigleux in the shape of a turtle under the exhaust that makes you cough, and are piled up on the terrace, halfway to the big dune below the house, Jack, Elliott, Emma and even Pong dragging his paws run toward the giant palm tree, and Doogie holds Janet's hand. He looks very carefully to see that there are no stains on his shirt, and he says, "hello Payne" and "hello McVey." They are very beard.

Mrs. Diane lies down, and the sun is low. Mr. Gardner on the terrace drinks a blue alcohol through a straw. The students go for swims in swim-suits, crying "Yippee!" in the many fingers of the waves that tickle the orange sand under the sun. Janet is always in her two-piece swimsuit, with the students who are laughing, but Doogie doesn't dare, in his pants, with his shirt and civilization, in the hot sand. He's afraid of the water.

"Doogie," says Mr. Gardner, leaning with Mr. Payne on the balustrade in green gardener shorts, "do you want to come with us to put John and Lilly in the ocean, out by the Cape?"

Doogie loves John and Lilly. John is smart, and Lilly too. He taps on the aquarium with the right rhythm, in the motorboat, before nightfall. Lilly approaches like a shadow on the side. With her round eye she looks at him, and she smiles. "Iiik, iiik." They play at who will be the last to stop.

Doogie says "Haounhh!"

Lilly says "Iiiik!"

Doogie answers, Lilly answers, Lilly answers, Doogie answers . . . "Are the two of you ever going to stop? That's enough horsing around. Come on, Doogie, stop playing the ape and come here."

The ocean is black. Doogie has black eyes, and sadness is there. The weather is calm, at last. Mr. Gardner opens the aquariums from the front, and John jumps into the sea, then Lilly.

Doogie plunges his big hand into the water, and he plays pink hoop with them. And then the whales arrived, and I opened my eyes wide under my eyebrows, with my mouth closed, shh.

The enormous humpback whale Bob Beamon was there. The water turned white, and Bob Beamon lifted his beak out of the water.

"Look, Doogie, he's fifteen meters long. Don't worry, he's nice, hold out your hand," said Mr. Payne in Bermuda shorts.

I held out my hand through the side railing of the stationary boat. Bobbie's underside was all black, and his head was covered with tubercules like potatoes, so I was startled.

"Those are hair follicles, Doogie. Don't be afraid. He wants to be your friend."

And then, suddenly, Bob Beamon swam away. I thought that Doogie had annoyed him, and I wanted to cry. "Bobbie, don't go away!" I said. He couldn't hear my hands. Bob blew all the air out of his lungs, and a cloud three times Doogie in the shape of a mushroom shot up into the evening sky.

"Take a look at that, my boy!"

The fin on Bobbie's back appeared at the surface of the water that was black like the oil that feeds cars. Bob Beamon rounded his back to dive, the smooth top side of Bobbie bent like a wet and pointy rock on the beach, and then his tail, like two of the spades in Mr. Gardner's card games, stood up and slapped, and he disappeared.

"Oh, Mr. Payne. Did you see that?!"

Another humpback whale arrived.

"Oh, I think we're going to be present for a joust," and he rubbed his hands together. Mr. Payne leaned against the rusted side of the boat, which was rolling this-way-that-way in the light of the Moon on which the humans live who have left the planet Earth fallow. Mr. Gardner was smoking a cigar under his mustache, and he placed his hand on my shoulder. "Look at how much intelligence there is in Nature," he murmured. Mr. Payne blinked his eyes while drinking from his plastic glass. "I think that's Caruso coming over."

Caruso was a black shadow on the surface of the water. He swam around the boat and Mr. Payne cut the motor so as not to bother him. It was getting chilly again.

Mr. Payne took out a big heavy machine with a flashing black and green screen, an old sonar, he said. He turned all the buttons and he said, "Look! The song has already been going for a few hours. Look through your ears!" Mr. Payne showed me a little graphic mountain and valley on the green line at the bottom of the control screen. "That's the length of the signal, one second." Then he gave Doogie a comfortable headset and Doogie heard the signal one time, two times, ten times, hearing the sound in the ears of his brain. He tapped his foot, and it's a sentence, two sentences, three sentences, five, and ten.

Bearded Mr. Payne, squatting down, smiled at me. "He wants to charm Zipper. Now Bob Beamon is going to reply. He's going to sing too, unless . . ." Other boy whales came up, ten of them at a time, and Bobbie Beamon jumped again! Jump and jump again, Bobbie! The water turned white, and his fins were like the wings of an airplane. He jumped out of the water, even farther, always farther as the night fell. Hooray, hip-hip hooray Bobbie!

Other boy whales stuck their heads out of the water, but all of them are less strong and less smart than Bobbie the best one. Bobbie wins again!

"What's going to happen now?" asked Mr. Gardner, who was standing, leaning over, and scratching his mustache.

"Ah," Mr. Payne smiles, "I think we should go back. This is not for little ones, for little men like you, Doogie." He stroked me nicely between my two eyes, which I closed. "Captain Zipper, the female, is going to arrive. Next year at Christmas, if the winds are favorable, you'll see a little whale calf swimming under this water." They both burst out laughing.

Then we went back.

Whale

—The memory of the whales.—The time of worries.—Poor Mr. Payne.—Where have you gone, Feng Po-Po?

Memories

Another Christmas, and a year had already fallen from the calendar. Doogie woke up in his room in the form of a big square, in his medium-sized bed which no longer has bars but has a comforter. He scratches his torso and runs to Janet's room. He knocks very quietly on Janet's big wooden door, which is half open. In the keyhole is a faded flower that hasn't been replaced.

"I don't have time, Doogie."

"Doogie!" Janet is sitting on her big unmade bed. She's wearing a white shirt that smells of her perfume for going away, and she is extremely very responsible. "We have things to do. Look at the sun in the sky." Doogie frowned. The window was open wide to let in a flow of already warm air, and it was almost clammy. It's Christmas! "Mother isn't here to explain everything we need to do. So you have to take care of yourself, little monkey! Go and pick your things up off the floor."

Doogie lowers his head. Poor Doogie, he does what he can. But what can an ape do? She took me in her arms, crying, "I'm sorry." She already had breasts. I snuggled, covered with hair like a fur coat, and she put her very long hand and the finger where the very thin ring was on my neck as if to scratch the lice that aren't there, prisoners in the bottle of thank you the shampoo.

"I'm sorry, little Doogie. I'm so hassled! Mother isn't here, and father is so worried. Poor Doogie; it's not your fault."

She put me down on the ground. The silence was big in the house, big on the hill, and Mr. Gardner was grumbling a lot at his students to carry the aquariums of John and Lilly, which were in danger of breaking, to the dirty runway of the Charles Bigleux. The new best student, Michael, took charge of loading the ship, feeding the animals, and meeting with the guards in blue caps who didn't have vacations. They had to wait for their salary, and the safe takes time to come from the banks on the big orbital station. The noise that was rising from the enormous cages of the Zoo made me deaf. "You have to put little wax balls in your ears, Doogie, instead of holding your big hands on the side of your skull." The animals seemed furious, restless.

Michael, as he prepared to speak, smiling, tapped the shoulder of the father who was sighing. "Don't worry, Mr. Evans . . . Up there . . ." and with his finger he pointed to the sky of the orbital stations, the satellites that blinked at night like the pine wreaths at the Pointe du Bec house at Christmas, the big human cities up at the gates of Heaven that you never see during the day. "He's in good hands. Your wife will bring him back to you. They know what they're doing at the hospital. My father worked there, as you know."

"Thank you, Michael."

I remember. Emma was sick, she was vomiting, and Elliott stayed at the Zoo. Jack was having really bad luck at that time. I wasn't in the lab with him anymore because he was so much less smart than me. He never knew how to do what Doogie did. Then he was locked up in the black cage, and he swallowed the pills they gave him. Mr. Gardner didn't have time for experiments like before, and Michael helped him with the mail, the money, and the papers. So in the meantime, Janet takes care of Doogie. I spend my time and I learn in the company of Janet Evans in the house with the blinds half-closed on the badly mown hill. She likes being the teacher a lot. She also likes Doogie a lot, and Doogie likes her enormously.

When the sun is at the summit of the top of the sky and the fog is light and cold, smoke and vapor completely cover the runway of the Charles Bigleux, which is cooled off by the automatic fire extinguishers that work one time out of two. There's a problem with the underground cable network. "Damn it!" Mr. Gardner always gets angry. "Don't listen to that—it's not good," Janet says, and she stops my ears while turning her green eyes as if they were black in the direction of her father who is fighting with the security station. "One day, everything in this wretched place is going to explode . . ."

Your attention please, ladies and gentleman, a bit of very dear respect: the Charles Bigleux is going to take off. From the foot of the deforested hill,

beyond the sheet-metal fence and the cabins, the little inferior monkeys—
"Doogie don't be racist like that"—the dogs, the cats, the bears, the lions,
and the idiotic birds make the most terrible noise there is because they're
animals, because they don't know or understand, hi hi. But Doogie is not
afraid, not he. He knows about aviation from the illustrated encyclopedia,
but he's still going to close his eyes. "Doogie, give me your hand." When
the Charles Bigleux takes off while roaring with the scream of its three
motors, we can't hear the beast animals anymore. They don't know that
we're going up into the air.

The trip puts me to sleep.

Pointe du Bec, through the porthole, is under the clouds, washed by water.
The weather is almost cold, and the house made of white tiles shines like fire.

Mr. McVey is there, but not Mr. Payne. "Alas, you poor man. I heard
about it, obviously," Daddy Gardner whispers while repeatedly patting the
hunched shoulder of McVey, who is very short.

"Yes," he says. "It's incomprehensible. How could he have been . . . Oh,
I don't know. But really, I mean, the way it happened . . ."

"Shh, not in front of *him*."

"Of course. We'll have to talk about this matter of a barrier. We need
to . . . I don't know, but there must be other ways of doing . . ."

And Mr. McVey looks at me with a tight smile in his two jowls, while
putting his hand on the top of my skull, which I never like.

"Gardner!" he says, very loudly this time. "We have to think first and
foremost about our security: about yours, Donald's, your family's . . ." He
looks out of the corner of his eye at where Janet has gone. At the humans.

"Be faithful to the human!" I say while jumping up to show that I have
understood, good student Doogie, while letting words fall from the gestures
of my two hands.

"Okay, Doogie, my good ape. All right, my boy." Mr. Gardner gives me
a very gentle fake punch, in the muscle of my arm, like a boxer of olden
times. But he doesn't seem convinced. "Hmm, I really don't know, McVey."
He agrees or he doesn't agree, I can't tell. There are no elements in the
speech to know.

"Come, Doogie."

He left his glass on the table made of episcia wood on the terrace of the
living room, and he went outside, forgetting his glasses. I handed them
to him.

"Oh, thank you . . . You . . ." He looked at me and didn't say anything. He liked me.

The students put on their swimsuits to swim while shivering, and I sat stupidly on my buttocks on the sand at the foot of the big palm tree with Pong, who was squatting down and who didn't say anything while eating his piece of bamboo.

Doogie said to himself: "Janet is going to swim again in the lapping water in the company of Michael's students." But Janet knelt down next to Doogie, who was pouting. "Isn't Janet going swimming?" I asked. The words came softly out of my mouth with the tips of my fingers. I was cold.

Janet was red on her two cheeks, and she said softly while sponging the roots of her red hair with her turquoise scarf: "I don't want to."

"Why?"

"I'm indisposed. It's . . . something new."

"What does that mean?"

"Come on, Doogie." She took me by the waist. "Let's go see the whales at the Cape."

Mr. McVey drove the motorboat, which sputters. The sun is red, it's fading, and Janet is wearing pants. She looks through her father's twins-glasses at the sparkling surface of the water far out from Pointe du Bec.

"The little one was born about three months ago, you know: she's a beautiful baby. Already four meters long and seven hundred kilos." Mr. McVey looked all around him, seeming anxious. "Captain Zipper will be breastfeeding her for six more months."

When the sun came back out, Janet tanned her shoulders. She tied her braids over the shirt with yellow and green checks. "What's the name of Zipper and Bobbie's baby?"

"Feng Po-Po," said Mr. McVey as he scratched the top of his skull like the belly of a lobster with no big or little hairs. He turned the tiller three times, and the boat went around the Cape.

"Feng Po-Po? What does that mean?"

"Goddess of the winds, of the four winds," Mr. McVey sniffled. "They're the winds that brought her to us. Payne wanted us to call her that, and since . . . The humpback whales live on reserves of fat in the winter, at Christmastime. Look! A minke whale on the port side! I think Captain Zipper must not be far off. They certainly make a beautiful couple, she and Beamon . . . Payne said so. You know, Janet, I don't understand it. I really don't understand it."

Janet didn't say anything.

Poor Payne! Oh! I wanted to go and give a hug to Mr. McVey because he was going to cry. Janet stopped me without even looking at me, one hand on the rail.

"Your father won't listen to me, but everything's falling apart. Soon we're going to have to arm ourselves, even at the Zoo. Like we do here." And McVey put his left hand on a gun, the holster of which was attached to the rudder. He looked at me sideways, but he was smiling.

"Look now! It's Zipper. Don't lean over. We'll keep our distance." I tried to put my big hand through the rusted railing to stroke the buttons in the shape of a potato on Zipper's head. We could already see the wound, like the zipper of Mr. Gardner's trousers that were badly washed because Mrs. Diane had left for up there. Mr. McVey pushed me toward the back, making me fall. I sought refuge in Janet's arms, near the lifebuoy. I glued my head against her two braids as I trembled.

"Mr. McVey, how do you know it's Captain Zipper? She looks like all the other gray whales."

"Look, do you see the big scar on her head, down to the base of the dorsal fin? Like a zipper on a pair of pants? The little ape, he understood." He pointed to my pants in vacation fabric. I made sure the buttons were done up for civilization. "It was the other whale that did that when she was born. Oh, I remember how Payne took such good care of her: he got up every night."

And he started to sob.

Far away, Captain Zipper surfaced again. This time, a playful and joyful little gray whale was stuck to her as if she was afraid.

"That's Feng Po-Po."

Zipper and Feng Po-Po lifted their faces out of the whitened water, making the foam move around. They called to us. They started to approach us cautiously.

"We'll leave now," Mr. McVey said, and the old boat launched its weak motors toward the back. We moved further away. Goodbye, Feng Po-Po.

Janet sang me a song to reassure me because the blackness of night was falling. Finally, she said: "Doogie, do you know what a marvelous ape you are?! Don't worry, monkey. Everything will be all right."

And I cried as I went to sleep.

For years now, the stones have been turned into sand under the feet of the calendar. Pointe du Bec is empty, Doogie didn't return, and Christmas is nowhere. Only Doogie's memory, I think, still counts the years of Christmas on the old calendars of his head, if they ever existed.

Dolphin

*—Feng Po-Po is cruising far away.—Help!—The dolphins
John and Lilly approach the ape and the injured man.—There
is no faithfulness anymore.—Memory of experiments in the
laboratory.—A drowning.*

From the Jungle

I breathe and breathe, and when I wake up a big white cloud like a cauliflower is flying over the water. Doogie rubs his eyes, and he places his hand on Michael's forehead that is covered with little pimples. Michael moans, and I lean over the side of the big flat gray rock.

Then a black fin splits the ocean in two, and her big open mouth comes out of the foam and makes a clap-clap like an applause. It's Feng Po-Po! Doogie can't believe his eyes. I jump with my feet together and I cry out "Hounh hounh!" Feng Po-Po has come to save Doogie, save Michael, and say hello!

Then Doogie takes Michael. I carry him on my back and Doogie walks into the water, clippity clop, clippity clop.

"Yoo-hoo, Feng Po-Po! Let the ship sail on and let the wave roll on!" But the whale swims away.

Doesn't she see me? What's happening? With fear in his stomach, Doogie puts Michael down. He floats, and the water carries us away. The Po-Po has left and I don't like water, it's bad for me, wet hair, you don't know how to do anything anymore, you're in danger. A sentence, a sentence, a sentence: the whale is singing from far to far, and we have drifted out into the water.

Farewell, beach of the crash. Farewell, Charles Bigleux. Farewell, Feng. Where are you? I can't see you anymore. Michael and Doogie, however, are in the water. The water dances, the dance of hello, the dance of goodbye, and we're lost out here.

The whale of your memory didn't remember me. Feng Po-Po, why have you left me in the ocean? Doogie didn't count on this: the cold of the night, the blackness of the horrible. Michael closes his eyes, Doogie hangs on, and what do we see? Moon, ocean, fear, air, swell, time, lost, and far.

Oh, I'm sinking. The shoreline has gone away in the night.

Gloop, gloop. Doogie certainly doesn't know how to walk on his back in the emptiness full of water. His lungs are exploding from the salty ocean that burns from outside in. Oh, Janet!

Janet. Desperation, helplessness, horror.

And then Doogie saw the tail and the soft-so-soft side of the big-so-big dolphin, and my hands slid toward the bones of his jaw beneath the fat of his skin, toward the water of his low forehead. "Iiiiirk!" he said. It's John! Michael, clamp your humanness to him, and hold on to the hold tight! John and Lilly, can you please help me?

What a beauty good old Lilly is! Hello John, my old friend!

While Doogie watched the line of the continent of the house swell on the horizon, holding on with Michael, John whistled a cry and I leaned to the right to see what was happening. Then, meanly, the dolphin let go of us when we had just gotten on.

Lilly turned her back on us. She's in a panic. It's almost daybreak. What's going on?

Everything is suspicion. "You're not very faithful, John," I say. The dolphin gives a violent swipe of his tail to Doogie, who staggers. He's doing bad things behind Lilly's back.

Where in the water did the Michael fall? I implore Lilly and I grab onto her flank.

Oh, she's trying to get rid of me too!

Feng Po-Po turns her back on you, and the dolphins aren't your friends anymore! What faithfulness is there in all this Nature?

Doogie is numb. After a few more minutes on the edge of the watch, he sees the shoreline of the black shore. He's suffocating. You must be faithful, fearless Doogie!

Oh, Janet, I never know how to swim . . . On the surface of the water, soon to be drowned, attacked by other mean dolphins, I see Michael, one foot out of the water, and I hold the air of my breathing inside my lungs. I'm trembling, I'm shivering. Go for it, Doogie! I jumped off Lilly at the moment when violent John was coming straight toward me, and I dived.

I grab onto sick Michael, the fingers of my big hand panicking, and under the water I open my eyes again. What did I see?

Three, five, ten gigantic dolphins, black with evil, their skin scarred, in rows, are encircling a school of a thousand thousands of fish, herrings, their fins wriggling. I can feel the air that suddenly shrinks in Doogie's insides, my hand around Michael's neck, my lungs smashed between the fists of the water, and suddenly I don't see anything, because as high as the highest walls of the biggest buildings of civilized humans, a vast net of air bubbles, moving from left to right, encloses the little fish, Michael, and Doogie in a prison of bubbles. And at the very moment when Doogie wants to open his mouth, he's caught in the trap of the air net, in Heaven. John, with empty eyes and black body, breaks the bubbles as he passes violently through the curtain. I think he's going to kill me. With his mouth open, he swallows up all the little fish like Hell, and they are soon dead like stiffs. Doogie is being clobbered. The water of the ocean rolls, mixed with a thousand thousands of bubbles. Roll after roll, he breathes, viciously spun like a knife on the anvil. Doogie, his arm tight around the big flaccid Michael, forever and always faithful, projected with the greatest speed into the disorder and perhaps dead in the foam, the mud, the sand, and who knows what. He swallows, he suffocates, he says farewell, and then I'm just a little packet of not very much in too many things, half dead and all of me in too much suffering, sinking here and there like blood.

Memories

I stayed in the arms of the scarecrow Janet for the whole day, pressed against the soft-as-fur mass of Janet's clothes, sniffing the odor of Janet's neck on a plastic mannequin, my hand in the knots of the long red hair of the snarled wig. Janet without Janet made me sad.

I was hungry, of course, but I would have stayed there until the end. Who knows? I'm a faithful monkey, but certainly not smart, no, no, no. I'd be in sad Heaven, at the end of my life, hopelessly watching the cold plate of food at the foot of the glass wall. But if I went toward the food, the scarecrow of Janet that isn't Janet would be gone forever.

From the other side of the windowpane, I heard a voice that was speaking in hushed tones: "So Skinner was wrong! My god! Emotions are not merely by-products that play no role in conditioning!" The young Doogie already prints words on his brain like the ink letters in newspapers.

I turned my head and I heard "Shh!" coming from the head of the scarecrow. I thought about it. Enveloped in the warmth of little Janet's sweater with the rolled collar, I did knock-knock on the plastic head under the wig. Well now! "Doogie, my little monkey, it's me!" It was the voice of Janet speaking, but without Janet! I opened the head of the Janet that wasn't Janet, and I took out the black voice with red buttons. Hou hou, Doogie, you poor imbecile! I didn't know what the recording of a loudspeaker was! Speak louder, loudspeaker! I turned the toothed control knob and Janet was suddenly yelling, but still in the same nice tone. "Doogie, it's ME! I can SEE you."

I can see you.

I turned my head. Where's the good behavior camera? Janet cried out, but in a very gentle voice: "I'm Janet, and you're Doogie." But I'm not stupid, and I wasn't stupid: it wasn't Janet. Janet has lost her voice! You need to be brave, Doogie, brave, it's an adventure. Be faithful to your teacher.

Way up high, above the two wooden chairs and Mrs. Diane's rattan armchair, I saw the eyes. That is called a camera, Doogie. It's like the good behavior camera: it's Janet's eyes without Janet.

Oh, no! Janet has lost her eyes!

Doogie thought about it. He left the arms of the scarecrow while wrapping himself in the hot fur sweater with the rolled collar that he took from the scarecrow. Cautiously, he rubbed the palm of his hand against Janet's neck, and he pulled the perfume from the plastic. He took it gently into his fist.

Then I walked delicately on the cold and smooth tiled floor, one step on one tile, one step on the next. I heard: "*Crackle . . . crackle . . .*"

"Good god!" said the voice of Janet, which belonged not to Janet but to Mr. Gardner. "Apologies to Skinner and Bruner, but what is he *doing*?"

After piling up the two chairs one on the other, I tried to climb up by holding onto the cord of the lamp with the paper lampshade. On my tiptoes, I grabbed onto the camera with eyes, the black cube that sees and that we don't see, and I pulled pulled, saying, "Excuse me, I'm not hurting you."

A piece of plaster came apart from the woodwork, everything cracked, and I found myself on my bottom with my head covered in dust and a little blood on my nose. Calmly, I wound the sweater and the red wig around my young ape's belly, I held my fist closed on the perfume, and in my other hand I held the pulled-out camera. Then I walked to the big smoky windowpane on the other side of the room, and because Doogie does the manners of being polite for civilization, I hit the knock-knock three times. Not more, not less.

I waited, while trying to dust off the timid little crest at the top of Doogie's head.

It was Peter, Michael's bald father, assistant number two of Mr. Gardner Evans, who opened the door. Mr. Gardner was rubbing his mustache, standing near a school table, with a notebook open, a pen in his hand, between two flat computer screens, and Mehdi, his mouth hanging open, had just spilled his coffee.

"Oh, my God!"

"I can't believe it!"

"Gardner," Peter said while turning around, "you've found the one we've been looking for!" I smiled while showing my white-from-toothpaste teeth, and I held out the wig, the sweater, the speaker, and the camera while trying to sign, with three or five gestures, tapping on my head, sniffing, showing with my expression that I was returning everything that Janet had left in the experiment room. Now she would be completely naked. The Janet without what Janet has is still Janet, but . . .

She arrived, running, wearing a little skirt and a cap, with no hair and without a sweater, in a shirt with puffy shoulders. "Doogie!" she said. "You're so nice, and so smart! I was watching you during the experiment! You won! Oh, I knew it!" And she took me in her arms.

She burst into laughter; she was a little girl.

"Look, daddy, he's so nice: he brought me back my sweater and my wig. But look, Doogie, I still have my hair." She let her hair down, splendid and smelling like shampoo. "And the camera and the tape recorder. Poor monkey, you thought this was my eyes and that was my voice."

"I'll have to explain it to you."

She made fun of me and placed her index finger on my nose. "Clever little one." I felt good in her arms, but I was hungry and my stomach growled.

"Oh, you poor thing. Come on, I'll give you something to eat."

She turned to her father. "Daddy, do we have to do more experiments? He's so tired."

She pressed herself against me, and I opened my fist under her nose as I timidly watched her.

"Oh, Doogie," she said. She smiled. "You thought you would give me back my smell, perfect little smart thing that you are."

Beach

—A big black sand beach.—In dead fish heaven.—How to dry the laundry.—Hunger.—First discovery of the Jungle.—The pleasures of nature.—Nightmares.

From the Jungle

When I stood up, Janet didn't take me into her arms. Instead, it was getting cool and the water was licking my feet. My head really hurt, and with trembling legs I took a few ape-steps in the thick sand that I sank into deeper the more I pressed my fat feet with large toes. I smelled the air, and without thinking I placed the closed fists at the end of my long arms on the gray-black sand while slightly arching my legs, my ears sticking out from under my badly combed hair, dirty and covered with algae and kelp. Then I blinked my eyes as I moved my jaw in every direction.

I found myself back on land with my buttocks soaked, dizzy after a few hours with my brain closed, in a damp area bordered by enormous opaque puddles with a few gray reflections of the white stars up in the sky of the humans. I was near the black and heavy ocean with its badly outlined fringe which was saying *gloop gloop* while it rolled sometimes white but muddy. I was lost along a horizon, near the coast of the curved continent, which, swollen like a cushion of black volcanic sand, followed rustling tufts of bushes, then shrubs, then palms with very high tree crowns, which looked disturbing in the dark green sky. The tree crown sways in the wind, toward the shadow of a vast mountain sitting on its butt on the forest.

The ship is nowhere to be seen, and we're on an extremely different black beach. Isn't that right, Doogie?

"It's the Jungle, Doogie," I said to myself. I sniffled as I noticed a bit of blood that had dried on my wrist.

I was afraid, and I remembered John's malicious craziness. How beast-like are the beasts of animals in Nature! I shivered. How lucky to have fallen onto the shore. Thank you, water that rolls and that brought me here like a stick of wood.

Puffing out my two cheeks, with one finger in my nose—"don't act like an idiot, Doogie"—I sprawled my buttocks on the gray-black sand near a puddle as big as a lake, like a mirror of the sky under the gray night.

"Aaaaah!" I said.

To the left of me, stuck sideways on the sand, a very frightening extremely awful beast was watching me, its mouth open with irregular triangular teeth, glowing, almost fluorescent, as if its skin had been torn off, with the head of a dragon, black eyes like marbles, and a little collar.

"Aaaaah," I sighed. It didn't jump on Doogie. Hee-hee, Doogie is such an idiot: it's a fish-fish. Little fish! Don't make fun of monkeys, of animals: it's Nature, Doogie. Oh, little fish. Trembling, I tapped on the top of its black skull. It was dead. Fish from Heaven, it's all over for you. And all around you are hundreds of fish . . . They and we are in Fish Heaven. They were struck and hit by the black dolphins who were chasing them in the net of bubbles. Poor, poor fishes.

Doogie wept. "Why is Nature?"

He would have liked to bury the very very ugly little fishes.

But where is Michael? I got up, wet from the water, and I called: "Yoo-hoo, Michael . . ."

Five or ten steps away I fortunately found Michael, cold and with his mouth open like a big purple fish on the beach of silence, the gray and black beach. It's getting chilly. What time has fallen? I looked tick-tock at Janet's show-you watch, but I don't see a lot much. I think that when one more hour falls, the sun will come up.

I leaned over Michael. Is he in Fish Heaven too?

I listened to the little animal in his heart under his chest and it answered me. The inside of his heart was still breathing. "That's good," I said, and I dragged him by his arms on his butt—heave-ho!—peeling off pebbles the whole length of the black volcanic sand up to the first green grasses and the plants and the flowers and the bushes and the hard brown earth, and into shelter.

I rubbed my two hands to wash them, squatting down near a puddle at the end of the night while listening to the groaning of the ocean, thank you water thank you wind. I washed my face, and in the darkness what did I see when I saw me? Oh, poor Doogie, what is your head if you even have one, you're so tiny! I lean my face down below my back, my shoulders covered with a beautiful black vest in tatters. My big hand to the right of the left is pressing into the edge of the pond, my flexible fingers pulled back. My whole gray brown pink hand is wrinkled. My lips are pursed as if for a kiss. The whole bottom part is naked like a mouth under my very small nose. I don't see my eyes, but I see a part in the middle of my hair. "Doogie don't move, I'm going to comb you." The part is a mess, my ears are sticking out, and there are so many hairs on the arm that is moving toward the water, which plays with the steady reflection and splashes me. I want to cry. Haounh, little Doogie, what kind of face do you have? Even the moon in the water is clearer than your head is in the air.

I turned around and I made out the shadow of the black mountain, like a very flat triangle under the slightly yellow-orange dark sky that had several clouds made of cotton-bud. Below, on the wet part of the beach, there are reflections that will soon be purple like metal, facing the ocean which climbed up blue beneath the darkness.

I turned my head again. Far away on the ocean I could see the big island with the two volcanoes and the dark mist.

I was tired, wiped out. What am I and who is me when everything all around me is more than everything, immense, more than me, oh, I don't know, Jungle and more Jungle, Nature is smaller than everything, I think? It's the everything that's so big. I'm suffocating, and then I breathe and I take off my clothes: my vest with the three gold buttons engraved with the cross, which are hanging off; my shirt, muddy and without a collar; my trousers with the pleat unpleated. I don't keep the dirty undershirt on, but I never take it off without putting on another. "Doogie, I don't want to see that"—what is "that"?—and unfortunately, I don't have another pair of underpants here other than these ones. I look at the watch: oh, I will never take *it* off. "Doogie, as long as keep your watch, I'll be with you. Don't cry, Doogie: I can see you."

I can see you.

Oh, Janet, I beg you, please see me!

Like Mrs. Diane used to do, I broke two fat branches on the ground on the carpet of tall grasses, and with a fork at the end I planted them in the sand, but they fell down.

Oh, what bad luck, Doogie. How much courage it takes. I wanted to let go of life. But Janet can see you. Janet is in my head, and I'm nothing when Janet isn't there. I tapped on the branch with a big flat gray stone to push it still deeper into the black sand which was oozing. First one branch and then the other.

Then I sponged the forehead of Michael, who is still breathing. He doesn't know, he can't tell.

Even though I'm tired, if I look hard my eyes can pierce the underbrush. Without advancing much I pulled on a thin hairy vine, and as I took out the six-times-blade cut-cut knife from the pocket of my big xxL underpants, I rubbed the blade against the end of the vine. "Do it on a stone or even against a tree, Doogie. Never put the big finger of your thumb under the jaw of the knife; it will bite you."

I pulled the vine between the two branches, and I pulled on the tongue to knot it once. "You make a circle, the head goes into the butthole of the circle, and you tighten the arms like around me. That's a knot: it's tight forever with no divorce, just like you and me."

I was quite happy with Doogie. I laughed as I placed my hands on the ground, and then I clapped. Good boy!

On Mrs. Diane's tight laundry line in the courtyard next to the terrace, bringing out the laundry basket when it was sunny in the morning, I hung the shirt, the undershirt, and the pants, and then the clothes of Michael, who was in his underpants because I had undressed him. Ha-ha, you're naked, Michael! Hey, Doogie, don't make fun! At least he doesn't have animal hair.

But the wet laundry dripped, *drip drip*, under the black of the shade, and it was not like in those days. Doogie turns around. Fortunately, the sun is arriving now to the side of the mountain: the red-orange-yellow sun in the violet tissue of the sky above the palms and the green tree crowns. Doogie places his hand like Janet does on his eyebrow to stop the sun at the exit of his eyes.

Doogie certainly likes the sun. He jumps, he screams, he picks up a few branches, and he pulls the fallen palm fronds to the edge of the beach. He completely protects naked Michael. He builds him a beautiful hut like with Janet on the weekend at the edge of the orchard.

Michael is sleeping. He lies down on the sand even when he's not tired, his head propped up on a pillow of dry leaves pressed into a ball and rolled in a soft palm frond which smells good to cool his neck. Doogie has placed a hollow stone filled with water from the dew of the leaves, covered with another palm frond, next to Michael for if he's thirsty, oh yes. He barely moves, and he doesn't say anything. He opens his eyes.

In the time that two very slow and lazy hours fall, in the sand in the hollow of the beach, sighing and sweating, Doogie has planted four twisted and groaning branches tied together by two vines and covered with three big palm fronds like the ones over Mr. Gardner's hammock on the terrace. Their laundry is drying nearby.

"What a genius this Mr. Doogie is," Michael will certainly say when he wakes up.

Now I have my you-are-quite-sleepy feeling. But the sun has risen. It's helping me, and I must find food for Michael and for me. Dress, protect, sleep, and eat. "Nature, which doesn't have civilization, certainly doesn't know that," I thought. Doogie, on the other hand, how much civilization you are, my friend, with your little ape skull in this whole universe. Oh, Jungle, you're not much of anything compared with me!

But as soon as Doogie puts his first foot into the Jungle to eat, he's not so sure of himself anymore. What does he know about the Jungle? He has memories, but they're from a nightmare. Come on, Doogie, remember. You were born in the Jungle, you come from here. You're from Nature, but you're very civilization now.

Do you remember the smells, the colors, what to eat? What does father eat, what does mother eat? What did they do since it's so much of a forest?

After three five and ten of Doogie's steps, I'm already submerged in the forest. How much of a Jungle this Jungle is! I can't see anything, and I can't understand anything. I don't want to get lost. Everything is without order, without speech, mixed up, jumbled, and upside down.

Here vines, there treetops, bushes, the ground that you can never see, tree trunks like the arms of giants, smells of everything and nothing. Nothing is distinct. I rub my eyes. What a mistake Nature is!

Then I see the first flower and I lean my head down. Between the heavy green leaves and the collar of orange lace, it's such a bizarre red tongue, with three five antennae and a furry dumpling. What is this shape? It's so fragile. Suddenly above the flower there's a green universe, three five ten thousand trunks and a ray of light that passes by itself under the humid door of the very tall tree crown. At forty times Doogie distance away, in the parasols of the highest trees, a cracking sound resonates. Does someone live in the Jungle like they're at home? I have a whirl of vertigo and I go down on all fours because—"you mustn't, Doogie, hands up feet down"—because I need to. I can't do otherwise.

If you can't do otherwise, it's because you're not human.

I am, and I'm not. Then, like a spiderweb, I see very long very thin leaves spread like needles on little branches in a star around a heart, and the pattern that is repeated three five ten million times above me, and a white flower like an octopus is opening its five tongues. I'm afraid to touch it. Will it close on my finger?

There are one two three yellow fruits, hard like pears without rumpled heads, that are hanging next to a branch at my height. I don't dare to pick them. I go beyond my steps, but there is never a path or a road in the Jungle, so I look behind me so as not to lose the light of the door onto the black sand beach, bathed by the sun in the air of the ocean that rolls. Blue, it encourages me. Breathe. Puff. Keep going.

I jump onto a shrub, I knock my head, and I slide my hand along a very long trunk that forms a coat rack underneath a ball of leaves far up above, green and yellow like a parasol for the yellow fruits of the little grape that I didn't know. I sniff. "Doogie, you have to know. Look in the encyclopedia; you can't eat just anything." Ah, hmmm, yes, yes, yes, it's true. But I whine. The book isn't here. What *is* that? You can't know: you need experiments, knowledge, and science. If I don't know anything about it, I don't eat it. I turn my back on it, I walk and walk and, oh! the light comes sliding between three five and ten small tree trunks with bald heads, above the soft bushes, covered with white flowers by the thousand millions, like in the painting of butterflies that Mrs. Diane liked. I stroked the flowers. If I take one, excuse me Mrs. Tree, I will give it to Janet. A big mister tree looks at me, his crown closed firmly like a coil of gray knotted branches in the shape of a mushroom. His bark is red, and I apologize to him.

I turn back and I bump my head. You must always apologize for a sorry. The always-green tree that is twenty times Doogie with Doogie standing on the head of Doogie, like a parasol with light twigs, young, soft, and gray, and with a few little needles planted on its trunk, doesn't say anything to me. Nevertheless, I feel the urge to climb it. "Don't climb trees, Doogie!" But it's so that I can eat. I look above my head at the little fruits like the ones for making jam, yellowish green, sometimes brown, the size of a fist, suspended in the air, too high for my hand.

I'm sorry, Janet. I don't even think twice about it, but I'm already astonishing myself. I'm climbing, my feet pressing into the pale-yellow pale-brown wood. Groping with my hands, I can't distinguish the wood from the bark, and, with my heart carried toward the top by joy, I'm still rubbing and climbing when suddenly there's a scream. A thorn hurts me and so on and so forth, and here I am, whining, having fallen fortunately onto my buttocks in a big green bordello—no bad words, Doogie, what are you saying?—of plants and branches and leaves with a frail rind from which move, oh! oh! plums like for making jam but yellow.

I take one, I take three. I will give one to Michael—he will recognize it—and then, exhausted, I climb down, pulling up my xxl underpants which bother me when I haul myself around on all fours.

Nevertheless, my stomach which is very hungry is growling. Oh, what to do? Don't eat the plums without knowing, don't trust anything that you feel or see. Hold yourself back. But when I hold out my hand like in Paradise in the lush plant underbrush, abandoned by the human, in the Jungle, I'm already smiling. I recognize it. Be careful, Doogie, you don't know. I push on the tree which is leaning down with foliage in the shape of a thick sphere, lush and fragile, the tree with buttery fruit in Mrs. Diane's orchard. Under the ample treetop, on its trunk of grayish and creviced bark, I recognize the alternating oval leaves with which I played at tickling Janet on her feet, and the fruit in the shape of a black pear with a plastic skin. It's an avocado, they're good! In the middle of the fruit, a fat pit that you take out to pour in the vinegar. Oh, Doogie likes that! But there's no vinegar. He picks avocados and licks his lips. This one I know and I recognize.

What should I eat with the buttery fruit? I could eat it with . . . Suddenly, Doogie dreams with his eyes open. He sees a fish, dead, on the beach. He wants to open it and eat it, to put in on the inside of him in his stomach. He . . . Oh, he's never had such an idea! He thinks he's going to vomit. The very idea of eating the little fish animal that is never faithful to the human! Janet said Doogie eats plants and fruits, grains. He eats fleshy fruits, arils, ripe and unripe leaves, shoots, flowers, and mushrooms. But not, oh not animals that are alive, never! Shocked, Doogie shakes his head and knocks on his skull.

I finished the harvest, because I recognized what I knew like an encyclopedia in my brain without trusting in the faithfulness of what I was feeling. I gently picked the mango from the mango tree without a tree crown, along the smooth bark, gray and brown, pulling off long leaves that, when I rustled them, smelled like the turpentine oil in the paint that was used to repaint Doogie's new room white when Donald left, the fleshy mango with the thick yellow skin and with stains of green and red.

I'll be eating at the dinner table with Michael, so I need to know how restrain myself. But when I saw—oh joy!—the fruit that I didn't recognize, I don't know what came over me. I jumped. I didn't think about it. Someone moved in Doogie who took, under the tall white tree, the fruit that looks like a plum-colored mussel, sometimes blue-mauve, sometimes light pink, stained with the blue of the sky, into my fat fist. And I opened the skin all at once to devour the pulp, the little skin over the pit, and I thought I recognized the taste of the smell of pork when it was hot at the foot of the Zoo with the scent of olive oil and aromatic herbs from the kitchen that however I had never tasted, letting the parts that are called the tartness of the kernel crack under my dirty teeth.

Oh, how good it is! What I had never known, I now knew. I stroked the resinous and perfumed bark beneath the soft leaves and the rounded crown of the tree. How strange it was, here, near the coast, to find this single tree, and I said to myself: "If you recognized it, is it because you knew it in the Jungle of your childhood even before you have memories of it? Why are you acting without thinking, Doogie? What's come over you?" Confused, I went back toward the light of the black beach, and I thought about my father, about my mother, about the father of my mother and the mother of my father, about the mother of the mother of my father. Did they eat trees and fruit? Oh, Doogie, is there something of the Jungle in you other than memories?

I gave Michael something to drink, and when he opened his pink mouth like a toad, I cut off little pieces of orange mango around the pit like a fishbone. Poor, poor fish. I looked at the beach with the cemetery of fish, which smelled bad under the sun. Never will I eat you, little fish, you poor thing.

I walked two, three, five to ten steps away, letting the sun dry off my damp hair and caress my nose. I took out my six-times-the-blade cut-cut knife, and I cut the plum that I knew well and the mango that I knew very well, and I no longer touched the fruit that I had never eaten and that I didn't know, the fruit of my ancestors.

The taste of the smell of fruit fibers was a delight in my mouth, and then I wiped my lips while closing my eyes. With a full stomach, I washed my hands in the puddle. Oh, happiness of the Jungle, isn't Nature perfect? Then I did what Mr. Gardner did on Sunday in civilization: I took a nap, sleeping with my fingers crossed on my chest. The moist cold of the hairs on my skin was dried hot, the emptiness of my stomach was full, and where my brain was in my head, I don't know. I loved Nature! Please forgive me, Janet.

Memories

All around me, it's nice out and I don't know anything. Speech has gone away. I think that I'm alone, but I don't know. I'm seated, scratching with a stick in the yellow grass, and I hold out my hand while grinning toward something, but I'm held back, and I feel good because someone is delousing me, someone who knows me and whom I don't recognize. She finds a parasite and puts it down on a leaf, the scent of which I recognize! Then she squishes it between her toes. My hair certainly doesn't smell like shampoo, and I only know how to say "Iiihihn!" I look, but I don't see anything. From behind me, someone gives me the fruit at last, and I bite into it. I know this fruit: I like to let it crack between my very little teeth, the dry part of the grains still tart, in the clearing that is getting darker. I turn around, feeling softly against my hair the person who . . .

It's Janet! She's waking me up. She's so clean and so combed, a redhead with green eyes gray eyes in a white apron embroidered in blue over an angora sweater that squeezes her at the waist. She's only fourteen years fallen from the calendar, I think. She looks me straight in the eyes. "What's going on behind your little eyes, monkey?" she says, pretending to be strict while picking me up from under my arms. "There's nothing to worry about, Doogie. You always have the same dream, you know." With the first words of my words, which have hatched like tree buds from my brain onto the branches of my two arms, I try to say what . . . what it is that . . . I have memories of.

She cuts me off and squeezes me in her arms. "It's just a nightmare, little ape. A nightmare and nothing more. The Jungle is only a nightmare. Look around you: civilization is the reality."

Then I try to speak, but she has placed her long thin hand where the first of her rings is shining and she strokes my neck where I never have lice but only the trace of the scent of shampoo. "It's all right," she murmurs, "it's all right," and I let loose beneath the caress that knows me.

Because nightmares are not memories.

Volcano

From the Jungle

Once the first day and the first night had passed, I had the idea of the memories of my plan. The beach, the shade, the sun, and the mangoes were sweet agreeable, but haggard Michael wasn't talking, his face was puffy, and perhaps he wasn't suffering anymore. He seemed to be knocked out.

"Doogie," I said, "you need to do something. No one's coming to save you."

Clean I was, my hair shining glossily, my trousers stretched and dry despite the xxl underpants I'd been wearing for three or four days, my vest torn in two over my buttoned shirt, my brain clear. My two hands were on the ground, my buttocks stuck out well toward the back as I grunted. Over the top of the forest was the mountain of the big volcano. I looked at it under the blazing sun. Hmm, I sniff, I sniff. I have to get back to the Zoo at all costs. Your home is the Zoo of civilization. Now that you're well rested, the road and the adventure await, and you need to take them. But oh! I shake my head while tapping with my fist on my too small skull. What course of what direction will ever lead to the house, Doogie? Because the Jungle reigns, deep, without road and without name, which separates you from the heart of the continent, where Janet, who perhaps thinks—who knows?—that you are resting in Heaven, is waiting for you, unless she isn't waiting anymore. Oh no, no, no, Janet!

Ah, but Doogie has more than one bag of tricks! When the second ray of sun was on the black sand beach, in the shade of the long fronds of the palm trees, I knotted my old and stained white undershirt at the four ends. I slid inside it two ripe mangoes, two hard avocados, some grains to crunch, and the only shoe I had left, and I filled the shoe with water from the nearest small river at two times one hundred of Doogie's steps from me to there, at the corner of the boulders. Doogie closed the shoe like a fresh gourd with the help of the laces, and the soaked map, on four times four pieces of stiff yellow paper, dried in the open air.

It's time to go, monkey. I said goodbye to Michael who kept his two eyes closed, and my heart pinched me like the clothespins on the clothesline. I'm still faithful and everywhere to the human, but the human might be you and it might be him. He's lying still. He's handsome, like a tall, invincible, and superb human. Then I lowered my head and I continued on my way. I think that Michael likes me, he likes me very much. Everyone likes Doogie, "oh Doogie, you're so cute." But they like Michael too. I'm leaving for just one spin around the watch, and then I'll come back. I raise my eyes. At the mid-point of the mountain, at the volcano, somewhere above the top of the bald tree crowns of the tall huge verdant trees where three or five thousand-colors birds are flying, I will no doubt see from up at the top where I am at the bottom. I'll compare with the map, and since there's no road down here, not from here to the house in any case, I'll draw the straight path that I hope—oh, I beg you!—will take me to Janet.

It's with a lighthearted spirit that I place one foot in front of the other, skirting the forest on the embankment of soft brown earth between gullies of black stones. The gullies trace a kind of arc after hugging the shoreline of the ocean waters. They shine like diamonds in the matte black of the ground. The gully turns, turns back again, and then digs through the forest. As it climbs slowly, the gully draws a shoelace between the trees and the bushes, toward the hill at the foot of the mountain. The blue air is silent as a bird chirps, and then it's repainted by three clouds. The fresh wind is getting warmer, and the trees are swaying gently. I climb, breathing hard, apologizing, on all fours now, the bundle of the tied-up sack knotted onto a branch that I hold against my back with one hand. I rush along the ground on two legs toward the gray rocks, the brown earth, and then the green and yellowish bushes that have invaded everything. Thanks to the lookout point at the summit of the hill, I didn't lose my way. But soon the path into the underbrush isn't one anymore.

At the summit, trunks of tall trees are squeezed together. Across the aisle to the sun, above the shoulder of my little white bundle on the vest cut in two where my sweat drips, I can see the little beach, black with a thousand reflections. The beach is flat and swept by the waters that glow like Mrs. Diane's frying oil, far from the mists over on the big island. Oh, the beach has shrunk on my eye just like an elephant that is moving away becomes an insect squished against the windowpane of the eyes that see and give orders.

"Poor Michael," I say. He's somewhere down in the shadows beneath under my feet, below the boulders at the fringe of the first trees of the forest on the shore. After two hours that have been let go by Janet's watch, which I'm looking at and speaking to, my only companion, grimacing, apologizing, on the palms of my hands, my knees bent, I climb to the discovery of a pebbly terrain on the naked flank of the big buttress of the volcano. I climb toward the forest that belts in the inaccessible summit, which is higher than the highest cloud, like hair on the temples of a bald man like Mr. McVey, you remember. I want to reach the forest and look situate from the height of a branch on a tree.

I go along a deep trench, the former child's bed of a torrent, of a river that flowed so much from its source in the forest that it fell down below. Maybe it's in the ocean now, who knows? On the edges of the trench, there are only pebbles and basalt, and I'm exhausted under the heat.

I'm so tired.

Sitting squatting on an enormous flat boulder, I open the bundle. I cut the juicy orange mango with the knife of six cut-cut blades to recharge myself, because the path from my lungs to my mouth is dry and hot like the bottom of a river that has fallen into the sea beneath the more-orange-than-a-fresh-mango sun.

Tilting my head down as I scratch the bottom of my ear with the end of my index finger, because "Doogie, clean ear clear mind," I see a very little ant, oh, like a baby ant, and I smile. She's walking on the boulder with Doogie, she's my friend. I watch her as I lean down closer, my eyes squinting.

She's a little animal with two times three thin legs with joints like Mr. McVey's robots. That's called a gaster in the shape of a heart, the head with eyes that are black points, and, on the thorax after the waist that's thin like Janet's are two oblique needles at a posterior angle. In a bit of earth around the boulder, some green plants have grown, and aphids are making their honey on the furry grooves of the stalks. The ant is eating behind her heart, but she seems alone and distraught, lost. She moves forward in this direction and that. She moves backward, shaking her mandibles, poor, poor ant far from your home, lost and no house. You understand, Doogie. Everyone is looking for where they're going or where they're coming from, you know. Since Doogie is nice, he takes from above him, from the messy tree with the frail bark, the small branch of a very very thin twig. Gently he peels it, and I take off all the knots and the needles. Then with my fat finger, reassuring the ant like a daddy, I help her climb up onto the stick and I lower my head toward the underside of the fat boulder.

What do I see? For a length of a hundred, three hundred big monkey steps, a colony of bustling lady ants are following the path at the bottom of the trench of the dried-up river. What a magnificent spectacle! The workers and maybe the queen in the center, and the soldiers, friends of my baby ant, are climbing on both sides while rustling with a big noise. On the smallest trunks lying across the smallest hollows, some of them group together and even serve as a living bridge for the ones behind so that they can pass over the obstacle and go forward. Doogie, that's an example for you. It's time to move yourself forward.

"You must run and join your friends," I say onto the stick to the golden ant with the bottom in the shape of a heart and the red head. She's little like a baby compared with the big adult ants and parents that are marching below. "You must not lose sight of your daddy and mommy," and I think of my own daddy and mommy.

To help the ant, I get her balanced on the very long stick and I lower the stick toward the infinite colony of brown ants with red bottoms that are nibbling and taking away the smallest minuscule twigs like a flow of crusty drool that has descended from the volcano toward the sea.

Then I smile. The ant is at least going to rejoin her people.

But when I put her down into the current, three five and ten warrior ants with mandibles in the shape of steel hooks, three times bigger than she is, seize her. I really think she looked at me one last time. They tear her up and devour her while cutting her up to share between all of them in a thousand and a thousand pieces to eat.

Aaooooouuunnnmnh!

Oh, unhappy Doogie! What cruelty! And now I understand that she was only a little red ant who was different from the big ants with the hooked mandibles that are marching, and I delivered her to the very ones from which she was fleeing.

Oh, misfortune, pain, grief, and affliction! Only stupidity and only despair cries in Doogie's heart! I can't stop weeping, and the tears fall onto my feet. I punch Doogie. Stupid idiot monkey, you killed your little friend the ant!

What a disaster Nature is! The ants are gone, and what has happened to the little one, cut up into pieces where she will never be in Heaven? Doogie descends from the boulder, and whining I reprimand myself. "Doogie," Janet always says, "I told you, that's what Nature is. You must observe Nature and say yes or no: that's civilization." I dry my tears as I walk, I observe and I experience, because as naive as you are, little Doogie, the good that you do for the smallest of the smallest ants in the Jungle is perhaps nothing more—in the scale of the forest of the world—than food given, neither good nor evil, to the biggest ants in their march. And killing, sadly, is no different from living.

Oh, I'm weary, weary, weary.

But now I'm more keenly interested in the Nature of the Jungle.

At the first shrubs of the ring of forest, I study the plants, the insects, and the ground, like Mr. Gardner does with his magnifying glass.

First, I notice a strange bush that's five times Doogie's height. In the undergrowth, in the shade, it covers the surroundings of the crown of the mountains. It's like a cluster of stems with heavy leaves that hang down toward the bottom, in the middle of which yellow fruits like lemons that have become thin after a diet attract the eye of Doogie, who breathes them in.

How does a tree work? Does it kill, does it live like an ant? I don't want to make the same mistake twice and take care of the wounded bush with the cut branches, with the trunk halfway twisted, and repair it only to make it worse than it was before. So I observe where trunks have fallen from their roots, and from under the powdery dirty earth full of earthworms I very cautiously pull out the feet of the plant. Between two vines that are hairy like two germinated potatoes is a big thick yellow root in the form of a vegetable, which on all fours I sniff suspiciously.

The smell of this thing is funny, very funny. A kind of earth with a very strong scent. For Doogie's science, I take out the cutting knife and I slice out a piece of the root without hurting it. With the edge of my finger, I touch the tip of my tongue and I taste it. Mmm. It has the very powerful acrid and bitter taste of deep earth. Is it yummy or yucky? What do I know?

I decide to peel off thin strips from the root, almost in a powder, and test it on my tongue. There's a feeling from a long time of calendars and calendars ago, or maybe of never, that makes me shudder. What is it? You idiot, Doogie! After what happened with the ant, and with Michael waiting for you, you're wasting the time that is running out of the watch. I get up, showing my teeth, but I'm not being mean. My arms are folded under my armpits because I'm scratching myself. It was high time for that!

What energy Doogie has! He must never, never stop. I don't even stop at the tall trees with thick trunks to climb up and look because I want to sleep there. I would sleep at the top of the summit, but I have to walk. It's as if the path is unwinding from under the toes of my feet. The precise eye of my brain is so clear that I can see very distinctly inside it. I can hear the voice of it and see the design of it because I know. How powerful the Doogie is! Oh, I'm better than you, better than all of you, you lowly ants and humans!

What are you saying, Doogie?

Oh, shut your trap! I'm the king.

Hee hee, I can very perfectly hear the sound of every leaf, of every leaflet of every one, each one different from the sounds of the others, and I can see every branch on another branch. I can see to the infinite at one step away from me, the summit of the black and gray misty volcano a thousand times a thousand steps away, and I run, I fly. Every smell of every flower, of every animal, fills one of my nostrils. Is there any limit to me? It's magic! Super-powerful Doogie!

I crossed the ditch, the tree trunk, the scree, and the ravine, because I'm big and strong and without hairiness, the enormous giant of Doogies, majestic, more immense than the mountain. I look at the mountain the way the moon looks at an ant. Die, ant! Doogie is here! Look, my friend! I can see all of you! My eyesight is marvelous, it's incredible!

But maybe this is . . . what if this was the powder from the root in my head? Like the stars made of dust, I have a light behind my eyes that's guiding me.

One evening, a student of Mr. Gardner at the Zoo smoked a kind of grass inside some brown paper, hiding near the vivarium under the courtyard. They were having a going-away party for Mehdi. You know, there weren't a lot of fun activities for the refugee students. They had red eyes, they sang with bizarre gestures, and they laughed all the time. I saw them through the window. I didn't say anything, and later on I think they tried to climb the bars of King the lion's cage under the moon. "If you're feeling sad about it, Doogie, you should know that they did it because of a substance. It's scientific."

So the substance transforms the brain.

And the brain transforms the world.

But the world doesn't change.

Lion King is not a bad guy, but his brain's in his stomach, you know. That's why he did it: he bit the student. "Bad substance!" I thought at the funeral.

Lion King was locked up in the shed in the reserve, and I never saw him again.

"Oh, Mehdi!" I said. But don't bury *me* too quickly. And I fly, I take off. "Ha-ha," I laughed, "I'm higher than the summit, and tough luck for the Mehdis of the world! Whatever substance in whatever brain of everyone in the world, you are only powder, all of you, but my eyes are stars. Hee hee, what a master this Doogie is after all. I dominate, and everything is at my feet!"

With the energy that I have, I could climb a thousand and a thousand volcanoes up to the orbital stations, and then I'll return as Mr. Doogie, dear very dear respect for the toasts and the champagne, going through the porthole, hee hee, and he poops on your head in the stars of the butthole of the blue sky. No, the black sky.

No . . .

Oh, never mind. What happiness! What power! What joy! I breathe. There's the scenery. It's a plate of food, and I'm going to eat it. And here, up above me, what is there? There's still something above me that dominates Doogie. That's not possible! I don't accept it! All the sounds of the silence are different in my ears. All I want is a big country beneath my feet, at the mountain of the summit, and I will pick it from above the sky, like a flower for Janet, at the root of my feet.

Of my . . .

On the last brown outcropping of boulders, I see a well-dressed Janet, two three five and ten times. Oh, there are a lot of Janets here at this hour! In a white summer dress, I think, her red hair tied up in a braided bun. I'm waiting for you with a wicker basket in my arms. It's breakfast, brunch, a summer picnic. She smiles at me and waves her right arm. "Come on, Doogie, I'm over here." Here is now. And you're there. I believe in it, and it's the greatest thing in the world.

So I climb, without using my hands, since I'm so strong, and I sit down at the summit. But where did Janet go? I look down.

Aaaaah!

It's the void of voids! Vertigo! I don't see anything below me except for nothing, and then, spread out toward the forest, I see black bands of basalt, and then the woods and the beach in the shape of a C. That's where Michael is. My head is spinning but my brain stays upright. Far, very far below me, the Charles Bigleux is smaller than the little mosquito of the night. You really covered some ground, Doogie!

"Doogie," I murmur, "what's happening to you? You have a lot of energy, but pull yourself together. What are you doing? You're out of control."

Frantically, I look in the bundle for the pieces of the map. But the wind is whistling, and I have to hold it tightly with my fat fingers.

And then, there she is. I turn toward Janet, you see. Hounh, hounh. Oh, oh! The substance of the brain of the substance crumbles, and I think that in places what I'm seeing is turning into powder. Inside my ears, the sound zigs and zags and forages around, turning like a bee that I'm chasing with my ten fingers.

In the foreground of the island in the ocean with the two volcanoes, the black sand beach surrounded by forests at the foot of the mountain forms an irregular crescent. But at the two ends of the land, like deltas, in little pieces like cookies that have crumbled into coffee, half-emerged vegetation is forming, roots coming out of the water and plants on the mud and the ocean, at the entrance to a long corridor that is gradually closed by two rivers of brown water. What is that called?

Doogie, still powerful, balances on one foot and then on the other. That's dangerous. There's an encyclopedia inside the brain of the substance. Janet learned it in biology. "Doogie, it's like near the big river where we go in the 4-by-4. It's called a *mangrove forest*. It's less than a swamp and more than a marsh. It's plants that have married the seawater to rivers without a divorce in order to make children from the air and breathe." There's a mangrove forest to the north and a mangrove forest to the south. Two mangrove forests.

Doogie spreads out the map that's broken into pieces, and stepping back, with his eyes wide open, his mouth moist, he studies it. There, and there. That's it. "Doogie," Janet says, "the big river that passes near the

Zoo at one hour of the watch away in the 4-by-4, where we get the crocs and the hippos . . ."

The river! I trace it with my index finger, and it empties into red and pink mangrove forests in the middle of the Jungle below the volcano mountain drawn in brown, definitely not further down than that because the other river goes down toward the bottom of the continent. Doogie, you smart intelligent monkey, now you know what you must do! You must walk with Michael to the mangrove forest to the north, cross the roots and the vegetation, climb back up the rivers, build a raft, and descend the big river until you're close to the Zoo. Oh, Janet!

But I can't walk, and I can't swim. Just look at me. I'll show you, Janet! There's so much energy in the substance, because Doogie is hallucinating and it's real. I know how to float! I can fly! Better than the best of the birds, the thousand-and-one-colors, hooking onto the sun with my chin, I hurtle above the lands and the waters, I fly over the Jungle, awake like never before, never sleeping and staying vigilant, stimulated like the most absolute monkey. I'm like the big Charles Bigleux in person, coming home and landing, the ship in the shape of a turtle returning from the stars. I'm flying . . .

I take off with the wrinkled map in my hand, but my foot gets caught in the bundle . . . Oh, Doogie, your brain has come out of your head! What are you doing with your arms in the air? Ouch, ouch, ouch! You can't really fly. But I don't want to see that.

And I *don't* see it.

Fire

—Hangover on a windy plateau.—The landscape far below.
—The sea, the river, and the forest.—Forest fire.—A crazy race.—
Arrived too late.—The disappearance of Michael.—
Clues, a deluge, and surrender.

From the Jungle

At first, I'm lying slumped over my arm on a big black and gray desert-like plateau, and I don't see anything other than the wind that's laughing at me, and it's flat. It's horrible what a terrible headache I have, and my left elbow is as stiff as a stone. It's getting cold. Where am I?

Nausea. Oh, Doogie's stomach is an old, irritated sack that is moving around. Yuck! I vomit, but nothing comes out. Am I the sack or what's inside it? I feel like I'm turned inside out like a glove. I notice that my two legs are wading in a yellow pool of orange clumps and bile, and soon the two muscles of my two arms won't move anymore, like the Charles Bigleux when it's broken down. The wings don't come out, the hatchways are blocked, and in my head commander Gardner mister daddy is crying in his plight. Oh stop, stop, stop! Oh, I beg you, I don't know, stop me.

I think that I'm having some hallucinations after the unfortunate encounter between the stomach of my brain and the substance, a short-circuit of my head through my eyes and my ears, because what Doogie is seeing now, the world is certainly not that. It's like a movie screen!

When I raise my head, a tall outcrop straight and black as coal is standing all alone on the gray plateau, swept over with oval pebbles by the sharp mocking wind. Up above me, like cotton plants without stalks, twisted like over-cooked pasta noodles in a spiral on the plate of the big dirty sky, the clouds are hiding the sun and the human orbital stations. They are white nearly gray, and I have the feeling that they're going to land, to come down and punish me.

The second thing I saw with the tip of the apples of my eye as I was coming down from the outcrop was the immense incredible crater down below, encircled by a flank of a thousand times a thousand times a thousand little black marbles on the ground. It looked like a soup plate. I thought it was rumbling.

Oh, never swear, Doogie. If you swear, you'll be a prisoner. But if you want to save your hide in the time that it takes for your brain to wake up and get back inside you one of these days, you need to get right back up onto your two feet and get down from here before long. But Doogie's muscles are numb because the substance has gone to sleep inside them. And he's dragging himself along.

The third thing I saw, at the end of the plateau, where the rock was crumbling like the morning cookie in the hot coffee, is that down in the void it's really a void. And the void is much more of nothing than you think. Houh houh, la la! What a trap of misfortune! Where did you go, and how did you do it, you poor fool of a monkey? How but how did you climb up onto this monster under the grinding clouds? Ouch, ouch. I need to think about not thinking, because this is desperate, and it's indisputably a fact. Oh, my goodness! Beneath me, fogged in, is the view of the big beach, below the mangrove forest of the river, recessed into the green indistinct darkness of the foliage of the continent that's stretched out to the horizon behind me, in the center of which, under the trees of the line far away, Janet lives. Oh, if I only knew how to fly! But you don't know how to. To the south, there's the other mangrove forest to avoid, but where is the map to draw and trace the pathway of the path of the river like a black thread in the green of the forest that serpentines and makes shoelaces? I turn around and I walk painfully on the boulders of the deserted plateau, and beneath the grinding sound I hear it. The wind whistles to me once, twice. The wind is gone, and the map isn't there. The wind has taken it away. The map has left with the wind, the map has betrayed me. Why wasn't your hand faithful to the bundle? All is lost now. Oh, what misfortune! For you there is never happiness.

You must write down the picture of the route in your memory, observing the mangrove forest with its thousand divided parts, the mouth of the stomach of the river that will poop you out near the Zoo.

But I squint, my hand pressed against my cheek, my jaw numb. Hou hou, what is *that*? Down where Michael is, in the hidden hollow at the bottom of the big C of the beach, under the foliage, an enormous big and big enormous column of black smoke has risen up. It's spinning around and flying slowly to the sky. What is it?

I sniff and I smell. Doogie, don't rely on your own understanding, but . . . There's danger, danger, danger! It's Michael! I must save him!

My breath has some hiccups. I moan a thousand times as I move my atrophied legs with the help of my very long and able-bodied arms which flog them—"get along, coachman, we need to get there, Michael is in danger, run, run." But filled with panic, I run in every direction. I rush and then I turn back, in one direction and then the other, disoriented. How to get off the plateau that Doogie has entered onto?

Oh, why is it that so many times it is so easy to go and so impossible to come back? It's the story of the cage, and it's the story of your life, poor, poor Doogie. Hi hi hi. I close my eyes with the help of my big hand, I unnumb my two legs under my torn trousers, and I pull back my breathing by closing my little damp nose with my other hand, trembling like when Doogie is in the swimming pool with the floating ring but you're scared of doing a poop in your underpants, and you'll never know how to swim because it's a nightmare.

I ran, hobbling, and I jumped from high oh yes from high to save you, Michael. I landed in the tufts of the very tall trees below the little cliff of the volcano. I tumbled, so oblivious, my shirt getting caught, I spun around and lost the vest. I'm scratched and hurt, but I hold onto the white shirt with one foot, I somersault, and Doogie grabs the trunk. He holds awkwardly onto the vine and slows himself down. He ends up headfirst in a shrub with round and soft-so-soft leaves that smell of lemon in the general poo scent of the entire earth. Doogie has his feet on the ground now. He's still Doogie, his buttocks on the ground, his head intact.

Oh, if you only knew. I looked at my watch to encourage myself; how many hours you will spend, monkey—Janet oh please help and forgive me—running on two and four legs, among the fruit trees and the palm trees, out of breath, my feet caught in the roots that came out of the ground like arms and knees. I think my nose is bleeding. I let one leg drag on the ground, and my black matted hairs come out from my unbuttoned shirt, my face scowling—what's becoming of me?—while stirring up the earth, jumping over obstacles, and going down the slope. Sometimes I somersault, and it hurts. Then, groaning, I'm on my way again, my mouth open over my mean teeth. "We don't show our teeth, Doogie." I don't have a pretty face if you saw it, but I'm faithful to the human to the end. Perhaps I have to get down by other means. Oh, sorry, I don't know anymore. Running like a crazy person, I think that I wasn't thinking. I was only a beast monkey, a fierce and violent monkey, but if I hadn't been one, I never would have been able to cross the forest to get there.

I came back to the trench with the ants, and from far above, going in the opposite direction, I followed them while holding my elbow that was scraped, red and without a shirt.

I might have been thinking, "Let's hope I'm not too late."

When I arrived, I spread apart the little fruit trees with my two arms, the ones with soft gray bark, after the mango trees and the shrubs with white flowers. I trampled carpets of mud, and I jumped up and reached out my hand across the curtain of trunks toward the light of the light of the ocean. The setting sun tapped me on my eyes with closed eyelids as I felt the sand of the beach under my feet.

I was still far from the hollow of the soft C where I had—alas, bad Doogie that you are—left Michael. At the end of the end of the arc of black sand, the yellow mango-orange sky was covered with a thick layer of smoke. It was the smell, the old smell of the oven of burned cakes.

"Oh Doogie, that was stupid! I asked you to watch over it! Everything is burned! I can't count on you." And again I cried while running heavily, my feet on the cool of the gray puddles of the water of the ocean, *splish splash*, my hands lifted up, then placed-pressed into the hardening sand, because in front of me, where there had been—but that was in the past—a beautiful camp built from civilization by Doogie—clothesline, hut, water in the gourd, and larder, all for you the human—there was only despair. Coughing, I could smell only the smoke of the fire of the smoke.

And waving my two arms to clean the cleanliness around Doogie so that I could see something, I understood. I fell to my knee, and then to my other knee. For a hundred of Doogie's steps, the fire had already eaten the most advanced vegetation on the beach of the woods. It's hot, it's hot, all around the shelter that was dancing sluggishly, crackling in the flames of the fallen night, already cinders and soon to be nothing. Where Michael had been, there were burned things, coal embers and carpets of nasty little yellow and orange flames that tickled everything that was falling down, crumpling and blackening, and then dust. Oh, it was really over!

Doogie takes the water into the hollow of his two hands. It spills out between his palms. He throws the water onto the flames of the forest fire to take care of it, but it's so strong that it isn't sick. The fire is doing very well thank you.

Oh Doogie, Doogie.

I stayed there facing the disaster, my feet in the water, on my knees and weeping. What's happening, and what has happened to Michael, Doogie? I never go back; I'll never go back to the house of the Zoo. And I cry and cry myself.

Only then, around the first hearth where the fire has left behind a pile of wood of ashes where Michael was sleeping, do I notice excavated footprints pressed into the still cool sand, at the edge of the beach before the forest, regularly one foot two feet. I approach, and I try to put my real foot into the hollowed absence of the footprint that I can clearly see. It matches.

"Doogie, what have you done? You were there when you weren't there," I say to myself. Oh no, no, no. But Doogie is already looking at his feet, the false ones and then the real ones, like an inspector in a police story. You know how in the evening before going to sleep Mrs. Diane liked to read the investigations of Agatha Grizzli in bed. There are also ten or three times ten absences of feet that are smaller. Those, I remember, are like the natural shoes of the little mischievous ones that Doogie didn't appreciate at all at the Zoo: the sapajous, the spider monkeys, the ouistitis, and one that I think is a gibbon.

Monkeys, little inferior animals, poop monkeys, nothing monkeys, have passed through here, yes, yes, yes. Don't be racist, Doogie. Hin hin. Haoounh! But nastily, filled with anger, I sniff the traces of the piss of the shits of these sub-shits, hiinh, violence, combat, fighting. In the sand is the absence of the dragged feet of Michael, and with my finger I can smell and taste the taste of his blood.

Aaah! Ouh ouh! Standing on my two feet, facing the burning forest, I pound Doogie's torso in rage. Soon the whole Jungle will burn, and the fire fires up Doogie's heart. He has flames in his eyes, blood and vengeance in his head. First, I groan, hulule hou-hou, and then I scream, I march up and down, I intimidate, my hair standing on end, and I dominate. I dominate and I yell in frustration.

Oh, Michael . . .

Kidnapped he was, hurt, dragged, taken into the forest by poopy little monkeys, sons of feces, and Doogie must find him again. But the fire, the fire that is burning, who did *that*? Because the shits who leave their droppings don't know about and don't understand the science of fire. Oh human, you who know, tell me, I beg you. Only Doogie, because he's a genius, knows the power of the match, of flint, of rub-rub, and of the wood that makes fire.

And what about the absence of *your* feet pressed into the sand?

Was it you? What does all this mean . . . ?

Doogie moans and groans, and as soon as I approach the absence of my foot in the black of the sand of the beach again, the sky weeps. It weeps three, five, and ten thousand times, because it's raining and the clouds that were touching down, twisted out of cotton like white ships in the sky, are pissing heavily.

All of that water fell, violently, wave after wave, onto me, onto the beach, and onto the fire.

The wet, soon-to-be-finished fire crackled like a mean person grunts when a nice person has chastised him, but the investigation is also finished, the absence of footsteps in the sand, the wet sand, warped, full of water, deformed, the ashes and the gullies of sand from which worms come out. And then the sand collapses and crumbles under the dark hopeless eyes of Doogie, who is soaked, freezing cold, his clothes in stuck-together shreds, cringing, his arms held in close. He's cold when he moves away from the household fire that is going out, without a house, without a home.

Farewell, clues. Cry, sky that isn't sad. Cry, Doogie who is cold. Who is there to know about it? Alone on the beach, the fire ended, the water fallen, Michael taken away, and the nasty animals by tens and by thousands in Nature in the Jungle are waiting for Doogie and are out for his hide. He needs to find Michael, to fight and plot, to be an ape and be faithful at the same time, to give and take blood a thousand times, and then to walk to the mangrove forest, to walk up the river and walk some more, and then maybe one day, moving further and further as the ape approaches them, to pass through the polished grills that creak under the sun of the Zoo.

You had only happiness, but now everything is only memories, and nothing will come back. Janet, you have forgotten me, and everything will forget Doogie. It's over, because everything is lost: the stars, comfort, the

Charles Bigleux, civilization, Michael, Mr. Gardner, Pointe du Bec, the friendship of the whales and the dolphins, breakfasts, Janet and perfumes. All lost. It's the end.

For the moment, Doogie, you're less than an animal, and there's not much of the human left in you. How, oh sky that laughs at me and that rains, and how will you, cry-baby Doogie, ever go further than almost nothing?

Dog

—The weakness of his sense of smell.—The science of the nose.
—An abandoned dog.—The master and faithfulness.

From the Jungle

I tried a try, and then I started another try. The sky above me changed, the rain dried up, the warm water became steam, steam was in the air, and the air was white, blue, black, and night. Oh, even in the darkness, in the dark darkness, like a blind man, I tried to act like those who know.

The absence of Michael's feet, and the feet of the little monkeys with shit on their butts, their absence pressed into the sand, into the mud, under the trampled ferns, on the earth. I looked at them closely, I smelled them, I sniffed them, and I followed them like a detective. "Doogie," I said as I shivered in the night, "if you're an ape, rediscover what you know: a thousand smells in the forest, the science of the tracker, the instinct of your apeness! Oh, to know how to recognize footprints, odors, the sounds of broken twigs, the echoes of the Jungle!"

But Doogie, I don't know the least thing about the science of the animal.

The sun rises, and after the cold comes the heat. What is the Jungle? It's the same all year long, but never the same throughout the day. Shiver with cold in the dark and suffocate from heat when the sky is high and even higher. Everything has evaporated, Doogie! Where did the smells go? My nose is stuffed up, my little nose that you have instead of a maw or a muzzle. Doogie, your nose like that of a human proves how little of an animal you are. I was divided in two: proud of the nose that Janet likes, of the nose with the two nostrils so close together like Janet's—oh what a charm, small and pushed in—but shame shame shame about the nose that is still too black, too smooshed, with a fold cutting it in two which wriggles Doogie when you sniffle, so blow your nose into the square embroidered handkerchief that Mrs. Diane sewed. Your dirty nose is running. You're still too much of a muzzle to be decent! What a dirty maw your face is, Doogie! Janet won't like it.

Aaaah.

But here and now, Doogie would like to change his smashed nose for a real animal face that can smell poopy buttholes! Because the muzzle of the face of an animal that smells, that sniff-sniffs—that face knows the good science of the track, of the smell of poops, and of the hunt.

When Doogie used to sniff his poop in the toilet, Janet would say: "Doogie, I saw you. I always see you, you know. I'm the invisible woman in the good behavior camera. If you want to smell your stools"—because Janet wouldn't call poop *poop*—"I'll have to tell daddy, and you won't have anything to eat and you will clean the toilets by yourself with the plastic gloves, the product that goes squirt, and the little pink brush. Is that what you want, ape?"

Oh, Doogie doesn't like that! He knows that the smells that come out of me are not for civilization, and Doogie we don't sniff people's butts either. If we did, where would civilization be? How civilized is the smell of sweet alcohol, of vanilla, and of the thousand fragrances from Janet's vial on her neck! Oh, Janet! If I smell civilization on her neck, what Paradise is next? Nothing nothing nothing. But . . . Doogie also likes the fragrance that comes out of Janet's mouth when she has had it closed all night long. "Doogie, my breath stinks!" Hih hih, Doogie glues himself to her when she wakes up! And the smell that comes from under her arms. "Doogie, where did you put my deodorant?" Janet is anger. And the smell of her feet that have been walking. "Quickly, Doogie, go get me some soap. Don't smell my toes, you stupid great ape. What an ape you are!" And the smell of Janet's moist butt! Oh, sorry, sorry, sorry: her buttocks. And when she forgets to flush the toilet and forgets about the soap and the product that goes squirt.

And the smell between her thighs!

"And what if I'm indisposed, Doogie?"

"Bad dirty ape!" I tell myself. "You're dirty and disgusting." And I give a slap to Doogie. "How can you think that way about Janet's thighs, in civilization and at the very moment when he has to save Michael. Be faithful to the human. Don't rub shit on Janet."

I look around me. What does a naked human do without objects, without machines or a compass, without the computer GPS and without the paper map, when very deep in the Jungle he has to find the trace, follow the path, smell the smells, and track the shit? I breathe in. There's only wet air, stinky earth, heat smoke, burned wood that has taken a shower in the drip-drip rain, and the thousand smells of Nature, which hasn't put in the squirt to smell good like civilization. Nothing is in my nose except the only smell that doesn't say anything: the smell of jungleness. Which doesn't speak. What good is language in the Jungle? Cursed nose that's not a nose, and stupid nose that's not even a muzzle.

Oh, there's fog between the vines and the trees, and there's a fog in your brain, you dirty ape.

Because I don't know anything, either about the monkeys or about Michael. Because I can't see tracks or feet or shadows. Because the noises I hear are only noises, and I don't understand anything. You're no hunter, Doogie, you pitiful excuse for an animal. Sitting on my butt, with my nose up in the air and my big eyes open, I know very well that without the science of shit that stinks, I don't know anything here.

"Ooooh!" I cry and I cried. What a miserable misery you are! Where are you, instinct, since civilization has abandoned me?

How I would like, naughty naughty, to smell the shit in my butthole, and that instead of my nose the muzzle of the maw of beast animals would grow, and then, stupid and mean, I would know how to sniff, smell, and hunt.

But I have too many ideas, and not the least sniff in my nose.

All around me is the Jungle of shadows that eat the light, the heat, and the water. Everything is bigger, everything is taller. Around the trees, beautiful flowers are growing on the trunks, and fruits as well, nuts, husks, and gourds. Look, Doogie, at how rich Nature is and how impoverished you are.

Thirty, fifty times taller than me are the closely packed trees on the little tuft on the skull far very far away, and the pipes of vines where the blood of vegetal things flows faster than your blood. I stretched out my big awkward hand toward the furry vine of the palm tree, above the ferns and the orchids, leaning like the back of a twisted tree that likes water. It's decorated with flowers, and it serves all the way up there as a sieve for the light when sometimes a ray of light falls, sliding down from the sun in the sky. And even if I don't have a mustache like animals, because my nostrils are so tiny, because I prefer my eyes and my brain to dirty nostrils, the yellow light above the grasses and the dark mosses where the dust dances tickles my moist nose, sniff sniff, my dirty nose that only knows how to sneeze.

And then I *achoo.* Filth.

Then I look in what remains of my pocket for the big, embroidered handkerchief with my name on the border. You need to wash it, Doogie, in the washing machine of a river. And as Doogie lowers his head to sniff, I see it.

What a scream I let out!

"What's *that?*" I wanted to say. Oh, oh, hounhn, it's a dog dog. Doogie, hihi, how stupid you are. Janet said, "Doogie, *dog* means dog in English." It's a terrier dog.

Aaah ah! He's coming toward you. What should Doogie do? Because I'm afraid of dogs that are very doglike.

He's an animal. How much like an animal he seems. No, no, dog, don't touch me. Hounh hounh. But he doesn't move back. I think he's showing his teeth like a hunting dog. He's as tall as half of me, he's all hair, and his hair is the color of dead leaves. Is this not a misfortune? You need to know that dogs bite, and Doogie knows it. The dog sniffs, he growls, and he looks at Doogie. He's going to jump on you. You need to run away to defend yourself, cursed monkey. I looked for a stick, a weapon, or a pistol, but I didn't find anything.

Run away!

The woof-woof, with his mouth wide open, had a dirty head, hair like a bush, ears hanging like a monster, fangs pointing down, and a snout that glistened with malice toward me. I know it: he wants to eat me. Then his tail stiffened. Aaah, I jumped up. He wants to stick a dagger in you! Poor, poor Doogie. Soon to be in Heaven in the Jungle.

How smart Doogie is. On my two feet, I jumped to the side, holding onto a vine, to escape.

But the vine said *crack,* and Doogie said "Aaaah." *Bang* and *boom* went Doogie's two buttocks on the brown earth.

What bad luck! Doogie doesn't want to see this. He presses his fingers against his eyes around his nose.

Ouch!

Doogie opens one eye, Doogie opens two eyes. The dog is sitting down, thin very thin, his tongue hanging out and his big yellow eyes empty, his hair badly brushed.

Hounh?

The dog licks Doogie's head. Yuck yuck yuck. Then he waits.

"Doogie, how stupid you are," I said to myself. "Ha-ha, the dog that is an animal thinks Doogie is human, so he's faithful to you."

"Faithful," I said, "is good."

And with the end of the tips of my fingers, because I was still wary, I pet him. "Come." He licked me. "Ha-ha," I laughed. "Dog, dog, you're such an idiot." And I made fun.

I looked him over carefully. He wasn't heavy, the English terrier dog. His blond tuft, his wide-open nostrils at the end of his very long, very wide and square muzzle, but above all, oh above all his fat mustache. Stupidly, he looks at me.

"What's your name?"

Woof woof.

I picked up the stick and I threw it like humans do, strong and far, and he went after it, barking joyfully.

Hounh. Pff. What's a dog good for? What a slave animal!

I got up, and then I thought about it. Alone as I am, no one here understands Doogie. The dog is like a watch that goes tick-tock inside the dog. He is only springs for running, barking, and sniffing.

"He doesn't have a soul, Doogie," I thought.

And I took out Michael's underpants that I had picked up from the black sand of the beach where the monkeys with poopy buttholes had abducted him. Those bastards! I looked at the wet and torn underpants of the human.

Oh, the human, Doogie.

Then the dog came leaping back, standing on his hind legs, one ear stiff, unclean, and muddy, his stinky hair the color of dead leaves under his mustache, with a stupid look and yellow eyes. He sat pretty and he stuck his moist snout, shiny and blond, into Michael's underpants, the blue striped underpants.

"Dirty dog," I grumbled, standing on two feet with my lips pulled back over my front teeth. Hou hou. "Don't touch what belongs to the human."

But the dog barked as if he wanted me to follow him, and cutting a path, his tail wagging *click-click* under the heather shrubs, his muzzle dirtily on the ground, he turned to me.

"Doogie," I said to myself, "he's trying to talk to you without language."

When I caught up with him, I saw the nearly effaced absence of the feet of poopy monkeys in the ground, and next to it, my own feet.

"It's a trail!" I cried with my two arms.

How animal is the dog who knows. As stupid as a watch, he reassembles the clues with the science of snouts that is so deficient in Doogie.

"Good dog," I said, and I stroked him with two fingers between his yellow and empty eyes. How thin and hungry he was. I climbed a tree to get bananas, calabash, and papayas. He ate without a napkin or fork, and he didn't wash his paws. He wagged his tail at the end, his chest hollow and his hair rough. Like a prayer, he raised his two eyes toward Doogie and whimpered, and I petted him to reassure him, the stupid dog.

Then I knew that I was his master and dominated him.

Mangrove Forest

—The dog looks for the trail.—The trail is lost in the swamp.—
What is a mangrove forest?—Fear.—Halloween and the fake
witch.—A nauseating labyrinth.—A parrot talks.—A suspicious
monkey.—The hunt.—Memories of school.

From the Jungle

Behind the English dog, Doogie follows.

They walk through the forest. The branches crunch and the noises tickle my unobstructed ears on the two sides of my skull. Oh, it's hot.

And when the forest becomes darker than deep, I want to say "wait for me dog," but I grumble and he stops. There's shade everywhere, and it's nice and cool. It's incredible how threadbare the dog is, how dirty his mustache. "Pull your tongue in," I tell him. "You really don't have toothpaste in your mouth. You stink." The dog sniffs with his nose, and he knows something. He's looking for something, his head lowered. He knows the way and the path.

"Doogie," I tell myself, "you're going to find Michael, glory to me, and save Michael. You'll pet the dirty dog, and then you'll move up along the first little river, then the big Congo River, and then you'll be at the Zoo and Janet will say, 'How faithful to the human you are,' and she'll caress me, because I will be clean."

Woof.

"What? Which woof?" I asked. What's going on with the dog? He holds himself stiff on all fours on the almost bald grass, his tail straight and one ear rolled up like a cheese crepe. "Oh dog," I say, "you have dirtiness in your mustache." Then, grimacing, haounh, I pull out his white hairs from his blond snout and then his hairs that are the color of dead leaves from his square muzzle. And he licks me. Yuck. I stand up. "Give me the direction of the trail, dog," I say, as I wipe myself off with the handkerchief in an embroidered square, my feet halfway in the slush.

But the dog, his thighs as stiff as bows, doesn't move. In front of him, in front of me, are broken branches squeezed like matches in a box, fallen by the thousands like in a game of pick-up-sticks. "Doogie, do you want to play with Janet?" Oh yes, yes, yes, but I have to pick up the stick pieces on my feet. The branches are blocking the way. Beneath where our feet are planted, the mud of the brown swamp is becoming black so black, and then gullies of green water, and oh! everything is so strange. The sun is cutting out shining clouds with scissors, and there's shade from the tops of very disordered trees. "Doogie, you have to clean your room." But in the Jungle, nobody does the cleaning.

Since the dog was barking *woof* without stopping, I said, "Shh! You're going to get a sore throat," and I explained it to him with the words of my hands. "This is the mangrove forest. The mangrove forest!" The dog paddled between roots that were higher than his hairy face, growling. Hundreds of badly tied wicker baskets were hanging upside-down over puddles, and roots crossed over crossed roots that were above Doogie's head, like vertigo all around the leaning trunks. I sneezed.

The dog yelped, because the trail of the monkeys with poopy buttholes continued into the mangrove forest. "Calm yourself, dog." I placed my hand on his head, and I was afraid that he would bite Doogie! "Look at me: the mangrove is a very strange forest," Janet explained a thousand times while taking a walk for fun near the big river on Sunday. "Doogie, the mangrove is the love marriage between Mr. Earth and Mrs. Water." She smiled. "Just like Doogie and Janet, Doogie. All the little trees eat the water from their mangrove forest when the tide rises and covers them, but the trees, the shrubs and the meadows are pressed into their daddy the earth below the level of the water, you understand, and then they climb up high to breathe the air, and the whole forest climbs, climbs, climbs, like a platform on stilts, like at the house at Pointe du Bec, you know. You know this, Doogie; I explained it to you. Look at me: it's the silt from the erosion of the earth, which is called *limon* and not the word for lemon in English, Doogie, which is *lemon*. The sediments from the river give strength to the mangroves, which grow quickly, strong, and close together. Don't be stupid, Doogie."

As the sun was going to sleep, I squatted down with my shirt open and I explained to the dog that this is a mangrove forest and that it's strange,

strange. The banks of sand and the wet earth mix with the water from the ocean and the river like a thousand castles of green-white beans. The roots climb up and all the trees have pointy heels. "Look at me, dog: I'm explaining it."

But the dog acted like an imbecile. He did his dirty pee onto the branches of the trunks that were knotted like the fingers of a hand.

"Imbecile," I said, "I'm not happy with you. You don't understand anything about anything, you animal with your disgusting mustache and your yellow eyes. There's nothing inside you. You can't just pee everywhere, and you always have to wipe. Be clean!"

He sat down on his bottom and lowered his head, sad. He didn't listen. I sigh.

Unfortunate sad misery.

The mangrove forest is a door that has no lock to open it. Everything is locked for the Doogie who walks on two feet, but the mangrove forest is a door that closes even on the dog's nose. The smell has fallen into the rotten water. The smell of the trail has departed: it has evaporated between the thousands and thousands of roots of the swamp.

Sadly, the dog sits down next to Doogie. He can't smell anything in the mangrove forest. The sun is yawning, opening its mouth in the darkness, and soon the night will be cold.

Of course, Doogie *tried* to follow the pathway through the mangrove forest. I climbed onto a thousand gray roots, above the water, the sand, and the swamps. I held onto the palm trees with both hands, and soon I stopped. The ground under the soles of Doogie's feet was as if the earth was covered with needles, gray pricking shoots like the bed of nails of an Indian fakir: ouch, ouch, ouch. There's nothing you can do about it. The mangrove forest is strange and dark. Above me in the black sky a pelican with a pink back flies up, and the voices of thousands of witches from the book that Janet reads laughed as they whispered: "Doogie, what is a mangrove forest if not the realm of witches?"

Oh, Doogie doesn't like witches! Janet so beautiful, why when Halloween falls out of the calendar do you draw a scary ugly head on your face, black and grimacing like monkeys?

"Because I'm a witch, Doogie."

The leaves whisper, and the thick mangrove forest cackles.

I'm lost, lost, lost.

Then Doogie shivers. The murky water is flowing in the distance. The deformed shrubs, like bones in a body with green hair, twist around and walk on roots like the gray claws of witches. Hounh! What can Doogie do?

Then the dog came to press himself faithfully up against me and sleep. He lay down on the bed of roots by my side, his four legs stiff, with the skin that covers the bones of his chest hanging down. He was still hungry, shivering, his neck long. He placed his head and dirty mustache against my knees that were pulled back over my poor chimpanzee stomach. You think that you're human, Doogie, but you aren't worth any more than the dirtiest of dirty dogs.

I sighed and I looked at the moon in the sky.

The dog animal is sleeping. He has neither a witch nor love for Janet in his heart.

I throw a glance at my show-me watch.

In front of us, in the darkness of the shadows, is a little island on the dirty water, like a cake that has climbed onto roots that look like cricket bats. Under a very twisted gray tree, in the fog of the night after the air comes out of the water, the greenish liquid is like squishy earth.

I would like, I would like so much for Janet to see me, to stroke my neck and whisper: "Don't worry, everything will be all right."

I think about that, and I see the dog sleeping. Then I look at him, I stroke between his two poor closed eyes covered with hair, and I say "haounh haounh" very quietly.

He opens his mouth and breathes. He's happy, I think.

How alone is the human, Doogie. How alone is the one who strokes, and how happy is the stupid animal that people stroke. And neither of them is you.

Memories

You're a sleepwalker, Doogie.

You didn't look at the watch that you wore on your wrist, and I went down the little wooden staircase at the end of the corridor of the house in the dark, not using the marble stairs of the great hall.

I don't remember what I did. You're big now, Doogie: you don't pee in your bed anymore, and you don't poop in your little pot. When I want to go now, I go downstairs to the double-you-see.

But when I opened my eyes, horror and shiver of woe, where was I? It's black within black, and I'm in soft blue cotton pajamas. Whining, I suck my thumb, my little head with eyes open turning to the right of the left and to the left of the right. With the tips of the fingers of my sweaty hand, I feel my way down the length of the hall like in an experiment, and I look for the yes or no of the light. "Doogie, that's called a *light switch.*"

Is this still an experiment? Is everything always an experiment? When will I have my grade at the end and finally get the cuddle? I turned on the light, and in the time it takes my eyelids to go flip-flop I can see all around Doogie.

I'm in the garage of the house on the hill, which I never knew about. The light imprisoned in the yellow neon rods on the ceiling that is as low as Doogie's skull blinks like eyelids above the cardboard boxes and the scooters, on the floor that is a color of blue like motor oil, as Janet always says, covered with slippery plastic like the top of chocolate éclairs but blue.

In a corner of the garage, one two three five and ten glass jars as tall as Doogie are standing under the greenish light, and in each jar—Doogie hesitates and then takes one two three steps in his pajamas—there's an animal.

It's Heaven!

Doogie sees the animal; he's like me.

There are one two three five apes in Heaven that are not moving, and how ugly, sad, and cold the yellow and green liquid of Heaven seems. Some of the apes don't have skin, just their bones with no covering, or horrible heads.

Aaaah! Doogie could jump or hide, but there's only sadness. Cast your eyes more precisely under the hair of this ape, Doogie . . . you know him. I come closer, squinting with the line of my eyebrows, when, deformed in the glass of the jar under the blinking neon, I see a shadow and a voice that says to me: "Doogie, what are you doing here?"

I turn around, and the witch has opened her mouth, her eyes coming out of their house, her hair black and her nose hooked.

Aaaaah!

I'm in Heaven!

"Don't be silly, Doogie," she says to me. "It's just me. It's Halloween. I went to the guard's house, the nurse's house, and the chauffeur's and gardener's houses. They didn't have any candy. When I got back, you weren't in bed. What are you doing?"

I looked around. I was standing close to the marble staircase, and the light was on. I looked in the mirror framed in forged iron: I had a red stain on my forehead. She laughed when I touched Doogie's forehead with my big hand.

"Why are you laughing?"

"That's an old experiment, Doogie! You recognize yourself in the mirror."

"Obviously," I pouted, shrugging my shoulders, "I know that I'm Doogie in the reflection and that Doogie in the reflection sees me at the foot of the staircase looking at you. But why is the stain there?"

"You had makeup on, Doogie. Don't you remember? You were Frankenstein."

Oh, that beast, that beast! I'm scared!

Ha-ha, very funny.

Doogie pouts. He's not the beast. I bury my head in my arms. Where are my pajamas?

"Don't you remember, Doogie?" And what about the green and yellow jars, the Heaven of bottled apes?

"Doogie." Janet squeezes her two lips together, grimacing like a witch. "What bad dream did you have this time? Come here, monkey." She makes the sign with her hooked finger.

Poor me. I was getting a cuddle in the arms of the black witch, who spoke and even smelled like the Janet I loved.

From the Jungle

When the next day fell from the calendar, Doogie climbed over the pointy roots, tumbled out of branches, and planted his feet in the sludge of the half-soaked coast. What a dirty place was this mangrove forest that was neither sea nor land.

Under the light, Doogie could see the maritime mangrove forest better, and the labyrinth of rhizophores—"that's what they're called, Doogie"—that live on stilts on the very disgusting ground of the low tide. With the blade of a cut-cut knife, in the bright sun of the morning, I cut into a white root that formed an arch out to the puddles of green water.

Yuck, that smells really bad! It stinks! There's a sap that sticks to your fingers. There's nothing to eat inside it and it's hot: the water is making smoke.

The dog stayed one two three and five faithful steps behind me. "I don't need you anymore," I said. "You can't smell anything here." But he scratched his dirty mustache and his brown nose of a terrier with yellow and empty eyes, limping behind me. When I stop, he stops.

"Stop imitating me," I said. "Don't act like a monkey."

When noon falls from the high sun, Doogie, wearing no slippers or shoes, avoids the dirty worms, crabs, and sponges in the sludge. He climbs above the salt water that smells like the rotten water of the containers of preserves in the garage of Mr. Gardner's house, above the roots that are the lungs of the white trees and the green tufts. And he jumps over the tubes and the stems planted straight into the ground like snorkels that dirty inhabitants under the ground use to breathe. I climb like an ape, with difficulty, my feet and hands on all kinds of wooden handles and shrubs that go *crack* and *snap*. *Tweet tweet*. The birds are happy in this filth, but not Doogie.

In front of Doogie, who is unhappy, dirty, and not washed, his sleeves pulled back and his pants torn, a big tree in the shape of an asparagus, enormous, immense, and leafy, sways in the wind that is coming from the right of the bottom of the compass of the sun.

Dazzled, Doogie, what is it? The dog growled and barked, and I calmed him down. "Shh," I said, "if this is a malicious enemy, we don't want to give him cries to eat."

Then, in the hundred rays of the sun that was throwing darts, burning my two black and white eyes that were protected by the palm of my big hand, hi hou hou, a big beautiful thousand-colors bird flew up, making the leaves of the branches speak—*snap*. His beak was crooked, his wings broad.

Tweet tweet. Thousand Colors is flying.

The dog, stupid as he is, thirsty on his dangling pink tongue, ran with a limp, jumping toward the flying bird.

"Come here, idiot," I said.

I ran on the soft ground, through the ferns and the hibiscus leaves that people drink as tea, under the palm trees, on the little hill that climbed as a refuge from the water. It's the tall and terrestrial mangrove forest. Then, *splat*, I fall into ouch.

Two little dry trees were hiding a disgusting ditch where dirty water from the rising ocean was trickling.

"Oh, yuck," I groaned. "What is *that*?" There's a fish coming out of the water with gray flippers as if it had legs, monstrous. It climbs up, hopping onto the low branches of the shrub near me. Doogie is afraid and he screams. I have to get out of here!

Where's the dog? I'm not very sure. Fish with gray faces are climbing onto the land, and worms are gliding through the water under my poor wading feet.

Doogie hears a noise. I turn my head and listen.

"Doogie, it's Janet."

"What?" I said. I think I thought I was falling down. Where is it? I feel my heart beating in the mangrove forest. I wade, I jump, I get on all fours like a monkey and I glide, joy happiness and Paradise.

"Doogie," the voice says, "it's Janet."

"Haaaaoooouuuunh!" I yell, and then I lower my voice.

"Can you hear me?"

"Oh, yes!"

"Doogie . . ."

"I can see you," she says. Two branches are still cutting my wrists with their prick-prick thorns, under the palm tree with a low butt, near the big royal palm of the king, tall very tall, which presides on the hill, and I leave the labyrinth of mangroves so that I can see behind the voice.

"It's Janet."

Oh, Janet!

And then I see *him*.

The dog, faithful, growls and wriggles his dirty mustache. Standing still, he barks like a hunter, his two ears stiffened at the foot of the very tall very royal palm tree. Despite the sun, I look at him, on the crown of the palm tree, and at the voice that is speaking. "It's me, Doogie, it's Janet," the voice says. "I can see you."

Then I see the Thousand Colors bird, with his crooked beak and his wings folded in, chattering. He repeats: "It's me, Doogie. It's me . . . Janet."

Rage of rage of misfortune! I took a flat stone that was drying on the ground, and I threw it at the lying Thousand Colors.

At first, he stopped talking. I was almost sad, because I got some happiness from hearing the voice of speech, especially of Janet, rather than the woof-woof, the tweet-tweet, the silence of nothing, and the wind of the wind.

Then he looked at me, at Doogie, and he said:

"The Rnimal."

"What?" I said. "What?"

"The Rnimal!" he, the bird, said. "You must go into Rnature, Doogie. The solution is in Rnature."

I didn't understand, standing on all fours under the sun which was playing a game of darts with my eyes. The parrot flew away, bathed in light, crackling the leaves of branches.

I was trying to sit down and think, when instead of Thousand Colors on the palm tree I suddenly saw a monkey with a fat nose, a little monkey with a poopy butthole. And in his hands he was carrying a piece of the T-shirt of a human.

"Houh houh," I cried, and the dog got excited. "Hunt, hunt," I explained, and then the monkey ran away from tree to tree. And as the faithful dog showed his teeth while running ahead of me, his lips pulled back and the hairs on his chest standing on end, I thought: "Hunt; hunt and kill."

Memories

On Wednesday morning it's dictation.

Whatever Janet says, Doogie repeats. Doogie is sitting on a wooden chair attached to metal, at a table that is the smallest of all the tables mister the gardener has cut off at the feet with a saw without hurting it, "specially for you, Doogie." In the morning, Janet plays the teacher, with Doogie feeling bewildered because the Mrs. is busy preoccupied with Donald who doesn't talk and who limps, because Jack eats tranquilizing pills, the poor duffer chimpanzee, and because Mr. Gardner is trying to save the Zoo.

As far as Doogie can remember, things are going badly, but Doogie is happy. His childhood is happy, and Janet is there.

"Doogie, repeat what I say. 'Lionel is a little boy. Lionel has a friend, and the friend's name is Edgar.'"

Haounh. Doogie moves his big hand around while wriggling in his seat. The collar of my shirt is scratching me and Doogie's balls are cooking in his Bermuda shorts. It's hot. "Lionel," Doogie says, "friend." And he adds the heart.

"No, Doogie," Janet says. "Lionel isn't a *lover*. He's a *friend*. Do you know what a *friend* is?"

Janet is standing on the wooden podium, wearing a skirt and suspenders over her shirt. She has tied up her hair, and from behind her glasses she's looking at Doogie to send him a smile. It's hot, and it's nice out. The old classroom on the second floor is small: four tables, a podium, a blackboard with chalk, the map of a map of the world, the clock, and the calendar. There are two windows that don't open anymore, and behind them I see Mr. Peter the Gardener and the nurse who is running on the gravel of the back courtyard, at the foot of the railing of the service staircase.

"Doogie?"

Hounh. Doogie frowns. His hair is not well combed; his cob is off to one side. "*Friend*," he says, "is like Janet to Doogie."

"No," she says. "Janet is Doogie's *teacher*."

"A *friend*, Doogie, means sharing everything without secrets and with equality."

"Ha hounh," Doogie says. And he holds out the index finger of his right to put it into the circle of the thumb and index finger of his left. "Hou hou."

"Oh, Doogie." Janet blushes. "Come on now, there's no sex! Being a friend is for the *mind*. Do you know what the *mind* is, Doogie?"

It's the brain in his skull, and Doogie pulls on his two ears as if to pull out the head of the big world from his little head.

"Don't act like a monkey, Doogie. Just because you know how to speak . . ." But the noise of a lot of noise was coming up the staircase. We heard the scream, and Janet came down from the podium frowning. "Stay here, Doogie." But I jumped over the table, little badly behaved Doogie that I was.

The door was partway open onto the landing of the staircase, the light from the window was attracting the dust that was flying around, and Janet asked:

"What's going on? You're disturbing us!"

"Miss Janet." The Gardener took his straw hat off his head, he sniffled through his beard, and from behind Janet he looked with a strange gaze at Doogie who was sitting up straight and not moving in his chair. He didn't like me. "What kind of an ape goes to school?" he murmured. "No offense, but did God want that?" "What is God?" I asked Janet one day.

"Miss Janet, it's about your brother." Oh! She went pale and her freckles turned red.

"He found a bird in the aviary: the parrot Edgar, the one we liked a lot. And . . ."

"Come on, tell me, tell me," said Janet, who was still just a little girl, you know.

"Well, miss . . ." The Gardener lowered his voice. "He killed him, miss, with his teeth. Oh! And then he *ate* him."

Then the Gardener shook his head. "It's the saddest thing. Like an animal! With everything that's been done to animals here."

And he looked at me. I didn't understand, but what a sweat I was in, there on the wooden chair held in by metal armrests, sitting up straight like a piece of wood. And Janet murmured: "But why? Why would he do that?"

The Gardener raised his eyes. He was looking me over from far away. I could see him through the half-open door.

"Your father has locked him up because, you see, he's having a harder and harder time tolerating it. Well . . . it's that this bird, Edgar, you understand . . . he talked, he knew how to talk. And your brother couldn't stand it."

Macaca

From the Jungle

"Hunt, hunt, kill, kill, bite him," Thousand Colors the mystery bird seemed to be screaming over the tops of the trees far from the mangrove forest.

He was a bird Doogie didn't trust and one that Doogie had seen before but that I had no memories of. He had a little crooked black beak under a sort of fatty gray wart on his completely white head. And feathers like wool necklaces in a thousand fluorescent colors: blue-yellow-green and yellow-green-blue and blue-yellow-green and blue-blue-yellow and yellow and yellow and yellow. What a plumage for the eyes! There was too much of it! The tail of the Thousand Colors is red like blood from the heart. You would have thought he'd been painted with a paintbrush.

Is he crying "hunt kill and bite him" to excite the faithful dog with the dirty mustache who is running far in front of me behind a monkey with a fat nose and now also a baboon with a face of smashed shit? Grrr . . . I pull back my lips, I pull apart the branches and—*crash!*—I fall onto a carpet of leaves under the big sun.

Then an enormous gigantic clearing opens up like a carpet under my feet. Around some very small trees with broken branches that were unloading fruits onto the flat plain in the shade of groves—oh, Janet, you wouldn't believe me: one two and maybe even three hundred monkeys are moving in all directions in the shade, in the light, on the moss, on the tops of boulders, and under the palm trees, in silence and in noise.

"Monkeys!" I said. Hin hin, poopy buttholes with tails! What strange ones they are! Other than a few baboons with faces like stingrays, there are only macaques. Heads with poopy hair, little monkeys with tails, mustaches, and black eyes. They're the ones who know nothing about the human. They're animals and good-for-nothings. Look at that, hounh hounh! They're small monkeys, gray, white, and brown, who are fussing around. Where is the intelligence, gentleman lady? There's one that's hitting another one! He makes off with the food and he poops. The smallest one squishes himself down, and the biggest one puffs out his chest. And what are the females doing? Oh, they're so dirty, their thighs spread apart, and between their thighs their peepee holes are all red and swollen. The males smell their butts, their fur is shiny or dull, and they all look alike, like puppets. "Slaves of Nature," I say, "you're not worth half of a quarter of Doogie, and I shit on you."

"Ouch," I say. My gray canvas trousers with two pleats are so torn up that they're shorts, and your thighs are hairy, Doogie, and striped with blood. You're not doing so well. Look at your feet, Doogie, without shoes and socks. You're hurt under your foot, you squeeze your big toe against the other toes to walk, with the gray callus and the thorns that prick you, and oh, I'm suffering.

"But Doogie, you've done so well."

I turn around. I look at my watch with the blinking dial. But it's just in your head, Doogie. The good behavior camera has filmed what you say about what you think.

"Doogie, I'm ashamed of you, you're a racist."

"All living beings deserve respect, all of them are smart and intelligent, each in its own way, each according to its needs, ape." Ape? Oh, Doogie doesn't like it when Janet calls him *ape*. He grimaces scornfully. "So, even the assholes are intelligent?"

"Bad words, Doogie!"

Phooey. All monkeys with tails are peepee, and Doogie wants them all to be dead. Forgive me, good behavior camera, but what idiots these lowly monkeys are! In the clearing, they're as stupid as yesterday, and they don't even know that it's today. *Woof woof.* I take a look. The faithful dog is barking and growling, standing on his hind legs, his front feet on the steppingstone of a gray and flat boulder. How panicked the macaques are. In the clearing, there's no order or civilization or progress. Everything is any which way with these savages. It's just forget-about-it.

"Nevermind!"

"Ha-ha, it's Nevermind here," the parrot cackles, the beautiful Thousand Colors with the black eye in a white circle whom I know and who is sitting on the branch of the half-uprooted tree near me and to my side. It's the kingdom of Nevermind: let it go, never think, and live their little monkey lives. But . . .

"How is it that *you* can speak?" I say with my hands to the intelligent Thousand Colors, who flares under the light, his tail red like a thousand bloods.

I repeat, I repeat again, and he chatters:

"It's the realm of Nevermind. But the Rnimal. You must go to the realm of Rnature. Rnature, Doogie," and he says my name.

"What?"

I repeat, and I repeat again.

Then he flies up from the other side of the green clearing where the macaques panic and take fright. They lie on the ground, showing their teeth, their ears sticking straight up, their chins forward, in disorder, and there's not even one that challenges the faithful dog who is defending me.

I descend, calmly, with the hands of my two long arms on the ground, and I give my poor feet a break by walking with the help of my hands. "Hands are for speaking, Doogie, and feet are for walking." Yes, alas, I know. But no one can speak or understand here, and feet without socks or shoes are not friends of the sluggish earth that pricks them or of the hard ground that pounds them.

Haounh. I pound my chest one time two times under the shirt that's dotted with stains. The dog sits, his nose in the air, and he obeys me. As I push my lips forward and click my teeth while whistling amicably, the idiotic females who are breathing hard, tired out from running away, in fear and dread, with flat stomachs, get up and growl, clicking their teeth stupidly.

Each one just does whatever, and it's Nevermind. The scene of all of them together is completely incoherent.

I'm shocked. Living like that, don't you have any dignity? The males, far from the edges of the clearing, are sluggish, and the females that are not women, with neither panties nor bras, are in the center of the clearing in a rectangular field. Suddenly and unexpectedly, a female who is taken over by a madness like Nature, grimacing, attacks another female for no reason.

It's all for no reason. I shudder.

She catches her victim and bites her on the back, pressing the poor female with reddish hair into the ground that is covered with pebbles, leaves, and nuts.

Then the beastly female with the white beard stares at the poor red-haired one, who flattens herself down and shows her teeth while smiling. How little dignity she has! Then the female with the white beard sees and perceives a group of young monkeys who are sleeping. She wakes them up and catches a stunned little orange macaca to whom she shows her fist.

A very young macaca with a serious look, the top of whose head is square, has let go of the food she was snacking on at the top of the boulder in the company of two older females. She goes after the female with the white beard, and they scream and get excited. With her beard on her chin, her ears flattened and in a frog position, she looks at the square-headed one, whose flared nostrils of a stupid animal without a true human nose wriggle. Another one catches her from behind and bites her.

Doogie comes closer, and the females spread out without paying any attention to him. What misery this life is! The ground is dry and dirty, covered with shit, nutshells, and nibbled leaves. Doogie frowns and observes two young ones, their faces hairless, their heads round and their arms thin like badly nourished children. I try to speak to them. They hiss and one of them grimaces, growling like an old man. There are scars on their arms. A male who is behind them shows me his butt, perverse. The perverse one has lost two fingers, and the stumps are pink. The ear of the female who is running behind them on all fours is slack, her tail stiff as she attacks a red-haired one with a crest and one frayed and cut ear. There are scrapes on her skull and under her feet.

As soon as one minute has fallen from the dial, one of the females gets excited for no reason, and they hit each other.

At the end of the clearing, between two naked tree trunks, the white-beard and the square-head have made peace. They don't remember anything. There's no intelligence or memories. For the macacas, nothing falls from the watch and nothing falls from the calendar. The dog is trotting along next to me, and I pet his head as he pulls in his tongue while whimpering.

And this is how they live.

The white-bearded one is glued to a woman who is kissing a woman—yuck, Doogie!—leaning against the back of the square-headed one, delousing the daughter of the female while looking through her coat for lice, scabs, and parasites. The other one is eating without sharing her leaf with the one who is tending to her, her eyes black and stupid, with an empty expression and a rounded back.

Then Doogie feels a cramp in the pit of his stomach because . . . despite civilization, how he would like to feel on his dirty hair, since there's no shampoo in the Jungle, the delousing of fingers and . . . Oh, but that's dirty, Doogie! Never listen to your thoughts.

I turn my eyes away, and I walk. It's chaos without reason or memories, this clearing of the macacas where baboons pass through, and green monkeys. They sleep, they eat, they fight, and when a child is born, what does it see? It sees this. This is what it will be, a poor macaca with a pitiful nothing life.

"Doogie," Janet used to say. "Don't make fun of the macaques, they're not poopies. Macaques come from Morocco, and we take care of them at the Zoo. Without them and the experiments of humans, a number of diseases would have killed humans, and Janet too. He's called a rhesus monkey, and thanks to him humans know about and can fight disease. Do you know about poliomyelitis, Doogie? It's thanks to the rhesus monkeys that we know about and can fight poliomyelitis."

"Ah! So animals sometimes give their help to intelligence," I said to myself.

The rhesus, the macaca monkey, never thinks before acting, as Janet has always taught Doogie to do. Just look around. The female with white hair climbs onto a boulder and presses herself against it. She stares stupidly, frenetically. She comes back down, and she climbs back up. During this time, the redheaded one has hit the smallest one in its muzzle that is a shiny triangle. They're all bitches. After a minute on the dial, one smiles when she has lost, and the two of them click their teeth.

What does it all mean? It's oblivion. And during this time, minutes hours days years are passing with no progress, while humans . . .

The dog barks, and I crouch down.

At the edge of the big chaotic clearing, in the clay, is a series of absences of steps pressed underneath the ferns, and hanging on the thorns of the brown bush is a piece of fabric from a white shirt.

I stick out my jaw, frowning, my ears trembling. Then the dog with the blond tuft sniffs the fabric from under his dirty mustache. He recognizes it and he barks.

"Good boy," I say. "If you could speak, you would say 'Michael.' You have memories, good dog. If you just had speech, you would be as much of a god as the human. Hunt and show me, dog."

Memories

Doogie is alone, but Doogie isn't really alone because he's big enough to remember.

"What is being if not memories?" he wonders.

Oh skull, oh too small brain of Doogie, squatting on his pine bed that squeaks in the square tower of the big house at the top of the hill. Doogie looks at the carpet and the stuffed animals, and Doogie looks out the window. The sky is blue, it's afternoon.

All morning, Mr. and Mrs. Daddy have been arguing. Doogie doesn't understand all the words, but he hears, and he knows. "Go up to your room, Doogie," Janet said. She was pale.

Mrs. wants something, and Mr. doesn't want it. Mr. Gardner says things. He talks about Donald and Mrs. Diane cries. Eventually the door slammed downstairs, Janet called and called, and Doogie sees her running on the gravel beyond the terrace and in the back courtyard. She's running toward the forest to catch up with them.

Then I'm alone. The Gardener is in the garden. The nurse is in the infirmary. Where is Mr. Peter? His son will come one day, but now the students are tired, and they don't have parties in the annex anymore. The Lion King's cage is empty. You could hear nothing and no one, because Jack takes his pills, except for the wolves who cry howl-howl. Doogie is alone; he's thinking. I'm wearing a Zoo University T-shirt with the cross, a pair of long white shorts, and shoes with tassels.

Doogie didn't dream it. He remembers the garage, the apes in Halloween Heaven, and when he goes to sleep because he's tired, certain memories chase Doogie like mean hunters chase their prey. I opened the door without making a single noise, and I gently put my two overly large hands on the banister. I went down the little staircase of black wood. I was looking for the garage.

For a long time—tick tock on the watch and re-tick re-tock—I looked at door after door for the garage. One door, whose doorknob was like a calculator with a code, was ajar at the end of the unauthorized service corridor.

It's unauthorized, Doogie! What does the good behavior of the camera say when it sees you? I think about that, and I hide in a corner. Sometimes, I think that the camera of good behavior doesn't see you. When I go into the garage, there are no big glass jars with apes that I know and who are in Heaven. It's different from my memories. Doogie is surrounded by five cages like hamster cages, except that inside them there are five apes like me, Doogie. But are they apes? They're smaller than little Doogie, and they have tails, black eyes, and mustaches. When Doogie opens the light of the switch, they growl and scream. Doogie covers his ears. How sad they seem.

"Oh!" says Doogie. They're all naked. I close my eyes.

After that, I try to speak. Doogie has never seen apes who are so backward in the brain. Not a single word, nothing from their head descends to their hands. On their necks are adhesive bandages. Wounds. Along their necks are tubes, and all around them are machines.

Doogie frowns. He smells a strange odor of sickness.

"You," he says, "what's your name?"

The monkey looks at himself, looks at me. What a little hairy head. He opens his teeth pitifully, he squeaks, and he whines.

"What? What are you saying?"

Doogie is astounded. Even if apes like Jack, Elliott and Emma are less smart than he is, all monkeys must be like him.

So who are these ones?

I lean forward and I extend my hand through the grill to offer a hello. The monkey with hair standing up on his skull, his eyes empty and his ears standing up, wiggles his nostrils. How ugly he is. He doesn't have a nose.

He bites, hard enough to make me bleed.

"Aaah," I step back and cry out.

And then I see *him*.

And he growls. On all fours, limping, he comes out of the shadows.

"Donald?" I ask.

It's Donald, my brother. He's handsome. He's very handsome, and how human he is. With no animal hair, redheaded like Janet, and with freckles, but snot is coming out of his nose. Oh, how beautiful his nose is, and the whites of his eyes. He might be stupid, but he could never be stupid like

Doogie, because he's human. His shirt is dirty, and he has bloodstains on his shorts. He's wearing the same ones as Doogie but without slippers on his bare feet that are covered in mud.

With my hands, I tell him, "Donald, you're going to catch cold on this ground covered in plastic."

Donald smiles. He's lovely. Doogie lowers his head. He knows it.

But the problem is that Donald doesn't know how to speak. "Droogie," he grunts, "Droogie . . ."

"Yes?"

"Hi hi hiii . . ." And Donald jumps, he jumps on me. I can't move. He's pinning my arms, he's strangling me, I'm suffocating, he bites me, I'm bleeding, I'm suffocating, and my head is knocked against the table under the cage of a monkey who is yelling and laughing. "Die, Doogie," I think he's saying. But it's just that he's screaming in his excitement. I smell the blood running down, and I think I'm going to Heaven.

Donald is killing Doogie, right here.

From the Jungle

Absences of steps in the earth and in the mud were pointing like the arrow of a finger in the direction of the trees at the edge of the clearing that loved humidity and that were getting taller. Then the faithful dog who was wagging his tail lifted his dirty brown nose in the direction of the trunks of high branches and of the wind, in the sky that you can't see because there are only leaves.

"Oh no, no, no!" I said. "Once again the trail ends." The dog can't smell the air, the branches, or the absences of steps going to the top of the trees with thin and gray bark. The dog looked at me. I think he was saying: "Monkey, you're the one who knows how to climb trees. You're the one who follows trails between the leaves along rotten vines. I've done what I can. Now it's up to you."

"Stupid dog!" I grumbled. I spread my hands. Hounh hou. "I'm not a monkey, I don't know how. I don't know anything, dirty dog. I walk like a human. Climb trees? No. I don't have the right kind of hands, and my feet hurt. I'm wounded."

I sat Doogie and his butt down on a log. The fog had just set in, and soon it was cold. The dog, since he was faithful, with fear of my anger, lay down in silence at three five steps away. He looked at me with empty eyes, and it was like when I see Doogie's meanness in the mirror.

"Oh, stop that, stop shooting your eye at me like that," I grunted, and I curled up like a baby and rocked myself.

As if that wasn't enough misfortune for me, on a low branch, above the stilts reinforcing the base of the base of the trunk of the fattest tree with the very high tree crown, the Thousand Colors bird landed. *Tweet* and *chirp* he said at first.

"Shut up and shut your mouth," I thought-growled.

With his beak, he pecked at his own plumage and his red-blue-red-and-yellow feathers. I noticed two gray stains on him. "Thousand and *one* colors," I said with my big hand.

He raised his crooked beak with its kind of wart, standing up straight on his feet with very pointy toes.

"It's the realm of Nevermind here," he cackled.

"I think we're starting to get that," I whistled. "Who told you?"

I repeat, and I repeat again.

Phooey. Damned broken record of a Thousand Colors.

"It's the realm of Nevermind here, but . . ."

"Yes, I know." I clicked my teeth and I spoke with my hands, but I don't think Thousand Colors the bird understood anything at all.

". . . but the Rnimal. You must go to the realm of Rnature."

Rnature.

"Yes, yes, yes." I was getting annoyed. I stood up in front of him and I said distinctly with my big hand, word by word: "I know. Who told you? Who is talking to you? From whom are you bringing these words?"

"Who, who, who?"

And he flew away.

I lowered my arms. The dog, faithful terrier, came up to me. With his dirty mustache, his blond tuft covered in brown mud, straight and thin as he is, he licked my hand and then, with his tongue hanging to the side of his head, he looked at me.

His saliva was yucky, but I felt his teeth. "Dog," I thought, "you understand me." Then he barked joyously.

I took my head into my hands. The bird spoke but he doesn't understand me; the dog understands me but he can't speak. Oh, what a misery of misfortune! And I sighed while placing the gaze of my eye on the show-me watch with the fogged-over dial. "Janet, human who can both speak and understand," I thought. "You're far away. And Michael. I know. I have to find him."

But how to do it, and who knows how? Without speaking, I asked the dog, who understood me. In the direction of the idiotic and cretinous macacas in the clearing who were sleeping, eating, fighting, and showing their sex with empty yellow eyes, he barked: *woof* and three times *woof*.

Oh, I blinked my pretty black eyes that have irises like humans have. "Doogie, you know, you have beautiful eyes, almost like a human," Janet always said.

But what about *them*? Who knows something about *them*?

"Doogie," Mr. Gardner used to say, "science is about first looking, then observing, and then finally you know something. I watch you and I have the science of Doogie. When you're older, look around you and you'll find science."

"Ha-ha," I laughed. "Who could believe that there's a science of the poopy monkeys?" Doogie, don't make fun. Okay, then: if there's to be science, science there will be. I squatted down, I opened my eyes, and it took a while.

Slowly, a female approached Doogie. Doogie watched. In the fog, she looked like all the other macaca females. She looked to the right of the left and to the left of the right. She quickly held out a leaf to Doogie and then she ran away on all fours. Observe her well, Doogie.

Doogie noticed that she was red-haired, more red-haired than the others. Not red everywhere, but on the underside of her disgusting hairy body.

Hmm.

Then I heard a cry and a fuss on the carpet of leaves and twigs. Another female had attacked the one who was red-haired underneath. What? She bit her viciously, and the red-haired one let it happen, lying flat on her stomach. What an injustice! Doogie, you have to intervene.

I jumped up on two legs, pounding my chest with my fist, and I showed my front teeth. It's been so long since I had any toothpaste. Doogie, you smell bad. The female lowered herself, her ears flattened, and she smiled nervously without really looking at me. Her poopy monkey tail curled. Then I noticed that from the front she didn't look like the red-haired one. She had a square head, and there was something insolent in her eyes. Tss. I remember that square-head. I looked to the right of the left, and in the chaos of dozens of dozens of macacas, who ran and who stopped, I noticed several square heads. "It's a family," I thought. It turns out that not all poopy monkeys are the same. They haven't built a cake mold like the one Mrs. Diane has to make them all alike. Hmm. Mysterious strange bizarre.

The red-haired female moved away from me without saying thank you very much, impolite, and she smiled at the square-headed one who was walking backward. "Imbecile," I thought, "you smile at the one who bit you, so you must not remember anything." But mighty oaks grow from little acorns, and now Doogie understood, his chin on his fist. I have the science of the patience of watching.

I see the red-haired female climb onto a round boulder in the light of the mist. She's happy, she joins two other red-haired females, they have very visible girl's privates, all round and red, Doogie, and you blush bright red. "Oh," I thought. "One of them is her sister. The other one has more hair, she's stooped over and is older. She's her mother."

But at the corner of the corner of the boulder, another brown-haired female with a square head who has a nervous look and who is making unpredictable gestures in the air is frightening her. The red-haired one moves back and descends to the ground that is rutted with nuts to do her little food gathering. She chooses food like at the market, and she nibbles.

By turning my head, I see that she can see the unpredictable square-headed one who like her is going to the market. Aha, she's intelligent: she understands that if the square-headed one is here she's not over there. She's either here or somewhere else, but not everywhere at once. The coast is clear. She rejoins her mother and her sister on the rock. She brings fruit, and all three of them move their lips and their tongues as if they were speaking without saying anything.

At the base of the rock, a white-bearded one who is holding a piece of wood in her mouth like a cigar has showed her fist while growling at a very little squatting macaca with dull hair, who is whining. She has no food. She holds her nostrils high and smiles nervously.

"Smiling," Doogie thinks, "means being inferior."

Then the white-bearded one turns her back, and the one with high nostrils grabs onto her to delouse her with both hands. Doogie closes his eyes. Are they happy?

I'm starting to understand. "Oh, Doogie," I thought, frowning, "even animals are intelligent in their animal way. Within the chaos, each one has its reason. Science is strange, Doogie: it makes you see and understand, and then you're disappointed. With science, everyone is right. Even the poopy monkeys are right to have poopy buttholes. Oh, the misery of science!"

Evening, with its fog, is coming. Cries echo, then it's calm, and then more cries. On top of the boulder, the mother and her daughters are making themselves at home. It's nice out.

The dog has woken up. Doogie says to himself: "Thank you for everything, science. But knowledge is not power. What should I do now? What should I do? Animals have an animal intelligence. What do they know about Doogie's intelligence? The dominant ones are number one. They're the ones who are the chiefs, they're the ones who know things."

Doogie gets up, and without frightening the macacas who are gathering or sleeping, I go in the direction of the mother who is breathing loudly, sitting on a boulder with her square head.

To show that I know their customs, that I know that she is a mother and a chief, I smile. She turns her head. Language is not for them. Doogie has seen correctly, he has observed well. Haounh. I imitate the macacas with their wiggling nostrils, and I turn my head toward the big trees while shaking Michael's dirty underpants, which I take out from my trousers. I hold out my big hand and I grunt while clicking my teeth like they do. "Where is *him*?" I tilt my head toward the piece of the human's underpants.

But night is falling, and the chief-mother and her daughters are chewing their food with their backs rounded. Nothing. She looks at me out of the corner of her yellow eye and wriggles. I see nothing in her eyes. "I have understood you," I say. "I have the science of you perfectly. I have observed you and I can talk like you, so now, please help me."

But nothing.

Oh. Doogie tried to communicate, and nothing happened.

The evening was a hundred colors in the sky, and Thousand Colors flew over my head. His crooked beak moved, he clicked with his beak, and he said: "Crooh, crooh, it's Nevermind here. It's anything goes."

Nevermind.

Nevermind.

"Oh," I thought. "Nevermind is the English word for *never think*."

Then I heard a little cry, and the naughty little one with the high nostrils jumped up and like a little bitch she stole Michael's underpants from Doogie. Clicking her teeth, she jumped back. She jumped, her tail extended, and then she climbed onto a vine and went into the forest.

"You dirty shit of a monkey, you macaca who doesn't speak," I growled. "You're going to pay for that!"

"Hunt, dog, hunt, and bring me back what belongs to me." He understood right away.

Nasty macaca, I remember her now.

Memories

Doogie was in Heaven, but Heaven wasn't inside Janet.

I coughed as I wept, and I got up from the floor.

Donald was moaning on the ground, dragging himself on all fours while showing the gums of his teeth. Poor Donald: he was sick, and he didn't understand what had happened.

Mr. Gardner had entered the garage, and his eyes were so round. He was so pale that even his mustache had turned white, and he was trembling. He slapped Donald once, and he hit him.

"Iiiink," Donald whined.

Mr. Gardner was sweaty, and the monkeys in the cages were jumping around. They screamed and clicked their teeth, their eyes black.

"Animal!" Mr. Gardner yelled between his teeth. And he knocked Donald to the ground. "Animal!"

Doogie, curled up in a corner under the table, closed his eyes, and I heard Janet coming to look for me.

"Go away, Doogie," Mr. Gardner murmured as he wiped his forehead with the handkerchief embroidered with his name while scratching his mustache. "Go away. I'm sorry; you don't know what this is."

He took me by the hand and led me to the door. The light from the neons blinked, and their reflections blinked back from the ground covered with blue oil-colored plastic. Donald, flat on his stomach, his nose bloody, grunted, and then he looked at me. He looked at me with the whites of his eyes, and under his lips I could see his teeth.

I shivered, and Janet wrapped me in a big checkered blanket. She bit her lip and her eyes wept.

Then they closed the door to the garage.

From the Jungle

Ooo la la, Doogie's feet hurt. He's all out of breath.

While the faithful dog barks and runs after the macaca with the high nostrils who stole Michael's treasure, Doogie squats against a big tree that is suffocated by vines. Puff, puff, my breath goes out into the chaos, and the sole of my feet has been cut by scissors. I winced.

Woof woof.

The dog is calling me. I'm coming. Suddenly, Doogie is tired with fatigue. What good is anything other than Never-the-mind? The evening is climbing up over the valley like the tide of the oceans on their banks, and you can see, hidden under the fog as if under the sheet of the veils of the clearing, some rhesus macaques. "Poor macaques, poor rhesus monkeys," I think. "The world is so big, and what do you know about it? All your life, from now on, in the clearing and in the forest, you will sleep and make kisses in the columns of a picture from science, but you will never see the whole picture."

And yet you live.

I took a breath, and the dog barked. I'm coming.

The fog tore itself out from under my wounded feet. On the boulder, I saw macaques that were gathered around a baby. Macaques were fighting on the ground, some in the lowest branches were sleeping, and others, after racing around, were going to sleep. Each one was different. Oh, Doogie, each one has his reasons, and where's the harm in that? Animals, animals, animals. "What else is there?" I asked myself. "Where are you, civilization?" I said goodnight to them, to the little ones, each one according to his name, and I got up. Farewell, valley.

Under my eyes, in the wash of gray-and-brown earth full of lumps that snaked its way along, I saw it. In front of me, climbing to the top of the embankment where the crazed dog was barking, there were footsteps of me.

Of me myself: of a chimpanzee.

Memories

Soon, the sixth of the hours will fall from the clock above the black table, but for now it's hanging on.

"Fall . . . fall . . . fall . . ." Doogie thinks as he watches it from under his eyebrows. "Doogie, you have to finish your homework." Phooey. On the table made of wood that was sawed by the Gardener, in the empty classroom, Doogie is fiddling with flat rectangles. On each card a mommy or a daddy or a little one is drawn, and Doogie must recognize them, divide them, and organize them by family to prove that he has the science of the family. The lion family, the dolphin family, the whale family: Doogie knows all the families. I smile. Doogie leaves the human family for last. Janet made it specially to please him. Mommy Mrs. Diane is in a photo under her umbrella, daddy Mr. Gardner is in a photo smoking a pipe under his mustache, and Janet is sitting at the table of her birthday dressed in a princess dress. She's smiling, and Doogie, dressed like a person, is in an ID photo facing forward. His mouth is open, and he has red eyes. Yuck, how stupid he looks! He's not a child or a human, but he's me. I'm sad. I look for a picture of Donald. Where is it? It's between the photos of Mrs. Tiger and Mr. Panther. Doogie gets the two felines mixed up.

Sad Doogie. One can see in the photo that you don't have a family.

And the sixth hour is still holding out. It never falls, and the sun is going down. Doogie thinks that the clock is stuck. I get up and get out of my seat. The camera sees you Doogie, but it's been long enough. The clock must not be working.

Then—*crash!*—Doogie hears a noise that is coming from behind the door.

In my overalls, I walk carefully to the doorknob, which is too high for me. On my tiptoes, I open the door, and what do I see?

Donald, pale, is lying slumped on his side at the top of the staircase.

"Donald?" I ask, but I'm afraid. It could be a trap.

Donald usually limps: he barely has the science of walking. But today he's on the ground and he's shivering. He says "eek," like a mouse. I don't want to touch him. The last time, he brought me too close to Heaven. That's over now, but when I touch the side of my neck I still have a bandage. His mouth was full of my blood.

But now it's Donald who seems wounded. He's groaning, and his eyes are small, red, and white, his upper body's naked, and he's wearing pajama pants. He's rolling around on the ground.

"Doogie," Janet had said, "my parents left to inspect the hippo pond. I have to finish my bio homework. You stay here until six o'clock; make sure on your watch. You know that the good behavior camera can see you." I looked at my wrist: twenty minutes had already fallen since the sixth hour. I had the right.

Donald swallowed. "Iiiih . . . Drooooogie," he said.

I leaned toward him, and he didn't do anything to me. Hounh, I separated his arms, and my brother was covered with red spots on this chest. He looked at me, I'll never forget, in despair.

I held Donald by the wrists and, sticking out my tongue, I dragged him into my room. He watched me the whole time. On my bed—even though he smelled very bad he's your brother, Doogie—I laid him down with a big effort and I covered him with the checkered blanket. He was shivering, and soon he wasn't moving anymore, stiff, with his eyes open. I touched him. How cold you are, Donald. I got water from the faucet, but he didn't drink it.

I sat down and waited on the stool. Evening came.

Ding-dong, and *creak*, I heard steps on the staircase. Donald hadn't made a movement, and I didn't know what to decide. Mrs. Diane opened the door of my room. "Doogie, I brought you your first banana." When she entered, she dropped the shopping bags and her handbag.

"Oh, my God," she murmured. "What is it?" I asked. She hurried to the bed, placing her hand with two rings on Donald's forehead, and then she looked at me, opening her mouth covered with lipstick. "Ape! Ape!" she yelled. "What have you done?" She shook me, hounh, hounh. "What have you done to him? Tell me!" she yelled.

She slapped me, and I lowered my head while curling up. "Oh . . ." she was weeping. "Oh, my God, I think my son is dead," she said. "I think he's dead."

And that word, it seems to me that it was the first time Doogie heard it. Since then, Doogie has forgotten it.

Death

—The word.—A cadaver.—Memories: first impressions of
Michael.—The hole, the weapon, and the burial.

From the Jungle

As soon as I had cleared away the ferns at the top of the embankment with my arms, I knew. The sun had fallen, but at the summit the moon was giving light like a flashlight, and it was getting cool. Faithful the dog had moved away, growling and even fighting with the hyena and the jackals that were walking there in the shadow of trees that were naked as if burned.

Oh yes, I saw it, and the word came back to me.

My memories are sad and my brain is sad, but I don't know which is the saddest. I knelt down. The word is *death*.

Stretched out naked, his two legs and his arms and the bottom of his face eaten by jackals, Michael wasn't there anymore. "Michael," I wanted to murmur, "where are you?" Night had fallen, and I can't speak in the night, even under the moon. My brain descends into my hands and my hands descend into the night.

The dog understood. He stayed seated, immobile, one two and three steps away. He prevented the jackals from coming again to make Michael into a restaurant.

But where are you, Heaven? If you are here, then Michael isn't there. Or else Michael is half there and half in the stomach of the jackal. Heaven, you are nowhere, and the real word is *death*. It's *death*.

And I wept, wept, wept a great deal on my knees. Because I knew. With my head lowered, I choked, and I had hiccups. Michael is rotting, Michael the human is no longer here, nothing, a void, nothing, it's over. And I wept and wept.

I halfway recognized him, dead and killed. It wasn't the jackal that had killed him. His head had been crushed by blows from a stone. His skull was open, his brain like brain meat that is dripping, a river made of blood. And he had been bitten on the neck by an ape, Doogie. Look around you: those are *your* footprints. I look, but I don't understand.

I think that I was crazy. Who is Doogie, and who I? Those are my chimpanzee footprints all around him. Who deathed him? I haven't forgotten the word, as craziness as I am.

All night, trembling, I sobbed. I didn't even see the hours fall on the watch of my dial.

Michael, dead as you are, you're nothing anymore, and Doogie didn't save you. Who it was that made Michael equal death I don't know and I don't understand. Those are the steps of my feet of the murderer.

Dirty ape, crazy ape, you don't know anything, and from now on nothing will be everything.

When I couldn't cry anymore, under the moon hidden by the fog, I caught my two ears between my fingers and I hit my head over and over against the ground.

And then I slept.

Memories

Donald stayed pale for one day. Donald stayed pale for two days.

"He hasn't gone to Heaven, Doogie," Janet said when she came, smiling, to sit on the edge of my very soft bed with pine legs. She didn't say the word, and Doogie didn't know, with his hands, how to say the word. He'd never learned it. It wasn't the black of night yet. Janet's two hands are around a mug. I wait for my herbal tea to cool off, and "gently, Doogie," I breathe delicately on the surface of the herbal tea made with good linden to cool off the molecules of heat. "Doogie, physics is amazing. Soon I'll teach you in class what I learned in the textbook at school."

"Doogie, all around you, it's incredible," she said. "If you only knew: everything is just atoms and molecules." Since I was frowning, she stroked the end of my bad nose. "Even you," she murmured, "even your nose."

"And what about Janet?" I asked, no longer pouting.

She turned on the bedside lamp as if to tell Doogie the evening's story. Her hands smell like beauty cream, she's a redhead, and she has breasts now. Doogie is very very very bothered.

"Even Janet," she agrees.

O atom, O molecule! Why are you Doogie, and why are you Janet? O molecule, what have you done?

"Janet, we have to go," we hear from the staircase.

Poor me, poor Doogie molecule, I understand that the Janet molecule is going to leave you. Janet put on her orange-and-blue down coat. "Ciao," she said, giving a kiss with the tips of her fingers. Her ring blinded Doogie. "We're going to be driving all night to get the bush doctor, you know."

Silence.

Janet lowered her head as she tied up her red ponytail. She was very worry. "Donald can't wait any longer." And then she hesitated on the step at the foot of the door. "Michael is going to come and take care of you. He's the new student, and he's so well-mannered and so cute, Doogie. Be nice, you're going to like him." She winked her eye, and the nightmare began.

At first her cheeks were pink-red, and she kissed him hello. She never kissed Doogie hello. "Good evening, Mickey," she said. He had his hands in his pockets, wearing jeans and a checkered shirt, with beautiful short blond hair and blue eyes. He said: "Good luck, Jane." Why is he saying "Jane"? And Doogie started to suffocate. Houh, houh. I was stuck in bed like a sick person. "Doogie," Janet said. "It's not your fault, of course, but you have to stay in your room until we know about Donald." Hooooouuh . . .

"Doogie! Be good! Look at your watch, and when you miss me, count the hours like I taught you, and count the days. Know that I can see you. Because I'm watching you. I'm always there."

And she left. Aaaah!

Then Michael crossed his arms. Doogie hid, whimpering under his blanket. I don't want to see this.

"Hello," he said. "How's it going, little ape?"

Huuuuuuh . . . Doogie made a face under the comforter under the blanket, in his Mickey Mouse pajamas. How many times does Doogie have to say it? Doogie doesn't like it when people call him that!

Hiiii . . . "Leave me alone," I moaned. But Michael, like glue, doesn't go away. He sits down and he speaks, separating the syllables as if Doogie couldn't understand the words, like he's an idiot, like he's talking to a baby. He says: "Look, I don't know you, it's the first time I've seen you, but I have a present. I've come from up there, from far behind the stars."

Doogie's not an idiot: he knows about the orbital space stations.

Michael whistled. Doogie doesn't know how to whistle between his teeth. "Hey, ape, I can't see you. Show yourself to me."

"Phooey," I said, and I lifted up my face.

Then I got hit by water in my face. What? He was laughing and his teeth were white. Shit. Doogie, watch your vocabulary. "Hey, don't worry, ape, it's just a plastic water pistol. Look, it's a water pistol, and I'm giving it to you. No hard feelings."

Oh, Doogie already hated him.

He smiled stupidly and—what a catastrophe!—he tried to stroke the top of Doogie's skull. He had a sad look in his idiotic eyes. I didn't understand.

"Oh, you poor ape," he said. "If you only knew."

If you only knew?

And then he wanted to tickle me as a joke. Doogie hates tickling, and Doogie hates jokes. His cheeks smelled like the shaving products that Mr. Gardner used, which Doogie is jealous about, but also like the smell of Janet's neck.

"Hey, ape, I think the two of us are going to get along well. Don't you think so? From what I've been told, it seems that you're a huge phenomenon. You behave yourself, and I'll work next to you at your desk."

Okay.

Doogie looked at him stupidly with the eyes of an ape, with his black eyes, while pushing his jaw forward, hounh, and then, as I watched him, *fart*, I took a shit on the bed.

"Oh! Oh, no!" he said. "This can't be happening!"

And while he was panicking and getting a towel, a sponge and the trash can, I jumped off the bed and ran away.

"Doogie . . . Doogie. . . . Come back here!"

"This one," I thought. "When he has trouble, I will have happiness."

From the Jungle

Doogie doesn't know all the subtleties of the science of burying, but what I know is that there is a hole in the middle.

To the dog, since he is faithful, I said "dig," and I showed him, and then he dug, in the early morning, because it already smelled bad.

Then I looked for religion, but I couldn't find it.

What's an ape who is burying a human supposed to do? I don't know.

"Goodbye from God," I said, but I didn't know what I was saying, you know. I explained with my big hand how I met Michael, how impossible I was, how because of Janet, you understand, I couldn't stand him. I said, "Michael, I don't know any of the stories about Heaven, I don't know anything about it," and I didn't cry.

Since the terrier dog was tired, I dragged the body to the very badly made hole, alas, in the black earth, and when I squinted I could see white worms that were moving around at the bottom. Oh, that didn't please me much as a restaurant for Michael, but the science of the hole is the only one that knows how to bury.

And he fell in. *Wham.*

I reached out my hand, and his leather belt was still around his waist. I unfastened it and pulled it back up. In the holster that was hanging from it, I heard a *click-clack*. I thought about it. I had found his pistol of a weapon.

"Doogie," I said, "you're far from being a weapon that has the science of the pistol," but I had a pair of xxl underpants and the little loaded pistol. I stuffed it into my underpants like a real cowboy, okay Doogie.

As I was closing up the ground of the earth, Thousand Colors with the crooked beak landed. He had three gray stains on his feathers. He cackled:

"Doogie."

"Doogie."

"Doogie."

"Yes," I said, "that's my name." He shut up, and I pushed the soft earth with my feet and my hands because no one wants to help me.

"Doogie, it's Rnature."

"Mm," I said. I wasn't listening to him. It was time to go back to the Zoo, and Michael was going away. So long, farewell, and bye-bye. After a while, the little macaca with the too high nostrils jumped from the branch of the dead tree while shaking Michael's dirty underwear that she had stolen the night before.

Feeling moved, I said to myself: "Is the dirty monkey saying goodbye and ciao to him?"

Then I understood that the idiotic rhesus macaca wanted to play and jump, she was so excited by the piece of fabric. "Grr," I growled, "give me that," and I hit her on the head. She smiled while lowering her gaze. The dirty monkey, I wanted to hit her again.

"You idiot," I thought. "You don't understand anything."

"You don't know anything about Michael the human. You didn't know him, and you don't know anything about Heaven or the end of life. You don't know a single word, so get out of here."

And then it was over. The sun climbed into the sky, and the mountain shone. I patted the weapon of the pistol in my underpants, and I petted the dog. I didn't know what to think, how to have the science of the cross and the cemetery. I just said:

"I think I liked Michael a little."

A branch snapped and I jumped. Where did that come from?

I wanted to do the same thing to those who did this to Michael as they did to him. Yes. I squeezed my fist on the heavy pistol. With the weapon, don't cry anymore: you have power.

The dog growled under his dirty mustache, standing straight on his four big paws.

"Shh."

Quickly, I hide behind the dead black tree, and I place my big hand on the moist and hairy mouth of the dog who thinks I'm petting him.

Someone is coming closer, and I lean my head behind the trunk that is as black as coal from lightning. Does someone want to carry the tomb to Heaven?

It's like a shadow, black and bent over, ungainly; it's like a reflection in a mirror. I recognize his footsteps, his feet. It's as if I see myself without being behind my eyes.

It's a nervous ape. It's another me.

I frown, and my nose rises like an accordion between my two red-orange eyes that are shining-burning, and I recognize him. He's not a macaca, he's a chimpanzee. Like me.

It was . . . it's Jack.

Jack

*—Memories of the second chimpanzee.—An attack
and the humiliation of the other.—The forgetting and the
memory of languages.—The assassin denounces himself.—
Memories: a tragic accident.—The Animal.*

Memories

On the advice of the bush doctor, Mrs. Diane left for the stars to get Donald treated. A month has already fallen from the calendar. I never see Mr. Gardner.

Every day I have class with Janet, but in the evening she leaves to smoke, to take walks, and to take the 4-by-4 car with Michael.

When the sixth hour falls from the clock in the downstairs classroom, Michael opens the door in a Hawaiian shirt. He smiles, he brings me a candy, and Doogie be nice.

Janet, wearing a blouse, gives him a kiss. "Hey, Mickey, don't you think it's hot this evening?" She turns toward me: "Doogie, you know, since mom left, Jack's been getting worse. It would be so nice of you."

Okay. Mickey gets to stay with Janet and count the number of shitty petals on the flowers from the fields while Doogie goes down to the control room of the lab to say "hello Jack." It bursts out of me: "Grrr."

"Thank you, Doogie."

When I close the door, cursing my babyish jean overalls, I hear Michael murmuring: "Jane, I know how hard this is for you, with your brother and all."

"Oh . . ."

"Shh."

"Okay."

I went down. Doogie spat out Michael's stinky mint candy, and I thought that one day I would show him my butthole and I would poop on his head.

I look for the key under the pot of the begonia flower. I turn on the light and I go into the control room. It's been a long time. I'm not in the lab anymore, I go to school now.

I haven't seen Jack since . . . since . . .

"Hello, Jack," I said timidly.

I saw him on the big velvet armchair, slouched, his eyes open. "Jack," I said, "are you okay?" I was afraid that, like Donald, he would jump on Doogie.

But when he saw Doogie, Jack grinned like an idiot. He twisted his arms and saliva came out from his lips.

"Jack. Well . . . What should we talk about?" He knew about ten words with his hands. "I'm going to get your plastic cubes," I said. "Do you want, would you like to play?"

Jack plays really well with the baseball, he can peel bananas, and he knows how to cook hamburgers.

But he's more of an animal than me, you know.

"He has a sickness of the mind," I thought. His head was leaning to one side, his fat nose that I don't like, that looks like mine, was a real germinated potato, and his lips were going sideways.

"Jack"—I held out my hand—"are you going to stay in the dark?"

Then, then, Jack held out his hand to Doogie. He wants to. He wants to delouse me. Doogie is embarrassed. "Come on, Jack, we don't do that."

But he wants to.

Doogie clears his throat and jumps from one foot to the other in his overalls.

"Well, I guess that's it then. I'm happy to have seen you."

Doogie notices the medicines and the pharmacy that is locked behind glass.

With difficulty, Jack gets down from his seat. He groans and looks at me. In his eyes I see, first pity, then nothing, and then he rounds his back. His fur is not very clean. He bends down in front of me. "Please." I don't know what he's doing.

"Oh, okay then, Jack, I'm going to go."

Jack the chimpanzee lowered himself down in front of me. What does he want? It was so shocking and unseemly to try to clear away the walls between us. So I left, leaving the light on, and as I exited the tiled corridor, I closed the door behind me.

What did he want?

And that was the last time I saw him.

From the Jungle

Seeming a bit desperate, Jack attacked me.

Houh! He was still a solid chimpanzee; he kicked up dust, and he ran after me. One time, two times, growling, making a lot of noise, he showed his teeth, his mouth open with a malicious look. I ran away, jumping on the ashy ground before I stumbled.

He dived onto me to bite me between my legs, but I got up quickly, scratching the ground which turned red when the gray dust flew up.

A piercing scream pierces your head! He tries to hit me, ah hounh, but it's only air that he finds under his fist. He missed. Such aggression! I protect my head, one arm on my hairy forehead, one arm extended. But you have to face up to this, Doogie. Because I understood.

Standing on his bowed hairy legs, one hand on his testicles, one hand on his shoulder, with the hairs on his skull standing on end, Jack lowered his head, his knees bare and his nose sullen. He pounded his chest with his hand.

"Dirty ape," I said, and I screamed.

Because I understood that he was scared. "Hi hi, Doogie," I thought. "As much of a coward as you are, you'll win without having to fight, because Jack is afraid of you. I just have to seem like his superior and I will be." Hounh, I stand up straight and I look at him. Already, Jack is ashamed of attacking me. His legs and feet are shaking, he steps back, tense, and he puts his two hands on the red earth and the gray ash from the dust that has just come back down.

From my underpants, I took out my heavy black pistol that belongs to the weapon of power, and I wave it above my head, grimacing. I focus my gaze on him, and toward the ground, defeated, haggard, he lowers his gaze. He smiles and shows me his uncertain jaw. He paws at the ground and flattens himself down. "Dog," I say. "Come next to me." And the faithful dog who is barking, his mustache moving, looks at me, poised on his hind legs, ready to bite your face, Jack. Oh, Jack, you shouldn't play at being the smart one, hin-hin.

Doogie is dominant, Doogie is the king. Repeat that back to me.

And that was it. Jack wanted to attack me, but he has a small impotent will, caught between his fear and his memories. He knows that Doogie is stronger, much stronger. He tested him a little, but he didn't know how to go further. I walk around, showing off the pistol in my underpants. The sun is shining and the ground is flat. The only sound you could hear was me, me, me: I breathe, I breathe, and I dominate. "Sit, dog." And he sits.

The dominator dominates. I puff out Doogie's shoulders, my head pulled back, and I look at Jack. I'm the one who has eyes; you have nothing. I'm the one who has the right. Jack is the same height as me, but he is more little-little. With his butt in the air, he shows his poop hole to the sky, he crouches down like a toad, his hair worn away. He flattens himself and goes down toward the dust. And now it's time to say "peace" to him. I grunt as I walk, I rub against him as I go by, and he gets up. "Jack, Doogie has humiliated you."

And he doesn't even know how to say yes.

I'm calming down. Be faithful to the human, Doogie, and don't drive a hard bargain. You also act less proud, monkey, when Janet is angry. It's true. I groan.

"So," I ask him, "what are you doing here?"

He's still scared, even if he's starting to relax. Panic-stricken, he looks behind him.

"What are you doing in the Jungle? Are you also lost?"

He doesn't understand. Poor ape, poor monkey. I give up with my hands: language is not for him.

I let out a scream, a pant from my good old past, and I bang against the trunk of a tree to remind him of it.

An abyss of nothing. Jack stays hunched over. I push the dust and twigs around while letting out a happy cry. "How've you been?"

An abyss of nothing is still nothing.

I mope. "Doogie," I say to myself, "what a filthy thing it is to be smarter than smart and the best of a whole species. All the others are as stupid as walls."

The only thing this idiot understands is domination.

"Jack," I grunt, and he jumps up. "Look at me, idiot: are you the one who did that to Michael?" I repeat: "Are you the one who kills him?"

He doesn't speak.

With his eyes wide, his mouth a triangle over his dirty teeth without toothpaste, he smiles, the moron.

"Jack," I cry out, "come forward, lower yourself down, recollect yourself, recollect yourself on the tomb of the memory of Michael the human. Do you remember Michael?"

He doesn't dare.

I slap him on the top of his skull while displaying my teeth. "I'm going to bite you," I say. I push him, and I lower his dirty head in front of the pile of blackish earth beneath which was what was left of Michael.

"Humiliate yourself in front of the memory of the human, dirty nose." And I spit as I grumble. I spit at his feet while making my hair stand on end. "Hunker down."

It's the temperature of night falling.

In the woods of the forest, high above the mangrove forest of the oceans, the air is cold. The dog is trotting slowly with his tongue hanging out. Leaning on a stick he picked up and peeled with his fingers, Doogie climbs and goes on talking: "Come on, Jack, follow us, come on, quickly." And since, sadly, Jack is afraid, Jack follows.

The land has risen, and the forest has changed. Yellow and red, the floor of earth that smells like iron has been ground up. From time to time, Doogie sniffs clay under his feet, and super-moist trees are shooting up in the direction of the sky, buffeted by the wind. Doogie follows the dog, and the dog follows Doogie. All of them are going up, climbing through patches of forest with boulders, toward the valley that is getting closer, the valley of the big river that flows toward the middle of the continent. Then Doogie will have to cross it blind and find the giant Congo that flows to the lake of the continent, not far from the Zoo.

In his head, Doogie is not devoid of the science of the feet and of the ground.

There is granite and basalt, as Mr. Gardner taught him, which swells underneath the thin layer of humus and the torn-up earth beneath my two feet. Rainwater has streamed, clefts and canals have made a sculpture out of all this Nature, and from under the fog of hopelessness I see the first green and black river that will lead Doogie and his companions to the Congo. "Congo King, Congo King," I laugh.

No one laughs with me.

How sad it is without language. Let's just sit on our butts.

It's raining, it has rained, and there's what is called mist. Brr!

On the elevation of the irrigated elevations are forests planted with bananas, with palm trees, and with the remains of old coffee plants from humans when they worked here long ago in the past, Jungle and Civilization hand in hand. But like Mr. Payne's bald skull, the trees are degraded and naked, and boulders dominate the skull of the earth.

Doogie also dominates. He's the one who found the spring water that is fresh to drink, and fruits, roots, and every single thing. The dog stupidly wanders off. Above us, Thousand Colors regularly flies, spins around, flies up and chatters some idiocies that he repeats. As for sullen Jack, he eats earth, along with the worms. The sun has fallen down, and we can't see the other end of our noses. I'm getting annoyed.

"This is far enough," I say.

Jack, his butt in the ferns, startles and then chews, slumped over. Against the gray barrel of the big naked tree, I put down my bananas and the wrinkled fresh palm leaves that I collected in the place of a sponge and dipped in the spring to clean myself.

"Jack," I articulate with gesture after gesture, "don't you remember speech?"

He stops chewing.

"The good old days," I say. "The two of us. Do you remember? An ape who can speak is a friend of the human."

"Blbl." He makes a face.

I was patient that evening. By the light of the moon on this open terrain, I took up my old ASL language, the language of apes who speak the language of the deaf and dumb in English.

English, please!

Jack knows ASL, *yes sir*, he's the one who taught me half of it. But who will learn it back from the one who learns it? It's a mystery, a mystery. An ape doesn't have ideas in his larynx, but he does have words in his hands, ladies and gentlemen.

I sign the word *flower* and I sign the word *smell*. I draw a wrinkly orchid and I wriggle my nostrils. "Jack, does that mean anything to you?"

Apparently not. Then I start up my act again. I sign *hat* and I act out a hat like Charlie Chaplin on the screen on the living room wall, like Mr. Gardner used to do to make us laugh, juvenile children that we were, ha-ha. Not children, not humans.

Everything came back to me. The PCM system. P is the placement of the sign on the body, C is the configuration of the hand, and M is the movement. I speak it badly enough that it's only for foreign humans who don't know me and for when I'm deprived of the keyboard, the screen, and the vocal translator. All of that broke in the crash of the Charles Bigleux.

Sometimes, as you know, the English words from ASL come to the surface of my well-ordered ape language, when I try to speak too quickly the way I do. Like the lumps in Mrs. Diane's yogurt, there are always bits of English in my speech. *You can't always speak like you want to.*

But Jack speaks zero.

I sat down, nicely, nicely, in front of the fat simpleton. Phooey. I squeezed his big intelligent hand, where the fingers are very far from the wrist. They have forgotten what the arm wants to say. "Jack," I said, "you were a model for me," and I modeled his hand like before. Mr. Gardner tried modeling, but it was only with Janet that it worked. Oh, how I loved it! She modeled my hand, you know: she constructed the sign with the tips of her delicate white fingers that don't have a single hair like on my fat foolish black-brown hairy hand. I'm a thrill!

I modeled *my, name, Jack,* and *hello* on his big hand. He looked at me emptily, and he seemed astonished. He wanted to eat. The dog lay down on his side. He was waiting to be petted before sleeping. So I massaged him, and his hair the color of dead leaves was dirty, rough, and crawling with parasites. Around us, mosquitoes were buzzing. What is this Nature? When the dog went to sleep, I whistled to Jack, and in the gray dust, by the light of the night, I drew the symbol of the moon, and then I drew lexigrams in the earth, in the clay.

"Don't you remember that? And that?"

I showed Jack the lexigrams of a dog, of the night, of the moon and of sleep. They were the only ones he knew at the time. But the lexigram of the thing doesn't look like the thing, and Jack has forgotten. Jack has forgotten.

How patient you are, Doogie the teacher. I looked at my watch. Janet, if you could only see me now.

But above all, how alone you are, Doogie.

You are a solitary alone one, for sure.

The clay hadn't dried behind the clumps of weeds, and with my fist I modeled a bit of the dirty clay that came from the crevasse, from the summit in the valley where the rainwater ran.

"Do you remember Lantek, Jack?"

Jack never liked the changeover to Lantek. Lantek was an artificial language.

"Well, do you remember the camera, the blackboard and the colored magnets, the strange kinds of language to stick on the board, looking for vocabulary words in the wicker box?"

Stressed, Jack chews the tips of his fingers. He looks all around him like a bad duffer of a student.

I sculpted the form of a lexigram in clay, a truncated cone, *banana*, and I asked again.

I really wanted him to remember. On the flat, cleared-off ground, like on an old wooden table, I placed a stone, a palm leaf, and a banana.

"Jack . . ." Slowly, I asked in English ASL, "*What is this?*" and I held out the clay lexigram to him. It fell apart, splat.

I knew that there was anguish in his eyes, but I went on. Jack has a panic: he stretched out his finger, he made the sign of the banana, and he pointed to the pebble.

Oh, I turned red with anger! "You bad dirty stupid monkey," I said. "Take this!" and I hit his hand with the stone. "That means you're wrong."

Smiling nervously, he assumed the dominated posture.

With tears around my two eyes, I signed "I'm sorry," and I said, "Jack, don't you remember how to say *friend*?"

It was the first word that I taught him, and he had never learned it.

Like a slave in the night, without language, he groveled before me.

I gave up and went to bed.

Only then did Jack tentatively get up. He came closer and he made a misguided gesture. "What is it, imbecile ape?" I groaned.

In the dark, trembling, I think he signed. No, he was asking me something. He turned around and presented his ribs to me, and then he opened his lips on his white teeth in the light of the moon.

The dog was sleeping like a stone.

I understood. He was asking me about a sign he remembered. "The sign that you have a memory of, Jack," I rapidly signed without him seeing me in the night, "is two fingers that move in a hook and a smile. That's the sign for *tickle*, Jack," and I wanted to cry. He lent me his flank, and as in earlier times I tickled him as I guffawed. The dog didn't wake up.

Jack vaguely imitated the sign, and he extended his arm to tickle-tickle me under *my* ribs, but . . .

"Go away," I told him.

He stopped. He didn't dare.

Memories

In class, I'm sad about what I've seen of Jack.

The day after the previous day, I don't know when it was, I raised my finger and I asked Janet: "Can we stop the class?"

"Yes, Doogie." She frowns. "Do you have a question, or do you need to pee?"

At that time of the morning, she's teaching me the past, the present, the tomorrow, and the difference between a conjunction and a disjunction, or something like that. Hin hin.

"No," I shake my head sadly, my ears sticking out from under the hairstyle of my hair divided in two with a part, with gel.

She's sitting on her desk and sighing as she pulls up her skirt over her long socks with red and white stripes, as long as tights. It's very hot. She makes her hand into a fan. Her cheeks are covered with freckles.

"It's about Jack."

"Oh . . . Jack." She raises her eyes to the ceiling. "Doogie, there's a problem with Donald, so . . ."

"But," I say, signing quickly with one hand, "why has Jack *stopped to speak*, Janet?"

"Be careful, Doogie," she said. "Don't mix in the English ASL of deaf-mutes when you're speaking Lantek. That's your own language. There are different languages, and there's language, Doogie. They're not the same." Janet is intelligent. I lower my head.

Patient girl that she is, she smiles, and she says: "Come on, let's take a walk in the woods and then go lie in the sun on deckchairs on the terrace. Dad is away, he's waiting for mom to return. He won't be back before tomorrow, so he won't know."

And she locked the door of the overheated classroom.

While sipping her orgeat syrup, Janet put her movie-star sunglasses on her long, thin, and very distinguished nose. In her white bra and shorts, she's lying on the transatlantic deckchair, and Doogie is swinging in the hammock.

"Doogie," she told me. "There's a whole story about language."

"I know." I lifted my torso up. "One day I'll tell it to you."

"Ha-ha," she laughed while picking up her lace fan. "You don't know anything about what you know, monkey."

Janet is as mysterious as a sentence sometimes.

"In the beginning, everything you see here—the financing for Project Zoo and the lab—daddy got it thanks to a new project on language teaching and learning that he had proposed to the orbital stations, to the eco-societies.

"The goal was to make Jack speak and to make the great apes evolve so that we could give the forest back to them. As you know, men have been living in the stars since the end of the war, and the Earth is a treasure that they are holding onto from far away. But we humans, Doogie, we feel so alone. We wanted to do something for *you*, you understand. After all, as dad said, if God created a being that speaks, and if that being creates another being that speaks, the conclusion is obvious."

I didn't understand. "What? Who is God? Is that the Janet of Janet?"

"Yes, you could say that." Sigh. She put her blue glass down on the ground, on the cement in the shade. "The conclusion, Doogie, is that we are *your* gods and that we are the apes of *our* gods."

With my eyes emptier than empty, I stopped swinging.

She burst into laughter. "Pfff . . . Doogie, you should see your face."

Then she cleared her throat. "Jack was the best . . ."

Doogie protested.

". . . until we got you, Doogie. Jack progressed quickly and well. Mrs. Diane, mom, had theorized the complete emotional environment. She wanted a child so, so badly, another one, not like me, a boy. She didn't look after me; it was all for *him*. For me, it's always been daddy."

Janet sighs.

"Jack learned the rudiments of deaf-mute sign language. Dad said, 'Apes don't have a larynx, but just look at their hands.' In two years, he knew a hundred and thirty signs, Doogie. He had absorbed it. Jack was so intelligent at that time. He knew negation relatively well, and the bases that you use today: agent, action, localization, possession, nomination, and recurrence. Dad told me that when I was still a baby, experts from the orbital stations, specialists in sign language, would come every day to carry out tests behind the glass windowpane. A sign was only counted as acquired when its utilization was spontaneous and had been assimilated for at least two weeks.

"So, it was all fairly classical, and it had already been done. 'We've already seen all of that,' the scientists told daddy.

"Then Jack signed by himself. The first time, he used an undifferentiated sign for both *flower* and *smell*, but when he had indicated the difference between them mom drank champagne. It was her victory! Dad wasn't very happy; he argued for another approach. Contact with Jack bothered him, and he was looking for something analyzable, something quantitative, you know. He was always like that, and his work on language led him to the following idea: you would have to compare, point by point, a child who has been deprived of language with an ape to whom a real language has been taught. You would have to have an objective comparison, you see, with a control subject. Do you understand me, Doogie? No, you don't understand anything I'm saying.

"Dad did more of the work with me. He always liked me, and he said that I was talented, very much so, you know: super-talented. Mom started modeling signs directly onto Jack's hand, and then, and then . . ."

"And then *what*?"

"Donald was born. We don't really know how. Dad and mom . . . well, anyway. He had a difficult birth; it was a miracle. Mom suspended her experiments and dad found you, abandoned. Oh, that was, you know, a real opportunity for dad. And, Doogie, an opportunity for me. Dad put Donald into competition with you right away. To please mom, who wouldn't let it go, and who was herself often tired and staying in bed, he taught you the bases in ASL, and he quickly got you to communicate. It was Jack, you know, who taught you to speak, to say the few English words that you sometimes mix into your speech."

"Jack?" I say, my mouth hanging open.

"Mm-hmm."

"The observers and the students had a strict directive of silence. They never signed in the cage or the lab in your presence. They only interacted with you orally, taking note of your gestures and the erection of your hairs. They wanted to know if an ape could teach language to another ape.

"In the beginning, for example, Jack taught you the signs for *come* and *gimme*. You repeated *gimme gimme*; you were so incredibly quick and smart. I have to say that in the evening we laughed together. I also respected dad's strict order of silence. I didn't sign. No, I only spoke to you with my voice, and I think you liked that. I should say that dad hid all this from mom, who was still convalescing in the evenings after work. He put you and Donald on parallel tracks for everything: for playing, eating, going to sleep. Except that you were working with Jack during the day, while Donald was taking a nap with mom. And very quickly, we understood that he was becoming strange.

"But when Jack taught you that first word, we were so moved. Jack liked to sign for *tickle*; he used to push his ribs against the bars of the cage so that a student would come and tickle him. Two days later, you, Doogie, started doing the same thing, and I would come to tickle-tickle you, and you laughed and laughed. Next, you made the sign all alone, all by yourself on the straw mattress. Then you imitated Jack's cries while associating the sign and the facial expressions. In the end, you made the sign on your own with a delighted look and then pushed your ribs between the bars and I tickled you, you clever boy.

"Jack taught you the verbs, and also location words and even adverbs, all in the English for deaf-mutes. You were moving faster, much faster than he was. You associated *hurry* and *gimme* so that we would give you a banana more quickly, or a cuddle, and especially, especially, you liked it when I modeled the signs on your hand. Do you remember? You loved that. It was so . . .

"As opposed to Jack, who almost never used language for anything other than requests, you, working with me, learned all the indicative propositions and descriptions. When mom was finally back on her feet, she mostly took care of Donald, while dad and I were focused only on you. Jack started to regress, and besides that you intimidated him. Very quickly, dad insisted that you stay in the house, and since we could see the limits of English sign language, he prevailed over mom by getting the scientific office of the Zoo to vote for phase two of an experiment involving a new artificial language that would be more flexible, that would allow you to assimilate a grammar. ASL didn't match well with you as a chimpanzee.

"Dad immediately brought a linguist on the Charles Bigleux—it was Mr. Peter, Michael's father—to work alongside him to create a simplified ideogrammatic language, Lantek, which was at first composed of lexigrams:

you know, the little symbols that didn't visually represent what they meant, and that were organized according to a very rough semantics. Oh, Doogie, I'll spare you the details.

"For Christmas that year, they gave you the computer screen and the keyboard with the big keys, the one you had when you were little, before the one you have now. Jack got one too, by the way, but he never learned how to use it. It was completely beyond him. This new language—he didn't understand it, and no one was interested in him.

"You tried to help him—you taught him the lexigram for *friend*—but you very quickly destroyed him. You were mean to him . . . You toyed with him and humiliated him.

"Little by little, you knew how to put together sentences on the vertical axis of your screen, you had conversations with dad, you assimilated relationships and numbers more or less well, the properties of different classes of words, and notions of metalanguage.

"And then, as soon as we were together in the evening, without the screen and the keyboard, since you wanted so badly to speak to me, we spent hours putting together a language of signs, one that expressed your own language, Monkage, the one you speak to us in, with your grammar and your lexigrams mixed with the old English for deaf-mutes.

"And that's when everything changed."

Janet breathed in. She sat up, still in the deckchair that was half in the shade and soon to be in the sun.

"You can't know everything, Doogie, but . . . No one knows why. I don't know why, even though I was there, and dad doesn't know. We finished the experiment, with very strong and consistent results, from the small stock of vocabulary that the better chimpanzees had, and you started speaking. Yes, you really did. With your hands, you signed sentences, with subjects, verbs, and objects. On the computer, which you used like a typewriter, you made a synthesis of your electronic grammar and the ASL language that you spoke with your hands. It became your mode of communication, and everyone who worked with us at the Zoo, all of those who were close to us, learned it.

"Except for mom, of course. She didn't want to. She never wanted to.

"But other than her, everyone talked to you, especially when we had programmed the translation software, with captors for your hands. Even if you and I still had our little words, just for us, right?

"But getting back to Jack . . . We had to do something, you understand, monkey? Dad put together some lexigrams that were like children's toys, plastic miniatures. They were words, including copulas and some quantifiers. They were colored, with baroque forms and a magnetized interior that allowed us to stick them to the blackboard. There was no grammar, but there was a big wicker box with a supply of vocabulary words.

"We asked you, who were so little, to play with Jack, to teach him at least *this* language in order to save him. Since you always obeyed us, you yourself learned the language of the plastic miniatures—yet another language!— but you didn't teach Jack anything. You just made fun of him. And then you abandoned him.

"He doesn't know how to do anything anymore, and he's so confused. We had to prescribe tranquilizers, and since he's afraid of the light, as you saw, he's unfortunately in the stockroom now.

"Oh, poor Doogie, if you only knew. It isn't your fault."

And because I lowered my eyes, she took me in her arms, she hugged me very tight, and she looked at the base of my neck for lice without shampoo.

"Doogie, you don't know it but . . . my little genius monkey, I love you so much."

Then I cry, and it's like I'm in Heaven.

At that moment, out of breath and badly shaven, Mr. Gardner comes out onto the terrace, and he has such a hard time talking, red-faced as he is, that he has to repeat two times: "Your mother . . . Your mother has returned."

And then things changed.

From the Jungle

I speak three languages, and I have a memory of a fourth. When speaking with you, a human who is not familiar to me except for your respect, I have to sign like a bad deaf-mute when I'm naked. But if I have the screen and the keyboard, I can type signs from my language on the keys and then a vocal translator will transmit directly to you the word of the idea of the fingers of my thought.

When I'm alone, alas, I often mix all of that up with what remains of my old *English*.

I sometimes have a memory of the language of lexigrams of plastic miniatures that I did with Jack. But he doesn't have that memory.

The day after yesterday, the four of us were going down—Thousand Colors, who is now accompanying us, Doogie, Jack, and faithful the dog who is really acting like a dog—to the foot of a finger of earth and stone that is standing above the valley. We always watch out for screes under our feet, and below us the river is green, wide, and slack. The big stone finger is hiding the sun from us, and we're walking toward the water so that we can go up the river on the swamps of its bank.

I make a joke to put Jack at ease.

Ha-ha, I imitate a stone falling, but the idiot is afraid, and he tries to jump into the void. "What are you doing, Jack?"

Cool and slow, because you're a chimpanzee, I catch him and I rub him for the don't worry, don't worry.

Then Thousand Colors chatters and repeats under his crooked beak: "Rnature! Rnature!"

And suddenly Jack freezes very stiff. "What's happening?" I ask. "Don't listen to him."

We hear the river moving, carrying pieces of wood and branches beneath our feet.

And, surprise of my astonishment, as if a substance had changed his brain, Jack signs while frantically looking to the left, to the right, and to the left. He signs phonetically, like a long time ago when he was teaching me the beginning of the alphabet.

"R-Na-Ture," he says.

"Okay," I say. "That's good, Jack, but the word is 'Na-Ture.'"

"No," I think he says, and it's like a shock. He knows the negative! With difficulty, tormented, looking haggard, he signs "R-Na-Ture" and "R-Ni-Mal."

"Animal?" I say, with a question mark. No, apparently it was "Rnimal" with an exclamation point.

Thousand Colors cackles, "The Rnimal!" And the dog who barks says "yip."

"What *is* that?"

"The-R-Ni-Mal-Wants." Jack looks at me, he's afraid. "Jack-Did-It."

"Did *what*?" I frown as I scratch myself, in the shelter of the big boulder.

He tries to jump into the void, but I hold him back, and the finger pointing toward the sky casts its shadow over the valley. I have a kind of vertigo from the sky.

"The-R-Ni-Mal-Wants." He's sweating. "Jack-Did-It." Then, after a moment of silence: "Mi-Chael."

"What? Articulate your thoughts. Michael?" I ask. "What about Michael?" and my eyes turn to him.

"Jack-Did-Mi-Chael."

"Oooooooooooooooooooh," I moan. Jack made Heaven for Michael! Jack doesn't know the word for what he did. Jack *killed* him. *Killed*. *Killed* is what you say.

And I fall to my knees.

"Jack-Did-It. The-R-Ni-Mal-Wants."

"But who *is* the Rnimal?" I ask, enraged and violently biting his wrist for domination, and the faithful dog growls and helps me.

"Who is it? Speak, speak, speak!"

"The-R-Ni-Mal-Is-Him." He curls up against the wall of gravel at the foot of the big finger.

And then I hit Jack with all my strength; I smack him in the face. Take that!

When it's over, ptui, I spit one time three times on him. I piss and I show my teeth. I say: "I forbid you to speak. Shut the mouth of your face." And Jack hunkers down.

I say: "I'm the one who gives the orders here. Only me."

And the dog barks to support me. "Shut up, you too." I scare your do-giness.

"We're going to go now. I'm the master. You're going to show me where the Rnimal is, and I'm going to kill the Rnimal. I'm the master and I dominate."

Jack has the shiny eyes of a slave. I know that he would like to speak. He raises a finger.

"Shut up," I scream without my hands. "Shut up. I'm the one who says who can speak." And to crush him I say: "You don't even know what the word is for what you did, chimpanzee."

I think about it, red with rage.

"But at least you *remember* what you did."

Memories

Mr. Gardner, his khaki shirt open, gave Janet the twin glasses that bring faraway things closer.

With his mouth open like a monkey, his two elbows resting on the railing of the cement terrace, he took his head into his hands, and Doogie came up to him to console him. Janet screamed, and she threw the twin-sisters glasses. There wasn't a moment to lose.

"Yes," Mr. Gardner said as he stood up. His very clean mustache had become slack, and his eyes were red. "The team is meeting in front of the garages with the equipment. We're leaving in two or three minutes. Janet, I really think that it's my fault as well," and he lowered his gaze.

"Doogie," Janet said to me, "go join Michael at the 4-by-4." I trotted off. They stayed behind. I was in my long shorts, a shirt, a cap on my head, and my watch on my wrist, poor chimpanzee. What could I do about it?

Far away, under the palm trees, you could see smoke rising.

Michael pushed on my behind, and I didn't like it. He made me buckle my seat belt and I pouted. What excitement! It was the first time I'd been part of such an expedition, even better than Pointe du Bec. The nurse and the doctor were in the white car, the gardener shot me a look while carrying the big crate of hunting guns, Naoki was driving, Sindhu had her two hands joined and was trembling, and the cook, the manual workers, the former cashier, the employees, and five, ten, fifteen people from the villages, neighbors who were scientists were all there talking, weapons in their hands. From time to so much time, they looked at me. I was sitting, well behaved, on the back seat. I didn't have my stuffed animals or a book or a toy.

Then Mr. Gardner Evans came running down the stairs and he made a sign: "Come on! Let's go!" Everyone took off. Janet, behind me, was pale, and no freckle outlined joy on her face. She came up to me and she undid the seat belt. "Janet, what are you doing?" She took me in her arms and said: "We're staying. We'll wait here."

Since I was in her arms, I didn't ask why, and they left. As she was cooking by herself in the stainless steel and silver kitchen, turning the spoon in the puree, Janet explained.

"Doogie, the Charles Bigleux, which was transporting mom and Donald, has crashed." Her voice slid out of her like through a flute. "We should have expected it. Dad knew that the right-side engine wasn't working properly. The Charles Bigleux is not too badly damaged, but we don't know if . . . if mom and Donald are hurt, you know . . ."

To please her, I finished my carton of soup with vegetables of leek, which I hated. "But . . ." She was thinking. "They crashed in the wild nature reserve of the Jungle. Near the Congo River, you know, to the south. Dad is afraid they've already been attacked by animals."

Doogie frowned.

"Which animals?" I smiled. "Animals are nice, Janet."

"Oh . . ." She turned around to speak to me and she wiped her hands on the kitchen towel with green checks. "Not all of them, Doogie; there are things you don't know about. The Jungle isn't what you think it is."

"Oh," I said, waving my embroidered handkerchief. "But the animals are going to protect mother and brother, don't worry."

"Doogie," she said, "we have a . . . dispute with certain animals."

"Which ones?"

"Hmm. Well, with apes, but they're not like you. They don't like humans. And then there are . . . animals in general."

When we went to bed, I was for once the one who told the story to Janet, sitting in front of her as she lay down. She was wearing a purple band in her hair, she stayed on her side, stiff like a picket in the fields, and I rocked her saying "ha-hou-ha-hou." "Thank you, Doogie, but let me sleep in my own space, please."

There was already a problem with the heating at night, and the house on the hill was cold, black, and immense. There were just the two of us, and since I couldn't close my eyes I suddenly understood that the world was too big for me, for my little head, that I was no bigger than a mosquito in the Jungle, and that without Janet the void was the void.

I saw the nightmare without sleeping. Everything is empty, no one is there, and without Janet the Zoo is like the Jungle of Doogie's first days: Doogie with no father or mother, curled up! What are you, nightmare? Even the Zoo is a Jungle.

I cried.

Janet woke up, and she pulled me against her heart under her swelling chest. "Shhh, little monkey," she told me. "You're my monkey; you'll always be my Doogie."

For two days and two nights, Janet and Doogie lived by themselves. They fed the animals during the day, and they visited Jack, who had become as stiff as a statue from the tranquilizers and medicines. Janet and Doogie were anxious, but they laughed. Such beautiful days. Memories, oh memories, where have they gone?

Despite the wretchedness of waiting, this was very close to Paradise: sleeping, playing, and eating, Janet only for Doogie, and Doogie only for Janet. He's not an animal to her. Animals are what is around them.

At noon, the sound of motors roared. We went down to the terrace.

Soon, there was disorder within civilization. The white car braked in the dust. The doctor, the nurse and Naoki were running. "Where are they?" Janet cried as she came down the stairs. "Oh my God!" On a stretcher, they brought Mrs. Diane's body rolled up in infusion lines, mummy bandages, and blood.

"Mom!"

The nurse reassured Janet with a gray face, waving her wrist. "Don't worry. She has broken legs, but she'll survive." And Janet followed her mother to the upstairs bedroom. Doogie was neither sad nor happy. It was just that the memory of Paradise was gone.

The medical staff operated on Mrs. for one day, and during this time Janet drank coffee and questioned father and Michael, who sat on kitchen chairs.

Mr. Daddy stayed quiet.

"Talk to me, daddy. What happened? What happened to Donald? Where's Donald?"

The Gardener, standing next to the door, didn't dare to say anything. He took off his straw hat, and the cook sobbed.

It was daddy's turn to speak, but his language remained mute. He tugged on his mustache and nothing more, like a puppet.

Michael's voice was broken like gravel. "Mr. Evans, if you can't say it . . ." And he got up. Suddenly, the kitchen became an almost dark kitchen in the afternoon. There was a cloud and black rain.

Janet ran up to Michael, her hair loose, and pulled on his hand. "Tell me, Mickey."

Michael said: "Donald managed to escape from the Charles Bigleux, which was badly damaged in the disastrous landing. The two pilots were . . . dead."

Doogie startled in his corner. I was listening like a spy behind the downstairs door that was half closed. I didn't have the right to be the camera. I'm not good behavior. But he was also Doogie's Donald, after all. I wanted to know, so I listened.

"All night long we looked for him. The gardener found his tracks. In the middle of the gorilla reserve."

"Oh, no!"

"Yes, where we haven't set foot ever since . . . you know . . . According to the tracks, Donald went limping off in that direction. He couldn't have known.

"Mr. Evans wanted to go search for him by himself. There was no question of putting the whole team in danger. After two hours, we heard a shot, and then another. We went after him. But we got lost.

"During this time . . . Well, Mr. Evans had found Donald, and he was . . . he was . . ."

Michael couldn't say anything more.

Janet had difficulty breathing; she was puffing her lungs. She was suffocating.

"He'd been massacred. Mr. Evans didn't want us to see it. He had buried him, and we found him prostrate on the tomb. So . . ."

Michael scratched himself nervously, where he could. Mr. Evans only had the strength to tell us that, to speak plainly, it was something other than a gorilla. It was some kind of animal . . . a terrible animal. *The animal*.

The animal.

Mr. Gardner got up abruptly, pulled the rifle out of the hands of the gardener, and walked toward the service staircase.

"Mr. Evans . . ."

"Dad! Dad!"

Doogie glued himself to the door. Michael opened it and everyone saw Doogie, who was squinting. But no one was paying attention anymore, because Janet, who was having an asthma attack and who had opened her eyes and was panting like a dog, cried out:

"My brother!" And she fainted.

River

From the Jungle

At the river's edge, I smell the green and I smell the gray.

I'm very angry with Jack, and I'm holding the knotted wooden stick in my hand. Sometimes I want to hit him. He's walking badly in front of me, and he doesn't speak. When he puts his hands on the ground, I grumble, "hands aren't for walking," and I hit the ground with my stick. He startles and he moans, poor Jack with his rounded back covered with scabs and scars under his thinning hair. I'm naked from the waist up now, wearing underpants as brown as poop in which Michael's pistol weapon is moving around. To the right of my right hand, the river of water is flowing in the opposite direction from where my feet are going. The river is moving in sheets of gray water, where pieces of the wood from tree trunks are floating like crocodiles at the Zoo. I don't trust it. All along the river there are only dirty greenish shrubs that hit you and scratch you. The dog leads the way, his hair so dirty that it's the color of leaves in mud.

Jack follows me. He breaks branches; sometimes he wants to stop, or maybe he wants to eat, hou hou. I bang myself into a tree trunk and I pant, and he trembles and moves on. I'm the one who gives the directions. I think that he has nervous tics. Sometimes he blanks out: he looks up at the sky and his two eyes cross like bees on a flower, he moves his head from back to front, and I smack his overly pink buttocks. Forward, lazybones!

Sometimes, I feel sad about being mean.

But I think about Michael, about his half body, about the end of Heaven for him, it's over, and I think about Nature. Nature doesn't know anything about meanness. Where are the good behavior cameras in the Jungle? The Jungle doesn't have eyes, Doogie. There's no God for you. Only humans have one.

And you, you don't have one.

Then I think about vengeance, or else I think about return to the Zoo, find Janet, and be faithful to the human. I lift my feet over broken branches, I hike along the river, and the silence grows larger, shrinks, draws circles, and sinks into the thickness of the forest.

I'm going to get revenge. I hold my pistol, even though I don't know how to use it. I'm going to get revenge. I'll go see the Rnimal in the Realm of Rnature and I'll kill him until death. Janet won't see anything. The Jungle is blind, farewell to the camera. Then, with the dog and Jack, I'll be at the Zoo again. Doogie, you're not so innocent anymore.

But then I'll forget everything. I would give anything to be able to forget the sciences that I have and what goes with them. I'll press myself into Janet's arms, and she'll caress me.

Doogie looks at Jack's dirty butthole in front of him. "I've had enough. It's too much, Jack, stop." I pound and he stops.

He barely looks at me. He's afraid of me. I put down my stick.

Then, slowly, I sign. I hope that he understands me, poor Jack.

"Come with me, your feet in the water, on the sand. *Come* and *gimme* your hand."

I pick up some curled leaves and I make a sponge in the water of the green and gray river while looking out for crocodiles in the distance.

I wash myself, I clean myself. Oh, it feels good, but it's hard to be human. Civilization is the best, it's sweet for the clean body, but when all around you there is nothing but the dirtiness of Nature, civilization is just good behavior. It's hard. And you have to wash your butthole. Jack is staring at the gray silver of the clouds. His mouth is open. "Don't look so stupid, Jack. Don't bring shame on our race." And I clean his butthole with the sponge, while the birds peep and preep on the branches around us. *Splish splash*, the river flows, and above our heads mosquitoes are hunting and Thousand Colors is still flying.

"There," I say. "Now get dressed." I take what's left of Michael's torn and dirty underwear out from my underpants. I put them around Jack's legs.

"We don't show the place between our thighs: it's an affront to civilization." I push my two lips forward and I smile at him. He lifts his right arm to protect himself, whining as if I was going to hit him.

Then I call the faithful but wary dog, and I give him the little bath of civilization he needed.

The day after the day after, I don't know anymore what the day before was, the landscape changed. The river runs straight now. The limp palm trees are falling down in the wind. Jack is shaking more and more often. Sometimes he drivels and I don't know what to do.

In front of us, the faithful dog barked.

On the other side, on the other bank, the tall and green trees were a wall that went down into the water. Beneath our feet, the now narrower river had accelerated. As it narrowed, it was scouring the banks of dirty sand like a rake, beneath strange kinds of rock like sponges. A pile of stones was blocking our way.

Oh, the bad luck of poor Doogie! Who will ever help you?

The sky was gray like a sheet of paper. "Where's the light?" I asked. Then, holding up my underpants by the waist, my jaw set, I waded into the wet sand. I was looking for a passage through the fat mean boulders.

Always walking around in the cold of the water, going up the river without being able to dry off, and then going back down and wandering some more.

Keep wandering, little ape!

When faithful the dog barked, standing on his hind legs, his mustache held up in the cool air, I knew where the danger was coming from.

"Come," I whispered, holding my stick against me while pulling on the arm of Jack, who, his back rounded, was twisting his nose and mouth around like a lunatic sick person.

From the boulders above us, pebbles were falling. A heavy breathing, a noise, and the presence of an enemy were increasing. With my muscles tensed, I was nothing more than Nature, and I held Doogie's breath while getting out my pistol in the power of the weapon. I signaled to the dog not to move.

That was the moment when, alas, Thousand Colors arrived on a branch, *crick-crack*, while chattering loudly: "Doogie! Doogie!" And then he landed on my head.

Stones were flying all around me. "Rooaar!"

Right above me, the lion appeared!

Big was the head of his face, his hair thick like wool and his eyes half-closed like a sage. He watched us from above.

He shakes his mane in the wind, his black tuft shining brilliantly, and when he opens his white mouth, triumphantly baring his teeth, the dog, faithful as he is, runs whimpering through the woods toward the fields.

I can hear the hard sound of flowing water, the pebbles beneath the feet of the lion were falling into the river, *splish splash*, and the birds are silent.

Suddenly, when he yawns as he approaches above my head, I recognize him, as I huddle fearfully into a corner between the boulders, holding Jack behind Doogie's back. It's King the lion! It's the lion from the Zoo!

I don't know if he recognizes me. Doogie is not a beefsteak like the others, but the lion has a pain of hunger in his stomach. He places a paw, he turns around, and he tries cautiously, under the sun that is ending—farewell Doogie—to descend the stacked boulders. But he can't. I think he's going to jump on me.

And then he turns sadly toward the flowing water.

Doogie sees how thin the former King the lion of the Zoo is. His skin seems like the beaten-up beige leather of Mr. Gardner's coat on the evenings when he plays darts with Mr. Doctor on the terrace. His hind legs tremble like those of a rabbit, and his tail is low. The skin of the lion's stomach is hanging down, his ribs, like those of a dog, are sticking out, and he's not very very handsome.

"Lion," I say, first with my hand and then grunting: "Lion king of kings, what is happening? What does all this mean?"

He turns toward Doogie and Jack, half fainting, his head still magnificent, and he holds out his paw to Doogie. Miserably, he roars. I understand. Oh, what misery! The old king is begging Doogie for something to eat. He's too weak to attack, he has lived his life at the Zoo, Doogie, and now he's in Nature. What is he doing there? The Jungle doesn't have cages, but the Jungle also doesn't have a Mr. Leo who brings red meat every evening in a refrigerator truck. King the lion, stuck on this boulder, is lost and he's hungry.

He's dying, Doogie, in Nature.

How sad Doogie is. But the faithful dog hasn't abandoned him. He comes back, his tail in the air. Between the trees and the bushes, he has found a path to get around the boulders. I follow him.

I carry Jack on my shoulder, and I turn around a final time to salute King the lion on his boulder. With his paw held out like a beggar, the skin hanging off his bones, and his still-red mane, he moans-whimpers. Then he looks at the water that is flowing and flowing beneath his boulder in the falling sun, and I feel that he feels that soon the king will also fall.

But whereas the sun will rise again—it always rises, I think—the lion will stay down. And I will continue on my way.

What is the mystery of Nature in this Jungle?

Doogie is worried. Jack, abandoned, hurt Michael and is wandering so far from the Zoo, and King the lion isn't in his cage but is thin and begging on a boulder on the other side of the continent, ten times a thousand miles from the house. Doogie stayed in the stars for so long. More than two full calendars in the orbital stations, far from Janet, oh, Janet. Receptions in the bright velvet living room, under the chandeliers, wearing the jacket, the shirt, and the trousers, wearing the tie, please, Mr. Doogie, total civilization, seeking glory and money. What's waiting for me now?

The sun has turned black, and the Jungle smells of rotten things. Doogie asks Jack and the dog to stop while he bangs into a tree trunk, pant, pant, and we stop. I see the thick forest that has climbed and that is climbing over the black fogged-in valley where the river is making a loud noise.

Tomorrow, I'll look.

Sitting, preparing the meal while the hungry dog keeps watch, on open ground, protected from enemies, I think it over. Something has changed during Doogie's absence. I can feel it. What is happening at the Zoo? Doogie shivers. And what about Janet?

I put pieces of banana into Jack's amorphous mouth, and pieces of ripe fruit and seeds, and I pet the dog's head. The Rnimal, I think, the one that Thousand Colors talks about and repeats, is the animal that forced Jack to the killing of Michael. I shiver. And what about Janet? Oh, Doogie, if your brain was bigger you would have the logical science of the connections and you would understand. You would hold the truth in your hand, just as you hold the stick.

But in *my* hand the truth is only wind, dust, and cold water. I lie down. I don't see any stars, under the crowns of the tall trees, and I hear the groaning of the wind of the river that is cold. Jack is behaving in an out-of-control way.

"Behave yourself, Jack," I say.

He doesn't answer. "Jack, speak to me."

But he doesn't manage to sign. His gestures are all mixed up.

I'm getting annoyed.

Then, in fear, Jack shits on the ground. Oh, this isn't a toilet! It stinks, it stinks, and now we'll have to move to another camp. "Jack is a piece of trash," I say. "Why didn't you say that you had poop in you?" Jack moans, he shows his teeth, he smells very bad, and he smiles. "Stop smiling, inferior, you're humiliating yourself." I mope and eat some fresh fruit. If the dog goes to sleep, Thousand Colors, up in the branches of the gray tree, will wake us in case of danger.

I go to sleep. It seems to me that the Zoo is in danger. Where has civilization gone? The faithfulness to the human is lost in the fog of a thousand mists. If the lion is dying far from his enclosure, and if Jack has run away, then the Zoo must have changed.

Will Janet recognize the Doogie?

I think that sleeping Doogie has started the night too cold on his bed of dried leaves. I have to sew together some broken twigs for a mattress of a nest to have nightmares in. What if Janet has become a chimpanzee in the forest? Hounh hounh. What if Janet doesn't know how to speak anymore . . . ? Doogie, what are you doing? Hou! Doogie, it's the end of humans. You're alone, and your faithfulness will lead to nothingness until the end of your life.

All day long, from the beginning until the end of light, Doogie, Jack, Thousand Colors and the faithful dog have wandered.

All around the waterfalls that are cascading down, in the fog of the first river that goes to the ocean, which for days and days Doogie's group has been following, the paths get lost in the forest. Enormous walls of green dampened by the splish and splash of water. Doogie grunts and trips over vines, leaves, and thick bushes. Below, water that is white like a fountain is bouncing back up, and waterfalls are doing peepee in the water on the other green side. Doogie can't find the way.

I'm getting a cold from the achoos.

Achoo! In his filth of a stomach, Doogie has a stomachache. Yuck. This Jungle of forest waterfalls is thick and wet, and the idiots the dog and Jack are following the steps of the feet of me. It's cold.

Water is running and running around the big green and white circus ring. There are little drops of humidity, and a noise of the noise of the noise. Doogie has to put a finger in his ears. Nasty waterfall. He sighs.

"Jack," I ask, turning around while leaning on the stick, "where are you?"

Oh, Jack has stayed back. "What are you doing?"

Jack is on all fours. He has climbed a tree.

"Jack," I say, "don't act like a monkey. Come down."

Since Jack is sad, he falls, *wham*, and he's sad. Then he looks at me. For the first time, tentatively, he signs, "Not-Ar-Rive-There."

"Who?" I ask.

He's reluctant to answer. "Not-Ar-Rive-There."

"Jack, look here and keep your eyes on me. You're signing a little, you can still speak a little bit. We have to get there. It's civilization. Yes, it's . . . We will return to the Zoo. This is it for Nature." Then Thousand Colors opens his wings in the humid air, under the greenest branches, and he *kek-kek* chatters:

"In the Realm of Rnature! We must go to the Realm of Rnature!"

Oh, he's getting on Doogie's nerves! "Hey, you damn Thousand Colors! I always hear the same thing. Yes, yes, I know: first we have to avenge the Michael, then we have to kill kill the Rnimal in Rnature for you with no Heaven. And then the Zoo, but . . ." I say, spreading out my arms in the cold, "where *is* the Narture of the Rnature? Where is all of that? It's just you talking and talking, and I see zero. I don't see it."

"Iiiiik!" says Thousand Colors. "Follow me."

"Follow me."

And he flies up.

Sigh. I'm tired and I want to poop. Forget about nevermind Rnature. Doogie, we must avenge Michael first. That's the first thing. Of course. But I'm tired and I want to fart out the fruits in my stomach.

I run and hide in the toilet behind a prickly bush.

Oh, I have a pain in my poop!

I look at my watch, but nothing shows itself on the dial that gives me courage in my heart. Janet, we're lost in the land of the clueless. The river from the ocean falls here, and then it ends. I have no idea where the Congo River is that leads to the Zoo, and I no longer have my courage to follow Thousand Colors into Rnature.

I'm a tiredness. My underpants are pulled down, and I hold onto the bark of the nearby trunk with my hand. Deafening enough to make you mute, the noise of the sound of the waterfall is banging on the skin of the skull of my brain. Oh, in the mist the air is like water, you can breathe again. Two times and then three times. I think I'm weak, Janet, weak.

And I don't know where I am anymore. I feel . . . In my head, the world is spinning, the poop is falling, the water is falling, the Doogie is falling, myself is falling, Michael's tomb, your baby, yours.

Memories

Janet was yelling on the staircase in her perfectly white nightgown.

I, who am Doogie, open the door and call for Janet.

I went down to the bottom of the stairs. In the kitchen, under the old gas lamp, Mr. Gardner Evans had grabbed his weapon, and shaking, he had dropped the box of shells that are the food of shotguns.

Now, under the full moon of Halloween, he was walking quickly on the gravel toward the 4-times-4—"that's not sixteen, it's a car, Doogie." It's a car that's always dirty and covered in mud. Janet, in her white nightgown, barefoot on the gravel, and Michael in Bermuda shorts— what is he doing there with the yellow stars on his briefs?–were running behind him.

"Dad . . . daddy," she said. I saw her.

"Mr. Evans, come back," Michael was saying.

Doogie has forgotten his slippers, and he doesn't want to hurt his feet walking on the pebbles. It's nighttime: you could bump your head in the dark, I'm afraid of the witches of midnight, and it's cold. I stay at the top of the pink staircase of the terrace by the railing at the edge of the darkness and I watch.

"Let go of me!" cries Mr. Gardner in the night. "I'm going to kill him." And there is the word.

Janet fell to her knees, crying "Ah!" Michael took control of Mr. Gardner by bringing his arm behind his back like a key, stop.

"I'm going to find him and kill him," hisses Mr. Gardner like vapor in the cool air. He's acting crazy. Do you know what crazy is?

"Kill who?" Doogie wonders.

And as Janet and Michael bring him back inside, Doogie hides behind Mrs. Diane's giant vase of dried flowers.

"I'm going to kill him," Mr. Gardner repeats, murmuring, "The Animal."

I shiver, and in the night air the moon is like the end of a tunnel that's moving away. I shiver, and it seems to me that I think I'm evaporating like smoke.

From the Jungle

I think that each second is the first. I think it falls out of the watch and then onto my head.

Ouch, ouch, ouch, it hurts! Massage your skull and rub your eyes: it's morning. You have your head in your own poop, monkey. The fog has lifted, but the waterfall of water is still hitting like a hammer: *splash . . . splash . . .*

I'm walking in a zigzag toward the river that is cascading on the flank of the mountain of greenery where I am, far above the river of white water. A few birds of two or three colors are flying above the natural sink of very white water that fizzes like mineral water, making bubbles of water vapor and drops of water on the leaves of the branches with which, on the edge of the rapid river that is sliding toward the bottom of the green valley, I wipe Doogie. I'm cleaning myself.

First, I wash my butthole, and then using sponges I take the grime of dirtiness from my neck, from under my arms, and from my ears. Then I brush my teeth with my finger that is dipped in the water that is flowing transparent blue and is clean but without toothpaste.

On the other hand, I'm still wearing Doogie's old dirtier-than-dirty xxl underpants that smell like pee, and I'm looking into the eyes of Michael's weapon. I rub it with the help of a green leaf with teeth, which I carefully fold. Everything everywhere is green here. It's too much green for me.

I have to think. Think, Doogie, think: which is it to be? Rnature or the Zoo? Which direction to go? What choice should you choose? What path should you walk?

"Thousand Colors," I call, but he doesn't come.

I whistle like Michael taught Doogie. The faithful dog runs like a terrier, and I see myself as human in his eyes. Sniff, sniff. His mustache is the color of mustards that prick your nose, and his dirty hair is like leaves in November. That's a month when it was autumn in the picture books, in those days, and when I see it I want to cry. How good you are, dog. I have only petting for you. That's something at least.

"Jack!" I call, and my "Haounh" echoes, bouncing off the stone walls between the drippings of greenery above the circle of mist that is rising from the water.

"Jack!" and the stones all around say "Haounh!" But Jack doesn't answer. Where's Jack?

In every place, I look for Jack, and the dog also looks for Jack. In the distance I see snakes, and my blood turns cold. There are snails and lizards, and Doogie wants to take them by the tail, and insects, and Doogie thinks that he is big when he sees such little, little ones.

I cast my eye behind the palm trees and the rows of banana trees. I advanced and retreated. I sniffed behind the trunk of the pineapple, behind the seed-bearing trees, and under the bushes of white orchids.

The sun has gone up, and Doogie has gone down. The dog smelled the soft earth, the hard earth, the humus, the pebbles that are cold, the earth that smells of iron and clay, red, yellow, ashes, and dust, and right up to the banks of rivers. Then the dog lifted his blond tuft toward the vines of the hairy trees, and he barked. He wanted to show me something.

"Jack's gone," I said. Jack has played the ape, Jack has been unfaithful. He prefers trees to feet, the naked to the dressed. I'm afraid for Jack.

I remember that he had signed, "Not-Ar-Ri-Ve-There."

"Jack," I thought, "you were never anything more than a chimpanzee. Of course. You will end up here without Heaven, damned." And since his faithfulness to the human was broken, I suddenly saw nothing in the memory of my companion but a chimpanzee ape.

And you know, I accepted it.

There will be no more medicines for him. He's not happy in Nature, and yet he's here. Jack, you're not a human, and the human in you was only suffering, pain and medicines, but never arriving. "Jack," I thought, "*be* a chimpanzee. For you, the human is just a nothing that will not get there, that will never get there."

And what about *you*, Doogie? What are *you*?

I looked at my watch. It was almost dead. Time had fallen down like the water in the waterfall. Only the memories remained. But where were they? In your brain, Doogie. Behind my eyes, I saw the face of Janet: "come here and cuddle, little ape, you've earned it." I saw her face on the watch, "to show you," she used to say. But now there's nothing there. And in front of my eyes there was only the end of the river that was coming from the flank of the mountains, in the crash and crash of the waterfall, and then forest without order or meaning and without the Congo. Ho! Ho!

I thought about it, and I didn't know what to do.

And looking straight in front of me, inside the thick Jungle that doesn't want me, hoping to loop back to the Congo River that would lead to the Zoo, I said "come" to the dog who has followed me, who is accompanying me, and all alone I went on.

Days upon days broke the calendar in ten.

Doogie and his dog didn't speak. They hiked, that is walked. Doogie with his stick, the thin and dirty dog on all fours and four by four. They went down the mountain, and then they climbed it. They met a panda who didn't move, like someone on drugs. "Stoner panda," I said. Ha-ha, I know the words from when the students smoked the substance at the Zoo. But Doogie and the dog were afraid of snakes. At night the dog kept watch. And in the evening Doogie washed the ape, looked for things to eat and drink and for how to keep them warm while the dog slept. They like each other.

And days and days climbed back into the calendar. Doogie had hardly any more skin left, just wrapping paper for presents on his bones, but he had more skin than the dog who had nothing left.

On the forest plain, the trade wind whipped us hard in the face, the nasty trade wind. We didn't do anything wrong, but we still got a spank to the face. The sky was disturbed, it pressed itself down on us, and the water made rain.

And when Doogie forgot the day and the calendar, walking and walking, we arrived at the summit of the peak of the hill of the mountain, densely wooded like Doogie's dry hair on his gray and brown skin. I breathed the air.

Doogie is standing upright in the shreds of his XXL underpants with his too heavy weapon of power, and at his feet is the faithful dog terrier, the hair of the moustache of whom, dull, was falling out like hair from a bald man. I think he'll follow Doogie to the end. Above us is a veil of clouds, the sheet flaking like from mashed potatoes into a mousse. The sky murmurs and Doogie understands. He leaves science behind, and everything that goes along with it.

But the dog growls. "Don't growl at the clouds. What can they do about it?" A day goes by, and the pieces of cloud have stuck together like accumulate-me.

With the dog, who was gnawing on a seal bone, I descended in the coolness toward the greenish and shaded valley.

There's too small of a skull in my brain for the world. What do I know about it? I'm sick to my stomach, I need to shit, I have a headache, I have no desire to think, and the filtered light from the yellow clouds anguishes the Doogie with a fear that he doesn't know and that comes from far away. He senses it. But what is it?

On a tree trunk that was broken by a thunderbolt of light from the old, exhausted sky, I sit down.

The faithful dog comes up to me. I hiss, but he licks me with his pink tongue and drools on Doogie's hand. "Oh, dog," I say, "you alone behind your mustache are faithful to Doogie, and Doogie is faithful to the human."

But what is the human faithful to? Oh, these are mysteries for the masters.

I feel bad, and I don't feel strong enough, but I get up and I walk until it's time to sleep.

I let go of my stick and I see, flowing green and smooth like a long boa constrictor at my feet, the wide and beautiful river of the Congo, silent under the sky of skies and under my eyes, blue and white with a thousand clouds in the water. I've found it!

"Dog," I say, "your master is a genius, and I will call you Faithful from now on, because that's who you are." I pet him. Without him, as alone and unhappy as I am, a poor Doogie would never have found, under the flowers of the branches of the twigs, the Congo of dreams and of his aims. "You're not good for anything, dog, but you have served me well." And I squeeze him tightly in my arms.

Then I think: "If I go up the Congo to the Zoo, I am certainly faithful to the quest for the human, and I will find Janet." But a contrary thought tears my heart in two and pains me. Because on the other hand, the Zoo sent Thousand Colors to Doogie to warn him and to tell him to go into Rnature. But Doogie didn't listen to Thousand Colors, and he doesn't know where Rnature is.

The dog whines. He at least is happy.

I lift my head, and under the thousand clouds, Thousand Colors is flying. He has rejoined us. He has grown paler, and he's tarnished. Like the clouds, he's stained with gray.

In the silence, it sounded like he cried: "This way, Doogie! The Realm is this way!"

"This way!"

With his wings spread, both colored and gray, his beak splitting the slack wind, he dives toward the waters of the great Congo River, and I see him from far away, chattering, beginning to go up in the opposite direction from the current, far above the heavy and green liquid that is flowing on the earth.

"Faithful," I say to the dog. "Sometimes the hand of the right wants to do something, and the hand of the left wants to do something else. But sometimes—and it's rare, dog—the two hands, click and clack, come together. You see, Rnature and the Zoo are like two hands, but they make a single fist." Hee-hee, ha-ha, I'm laughing. They're in exactly the same direction!

The dilemma is over. Running, I descend and I descend, ready for the river of the river flowing backward, ready to follow Thousand Colors and the direction of the Zoo which is also that of the enemy. I jump in the air with a "Yippee!" Happy Mr. Doogie! But the air is heavy, I have a stomachache, and I quickly fall to the ground like the hours of the watch and the days of the calendar. That's life.

Congo over here, Congo over there, and good behavior camera that no one can see: I'm here! I would like the sky to see me. I wave my two arms. I cry out: "Poor Doogie, I'm here."

But alas, no one's there for me.

Raft

Memories

Every morning and every evening, Mr. takes Mrs. Diane onto the terrace
near the pots of her plants, which she waters. The ground and the walls
covered with ivy are pink when it's the time when the sun rises or when
the sun falls. Mrs. Diane places her two wrinkled hands on the blanket
that covers her knees and thighs.

Doogie, there's nothing underneath!

Sitting in the wheelchair, she never eats. Mr. Gardner, Michael, and Janet
are extremely worried. In the evening and in the morning, rolling on her
wheels, Mrs. Diane stays behind the banister of the guardrail. She watches
and she waits. She looks toward the river of the Congo River, behind the
forest at the foot of the hill, where the workers have repaired the Charles
Bigleux.

She doesn't speak to Doogie when I pass by. *Hiss*, she chases me away
like a cat with her hand, showing her teeth. Then she tries to hit me with
her fan. Doogie never understands why.

"Doogie," Janet explains, "you should go in through the kitchen staircase
entrance." Doogie has grown up: he's a big monkey now, an adolescent.
I'm wearing a Save the Planet T-shirt and a pair of Bermuda shorts with
palm trees like Michael, but size XXL. "Doogie, you really don't look good
in clothes that are tight: you need big sizes."

As for Mr. Gardner, his mustache has turned white, and we don't really
see him anymore. He is often hunting, he misses Payne, and he talks on
the telephone to McVey without saying much. The Zoo is beginning to

empty out. Of the students, only Michael has stayed on. For Janet. "I'm doing it for you. I love you, Jane," he said.

Grrr.

The Gardener and the cook avoided Doogie. I'm on my own quite a bit these days, but Janet is with me. As the universe grows, no one loves Doogie anymore and Doogie's heart shrinks, but Janet is still here. "I'm here for you," she jokes, her mouth like a heart of happiness.

So I'm still happy.

What a funny Zoo! The children from the spatial stations haven't landed here for a long time to discover the old Earth on the big vacations of their lives, coming by rocket onto the dusty runways of the Congo to visit our Zoo. The science students from the University of Etho-Ecology are few. Under the direction of Michael, there are Li Yang, Sindhu, and Naoki. I even run into workmen less often. The sunset of the sun is falling slowly onto the Realm of the Zoo. It's nice weather and the animals are sleeping. King the lion is in the solitary enclosure and is being punished. The sea lions have eaten; they're looking for the ball of earlier times, and the joy of it as well. I think that the nice all-gray seals are asleep. I walk down the deserted white gravel aisles. I'm on the other side of your cages, my friends. The white teddy bear comes up to me. How beautiful he is. He dips his paw in the swimming pool of his pond and then he lies down, his fur clean and very muscled. "Nice, magnificent teddy bear," I say. "You live in peace."

It's summer.

Doogie stole some popcorn at the entrance. The entrance is closed. Only the sweeper greets me hello. I walk in flip-flops down the aisle that twists like a boa along the windowpanes of the vivarium. It's morning, and I don't have homework.

Suddenly, I think the good behavior camera must have seen me.

"Doogie," I hear Janet call, far away, on the promontory near the service exit, next to the warm springs, between the storage sheds at the foot of the hill.

"Doogie," I say to myself. "Hide the popcorn, it's not allowed. Wash your hands at the little sink on the aisle and be good. The camera can see you."

Janet is wearing a candy-pink tank top, her hair tied up, in sunglasses and mini-shorts, sitting on the hood of the 4 times 4 how much does that make, which is shining and reshining under the sun, and the golden circle engraved with the cross glares in my eyes. What's going on?

Michael has cleaned everything with the water jet, and Janet is smiling. "Thanks, Michael." Michael is there, him too. He's holding a wicker basket in his hand, and of course, blond and hairless as he is, he's there with his naked torso.

"Hello Doogie, little ape!" He holds out his hand and I take a step backward, my back pressed against the steel grille.

"Doogie, be nice!"

I sniff out that something is wrong. "Come on, monkey," Michael smiles, "let's make peace. You get in back and we'll go for a picnic!"

Picnics were good memories, despite Michael. I remember everything, you know: the position of the sun, the shape of the car that was driving in the ruts under the palm trees. And music, Doogie, you like that! "It's old music, Doogie, The Beach Boys!" Doogie can't hear anything. Janet is singing. She has put her fanned-out toes onto the bottom of the windshield, her hand on the car door, and her head back. She's laughing.

Michael, at the wheel, was laughing too. "Come on, Doogie!"

I don't know how to laugh like they do, but I pretended I could.

"Yippee," Janet cries out, and she yells, "John B!" Personally, I don't think this is very human, or very Janet.

"Relax a little!" Janet tells me as she turns around and puts a cap on my already mussed-up skull.

"You need to laugh sometimes, enjoy the good times. Today we're in Heaven! We don't have to give a damn!" she exclaimed.

Doogie lowers his eyes. Those are bad words.

"Come on, Doogie; bad words are allowed today."

Doogie doesn't understand.

"But what about the good behavior camera?"

"Oh, the devil take the camera!" Janet grins, turning up the sound. "We're having fun, just a little fun." So, with a click we can turn off the good behavior camera and it doesn't see anything anymore.

But Doogie is panicked. Because I'm faithful to the human, I know that the good behavior camera is never turned off.

As the sun rose, the car jumped over bumps in the road. "Yeah!" Michael said, sticking out his tongue. "That's called the accelerator *and* the break."

"Man, this is great! It's really super nice weather!" Michael exclaims. And the 4 times 4 stops at a long strip of sand that leads to the creek of the water hole. It's a small blue tributary of the Congo River, lined with boulders, and Janet says that this is Heaven on earth. She takes the towels, and Michael takes the basket. "Doogie, you bring the bag with the suntan lotions and stuff."

Doogie thinks it over. Heaven can't be down here.

Janet undresses her back. "Turn around, Doogie." And then Michael is in his underwear, and it's hot. Doogie knows that he can't spread suntan lotion on his black hairs, but "let me do the end of your nose." Ha-ha, he looks like a clown. It's not funny at all.

The humans swim, but not Doogie. I'm not a fish.

"Come on, just get your feet wet!" The gray rocks are slippery and sharp, and the transparent water lets you see the beautiful though distorted legs of Janet, who is laughing and looks like a siren. She draws circles around herself to celebrate.

Michael is lying on the highest boulder. He's tanning his back, he's muscled. "Hey, monkey," he says to me. I force myself to smile.

"So, this is it," I think. "This is Heaven for Janet, but what a shame that Michael is here." I count the reasons: no worries, we're off by ourselves, the sun, the boulders and the water, the towels, and we're laughing. Therefore, it's Heaven!

Doogie knows that for him only Janet's arms and her hug are Heaven. "But," Doogie thinks, "Janet can't take herself into her own arms and give herself a hug. She can't be her own Heaven."

"Hey!" Janet cries. "Hey you, Michael!" She kicks her feet. "Come on in." She reaches out her hands to him.

Oh yes, Michael's arms are clearly *her* Heaven.

"Oh," Doogie thinks, "does everyone have their own Heaven?"

Michael stood up. He puffs out his chest and he acts crazy. He stretches out his arms, and he jumps from way up high into the depths of the water that is as green as the jewel Janet has on her neck. Is it all over for him? No, he comes back up. Janet is laughing, astonished. She holds out her hand to him. He shakes his head and rubs his eyes, and then with a big gesture he says, "Yeah!"

Doogie, I close my eyes. I want Heaven. I take two steps on the fat gray boulder. I keep my flip-flops on just in case, and also my Save the Planet T-shirt. Phew. I close my eyes and I squeeze my nose. When you have to go for it, you go for it.

Of course, Doogie doesn't know how to swim, but Heaven is there, and Doogie wants Doogie to go. I don't know how to do it. I walk, I walk, and finally I cut the air in my lungs. Oh, oh, I open an eye. I really think that Doogie is walking into the void.

I hear Janet and Michael yelling: "Doogie! What are you . . ."

And . . .

With a splash of splash, I said hello to the water and goodbye to the air, but I couldn't speak. Someone had knocked me out, and even though I wasn't tired I think I went to sleep.

From the Jungle

At the water's edge, there's only one solution: to build a raft.

I rolled up the sleeves of Mr. Gardner's shabby old dirty shirt, and I pulled up the elastic waistband of my underpants that were falling down. Thanks to the power of the pistol, I tapped on some tree trunks to have the science of their resistance and solidity.

Soaked, sick with a cold, but washed like a civilized person on the edge of the Congo River under a stormy gray-black sky, Doogie sniffed three times to smell the fresh air. He put his feet into the slush toward the dog who was paddling around, and he explained.

"Building a raft, Faithful the dog, is putting the forest onto the water." I thought about it. Michael had the science of rafts. "One day," I told the so very faithful dog, "we went to have a little fun with Michael and Janet. No, you don't know Janet, dog that you are. But you know Michael: with your nose you smelled him dead. Doogie wanted to annoy Michael when he was alive. Doogie acted like an idiot and Doogie fell into the water."

He remembers.

At the end of one after-the-noon, Michael had built a that is called a raft. You need wood. Not wood from banana trees: it dissolves in the water like sugar in coffee. Pay attention to the be careful. But I do collect the wide woody leaves of the banana trees and some fruits for provisions.

Then I look for three or five mangrove trunks from the small mangrove swamp of the river. The mangrove, Doogie, is the tree that walks on stilts, a big gray tree with a thousand roots like feet on the earth. After a flood, ten or more gray broken trees have fallen. Doogie drags the smallest and the softest of them onto the mud beach. "You see, Faithful the dog, I choose five trunks and I attach them one to the other." The front of the raft, as Michael said, is narrower than the back. You have to put the trunks together like five asparagus stalks, and the end of the asparagus is thicker than the point. It's an asparagus raft.

Then I collected beautiful, sumptuous bamboos. For a whole day under the heavy sun, I crossed long straight bamboo stalks over the trunks that are like green asparagus. After which, with the help of vines that the dog Faithful pulled through the trees in his mouth, I built, knot by knot, a sausage of bamboo and tree trunks. Over and under I pass, pass again, and knot. The science of knots has a thousand magics, but sadly Doogie doesn't know them. I only have the science of shoes and laces, and the ones that are pictured in my encyclopedia. Let's hope that will be enough.

The day after the night of the former today, the sky is covered like the lid over vegetable soup. The gathered clouds, lively and fast, have climbed onto the summits of the sky, and they're forming layers and layers. Those are stratus clouds, Doogie. I don't know why, but I don't trust them. Nature is always changing.

I gaze at the raft, and I'm proud of proud of myself but also proud of you who taught me. At the moment I let it glide into the water that is flowing, with the frightened dog sitting under me and me holding onto his behind, I decide to call the raft the "Michael-half-Doogie."

And I close my eyes. Farewell forest, hello water.

So as not to have a big pain in his little butt, Doogie covered the mangrove trunks with the leaves from the banana trees. And with the help of a pole made from a very long stalk of bamboo, in the current that is moving very fast, I try to orient myself. Hey, monkey, this is the life! Bye-bye to the earth of the ground!

Already, the dog who is as faithful as he is a dog isn't barking at anything anymore. As terrified as he is, under this dirty never-cleaned sky, carried by the slow and heavy flow of the Congo, I must row at times, and at other times I let us float along.

How my stomach hurts! Doogie is no longer able to make poop. Sitting on the raft on a banana leaf, he's going down the wide river that will one day empty into the Congo. And then he will have to go back up the water like a watch that has let go of time.

I have a cramp above my stomach, but I paddle with the bamboo. Finally, I think that I vomit, dizzy, without letting go of the pole. Yuck, my throat is dry and I'm thirsty. Hounh houh.

But when I lift my head, it's almost nice out. The sky has vomited its clouds, and the river is descending toward the influx into the Congo. It's worse when I breathe. Tapping with my feet, I test the solidity of the raft. The raft sails on, and even the dog gets up.

He comes over to lick Doogie's vomit. Disgusting!

"Yuck, dog!" And now he's licking Doogie. "Stop that!"

The current flows along. Far away, on the muddy river's edge, a few crocodiles and some boulders or hippos. The greenish waters allow Doogie to move past them on the raft.

All day long, nothing to report.

It's while going around the elbow of a big turn, with the thick and hairy flanks of mountains and the brown forest above us, that Doogie, beneath the cries of the birds, the sound of the silence of the trees, and the once again blue sky, so calm and blue, senses it.

Up there, over there, somewhere, Doogie senses the Enemy, the Animal.

And with the tip of my finger, I search for the pistol.

Memories

"Hurry up, Doogie!"

It was panic. She pushed me onto the staircase, and I woke up.

The whole house of the household had been closed off. The lights were turned off and plunged into darkness. Only the pocket lamps in the pockets of the students—Charles, Norbert, and Naoki—lit the big living room. Mr. Gardner's big leather armchairs had disappeared. I turned my head in the corridor, and I realized that the armchairs were blocking access to the entrance, both from the terrace and from the kitchen. I shivered.

Janet was holding a large stick in her hands, and she was wearing a furry shirt. She was arguing with Michael, and that's when I noticed Michael's powerful pistol, which was loaded with bullets.

Then there were cries. Mr. Gardner had wanted to go out through the kitchen, and the Gardener, two workers, and the cook had held him back. He was yelling: "I want to go and kill it by myself! By myself!"

And from outside, we heard the sound of hell. A thousand thousands of cries, and then stones were banging into the walls, the shutters, and the roof. No one was speaking, and Michael brought Mrs. Diane into the middle of the living room, between the glass bookcase and the fireplace. She was weeping and weeping.

She only spoke the sentences: "Get that ape out of here! We're humans! Kick him outside with his own kind!" Then Janet gently took my hand, and she led me to the study behind the living room. Sindhu and the nurse who was drawing a cross on her forehead while moaning also came with me. Then Michael came.

He tapped me on the skull. "Don't worry, monkey. What we need now is courage." And since I seemed doubtful, he swallowed and said: "The two of us don't know everything, my boy, but we have to be faithful to the human no matter what happens, right?"

Then the wall shook. Behind it, in the black of the night, we heard a roar, grunts, and cries of screams that I had never known.

"I think it's a revolt," Michael said. "It's the animals."

I had no idea what was happening. Rocks and scrap metal. They were breaking everything, and they had surrounded us.

Janet came back from the living room, and she slid her head through the doorframe of the big door. "It's the Animal," she murmured. Michael agreed.

A yell cuts the silence of the night in two. Doogie plugs his ears, his bottom on the thick rug at the foot of the desk.

Then Michael concentrates. He frowns like a human hero, Doogie imitates him, and Michael slides the end of his pistol between the big venetian blinds.

Bang!

He shoots once.

Bang bang!

He shoots twice. He reloads his pistol weapon, and in the living room I hear Mr. Gardner and his shotgun attacking the Animal and all the other animals. *Crack* . . . We hear the door splitting.

"Block the staircase," Michael yells to Li Yang and Naoki, who are running toward the stairs in the front hall. They go up to the second floor.

Oh, Doogie is scared, and Janet comes to pick him up. "Don't worry, Doogie, we're going to win. The humans always win in the end," and she gives me a hug.

But she's also carrying a smaller pistol-you with bullets in a matchbox in her hand, and when Li Yang cries out for help at the top of the staircase, she turns over a chest of drawers from the front hall to block the descent. But Mr. Gardner sneaks through first. Li Yang is yelling, and Michael is trying to catch Mr. Evans. It's chaos.

In the living room, the pocket lamps break down one after the other. We don't hear the noise or the rain of projectiles against the sides of the house anymore, and there is light from the moon through the venetian blinds. With the windows closed, the shutters are clacking and creaking.

From the second floor, there are one two three gunshots, and Mr. Gardner comes back down covered in blood. Then Mrs. Diane splutters and chokes, and he says, "I missed."

The Rnimal.

Michael cries out, and the nurse and the bush doctor go up to the second floor. I think Li Yang has gone to Heaven. Then the light comes back on, the noise isn't there anymore, and finally the sun comes up and everyone is crying, standing over the students who are laid out on the kitchen table. Doogie goes up to the second floor and he finds that his room is a battlefield: stuffed animals gutted, toys broken, books torn up, the pine bed killed. There's poop, blood, and pee, but no one is there. Through the window with a broken pane Doogie sees absences of footsteps that he recognizes, and outside he sees open cages. At the foot of the hill are dead animals, crazed animals, animals that are wandering around, and others that have escaped. They're traitors to the human. Nothing is clean anymore and everything is chaos: bars of cages, aisles, garages, buildings, kiosks, and potted plants. The door of the glass vivarium has been knocked in with a big torn-up tree trunk.

Then Doogie goes cautiously down the staircase. Sadly, I go into the deserted living room, I open the big window, and by the light of day I see the books on the floor, the overturned chest and tables, shotgun shells on the ground, and the rug that has slid. I see Mrs. Diane in her wheelchair, her head lowered, her bun at the top, her arms gray and stiff. I get up the courage to approach her, and I ask, whining:

"Is everything okay?"

I touch her, and she falls onto her side in a pool of red. "Aaaounh!" Doogie yells. When Janet runs up to him, in a blue shirt and jeans, she opens her eyes wide, and she falls to her knees.

"Oh, Doogie," she weeps. And then she says the word and Doogie understands.

From the Jungle

The rain is falling the rain is falling the rain is falling.

How tedious the rain is! Doogie shivers under the gray sky that's like the open mouth of a giant above him. I took the dog who is afraid onto my stomach, and I tried to close the shirt, but the buttons have cracked, the buttons engraved with a cross. With my big hand, I guide the raft as well as I can on the water that is descending rapidly, always more rapidly. The water is increasing, and so is the current. I think that a storm is cursing Doogie, and Doogie curses the bad weather.

From the banks of the river, the wrinkly skin of the dark green forest climbs, and no longer does any sound come from the house of the trees, while the edges of the arms of the river are spreading, and Doogie, lost in the middle of the water of the Congo River, carried along, suddenly feels that the current is doing the work for him.

I'm dejected that I can no longer control anything. Rudder, you are the river, and the dog and me are heading into the big mouth of the unknown, while above us the sky is a naked butthole that is clouding over with poop that is falling on you.

Water

—Storm and rain.—The waterfall with its open mouth.—
Memories: the mourning of Mr. Gardner, the failing zoo,
and sadness takes over our minds.

From the Jungle

It's not a storm: it's a whirlwind and a tornado! The lost raft spins directionless on top of and underneath the liquid. Poor unfortunate Doogie: the sky has done peepee and the river is swallowing you and swallowing you. Under the rain, under the wind, I can't see anything. Everything is gray. The tornado of wind carries the raft of asparagus trunks that are cracking and now are bouncing on the blades of the waves of the river.

"Aaoooouh!" the dog howls, and I would like to howl along with him. But only silence befits a master. So I reassure him: "Be faithful to me, dog, and everything will be all right." I think that I console him. He squeezes in between my arms and puts his very dirty mustache on my knees while closing his eyes.

Sick as I am from eating fruit, I can neither poop or pee, and my stomach is like a rock. My head is spinning along with the wind. I'm dirty and poor and alone, like a leaf under the breath of the god of humans between his teeth.

Oh! Everything is moving faster, the water is turning white, and above me I think I see the eye of the sky that is staring at me and saying to me in a biting breath:

"I can see you, Doogie. It's me."

One last time, I look at my show-you watch, but the waves have already slapped me. It's all over for the tick-tock. It doesn't work anymore.

I yell and I scream: "Janet! Janet! Why have you forsaken me?"

My watch isn't showing anything anymore.

Then I lift my head and I see that the green and blue water is quickly becoming a faster white than white. Then it's just fast, and in front of us there's no river anymore, there's nothing anymore.

What's in front of us? A void.

It's a waterfall cascade of waterfalls of water, and Doogie says farewell to the raft. It bumps into a rock and cracks. Goodbye. It bumps into two boulders and the vines rattle. You're holding onto one or two crosswise tree trunks, trapped between two gray teeth above the great void of the waterfall of the cascadings of white water. Even the air splashes me, and the thunder of a thousand rains growls above my head. You turn over onto your back, and the water is running everywhere on your engulfed torso. Lift up your head, Doogie, and be faithful to the end. Be faithful to the end. Be faithful until it's the very last piece of wood, and hold on.

A thousand times the height of Doogie the precipice plunges, hungry for me, for poor, tired, sick, wet me, wanting to eat me. But Doogie won't let go of the last tooth in Nature's mouth and fall into its stomach.

With my big hand on a knot of mangrove wood between the two boulders, I try to catch the other boulder to climb out toward the riverbank. The riverbank is very close, Doogie.

I lift my eye, and the eye in the sky has closed. A cloud cracks open and there's a torrent falling from above me. A pressure as if the arm of a monster is pulling me upward. The wind clobbers me and the rain scratches and bloodies the Doogie. A whirlwind hits above the river, and Doogie keeps his eyes closed against the drops of water, dry leaves, and bits of gravel.

Suddenly, Doogie feels a branch bouncing off his foot, and Doogie wonders if his leg has been torn off. The water around me has turned red.

Nature, Doogie, wants your death.

Nature, Doogie, won't be your Heaven, it will only be the end of your life.

No! Help me, Janet, I can do it. And I throw my arm to catch the boulder to the left of my right, to climb, to climb up onto the riverbank under the storm, before I fall into the Nature of the Waterfall, oh nasty Nature, into your white stomach, wet with swirling.

I open one eye.

And then I see, going past me like a piece of wood, distraught, his eye staring and his mouth open, in fear, in fear, in fear—oh Doogie, you are his master and you have abandoned him . . . Dog! Dog! Dog!

He's barking! He's dying! Into the mouth of the death of the waterfalls of white water, silent amid the too enormous deafening noise, he topples.

And since Doogie can't abandon the one who is faithful to him, I moan: "Haaaoounh! Dog!" I let go of the tree trunk and, powerless, just a cherry pit in the too large ocean of the river, I also topple, my leg bleeding.

Doogie, I think that when you were released into that white mouth, a poor piece of meat with a little pack in your brain of memories, you became something people forget.

And I lost the science of my sensations and of my mind. I was gulped down.

Memories

Drip and drop, click after clack. It's not the sound of rain falling, because the sky doesn't need to pee. At the end of the courtyard behind the house on the hill, the sewage pipes of the Zoo are broken. Is it from the storm, from old age, or because the animals have repeatedly attacked it? From this point on, the animal beasts will attack the house of the Zoo umpteen times. Doogie is scared, and Janet is preoccupied. She's very busy.

The Zoo has been secured. They're putting up barbed wire, there's a night watchman, and you never go out.

So stay home, Doogie, stay home and do nothing. "Doogie," Janet says, "you're an adolescent, and you're going through a crisis." Doogie pouts. One day out of two there's no class, and there's nothing to do. The sky weighs on your head. It's bad weather and soon there will be a storm, and Janet has to take care of the Zoo with Michael, Naoki, and Sindhu. There are no employees other than the cook and the Gardener. Dirty weeds are growing, and everything is deserted. What's going on?

Doogie is well dressed. What a beautiful shirt you have on, and shoes made to measure, even if they hurt you on the soles of your feet, Doogie, when you walk straight without wrinkling the pleated trousers. How faithful to the human you are today. But why, and for what purpose? Doogie is alone in his solitude. Sitting on the last step of the service staircase, I pick up one two three five and ten pebbles in order to make them dance ricochets on the dirty brown puddle in the mud. Drip and drop, the broken pipe spits out ten drops and the water runs runs. Other than that, there is silence. A hundred Doogies away from here, the forest begins, and Doogie is afraid of the beginning of the trees, so he watches. Drip and drop, and then it starts over.

How heavy the air is, and the garbage cans have fart breath. Doogie, bad words will fall onto your foot, ouch! Don't use vulgarity.

Okay, okay. But Doogie is tired of doing nothing.

I watch the skies that aren't very skylike anymore. I have to go back inside.

"Doogie!" I hear again, and I know that my name means that I will come. Farewell, rick the cochet. See you soon, drip-drop. Oh, darn it, Doogie, I got a stain. I drag my feet so that I can tuck my shirt into my pants, heh-heh. Doogie is smarter, Doogie knows how to lie. He's hiding the stain from you, and you think there is cleanliness.

Walking around the house, Doogie goes past the bird cages. Not one of them is singing: it's a deserted silence. Then he passes in front of the snake apartments. Nothing is snaking: just broken windowpanes, dust, and trampled branches. There are bolts on the locks. Everything is rusting, and you, Doogie, are the last one who remains.

Janet, in her cap and overalls, is sniffling, and her hands are full of earth. Hou hou, Janet is dirty like a stain, and Doogie is clean! But even when she isn't pretty, Janet is beautiful.

I see Mr. Gardner behind the window. He doesn't fit behind the curtain. How strange he is. He's watching. He just stands there.

"Doogie," Janet says, "come here, monkey." I don't know if she's happy to see the tip of my nose anymore. She speaks to me, and she washes her hands in the sink under the terrace. She doesn't have the look anymore, and she doesn't have the cuddle anymore.

"We have to put the feed away, Doogie. Michael is waiting for me at the stables. I don't have time. Have you done your homework? Tomorrow, you'll have to start doing experiments again."

I lower my head. Hou. "But Doogie hasn't done anything wrong!" he wants to scream.

"Doogie!" She doesn't want to do any look-at-me. "We don't have time to play anymore, Doogie. You're big now. You have to help me."

Hi hou . . . Doogie is angry. I stick out my tongue at her and make the sign for annoyed.

But Janet drops her buttocks down on the staircase, her cap falls off, and she's crying between her two hands. How her tears bring suffering to the little monkey that I am. "Janet, don't cry, I'm here." And with something like a hiccup, as if she's a little girl, Janet does look-at-me into your big eyes. "Doogie doesn't need Janet anymore, but I need *you*. Nothing is working out, Doogie. Just look around you."

I look to the right of my left, and Doogie turns around on all fours at the foot of the staircase of the terrace. Then I look at the sky, and there's a drip and a drop.

It's raining. The pipes in the sky are broken too.

"Doogie," she murmurs, her cheeks black, "I won't always be here. Soon I'll have to . . ." And since she's crying, Doogie throws himself into her arms.

Sometimes Janet is very little, but Doogie never feels like he's bigger than she is. It's only that the pipes of her eyes break when sadness roams. And I sniffle in the shelter from the rain. Because sadness will soon be here forever.

Heaven

—Opening your eyes.—A wound.—The unexpected visit
of a female.—In the clearing of a forest surrounded
by the waters of the river.—The bonobos.

From the Jungle

Where are your eyes, Doogie? You can't see anymore. You lift your buttocks and you feel better. But oh! Doogie falls back down again. He can't walk, he can only crawl.

If you take in air through your nose, it feels like it would be too cold, but if you breathe out air through your mouth, you're too hot. You're under the sun, and Doogie sees orange circles and something like butterflies that blink on the screen of his eyelids. Your eyes are open. If Doogie squints, and if you're calm, you can see where you are.

It's a clearing under the bosom of the sun. Around the clearing, like curtains, gray trees are climbing up into the green, and way up above you it's blindness. Doogie closes his eyes.

Is this Heaven?

Doogie sniffs, Doogie smells. Down here, everything is mint, and the fresh grass smells like crystalline water.

Doogie opens his eyes. His head is stuck in the humus that's like a soft cake on the ground. He turns his neck and stretches his arm, and you say "ah aah!" There's a white-blue and blueberry butterfly moving across your two eyes. Behind you, under the sun that is repainting the clearing white, there's silence from the noise. One two, you hear the cry of the leaves that are taking a nap, from time to time a bird flies up, brushing against the branches of the greenery, and then there's a lasting silence.

The more Doogie leans his head to the left, the less he sees the trees, as if a hole had been cut in the big soft gray-green curtain of the virgin forest.

In that hole, you can see only rays of light, a big blinding white, and then blue. It's the sky, Doogie. How did you end up in a clearing suspended from the sky?

Is this Heaven?

With his nose in the mint of the herbs of the freshness of the field, Doogie picks a caterpillar curled up like a snail shell, like an orange and black chocolate jewel, from his shirt. Then you tap with your big hand on your leg. Ouch! Your leg is a machine that doesn't work anymore. It's stiff hard and it drags.

When you bring your big hand to your head, Doogie, you remove a big palm leaf. Who put that on your head? There's blood underneath.

One two, and you throw your eye into the blood that's like mud on your black finger. You know that there's a wound. You breathe, you open the door to the air, and then you chase it out through the window. Then, Doogie, in the center of the beautiful clearing and the green and white silence, while blowing air out, you crawl, with the palm leaf on your head, toward the hole in the curtain where the white then blue sky is the horizon. One two three five ten and you don't know anymore. Where is the ground, Doogie, and where is the picture? You can't see anymore. Protect your eyes. You're lying at the edge of the earth, as if on a plate, on a high very high plateau where the wind is blowing. It's cool here. Below, beneath your eyes, is soft ground, and then the hard ground of a cliff descends to the water of a river that is white in the fog. You're floating in the silent sky, higher than high, and you turn over onto your back where, blinded, you see only the sun above you.

Doogie, this *is* Heaven!

One, two. Do you remember? Remember what? You don't remember anything. You're wearing a shirt and a pair of XXL underpants, and how big your hands are. Remember who? Doogie, do you remember? No, you're not human.

If Heaven is here, then you're not in it. It's not for you. Breathe in the mint, see the white, and listen to the wind of almost nothing. You don't have memories of anything. You don't have memories of where you're coming from or where you're going or how you'll get there. Only memories of the Jungle as Jungle, memories of the dirty forest where there's nothing good that you belong to. You groan from your head, and you groan from your leg as you crawl. You try to lift your butt, and you try to hold the head of you don't know who you are. Houh, it's too late. Everything is spinning, and you fall down.

Doogie barely has enough time to see her. She comes toward you from the trees, and she stops when you stop.

Doogie opens his eyes again. He sees the blue of the white of the sky, but first he smells something.

Next to Doogie, there is someone of the female sex who has sat down while the birds are making bird-sounds above the clearing of Heaven. Doogie has a name in his head, but he doesn't know which one it is. She has placed her hand on his head, and with her other hand she's holding Doogie's wrist. The weather is mild, and Doogie is not afraid. She lets out little cries that are perched high in the air and that penetrate his ear as she gently yelps, "Shee-shee!"

He looks to see who "Shee" is.

Shee is like him, but more elegant. She's a small one with red lips who is trembling, her hair black and her ears small. She has wide nostrils and a flat face, fine hair and a well-combed part in the middle, but she's not a chimpanzee. Doogie picks up her hand and looks into her eyes. She's like a mirror of Doogie, a beautiful one covered with hair, but when she opens her mouth, her hand stretched out while she opens and closes four fingers, calm, she's a female Doogie but more like a cousin.

Doogie turns over onto his side on the grass. He's wounded, he moans. He stretches out his leg, and so as not to frighten her, since she runs toward the trees while looking back behind her, Doogie offers his hand and grins. "Come back." Very cautiously, Shee comes back, with a little agitated but friendly cry. She pouts. Doogie is hurting, he needs her. He pulls back his lips while halfway closing his eye. The sun hurts him, and blood is flowing from his head.

She-shee comes over and walks all around him, her cheeks hollow, her lips swollen, and her jaw moving. She's tall and straight, with muscled thighs, as naked as in paradise. He sees her breasts and her thick nipples. She smiles timidly and approaches Doogie on all fours with a palm leaf in her hand.

Under the silence, far from the base of the trees of the clearing where the birds whistle and the wind blows, Shee-she leans over and places her delicate palm on Doogie's bleeding skull. His leg drags, and he tries to crawl toward the shade.

With his lips pulled back, Doogie asks her: "Who is Shee?"

As if to say "shh," she places the back of her hand on the mouth of his lips and caresses the top of his head and then his neck.

When, her arm around his back, she gently helps him to limp to the shade of the forests of Heaven, Doogie follows her odor of grass, sweat, and earth, and he can smell that she smells good. She-shee is more than a chimpanzee like Doogie, he thinks. She's a bonobo, the best, most beautiful, sweet, and good among us. She's a bonobo, and she's caressing you, and then your head turns, and it's over again.

Doogie sees her, naked and fearful against a tree trunk, her pink buttocks in the fog and her gaze moving around. Doogie lies back against a big tree in front of her, and Shee disappears.

Everything is calm of calm, it's in the shade. And Doogie sleeps.

What is Heaven, Doogie? Is it the end or the always forever? Is it something good, or is it nothingness?

Doogie is resting, sitting on the ground near a tree, and thick tufts of grass are growing on the ground in the place where the light from above caresses the floor of the forest through the foliage.

Doogie breathes, and even though his leg is sick his head is doing better. He sniffs, and an old ape, letting go of a vine, approaches him without making noise. Doogie has vague memories of speech, but he sputters with his hand because of the pain in his wrist. Then Doogie pouts, his gaze into the void, and he grins rapidly. He's an old bonobo, and Doogie calls him Bob. Since his shoulders are narrow, his neck thin, and his skull small and round, he's not like Doogie. He has wrinkles on his forehead and between his nose and his cheekbones. He wriggles his nose. Doogie lets him pass. The Bob from Heaven sits cautiously against a broken tree trunk one and two steps away from Doogie. He watches and watches. How curious you are, Bob the Heaven. Doogie smiles. Sometimes Doogie senses aggression in himself, anger and fear. Alone and abandoned, his skull emptied of its brain, he would like to roll boulders like a real chimpanzee, to prick up his hair, uproot shrubs, and stand erect with his fur coat poking straight up like needles.

But here in Heaven, everything is much sweeter. It's the sweet life. Tired, Doogie holds out his hand, and the old Bob, slender and wriggling his nose, relaxes. He breathes with his mouth open, and then, since Doogie is hungry, he gives Doogie a ripe fruit the size of a fig, a handful of shoots, and some caterpillars. He grunts, and the old Bob presses up against him. His hand is in your mouth, Doogie. He's feeding you, he's nice. Doogie would like to cry, but he doesn't know how anymore. Then the old Bob looks at Doogie for a long time, and Doogie wants to show that he's not just a monkey. He wants to give the word with his arm to show that he's not just himself. But the gesture is simply impossible.

The light of the end of the day is slowly going down in Heaven. At the border of the clearing, in the airy red-and-green forest, a Bob is standing up straight, with arms that are longer than the chimpanzee you are. He's walking slowly, watching me. He grins for you to come. They're not coming to you, but you are going to them, dragging your leg. You blink your eye, and when the forest becomes deep and shiny and green and tall and soon to be dark, Doogie hears noises all around him.

One and two and three and five and what is the number of the word, the word of the number? Doogie has forgotten. There's a lot of a lot of rustling of feet and brown silhouettes, secretive, then little cries of *hooo, ho, hoa* coming from high perches that cross each other, cross over vines, trunks, and branches and meet in high places, climb, break up, and cross and weave through the branches. They're making their nests for the night.

Heaven belongs to the bonobos, to the bobos. Doogie looks at you, and the old one climbs up, and then a female—it's her, it's Shee—pushes on your back and gently helps Doogie to climb. No one speaks, and everyone says "hoo hoa," then "haa-ha." Doogie grunts, his leg that is becoming paralyzed limps, and he snuggles in at the end of the bed, a little nest just for the night. She looks at him and, with her feet in the air, she caresses you, one finger in your mouth. It's cool here, and her big, long foot bends and unbends. She shows him what is between her thighs, then wavers and closes her legs. He hears the long-distance calls, hoots, loud cries. Then, just like the day, the evening comes, and the hours pass by and where did they go? Among the bobos, Doogie goes to sleep and takes care of himself. He doesn't need a word to say what he feels, he just feels it.

Bono-Bob

—Weapon and clothes.—The cycle of days and nights.
—The temptation of Heaven.—Sexuality.—The affection of a
female.—Her and him.—Violence, reconciliations, and rubbings.
—Without memories.—The return of the faithful dog.
—A passage to the exit from Heaven.—Love in the night.—
Obscene memories.—The farewell with no return.

From the Jungle

Day evening day night morning night morning evening. Everything is flitting by, and Doogie's pain as well. Things are good in Heaven, all is well. When Doogie wakes up, She-shee has left, he's wearing palm leaves that protect his skull, and at first he limps awkwardly on the rough tree trunk. Doogie likes the bark, the smell, the cracking sounds, and the hairy vine. Doogie in his shirt doesn't like shirts too much anymore, but he likes bare feet on his tree friend. Beneath him, down below, there are bobs who are going about their daily lives. They are doing . . . what do they do in the morning? The light pierces the ceiling of the leaves, and the little bonettes are walking and rocking a baby bobo with the left hand while grabbing fruits and petals with the hand of the right. A bono-bob runs toward the clearing, his long arms folded in, his back tilted forward, his face calm. And the others along the big fallen tree trunk in the forest are kissing each other. Are they fuck-me kisses? Doogie turns his eyes away. It's something he shouldn't see. And now Doogie, grinning, has reached the height of the heights. Solid against his friend the trunk, Doogie watches and observes all around him. It's an enormous patch of green entwined with the blue-gray-brown of the water of the rivers. It's a big plateau in the basin of the sons and brothers of the river that's flowing down below. Doogies can't swim, so Doogie is stuck in the middle of this green Heaven. But he's not worried. There's nothing he needs to do. He stretches his knee and brings a little fruit to his mouth, cracking the seeds.

Doogie tries to . . . what's thinking? It's far away. He has forgotten everything. Who are you? Doogie rubs an eye while showing his teeth. He's hot in his it's a shirt. The basin of the plateau of Heaven at the foot of the summit of the big tree is swimming in the white, and everything is slow. With his arms crossed and his head pushed forward, Doogie is still. He moves, and he waits. In his hair he senses the desire to be deloused.

But in his skull, Doogie understands the facial expression of a big aggressivity, of fear, with his lips pressed together, his face tense and frowning. He shakes his face, and beneath his feet he sees the bobs and the little bobbies, so little oh so little, who are snacking. A little one is playing, and another she-shee is kissing. Groan.

Doogie climbs down while scratching his back on the tree: oh Heaven! Without thinking, he catches the hanging vine. He thinks he will fall, but he doesn't even have to think about it. He holds on with his fist, he bends the correct leg, he juggles and one and two and there, he's on his feet, it's the earth, his hands on the ground, and he sniffs.

He meets one bob, two bobos move away, and three bono-bobs continue along the big broken trunk. He goes deeper into the forest and hears the echo of cries: "aoah! oh! ah! ah!" It's warm, less humid than the night but more humid than it was up there. The open sky is protected by two clouds, by mists and storms, and everything is soft. You separate the undergrowth and sniff the branch. A bobo brushes against you. You are among them, near the swampy terrain where the trees are low and the ground is soft and muddy, going down toward the little stream that runs to the cliff. Doogie hears the rain falling from above, and thousands and thousands of caterpillars, the droppings of caterpillars, fall onto him crisscross from the trees. He holds out his hand, catches, eats, crunches, and then moves on.

Behind the embankment, Doogie discovers a pile. There are two pieces of cloth covered with earthworms, bloody, and a cold black object. You recognize it: it's a pistol. Hmm, Doogie shakes the weapon of power. He doesn't understand. Then he makes a sack and puts the pistol inside, and without thinking he puts the sack behind the boulder covered with moss, hidden.

Beyond the little pile, there are steps without the feet in the ground: one of them is being dragged, going toward the little burbling river. Doogie, those are *your* footsteps, *your* feet.

Hmm. He remains standing, his hands in the mud, his mouth closed, his eyes blinking. Nearby, there are other footsteps without feet: longer and thinner. He raises his eyes, and she it's Shee hisses and watches him from behind the gray moist tree and looks at him from below while chewing on a grassy shoot. He sees the nipple of her breast. She's leaning forward behind the tree behind the bush. Doogie looks at her, and she sees him, holds out her hand, hmm, oh oh, lowers her head, thin hairs on her face, and she turns her butt toward him, pink and very thin, then quickly, gliding, afraid, not afraid, she moves away and pushes into the tall grasses.

Doogie stays, sitting, not moving, his finger in his nose. He is him.

Eat nest sleep eat delouse and kiss. There is pebble, leaf, tree, and the bonobos. Doogie rubs his back with his shirt now in threads against the trunk that is lying on the ground. He eats a shoot; he moves his thumb and chews. On the other side of the soft brown tree trunk a female is eating a fat fruit and, ha-ha, a little one is climbing onto her back, his legs stretched out on her shoulders as he tries to open the larder of her mouth. *Hoa hoa* a male runs the length of the trunk and Doogie turns his head. The male's sex is straight like a white feather and it's an erection, his torso puffed out. A rustle, leaves and wind. Doogie picks up a piece of fruit. Around him, he recognizes one two three bobs, but he doesn't know how to put a name to their faces. He can only sense who is who. Sometimes, one two five females from the length of the river further away in the forest are here. They weren't here before; they come and go. When dusk falls, each one of them goes back and climbs up to the nest.

Sometimes there's a female. The one who was here before is no longer there. Doogie doesn't know, but he senses it.

Climbing back up the big trunk, he sees an armrest for one bob, a chair for the other bobby, and a bed for another bonobobette. Doogie smells two females who are rubbing hands. A little one climbs onto the back of a bobinette and looks at him. Then the bobettes touch each other: it's sex. Oh, Doogie, close your eyes! He senses anger inside his own dirty Nature. Everywhere there is kissing and fuck-me, but Doogie doesn't know, he doesn't want.

Who are you inside of Doogie?

When Doogie leans his head out it will soon be dusk. The air is soft and the light is soft. He sees that he is not like them. Doogie, you have underpants, and they watch you, they sniff.

And under your white-brown dirty underpants, Doogie, your sex is straight. It's like a hand in the middle of you that comes from your Nature toward . . . what? It doesn't have fingers. Toward whom is it stretching? It hurts, it hurts.

Oh! Shame! But what is it, Doogie? Your head is on fire, and you have both hands on the hand of your sex. How hard and straight it is. What do you want? It's shameful, Doogie, but you have the word and you don't know what there is inside it anymore. It's an empty chocolate box of the word, empty. What is there inside of you that is called *shame*?

Doogie runs toward the river. He feels that there is something he wants, but he doesn't know what it is.

Before the evening, at the place where the river arrives to vary the reflections of the big green, and flows softly, *slosh slosh*, it's getting dark. Doogie sits down on a boulder.

In front of him, on the carpet of yellow grasses, there's a sex party. Doogie, where does that word come from? What's inside it? Where did you hear it?

Bob and Bob, the two males, are squatting down and rubbing each other behind the rump, and the older Bob cries out as he takes the it's the penis of the young one. Then the young one is on his back on the grass of the evening and Old Bob gets active on him, rubs and rubs. The little she's a Bobette gets onto her back. She likes it. Bobinette presses her vulva against the fat pink lips of her it's her mother while sniffing. She's busy rubbing the pink mouth of her sex nicely onto that of the other female.

Doogie watches. Doogie, you're a voyeur, you are seeing this.

There's movement, and then the movement shifts. The females get up, and it's finished. Toward the forest, a male descends from a female, and another female with her foot in the water invites him with her butt. He jumps and jumps, his sex feather is in the pink mouth of the sex of the female he penetrates. Doogie sees. He's affectionate: "look at me." A kiss on the hand. Everyone is loving, Doogie, everyone loves each other.

You sense it, Doogie: Heaven is sex.

When you move your eye along the river, the water is flowing and night is falling. It's nice out. You have what you want.

You see her lying on her back on the stones, half in the water on the beach of the clear water, her muscled legs spread. You know those legs, Doogie. Look inside the water: a beautiful so beautiful hand of it's a woman is playing with the pure water, her fingers black. She places two fingers in the pink of the mouth of it's her sex like half of an orange that is filled with blood. Then, outside of the water, Doogie sees the point of one of her smooth brown breasts, and the plume of her smooth little hairs. She-shee cries out and lifts her head, the head of a woman, a female. She's holding a white flower in her mouth, her ears thin and her eyes half open. Flirtatiously, she chases away a butterfly with her other hand. With the left hand, her fingers on the stem of the mouth of her legs, she is masturbating. Doogie, where does that word come from? How good it is: she loves the water and the water is flowing. She calls you, saying "come here" without saying anything. You sense it.

You're like the water, Doogie, and she is Shee, like the flower, like the mouth.

Your hand is hiding your underpants, hiding the hand that is stretching. Her mouth opens, it's pink and you smell it pink. She doesn't say anything.

And you run away. Night has come, and you're naked there.

When the sun has gone down, will it rise again? The morning answers yes and Doogie descends from his too poor badly made nest. He is healed now, and when the sickness is doing badly, the patient is doing well. Doogie feels that his head is clear, but the foot of his leg still drags and Doogie limps. He will always limp. Hobbledy-hobble, Doogie crosses the little clearing and goes along the tree trunk that is lying on the ground. Which trunk is it? As with all the trunks, there's a bob, and bobbies, and kisses.

It's bright in the not very thick forest, and the trees are like broccoli. The sky is open, and up above is blindness. With his feet, Doogie picks up the caterpillars that shit from the branches and fall fall. He eats, he limps, and he sits down.

With his big sure hand over his eyes, his gray, wrinkled, thick hand, sitting in the shadow of little trees between the river and the forest, he watches the plain of yellow grasses, and there are two bobettes doing gymnastics: they stretch their legs and say "ha!" One smiles, and the other touches and strokes her. A little baby belongs to one of the bobettes, but Doogie doesn't try to understand anything. One of the bobs catches the baby and lays him down on his feet, lifting him as if he was flying, pretending to be a bird, and little Bob pouts his lips toward the front, the crown of his hair in the wind.

She-shee is next to him, and she smiles. A flower is in your mouth. Crouched down, she comes out from the shadow and the silence and she holds out the arm of her hand, almost making contact with you. Doogie who limps got up and took a step to the side.

When he looks her in the eyes, he doesn't know if it's Shee. He wants to recognize her, he wants to speak, but she doesn't want to, doesn't know how. He tries, calls her Doogette. It must be you and not another. I don't want . . . I mustn't confuse you with another.

She-shee or another, what does it matter? She wants contact. She has flowers between her teeth, and when she stands up, naked, arched, the mouth of her sex swollen under your face, she walks delicately, and she goes down toward the stones. Doogie is captivated. She turns around and Doogie smells his underpants. She is open, she is soft and clean, she loves the water, she loves the water so much, and she is attracting you. You look at her eyes and you don't know anything, but what do you feel?

Go take a bath.

She takes Doogie's hand. At the same time, she looks the other way, from the water toward her knees. Doogie tells himself: the other bonobos don't like the water, so this must be her, it must be Shee, I must be recognizing her.

But maybe she's a different one.

She-shee with few hairs and a flat, thin face and tight thighs, is paddling, she's making a sponge, a kind of sponge, with leaves that have fallen into the water. Doogie takes the sponge in the green light. He makes a ball, and he comes toward her to wash her.

Then, suddenly, she turns around, her head above her long, straight, and beautiful back, and her mouth that seems wide open above Doogie's. Astonished, he offers his teeth. She slides her tongue, and for a long time she moves her tongue slowly toward his tongue; it's hot and moist. It is me it is you. He trembles.

Then Doogie is afraid. He limps, he jumps, and now here he's out of the water. But she follows behind him, and in front of them is a field of flowers and openings of green.

Night after night, Doogie sleeps with her in the same nest; it's a bed.

When the light has left for not there anymore, but the moon remains across the branches and twigs, Doogie hears the trumpeting of the elephant from across the river, in the muddy baths, and he doesn't sleep. No, Doogie sees, Doogie keeps watch.

What are you looking at, Doogie?

She's one of them, she's her. How strange, when seen from up close, is the mystery of one who is like you but is not you. Doogie looks at the flat little nose and the half circle of the hollow of the nostrils of the Doogette. Because Doogette is sleeping, she doesn't know anything. She smells like sleep, pressed up against you. Doogie, why can't you sleep?

On the bottom of her chin, she has some black hairs and some white hairs. It's elegant, and the leather of her skin around her eyes is wrinkled like water that flows from the waters.

Suddenly, she opens her two eyes, and they are black moons in orange reflections. When she sees you, what does she see? She shows her teeth, so white. Is she beautiful when seen up close? Doogie doesn't take his eyes away from the Doogette. She yawns, she curls up, she needs warmth. The temperature on the ground is falling. On the fat branch, next to the birds who go *cheep cheep*, it will soon be cold. You'll have to protect her.

He sees the very thin line of her lip. It's red, and he wants to. When he sees her buttocks and the pink number two mouth in the fingers of black, Doogie closes his eyes.

Doogie, she doesn't have a daisy between her teeth anymore. Is she dreaming of the water that flows-cascades and that she loves so much? There's a hand on her mouth and on her legs while she sleeps: is she dreaming of Doogie?

At the moment when Doogie thinks that he understands that he knows what she is, that he knows what is inside you, he loses the word, he loses his understanding, and when he finds the word again, he looks and there's nothing inside it.

Doogie, when you feel it you don't know it, and when you know it you never feel it.

Doogette presses herself closer, and it's stupid, but you feel like Doogie.

One day, on the green hilltop, a big female Bobette meets her little Bobby who is coming down in the morning on the carpet of dry leaves.

Doogie jumps out of the nest, with one leg that limps and the other that walks. Letting go of the vine in midair, he lands on two feet. Old Bob the old male shows his teeth and smiles at Doogie while gathering his fruit. Do you think that Doogie is going to stick out his hair? You feel anger, you're defiant, you're a chimpanzee, but he just walks by. The Old Bob dominates the bono-bobs, but for the Doogie who is a chimpanzee this is Heaven.

Bobby, the son of the big Bobette, is dragging a little branch and yelling. Then *hoaa*, he jumps in the direction of Old Bob. Doogie watches as he climbs the green hill. Old Bob is surprised; he slaps the little Bobby to defend himself.

Then Big Bob, the dominant of the dominants who gives kisses to all the bobettes, comes down, grunting. He's coming from the river. He's big and brown, and he ignores Doogie.

Old Bob is stressed, and Big Bob calms him, one hand on his shoulder. Then he rubs himself, he climbs on top of him and kisses him and back-to-back, rump to rump, he calms his calm, and the little Bobby goes off toward the hilltop with the little branch, no worries.

Doogie, who is chewing his fruit and one and two, looks for Doogette, who is always holding hands with the big Bobette. She watches over the little Bobby when Doogette goes to the river because she loves the water so much and so much.

Then the young Bobby comes back and charges. He knocks the old Bob with white hair into the air. Doogie frowns. Old Bob responds: he gets up and runs quickly between the bushes and the trees toward the thick of the forest. Bobby charges again, and when the old Bob picks up a branch, his teeth to the front, the mother, the big Bobette, takes off, a little one on her stomach. She helps her Bobby, and Bob the Old runs away with a big scream. Two and so many and so many screams echo each other. Doogie jumps up. Are all the females coming from the woods, and from the river and the embankment? Running along the tree trunk, allied with Bobette, they chase old Bob the White. One and two and ten times Bobby attacks, until they reach the clearing. Then Bobette hits the old guy, and he ends up being quiet and climbing high up in a tree.

Now, as soon as Bobby drags his branch into the area, the old Bob climbs the tree. If he charges, the old one runs away, and finally he offers him his rump while whining. Now, when Big Bob comes back down with two females, he ignores the old one. He sniffs, he rubs buttholes with Bobby, and afterward Bobby bangs the females.

By the end of the day, the big Bobette is dominant. Doogie is looking for his Doogette, but he gets her confused. The doogettes come and the doogettes go.

He walks on all fours to the summit of the green hilltop where the sun is falling. The big Bobette chases his Doogette away, with a little one on her back. She is her friend, but she doesn't like Doogie, and now she reigns in Heaven with her Bobby.

"Are you Doogette?" Doogie wants to ask. She is screwing, and another is screwing her. Doogette yelps with pleasure. The mouth of her sex is in sideways friction with the sex of the big Bobette who is rubbing herself there. Her lips are swollen like a balloon, and Doogette is stretched out on her back, her arms behind her head in surrender. The Bobette on her stomach picks her up and moans. Rub your sex.

Doogette smiles. She sees Doogie, she picks up a flower, and she brings it to her mouth. She comes out from under Bobette, who leaves with her little one.

Without any memories at all, she takes your hand and climbs into the nest. Limping, they meet Bobby, his lips pressed together, his face tense. He grunts in the darkness, and Heaven softly slips into night.

Hello, morning. How many times it's been Doogie doesn't know.

Bobby is the king here now, and it's the big Bobette who dominates. Doogette delouses Bobette against the big lying-down tree trunk, and then she gets up and crosses the prairie of the savanna of yellow grasses. The sky opens its cover. It's green weather.

Doogette—are you the same Doogette or a different one?—bends her legs, and Doogie sees under her hair the pink covering of her muscles, her fat straight calves which move in a zigzag toward the stones, toward the river of the plateau. She carries her food: shoots and leaves of ginger that are red like she is. Shee sees you, Doogie, and she turns her head, her high little ears, her flat face. She pouts and lowers her eyes. You see her breast without hairs, and with a gesture she touches her buttocks. She gets into the water and cools herself off. Doogette has picked up half of a red bell pepper, and she draws water into it.

What is love, Doogie? You jump, you who are lame, and you walk into the cold river. How good the bath feels on your sex, Doogie. You lower your underpants, and the sun of blindness is high above.

With your eyes closed, you feel it. You open your mouth and she puts in her tongue, and hounh, Doogette rubs between your legs, pulls your back toward her, and spreads your thighs. You see her. She shows her teeth in the sun, and you try to go inside.

A cry, and she has turned around. Splashing, she lets go of the red pepper. Long and thin, Doogette gets out of the water and dries off her buttocks with wood shavings in the shade. Doogie runs after her. She pushes him away and gets on all fours. She refuses to look at him. Oh, Doogie is annoyed with anger. He pulls up the root of a briar, ruffles his hair, and rushes away.

Bobby barges out of the forest, along with two bobettes and the big mother of Heaven. Bobby is dragging his branch, and Doogie grunts. He turns around and Bobby rubs him, touches his butt. Lick my butt.

Then his mother the big gray Bobette lies down and offers him the hole of her sex, but where is Doogette? Why, why? He wanted to, but She-shee left. The big mother wants to calm the Doogie. She has come to do kissing and fuck-me. But your pink sex is like shame. Doogie trembles and runs away.

Another bob who is passing by squats down. She yelps, and he goes inside her, yawns, rubs, and gives one last push, hin hin. It's just a hole.

The emptiness inside Doogie's head hurts him.

Doogie is up in the tree, and beneath him the bobs and the bobettes are barking: *hou, ha ha, hoa.* What is this Heaven? Where is the hole that would complete it?

Somewhere, there are memories. Doogie, oh Doogie, I beg you to remember. Who is what, and who are you? Fill in your hole, Doogie. The shame of sex is not for the ones who are barking. It's only for you.

Doogie falters. He breathes through his bitten lip, and he hides the ears at the top of his skull with his arms, pressed against a branch that is swaying. Who are you?

Screw them and screw me. Down below, they're still barking.

From beyond the outside, far from the woods, there's a *woof woof* bark.

Shut up! Shut your faces and shut your holes!

They're barking like dogs!

Like dogs!

Dog!

And then Doogie remembers. You have filled up the hole inside me. I climb down the branches, limping, running. Now I know, because I have the solution.

Across clearing, across forest, now I know. I descend from the hilltop, I limp on the stones, and I recognize you. He's barking, he's barking! At the edge of the river and in the morning, he's growling. He scares the bono-bobs who run away, gesticulating. How stupid they are: they don't have the science of dogs! Bobby who dominates drags his branch far away from the dog. He cries out as if he's also barking, and the big Bobette limps to the gray tree. The dog crawls and comes out of the water of the river. Oh, even with a broken leg he's chasing the bobbies of Heaven!

And oh, now I know who *you* are: you're Doogie! I put my hand around the waist of Doogette, who is trembling at the foot of the gray tree, her lips pulled back, her teeth showing, smiling. She's filled with fear. What's all this nervousness about? Doogie stands up, strokes her, and reassures her. "This is just my English dog of a terrier!"

Doogie has rediscovered the words of the I that is me. Doogette opens her round eyes; she doesn't understand. She presses herself into me, far from Bob and Bobby. I take her hand and I escort her, "don't be afraid," and I hold out my hand to the it's my dog.

"Have no fear. He's my faithfulness!" And I look at the bobbies, at Heaven. I, me, I'm the master. "Oh, dog, what a joy it is to be me again and for you to be you!" He looks at me, a goody-two-shoes expression on his eyebrows, his eye swollen and yellow, and in his eye I see absolute faithfulness. "Faithful the dog," I say, "I'm proud of you. You are wounded, yet you have looked for and found your master. Doogie knows that he is Doogie when he has his dog." Limping, he puffs out his chest, his hair standing up, and he pants for a long time. "Haooounh! Long live the dog of long live me!" The bobs lower their heads and scatter. Only the Doogette remains under my arm. She blinks her eyes and rolls against me.

Then I pet the head of the good dog with a mustache, thin and with a broken leg, who is sticking out his tongue, so happy to be with his good master. And since language is mine again, I ask:

"Where have you been, dog? Where is the entrance to the exit from Heaven that you have found?"

Doogie is walking as the master, to the right of the left of the Doogette and to the left of the right of the dog. He walks and climbs up the course of the water, pouting with contentment. Soon the little forest around the little river clears away, and the river is flowing in the middle of a big green plain. Doogette squeezes her little body against Doogie. She clings to him and clicks her teeth. Doogie looks at her. She-shee doesn't have a flower in her mouth. Is it really her? She's nothing more than a female ape with hair and a smell and a strange body that isn't faithful to the human.

The human. Doogie looks at his hands. He pets the faithful dog and gives him a piece of fruit and a dead bird to eat. The dog eats his meal while wagging his tail, wiggling his tufted head the color of dead leaves. *Woof woof.*

Long before he reaches the fog, Doogie stops to think. Standing up, with his head toward the horizon, in his underpants, he holds Doogie between his hands. Doogie, where did you come from? And where did *you* come from, dog? Heaven is a big plateau bordered by the water of water, and monkeys don't have the science of swimming.

Suddenly, they're advancing toward the green and yellow plain of the plateau, which is climbing, and the river is descending. The stones at the river's edge become a low wall, a higher wall, and then a cliff. At the end of the end, Doogie smells waterfalls and the cascade of water. And he remembers.

Doogie fell from the water that falls! The river cradled Doogie and took him by the hand. I was injured and I ran aground on the river's edge. It was Shee who found me.

But when I turn around, Doogette is running away. She's afraid. We're leaving her territory. "Doogette, come back," I say. She doesn't understand. She runs like the dirty ape that she is, on all fours. Doogie, don't say bad things about her, she saved you. Hmm.

I climb the plateau that is rising, and I glance down at the water that is flowing and descending, running backward. Heaven is a prison: there's no way out of it. And I sit down while breathing hard from the pain in my leg. The sky is covered by a tablecloth of clouds. You too, dog, you have a pain in your leg. I pet you. I took palm leaves, and I built you a bandage for your blood. Hou hou, you're licking Doogie's head, you idiot. I'm taking care of you.

And Doogie thinks: "The Doogette also took care of Doogie as well as she could. How did she do that? She's just a little monkey, and where is your gratitude, Doogie?" I think about her with sadness, and I see the dog who is running in the mist, who is limping. He barks, he wants to show me something. Woof woof what?

And then, how about that?!

Underneath the mist on the river below, beneath the cliff that is climbing up, there's a bridge that crosses the water, a wooden bridge, a bridge that's still standing.

It's human. It's a trace of you, human. You have put your finger in Nature. I ask the dog: "Did you go through here to find your master? And then climb the cliff of rocks and vines to the plateau of Heaven surrounded by the waters of the Jungle?"

And he barks one two three times in the fog, happy, his hind leg wrapped in the palm leaves around the splint of a branch. His hair is dirty and wavy, and his snout is long and wide. I can't see your eyes very well, but I pay you back with love, with faithfulness, and I stroke your snout and under your stomach for a long time, my dog. You've earned it. Because here is the door of the exit from Heaven.

But Doogie, who will stroke *you*?

Sitting in the mouth of the mist of the cool heights, I hesitate before the departure of the solitary traveler, and I think about Doogette the flower, about the one, Shee, who presses herself into you. There you had a nest. I close my eyes.

First, Doogie, get your weapon from Heaven. Then say goodbye to the Doogette. Tell her, though she won't understand.

"Oh, Doogie," I think, and my head is spinning. "In the forest you have love and happiness, and in civilization you have faithfulness. Why do you have to decide to leave and say farewell to Heaven?"

Then I look at the faithful dog under my caress and I understand. I know. You, Doogie, are the dog of the human, and beyond that you're nothing.

Before the after the afternoon, lame Doogie stands up straight, and with the too short arms of a chimpanzee he leans on a stick that has a thousand knots of wood. By his side, Faithful the dog licks a puddle of water out of thirst, and our shadows grow like children of the sun. The weather is nice. Doogie knows that he knows that he doesn't belong in Heaven. Heaven is for you, monkeys and bono-bobs, and Heaven, I can tell you, is nothing important. Is it less good or better than real life? Each one does what each one does, Doogie. Look at them and then look at yourself.

Like a shepherd, I hold the dog against me at the summit of the big green embankment, the forest with the clearing on one side and the river with the rocks on the other, and then the plateau rises. Doogie sees Bobby dragging the branch of his victory. He is dominant: he attacks the Bob who is missing a hand, and the old Bob hides in a tree. Doogie could give them names, but what's the use? Civilization, Heaven, what's the big difference? Doogie doesn't have the answer, and they don't even have the question.

There is violence to the left and cuddling to the right. It's Heaven, and not everything is black and white, Doogie.

Now Bobby reconciles with the Bob who is missing a hand. He rubs his scrotum against his rump, with a stupid look, a happy look. They're doing homosexual fuck-me. Does Nature disgust you, ape? And I look at my own black hands under the tattered brown shirt from the Zoo. What remains of the human?

I remain. I lean on the stick for the last night, and I grimace. I whistle to my dog the dog to come. At my feet, Heaven is going to sleep. Doogie, go and find the nest where you don't belong to anything. A female yelps with pleasure: is it Shee? I can't tell. The cry is coming from the water. An adult is rubbing the sex of an adolescent, his back straight and his legs spread against a tree. His penis gets hard and the old Bob walks by. The female rejects him, but he takes her with the in and out.

Under the lowest of the lowest branches, the big Bobette and a new female who has come from the forest beyond the plain are touching each other. She shows her teeth with pleasure when the other one slows down when Doogie sees her through the big leaves.

Piercing cries, pierced buttholes. Hugs and kisses. Doogie, all alone, leads his dog to the little bed that he made him for the night so black. Dive down between two fat roots and sleep well.

And then Doogie climbs up into the darkness, into the tree of his nest with his good leg, poor monkey. I look at the moon and I ask: "Human, why did you take me out of the Jungle of animal Heaven? Why did you put me all by myself into language, on the threshold of the door of the human but not inside it?"

At the door, Doogie, it's impossible for you to enter and impossible for you to leave.

You're all alone, oh Doogie, but you're not the only one like you!

I hold out my big hand. She-shee is there, and she presses herself against me. When the hairs of another skin meet the poor hairs of my poor skin, I'm not a brain anymore, I want to cry and say "love me." Is this the same Doogette? I try to touch her head, but it's not a face I can tell by feeling. I look for the flower between her teeth, but it's not there. I'm not sure it's you. I don't recognize you.

Oh, Doogie, you don't recognize the animal you sleep with! How low the beast has fallen! I hate you! Human to whom I am faithful, do you feel the solitude that is mine and the Nature that is tearing at the stomach of my underpants? I'm alone and I need Nature in me, in the underpants of my sex.

Shivering in the darkness of night, I ask for a cuddle, sliding along the nest of twigs on the branch that goes *crack-crack*. She has opened her mouth and opened her thighs. For her, it was business as usual: smell, kiss, and screw. But not for me. Please tell me it's different.

A lamp in the pocket of the moon falls onto her through the leaves. I look at her and I feel that it's no different. Put it in me, screw me: it's just kissing. She grimaces with her nose and opens the fat orange swelling of it's her sex. It's time to go for it.

I'm sweating, Doogie, and I want to, oh I want to so much, but Doogie she's an ape, she's an animal! She hangs her long black arms around my neck and lightly suspends her thighs on my sides, and she says, "go ahead, enter." Oh, I see her with her mouth open and her facial expression. With a thrust, she turns her head one way and the other and looks for a twig in the earth at the elbow of the tree trunk.

Then she looks at me. She has slid a red flower into her mouth, and I think I smell running water. I hate her, hate her! What an anger there is in me, my hairs standing on end. What misfortune! I want to hurt her with my sex. Take it out of your underpants. I tear the flower from her mouth, I pound my chest, and she curls up beneath me.

I'm doing violence to her.

One two three, breathe. She's so small, like a twig of hairs. What does she understand? She implores me: she wants to take a break. She holds out the pink of her hand in the darkness. She wants to press against me, she wants to make up, sex, peace, and Heaven.

"She's an animal, Doogie. What are you doing?" It's a woman's voice, but where is civilization? I look up above me in the sky above the branches, at the moon, and I think that she can see me.

I'm about to enter her, Shee is pressing up against me, but I hear: "I can see you."

I saw eyes in the dark. Doogie panics. I look above me and to the side and I push the Doogette away. She's scared.

Then beneath us under the branches I see two shining black eyes and they're looking at me.

It's your dog, Doogie. He woke up. He saw you.

"I can't," I say. I tremble and I leave the nest.

He saw you doing that.

Memories

I can't sleep. It's too hot, and even the sheets are sweating.

I'm sitting on my white pine bed, and I give my eye to the moon through the blinds of my bedroom.

It's an evening of night, and on the staircase below my big oak door the heat smells like whiskey. It's Mr. Gardner, who has been drinking. When he drinks, he says stupid things.

The sweat is sticking to Doogie's hair, oh, too much hair—what is this curse, Doogie?–and Janet laughs. "You wear a sweater all year long!" Ha-ha, that's a good one! I have clothes, pajamas from civilization on my back, but I already have animal hair on my skin. Thanks, thanks for everything, Nature! Haounh phooey. . . . *Crack!*

I hear a noise. *Crack!* What is this termite doing under the floor? I lower the little ear of my skull to the mattress. *Crack*, and again *crack*. Hmm. Doogie doesn't like that. I get down from the bed with water pissing out between my hairs, and I glue my ear to the off-white rug on the parquet floor. *Crack.* Doogie took his adventurer pocket lamp, pulled up the waistband of his pajamas with the golden circles and the cross, and went down the stairs. "Janet," I wanted to whisper, but the big mute hand of the ape can't be seen in the darkness, even when it's speaking softly. The door of Janet's room is open, the light turned off. Doogie is afraid.

I go down toward the living room. It's dusty. No one is doing the cleaning at our house anymore.

I hear a noise that is saying "shh."

"What?" the noise that is saying "shh" says. "We're going to wake up Doogie!"

Hmm. There's a funny noise on the couch that's like talking. I turn off my pocket lamp and I open the red door of the big television reception living room.

The lamp is covered with a white T-shirt, and the light is saying, "shh, I'm dimmed." Under the lamp with Janet's T-shirt on it, there is her brassiere. And I saw Janet wearing only panties—she's almost naked, Doogie—on the black leather sofa, lying underneath Michael in his black underpants.

Doogie didn't move.

She's crying, her right arm on her chest, and she's looking for a handkerchief in the Kleenex box. Michael is holding her gently in his those are his arms.

"I can't," she says.

"Why not, Janet?" Michael whispers.

"Because . . ."

She turns over abruptly and I see her, her red hair disheveled, and she sees me. In the darkness, through the half-open door, she saw my two black shining eyes which saw whatever that was.

She shivers and gets up from the sofa-bed.

From the Jungle

It's morning, it's hot, and it's time to go.

After the breakfast of fruits and caterpillar droppings, Doogie brushed the dog's hair. He leaned on the stick with a thousand knots, and he descended limping toward the plain of yellow grasses and the river of riverbanks and worms.

Doogie didn't look back. Those are apes, Doogie. And I don't want nostalgia for the bono-bobs of Heaven in my stomach. Doogie rediscovered his lost memories in the Jungle, but he holds his faithfulness tightly in his hand.

I will go to the Realm of Rnature, I will kill the Rnimal, and once back at the Zoo I will ask for a cuddle from Janet, and she will say what a good ape you are. And that will be *your* Heaven, Doogie. I sponge the forehead of me with the help of a sponge of wrinkled leaves dipped in clear water. I look at the sponge and I think about Doogette.

Then I spit, I close the brown shirt over my torso down to my dirty xxl underpants which cover me like civilization, I grunt, and I move away from Bob and the bobbies who are walking around nervously on all fours. I go behind the boulder—follow me, dog—where I take the bundle with Michael's pistol out of the muddy earth. I feel its weight, and I look at the bobs with scorn. I have power. Bobby acts like an imbecile with the branch, and the big Bobette his mother the female runs around yelping, with shoots in her hands.

Animals.

I clean the weapon of the human, my feet solid in the mud of the water that is flowing and burbling over the gray stones. The dog barks.

Behind me, lying down with her eyes open on the stone patties in the water, She-shee is watching me while biting her lower lip. She doesn't say anything, and her legs are spread as she moves the water below the mouth between her thighs.

"Close that up," I grumble.

Does she know? What does she sense? I don't know anymore, and I don't know if I ever knew. She's another kind of animal. Each one is his own animal, and no one is the other.

She doesn't move at all, and I think she's sad as she watches the lame dressed-up chimpanzee who is walking away from her. If I look at her, I think that she loves me, and I do too, but I tell myself: forget her. She will forget faster than you will.

I sigh. The dog is in front of me. At the beginning of the prairie, I pick a white flower. I think about it, I hesitate, I retrace my steps, and I give it to her with the tips of my fingers. Is she pretty, is she beautiful? She's a lying-down ape, she loves water so much, she bites the flower and moans. Does she hold out her hand to me? She smiles. I think she's crying but I don't see a tear. I don't know. I would like her to tell me something or embrace me. Solitary ape that I am, I have loved the company of press-against-me with you. She does a kiss into the air of the void. And, saying "ha ha" as if she was singing, she bats her hands on the water, happy. Doogette opens her mouth and tickles herself. I see her open sex. I beg you to close that.

Where are your eyes, Doogie? I close them, I turn my back, and trembling I go away. The dog is waiting for me.

Behind me, behind me, what do I hear? A long cry of sadness and complaint in the lapping of the flowing water.

I climb the embankment, and my heart drops down inside me.

When the mist isn't very mist anymore, the storm becomes a rage.

Doogie smells the storm as he walks through the dry grasses and into the green grasses. He drags his right leg—one, two, stick, three, five, breathe—and I look up high in the sky. Then I see, at the summit of the embankment of the plateau, on the cliff that is crumbling into the water of the river, the bridge of the human that leads to the other side in the direction of the exit. I drink a little water from the bell pepper that I filled near the stones, and I give some to the dog, master and adventurer that I am. The fat heat of silence weighs on the shoulders of the Nature of the plateau. Back behind my buttocks, I see the green forests of trees and the clearings of Heaven. But that was yesterday. Squinting, I can still see the Bobs and Bobettes milling around, eating, and playing at fuck-me. I smile with a grin of all the better for them, and too bad for you.

I look harder, and I think I see her in the clearing where I once lay as if dead. Is she alone? Is it her? From so far away, I can't see very precisely in the heat. She's a doogette like the others, lying down and stretching her arms behind her.

Does She-shee miss you?

A Bob has jumped onto a tree like a trunk, and he has come onto her. He is doing penetration to her. Doogie watches the you-screw-me-I-screw-you. He likes it and she likes it.

Poor Doogie: she already doesn't remember you. You, I think, will remember her as long as they don't pull it out of the brain of your skull.

How unfair remembering is.

Then the fuck-me is finished. A Bobette passes by, and it starts over. The wheel is turning, and there will never again be the time, the minutes and the hours, that have fallen forever. All around the Doogette, I see the clearing, and around the clearing the forest, and around the forest on the plateau is the river and the Jungle and the earth and the sky and the stars and the humans in their orbital stations.

The little bonobo doesn't know about all that. You do exist, Heaven, but you're very small.

With the bundle on the shoulder of my back, leaning on the stick on a gentle slope and then a steeper one, I descend with the dog to the bridge in the fog. And please forgive me, but when I see it again it's in memories where I stayed with her as an ape for my whole life.

Putting weight on the bridge, I place foot after foot on the planks that squeak.

With my finger I rub off the sand and the dust on the railing, and I shudder when I recognize the white water without Doogie in it. With my foot I clean off a dirty plank and I see the golden circle engraved with the cross.

"Doogie," I think, "the Zoo had a bridge in the Jungle, and I didn't know about it. Between civilization and Nature, there was something in the past that makes you feel cold in your back. Poor ape with your brain in your little skull, you sense that it eludes you."

In the gray sky like marble with lizards, a bird's shadow floats, and you place your hand on the back of the panting dog who comes hobbling to your side.

"It's Thousand Colors," I murmur.

"Keep going, keep going!" he cackles. And I follow Thousand Colors with all my eyes as he says in the air: "Find Rnature!"

"Find the Rnimal!"

"Yes," I murmur to myself with my big hand. And squinting the fold of skin down over my eyes, I noticed that Thousand Colors was no longer more than one color. He was gray, just gray.

I searched in my memories as I crossed the bridge, and I forgot. My sex called me from under my big underpants. I touched the hard hand of my sexuality, and I sighed: no.

What a stomachache I had about my faithfulness, but I started my very long hike, my pistol on my shoulder, to end things with the Rnimal of the death killer of Michael and return to the Zoo.

Inside him, the vengeance of hate filled Doogie like a balloon, his stomach broken in two by his sex that wants and his faithfulness that doesn't want. And to the dog I said: "A Thousand Colors bird of only one color! What do you think about *that*?"

Happy, he barks.

"Hmm," I think. I think I believe that there are mysteries in Nature and civilization that they're hiding from your wisdom. Hin hin haouh. Doogie is going to astonish you. He'll discover all the secrets, he'll kill all the killers, and Janet oh Janet will say: "Doogie, what an incredible monkey you are!"

And then I'll have a right to her cuddle.

And giving a punch to the hand of my sex, I said "go back home," and I pull up my underpants as I walk. "You'll see what you're going to see, isn't that right, dog?"

Woof.

Pongo

—Memories: a red dress, the bankruptcy of the zoo, and the visit of an administrator.—The watch and the old orangutan.—The plan.

Memories

"When we host an administrator, Doogie, we put on a very beautiful dress and we're extremely pretty like a princess." "Why?" I ask. "Is he the administrator of the dress?"

"Don't be an idiot, Doogie! It's the science of seduction." In her bedroom in front of the mirror, Janet has put on the red dress that makes her breasts show and that looks like an invisible hand is squeezing her waist. Doogie is sitting down, wearing a shirt without a stain. Your slippers are polished on the bed. He watches Janet adjusting her earrings, her necklace, and her three bracelets. She sees you in the mirror, your mouth open, poor monkey, lying on my back. "Tell me, am I pretty?"

Oh, Doogie won't tell a lie, but Doogie is not very handsome. Does he have the right to say that Janet is pretty? I think that if I look at her I'll soil her.

"Look at me, Doogie. Am I beautiful?"

And by the light of the evening, Doogie's heart hurts his chest. I feel my sweat, my hair, and the poor hairs on my skull. Houh, Janet wants Doogie to say it, and Doogie says it, but Doogie is still smaller when Janet is big. Oh, Doogie loves the prettiness of Janet, but the more distanced the beauty of Janet is the less close she is to you, the less she's your friend. Doogie lifts his eyes. Compared with the red beauty of her throat and her red hair cascading down, with earrings like crystal tears, Doogie is only a black animal with balls of hair wearing a shirt. Who is Doogie to say that you're pretty? No one, ever.

But to make her happy, I say, "Janet, you're as beautiful as the evening is. And I do not find the like of her beauty."

"Oh, Doogie." She picks out from her beauty case the secrets of makeup, and she holds up the red frills of her dress; it is carmine of do not crease it when you sit down. Janet is happy. She's not happy every day, you know, and Doogie must show how happy he is with her beauty on the day of the party.

I show my teeth but not too much, smiling like humans do, but inside me it makes me feel anxiety.

"Doogie, when you see a princess like me, isn't it like Paradise?" "Paradise?" asks Doogie. "What's that?" And I hold back the respiration of my lungs because her perfume is too beautiful.

She bursts into laughter. "Oh, Doogie, haven't I taught you that?"

Doogie shakes his head no. "You need to come down now," Michael yells from the staircase. Janet holds my chin between two fingers, and I give my eye to each pearl on her neck so as not to look at her breasts. She says, "You know, there are men way up there, in the stars . . . They left, and they left Nature all around us. They're living . . ." and she starts breathing again, "they're still living like princes and princesses, and they're very rich in the orbital stations." With the hand that has her ring on it, she shows off the red flower of her dress and she says: "They dress like today every day, and they're always happy." And her gaze blinks. "As for me, just look at my hands. I'm condemned to stay here with dad, so what do I know? I do the gardening and destroy my hands. There's never a party, never anything fun. It's a hole."

Janet looks at the star of stars through the window. "Paradise, for me, is up there. I would so like to meet people, to speak with them, to see artists, singers, pop stars."

And then she laughs and puts her index finger on my dirty nose. "What a beautiful star *you* are, Janet." "Let's hope so. But for the people up there, I'm sure that Paradise is here, on Earth. They have greenhouses and vegetables, but they come from Nature, from the forest, from the rivers and the ocean, isn't that right Doogie? For them, up there, Paradise is *here*." And I say yes.

"Stand up straight and fix the pleat in your trousers." She gets up and spritzes a little perfume onto the odor of her neck, and then she grabs a cardigan. Brrr, it's cold on the veranda. "You know, the administrator who is coming this evening is coming from the stars. It seems that up there he knows some stars, and he's coming to talk to dad and me. An administrator means money, Doogie." She snaps her fingers, and her eyes with their long eyelashes like toes close. "And the fact is that there's no more money. No money, no more Paradise, and well"—she sighs, puts the cardigan on her shoulders, and turns out the light—"this might all be over soon, little monkey."

In the dark, Janet, tall and dressed in red, leans toward Doogie. Before going down the staircase, she squeezes me tight and I think I'm going to fall. She whispers: "But we know that Paradise is when we're together, just the two of us, right?" And she says: "My little ape brother."

"Give me your hand and pull up your belt. We need to make a good first impression."

From the Jungle

One day, Doogie and his dog reach the source of the river.

In the company of the most faithful of faithfuls, Doogie climbed the mountains and walked the steps of the slice of white water that cascades and flows between the boulders and between the trees. He hasn't counted the days and the minutes.

I say "houh" for having the courage. My shirt is open, and at night when I'm not tired of being tired I wash my xxl underpants, and I let the dog keep watch while I take my nap. When there's too much hot in the middle of the afternoon, and the burbling of the water doesn't cool off the path to discovery, I sit in the shade of a thousand green trees, and I let the dog have his own sleep. I watch over him while I gather fruits for the meal. In this way, as the water comes down, we go up.

After the waterfalls, the water having evaporated, by climbing the boulders and the soft earth Doogie has arrived in the middle of a forest at a place with a little quivering noise where the water of the river is like a baby that is coming out of the stomach of the ground. Here it is: the end of the river. It's nice here. Doogie forces himself to talk to himself so as not to lose what remains of language in his hands. I make a tour of the area of gray boulders, of trees battered by the tempest, and of little peepees of water that are running down from the summit of the mountain while singing their song. Is this a dead end? "Stay here, dog; I'm going to look at the summit of the very big white-gray boulder."

Doogie grunts and limps on the leg that drags.

Then I see the person who is watching me from on high, squatting on the head of the boulder. Someone is way up there, and he sees me.

And I recognize Pongo.

"Pongo Pong!" I cry. "Don't you recognize me?" Pongo Pong is a red-haired ape who was in the class above me at the Zoo, very skillful with his hands. Pongo is a technician: he always has the science of the tools that Doogie breaks. Long are the red hairs of Pongo; there's a goiter and a face in front, and he has a fat belly, Pongo does.

"How is this, and what are you doing here? Did you leave the Zoo?" But Pongo the old sage with his fat all-red belly is staring into the void. "Phoo-ey," I tell myself. "He's regressed like all the others. Like Lion King and Jack. It's all over for them." I pick up one or two bananas to give him as a present, and I want to leave, but in what direction? I squint. I'm looking for the Rnimal of the Realm of Rnature, and Thousand Colors who has been all gray for a few days isn't giving Doogie the route anymore.

I sniff. "Pongo Pong the wise," I ask, "you who have placed your butt on the butt of the sack of sources, do you know which direction to go? You know Rnature." To the maximum astonishment of Doogie, Pong the disgusting orang with orange hair got up, he walked forward on one arm, two arms, and from under his hairy coat he took out something that he was holding tightly in his fist. He tapped me on my back, old friend.

Roaring, old loner that he is, he drew for Doogie the valley behind him which snakes along, green and yellow and green. "Yes," I said, and he said "hou-hou."

"Far, far away I've seen a lake that mirrored the sky."

"Hou," he said.

"Down there?"

He didn't say anything. He was intolerant of my presence, the wise old man. He grunted and opened his fist while moving away from me.

As I was leaving, I looked back at him.

"What?!" my eyes said. In his fist, as if it had been repaired, dirty but still letting the hours fall, he held the dial of my watch, recuperated and ready for my wrist.

He gave it to me. I took it from Pongo, and old Pongo went back to the source.

Memories

Doogie looks at his watch. The administrator has left, and Papa Gardner is already escorting him onto the landing strip of the Charles Bigleux for the stars. It's still night.

It's cool out. Doogie is taking advantage, and he isn't in bed. He's all alone on the big veranda because it's party day. But the party was not even eat the dessert, and Doogie must have seemed like an idiot of civilization in front of Mr. Administrator, who didn't shake his hand politely. When he looked at me, I saw what he was thinking behind his suit: *animal.* And Doogie *was* an animal. Isn't Janet happy? Farewell to the red party-day dress, her hair undone, she locked herself in the study with Michael, and Doogie is waiting for the results while shaking with worry. Through the glass of the skylight, I watch the stars of the stars of Janet's Paradise.

She came out in a pull-it-over, no more red dress, and Michael went upstairs while clearing his throat. He didn't seem to be in agreement-agreement. Oh, Doogie doesn't like that.

Janet sits down next to you under the veranda. No one has cleared the big table with the tablecloth that Doogie ripped in anger.

"Doogie, monkey," Janet said. "That was a good start." She took my big hand from me, and I couldn't speak anymore. I listened. I was sweating under my shirt, and mosquitoes were buzzing around me.

"I have . . . we have a Plan, Doogie. Listen to me carefully. Do you want to save the Zoo?" I didn't say anything, but you want Janet to be happy, so with my head I made a sign of yes.

"We need funds, money. They've cut off all our resources, and daddy is at risk. Everything will be over soon. The people from up there . . . yes, the ones in Paradise, they don't understand about the money . . . They don't understand what *you* are, the importance of what we've done, you know, your experiments. It's all about *you.* They need to see it, and they need to pay for it."

I didn't say anything at all.

When Janet starts breathing again, as redheaded and beautiful as she is, what she's going to say to Doogie won't make him happy.

"Here it is. Here's the Plan. We have to do it. You're going to the stars. You're going to leave for up there. You're going to do a tour. You're going to show what a miracle you are: Mr. Doogie, an authentic educated ape who is faithful to the human."

"You will take Charles Bigleux and you will fly up to the sky. That's *his* Paradise, you know. I've always dreamed of going to meet the stars . . . You'll make Janet proud, and they'll give us money. And then we'll be together."

Here we go. Doogie had suspected it. And she smiled under the midnight as if I couldn't see the swimming pool of her red freckle stains. "Oh, I would love to be coming with you, Doogie."

And then I understood what the Plan was.

It was no more Janet for Doogie.

Thousand Colors

—*The parrot shows the way; he has turned gray.*
—*A cry to attract the wild animals.*

From the Jungle

Goodbye, Pongo. Doogie is going down toward the valley of the emptiness with the dog when a sky-gray Thousand Colors joins them.

"Hello," Doogie grunts. What a funny Thousand Colors who only has one color left. He's completely gray.

"The Rnimal! Rnature!" Doogie says. "You always repeat the same words. Shut your mouth from opening." I look at the emptiness that is approaching, and I feel something that is coming from my Nature rise up everywhere. I don't know it, but I can feel it. I close my eye.

Then, limping, I put down the bundle in the shade, and, watching out for the snakes that are wandering around I go down on all fours, my shirt open, and I do some sniffing. An ape I am and an ape I will be.

The dog is sitting waiting for me, and Thousand Colors who is only gray has closed his mouth on a branch. "Companions," I say with my big hand, showing some teeth, and I can feel it, I can hear it. This is the moment. "I have my plan, and here it is."

"Hi hou hi," I laugh with derision. They don't understand anything, but I have understood. I tighten the watch of faithfulness on my wrist by one notch. Janet, I think of you one last time. I breathe, and I remember the Paradise that my happiness and the veranda were for me.

Then I take courage between my two fists, I listen to the leaves around me, I pound my chest one two times, and I let the noise out. I scream, and filthily I let out the monkey that I am.

Monkey!

Just a poor monkey, I also have a Plan, and the small amount of human-ness that's inside me self-destructs.

In the hollow in the depths of the pitiful, thick, and nothing Jungle, Doogie plays the ape by taking off his shirt. He's in training. Doogie sees that he's worrying his faithful companions, the all-gray Thousand Colors and the more-than-faithful dog. They give their eyes to you in a strange way, as if you were playing at being a kind of monkey that doesn't exist.

"Be calm and tranquil, companions," I grunt. "This is the Plan. Hou hou. Do you understand me?" Then the terrier dog raises an ear, and all around us he hears rustling, then soon crunching, then cries. It's animals.

"Houh hou," I say. "Have no fear. The Master is here, the master and dominator that is me. I'm following the Plan."

How much fear I have, and how little security inside me. Did Janet have so little of the peace that reassures inside her when she used to reassure Doogie? I breathe and I throw away my shirt. I'm an ape. I knot a fat bundle from the shirt for the pistol of Michael the human. It isn't too heavy. I lower myself down onto my knees, I pet the dog, and I put the bundle in his mouth. The screams are ever more screamlike in the rotten forest.

"Dog, I know your faithfulness. I'm entrusting the treasure of the hu-man between the hands of your teeth. Never let it go. I don't give it to just anyone. Stay far away from me. Roam. Go with the gray Thousand Colors. You have understood, gray Thousand Colors."

Because the gray Thousand Colors has the key to the path that leads to where we're all going.

He understood.

"And look at me, dog, look me in the eyes. Don't listen to the noise of the enemies. On the day when I will whistle for you, perhaps far away from here, you will have followed me at a distance. On the day when I whistle, you come." I smile.

"And you will bring me *that*." I try to pull the little bundle with the weapon from between his teeth. He growls and doesn't let go. That's good. "That's good, dog. You will bring the power of the human when I need it."

Screams like a cemetery of myself mark crosses all around us. They're holding my chair and I'm getting up. It's fog, it's gloom.

"Now scat! Go away. Leave the Master to take care of business. This is goodbye. Fly away, Thousand Colors."

And, chattering, he flies up into the sky.

"Go away, dog."

But the dog takes a step and he stays there. The bundle with the weapon in his mouth, he looks at me. He doesn't want to abandon me. I moan and I open my teeth. "Go away."

A step and he stays there, his eyes toward me. Hmm hou. I jump up with my feet together and I uproot a shrub. "Dog, get out of here!" I'm mean, very mean. I let all the anger of the Nature of me come out. Rolling boulders, I'm going to hit you, kill you. Houh!

Two steps; he's afraid, he looks at me. He has to leave on all fours.

"Hiaaaaaaaaaaaah," I say, and I pound my chest and I pant, I howl. I move toward him, and he moves away.

Ha houh. Alone as I am, I break some wood and I wait full of hate for the enemies, the animals, the bad ones.

They're bad like myself, a dirty filth of a monkey.

Ready to fight, I wait to see the face of their screams.

Chimps

—Wild chimpanzees.—A violent battle.—A definitive loss
of the watch and of time.—Memories of a departure for the stars.
—Last images of Janet.—A slave of "renatured" apes.—Arrival.

From the Jungle

What a dirty face they have! Doogie, you're losing your language.

One two and three and I don't know how many chimpanzees come out from the undergrowth on all fours in a big very big anger. It's all *ih ih ih ih* and *hou hou* and *ah ih hin hin*, pound your torso and show the filthiness of your mouth. That one raises his head and displays his teeth. "I fart on your teeth," I say to his face as I stand up. "I ain't got no fear of you." He comes close to me, he moves around me, and he circles around me. "What do you want?" Don't show fear! He's getting aggressive; he pouts and his nose wriggles. Another one is dragging a branch. He lets go of it and then picks it back up.

I look all around me and I watch them. One asshole, two assholes, three apes. Big strong chimpanzees like me. I'm big more than them; I'm strong more than these weak ones.

Let go of Nature, Doogie: it's just faces of assholes. Hi hi hin. Who's this one? He advances and sniffs. You stink of yourself. He moves back and another one gets up. He gauges, extends his arms, and pulls back, like the asshole of a jerk that you are.

"Ha! Come on! Doogie in your face!"

It's from the back of my side that the first one attacked, *pow*, and ouch, it hurts. It doesn't hurt me, and I'm not hurting you. Doogie slugs the emptiness, and hou, it's an in-your-face rumble that's starting.

It's hou hou, and I run, I hit, and the other one hits me. Bite him, you asshole. And clobber your rumble.

Hin hin, blood. Doogie is bleeding and he's limping. One of them jumps and—*crack*—he bites your leg. There's another one who, the asshole, twists and turns his fist in your stomach. Ouf, where did my breath go?

I grunt, blind, my eye hurts, and he's grabbed onto Doogie's butt and has put two fingers into it. I swing my arms, and there, I catch him, and there, I catch the first one I can catch, I smash I grab his balls and shatter them. I shatter them. Hi hi hi, the asshole crawls on the ground, he runs toward the trees. I have a piece of his balls in my mouth, and I spit out blood. It's yours not mine. Come and fight. I'm limping a bit, but I fight. There's one, and there's one, and there's another one. Doogie in his underpants closes and opens his fist in the face of the jerk and clobbers him, grabs, goes for it, a finger in the nose a finger in the mouth, and *crack*, he breaks your mouth, he smashes the asshole's teeth. Another one, grabbing from behind, twists Doogie's ball through the underpants, but the underpants protect Doogie like a human. Then a kick and I punch your shit, I mess up your butt. Come on, come on!

One asshole of a chimpanzee like me runs and then retreats. Another one attacks and shows his teeth. A punch to the face, and he retreats and retreats.

Now Doogie is bloody, with one and two fewer teeth. His underpants are red, his leg limps, and his shoulder is dislocated. I get up on the boulder and I pound my own torso. I impress them and I dominate. I "hi" and I "hou." I "hou hou." Is this victory? The assholes are retreating on all fours like toads.

But I sense something. When I turn around, there's a bigger and much bigger ape behind me. He's a black and silver gorilla, a monster. He grabs my arm, and it cracks, ouch, hin hin. Doogie's arm is breaking against the boulder, and I have time to see the watch from the house breaking into a thousand and a thousand pieces on my wrist, the dial wrecked. I don't have any faithfulness on my wrist anymore.

Then I lift my eyes.

A whack to your mouth, and a tooth goes into Doogie's lip. It's all over for you. I'm destroyed.

Now who's the asshole? I'm the defeat.

The end of the party is here.

Memories

It's a goodbye in the dark. It's bye-bye, and dark Janet has let go of Doogie's hand in the middle of the gray landing strip. It's morning. The last time I saw Janet, she had a ponytail for her red hair like she always did, in such a white shirt with puffy sleeves, and the wind was blowing. She was wearing a skirt that she had never worn before, pleated, blue and blue and blue. And she said farewell. "This is goodbye, Doogie. Do you have everything?" As if Doogie was still little, at the foot of the iron staircase of the big Charles Bigleux, the space airplane that was smoking. And suddenly, Doogie felt panic. "Janet," I thought. "Where did she go?"

She's behind you, saying bye.

I ran, letting go of Michael's hand. He didn't even kiss Janet. Is he angry? I ran, and like a poor nothing ape in her arms I didn't want to separate from her. "Doogie, you're big now." No, no, no. I just wanted her caress forever, and to keep being Janet's ape who is nothing when he's not with her. And showing my teeth in a dirty way I felt myself grabbing at her skirt, at her shirt.

"Doogie," Janet begged as she stepped backward.

"Doogie! That's enough!"

"I didn't want to go, Janet. You know I didn't want to." And I asked her with my little arm while panting: "Keep me; don't explain to me but keep me."

"Oh, monkey," she whispered said. "You won't understand." Janet cried, and Doogie too. She took my wrist and she repeated: "Doogie, the watch that we just gave you: it's *my* watch, you know. Look at it, and, you understand, it's a watch that watches over you and protects you. You'll never ever be separated from it. Don't break it."

"Doogie, I'm proud of you. Look at it as if it can see you. It's a piece of me. The hours fall out of the dial like I taught you, and I will think of you, little ape. I'll be there. When you're sad, look at your watch and count the hours."

"Never lose your watch, count the time that's left, be faithful to the human, and think about me."

That was Janet. Michael stopped Janet's mouth. He saw me, and in his eyes . . . "Oh, Doogie . . ." It was Janet. And I heard, "poor Doogie, poor monkey," and then I didn't hear anything. Did I let go of Janet? Doogie, did you let go of Janet?

I think that a syringe was giving me a shot in my back.

And then, like the hours from the dial, I fell out of her arms forever, gone.

From the Jungle

Hi hi hou and move.

They're marching me I don't know where, I have a lot of fear and a solitary aloneness, and one and two and how many chimpanzees are marching me like cattle. They push me, and they pass me. I'm moving slowly, limping and begging: "Let me go, I feel sick, I want to drink and rest." They tell me "hou ho ho." You can't talk to livestock.

I want to stop. My leg doesn't respond any more when I say walk, and I'm disfigured. There's a pain that hurts the face of my blood. I stop, and when I fall he hits me and I get up. It's the gorilla. He's black, he breathes, he's calm, and when he opens his teeth and looks at me, I walk. I go to the left of the top of the right of the bottom of the Jungle without a river or a clearing, and from time to time there are birds, branches, and more branches. Blue head, long tail, chocolate back, white stomach, brown ears, gold crown. A thousand birds on the branches and under the leaves. No trail, rustling and never silence, screams of apes, and they clobber my face when I moan. I drag myself until it's the end.

"Doogie," I moan, "you're a prisoner."

And it seems to me that even the birds are laughing. And "move," the gorilla grunts, grabbing on to vines. The chimps are like ants around me, and they stab and bite and hit you in the face.

Fall, bleed, get up, and walk until you fall, Doogie.

Long is the trail, small are my feet, and long is the pain of suffering.

I couldn't feel myself anymore. Poor Doogie, poor who? Like a slave of Nature, you drag your legs in their underpants in a more and more hostile foreign forest. Dark and dead, it's ugly.

How mean the other chimpanzees are! They don't give you any eats. They come and go, like chaos, and they drag me. Doogie . . . I don't feel anything at all. The brown forest has been degraded, and big holes poke into it. Big trees still hover in the air, but on the ground it's as if the virgin growth has been deforested. There are little palm trees, weak and hot, grasses that cut my feet, and filth.

It's the forest that humans abandoned.

Humans . . . I throw my eye that still works into the sky of my stars, and for the first time I feel that nothing has its eye on me. Doogie, how alone you are as you walk and walk and walk. A monkey bites you, a monkey climbs and pants, another bangs into a tree trunk, and we advance.

Here, it seems that humans fled and Nature returned. The ground descends, the valley climbs and descends, and I understand.

"Here," I say to myself, "is the Realm of Rnature."

They grimace, the chimps that walk and run around solitary Doogie, and one of the chimps has two missing fingers and a stump. I'm the one who bit the hand of that asshole. I look at him defiantly, and I lift up my cheekbones as I limp like a slave. I display my teeth. Hi hin. He runs into me, pummels my back, smashes my shoulder against the boulder under the tree trunks, and slugs me. I hiccup, the lone gorilla puts a hand on me, two hands, I fly toward the ground, and when I lift my head, one of the eyes of me is full of blood. "Get up."

Hmm. The gorilla walks on and Doogie staggers behind him.

With the only eye that I can open, moaning, I see Rnature all around me: shrubs that are growing with no order or discussion or purpose in the big and ancient clearings that are like the dining rooms of humans.

I sniff, smelling the blood of me, the blood of you. Hmm. I recognize this. What and where is it?

Memories

And the fat Charles Bigleux, the spatial vessel of the stars in the shape of a sea turtle, went up, sailing on the white fumes and the white cloud. All the air is squeezing Doogie's arms, legs, and skull. I open half of one sleeping eye. Where am I?

The good Doogie is a prisoner, attached by the hands and feet, sitting in a purple armchair. Through the round and badly washed porthole, asleep in my sleep, I know that the Earth is going away beneath my feet, but it's really my feet that are going away, and the Earth will still be there when I'm not.

And the Earth gradually turns into a ball, a little ball. Where is Janet on the ball that's as small as Doogie's hand? You're becoming a giant, Doogie, but now, alone and without her, you are nil.

This is how I became Mr. Doogie for the stars, whom you know, and Janet was never again to be anything more for him than memories.

I set my two eyes down onto my watch, so low I was, and I thought about it, and I spoke to it. I told it about the flight of my voyage and about what was in my heart.

Doogie, Janet, atoms, and molecules all far apart. They were closer when I thought about it, but that's just something in the past.

From the Jungle

Hunger has no end, Doogie, and the mouth has no morsel.

You sleep and you eat, but when the chimpanzees stop moving, other naked chimpanzees come down from the thin trees of the forest which has grown back from Rnature, and they march and march. Doogie never stops. Doogie eats when he pulls rotten berries off with one hand, or leaves, or a caterpillar. The other arm with his big hand is frozen, broken, and his leg is dragging. Doogie can't feel the half of his face to the left of his mouth, and beneath the idiotic tweeting of thousands of birds, like a cloud, he advances toward . . . Where is the end?

For how many days and how many nights Doogie the prisoner has walked alongside his brother chimpanzees, who hit me and who sometimes laughed like animals. The gorilla went away, and the gorilla came back. In the Jungle with neither here nor there, the troop of animals went on with no direction, Doogie. But even if I want to leave, I don't have the strength. They hit me. I'm only a monkey like them, and I jump up grabbing onto tree trunks. There's only a tiny voice in my half bitten-off ear that says: "The Rnimal, Doogie. Just don't forget that, remember it. And when you see him, kill him, and it's over."

The voice speaks, and Doogie is quiet.

Why this chit-chat? Just be an ape and the words will stop.

From time to another time a word comes back, one word at a time.

How many watches Doogie has crossed without counting the days, without saying, without thinking. I don't know . . . I don't feel much.

A column of chimpanzees climbs, descends, moves on, runs, eats, sleeps in nests at night. A fight, alliances, a brawl in Doogie's head. Doogie follows. Bands of them. One, three, ten, five, stop. When the counting ends, the ape goes on. It's night, it's naked. Dirty forest of Rnature, stones, lakes, savanna to my left, Jungle to my right. Right or left, you bastard, just mix them up and go on.

And I found the word again. I looked for it, and then I didn't look for it.

I touch the boulder with my foot. I step onto it and I see that there's a circle and a cross.

I lift one eye and the other closes.

And I say: "No!"

Zoo

*—Despair and the death of the past.—The beautiful house of
bygone days is now in ruin.—The renatured animals surround the
ape who is faithful to humanity.—He rids himself of the last of his
shame.—Memories of the stars and of his return to Earth.*

From the Jungle

Doogie staggers between three chimpanzees. The trees have fallen. There's just a path of weeds, heat, gravel, and the thing that I see. It's iron. It's a gate made of rust and bricks. It's the bricks of a wall, a low wall.

I look at the iron. It's the iron of bars and the hand of a human, dead. I see the ruins, and underneath the ruins, a hill.

The hill is yellow and gray, and at the top I see a black pile of destroyed walls and ashes and the sky, and then nothing.

I stop my stop. On my hand to one side, and on my hand to my other side, there are ten and a thousand and even a hundred chimpanzees, grunting and screaming. They're animals. I see the elephant, and everywhere in the middle are apes and more apes.

And at my feet, underneath my gray blood-soaked feet I see a bit of steel leaf. On top of it is a word that is coming back to me. Under the gilded circle engraved with the cross is written "Zoo." You made it, Doogie.

It's the Zoo, my destination.

Today, it's chaos. A gorilla, macaques, chimpanzees, and baboons, all angry and behaving badly, neither civilization nor Nature, are pushing and dragging me. They growl, and there's a kick-ass fight. Alas, they reign over the ruin. It's death to the old civilization. Nature is back, and you're back here again.

This is what Rnature is! And out of the only eye that I still have I see the ruin of my voyage, the end of the effort of everything, and something worse than death. I think "Janet!" but I don't see her. Either you're dead or you've abandoned me. And I see ruin in the place where my memories stopped of what was your childhood and your adolescence, poor little ape of me.

They're screaming screams! Destruction and food on the ground, and they pick up what they can to eat, *iiirk! iiirk!* Everything's mixed up, and Doogie is walking in the middle of Rnature. What a realm of the death of everything and of the human it was.

Aaaaaaaah! Animals are jumping! Victory over the human! And the Zoo is dead.

Doogie looks at the house that was on the hill. He tries to remember, but hardly anything comes.

He sees a little girl in a white shirt and big staircases; he sees cages and children; he sees some language of words on a blackboard, a bedroom, and a pine bed; he sees the door of the smell of the kitchen, of the smoke of black ruins, and then nothing. There's a baboon in front of him. Two, three of them are challenging him and grimacing. There are droppings, and an old panther who's wandering among the crushed stones.

Doogie tries, but he can't see anything. Nothing.

He sees Nature that has returned but that isn't succeeding. Animals that are hungry are turning circles on the concrete ruins, and there are cries and movement.

Doogie senses aggression, and he senses those that are assembling around him. He blinks his eye, and something shoves him.

Houh!

You're finished, Doogie. This is the only company you will ever have. The dream you had about your house is here.

Memories

The rocket Charles Bigleux said goodbye to the planet Earth in the black so black, but the Earth didn't say anything back. When and when the Doogie wakes up, he's already gone. The motor shakes and vrooms, I'm attached to the armchair, and it's hot like inside a coffin. I turn my head, and in the eye of a porthole made of blue glass beneath my feet I can see the sky. It's like night, here, there, and everywhere.

Then Doogie recovers the memories of how Janet stayed behind and Doogie left. And just as alone as I am now, so alone I was then. Doogie's peaceful cabin covered with the orange and blue carpet hurts my eyes.

Someone said yes to the lightbulb, there's light, and he speaks to me, standing near the red armchair. He moves. It's Michael.

As the night of the sky flies up, there's a *psst* and it's scientific. O stars, now is the time of rockets!

"Doogie," Michael tells me, "you need to be very strong. There's going to be, there will time that passes and that doesn't come back before we return to the house."

"Why are you talking, astronaut?" I grunt. He leans over, in a military outfit without a helmet, and I grumble. "I too," he says, "am sad to be leaving Jane far behind us, you know. I love her."

I *what*?! "Houh," I say. For Pete's sake, who made Doogie the prisoner of this idiot that is Michael? I wanted to sleep, and for him to leave the ape alone with his pain.

He turns on light number two, and Doogie closes his eyes. "The two of us really need to have a serious talk one day," he laughs.

"Oh, talk to your own mouth," I grouch.

Michael clears the inside of his throat while chewing a piece of gum. "You don't understand . . . You don't understand everything. I would like to be able to talk with you, monkey."

He seems sad, but Doogie is revolted by this moron. For how many calendars will I be his prisoner?

Houh houh. I get excited like the space monkey I am. My ears hurt, and I'm not a monkey! I understand, so shut up.

"Doogie, we have to keep the safety straps on while we're in the acceleration phase. I'll let you out soon."

And he turns off a switch of the light.

Then he stays there with his forehead against the porthole of the orbital sky. "Get out of my orbit," I say to myself and to the straps that are holding my hands. "Doogie wants . . . I want Janet!"

He murmurs: "I shouldn't be telling you this, but this whole thing's an experiment. That's just the way it is. I don't know if you understand, but . . . you shouldn't get any ideas, I mean, if you *are* getting ideas. I really don't know what to do. I promised Jane . . . But I'm worried about you. I don't think we can do this to you. I think you have more in your heart that we believe you do. It's . . . well . . ."

Do *what* to me? Just give Janet back to me and shut up.

And he turns off the last of the lights. It's dark, and the motor is speaking louder than he is.

He's saying, ". . . Decay . . . experiment . . . recovery. . . ." And then, ". . . guilty, you know, I get it."

"Who the heck are you talking to?" I sniffle, and as the nausea of the porthole, the stars, and the metal of the machines accelerates, the noise rocks me to the point of vomiting.

". . . Poor ape . . ." he says. ". . . memories, but they aren't true." And the Charles Bigleux roars like a tiger in chains in the vast and empty space.

Then his last words. "Doogie . . . You will never be . . ." And then he says, "She . . ."

She . . .

And then it's the machinery of the motors of the rocket that has its conversation.

From the Jungle

Oh, dead former Zoo, where have your animals gone? They're free, and Doogie, loosed from the memories of his past, is nothing anymore.

But I sense my Nature.

The yellers and butt-rubbers form a circle at the bottom of the hollow of the old hill, where Doogie used to go when he was what he's forgotten about. The circle of all of them makes an arena where Doogie is standing by himself. The black apes—what are they called?—are grunting, the felines are walking and roaring, the squawking birds are flying and landing, and the snakes are crawling and sliding. I understand.

One and two parrots that are perched on the old wall of the broken burned-down storage shed are chattering.

"Human!"

And the circle of the arena closes in. Doogie sees another myself of a chimpanzee who's looking at you with an I'm-going-to-clobber-you stare, and there's a lynx behind me who's showing me how many teeth he has.

"Hu-Man!"

I think Doogie understood. I get down on all fours and I smile, fearfully, animal that I am.

Then the parrots try laboriously to fly up, and I hear:

"A-Ni-Mal!"

And the circle of the arena grows larger, always with noise, always with cries. "Who are the animals that I am one of?" I ask myself. But the blackest apes sense it when I'm thinking, and from beneath their lips they display the hatred they have of the human.

"Hu-Man!"

I submit the Doogie by squishing myself down in the center of the arena like a hairy frog, and I smile, and I think:

"Don't think any more. It's over for you."

And the circle of the arena relaxes. These aren't *wild* animals that are crawling and wriggling, breaking stones, walls, and rubble in the black circle at the foot of the legs of the hill. These are animals that were the Zoo and that want to return to Nature. "This is Rnature," I think. "But they don't know how, they can't do it."

Did they sense the thoughts in my too-little skull? The circle of the arena closed in again: cougar, jaguar, owl, elephant, tapir, and the black apes like the false Nature that they are. Oh, baboons! Oh, felines!

Then I look at their gaze with my single eye, and I see my stomach. At the butthole of my body were the big dirty white underpants that protect my faithfulness.

My underpants!

And now the circle was just a dot.

"Hu-Man!"

It's time to get completely naked, I think.

Memories

"4, 3, 2, 1 . . . *Charles Beagle*, blastoff!"

And the big Charles Bigleux took off. Doogie couldn't hear the voice through the loudspeakers anymore. Close up your plug your ears! It's good-bye to the last of the orbital stations. Seated in my seat, looking through the blue porthole, I can see the big houses of space where the rich men I have met a thousand and a thousand times live.

One calendar, two calendars I spent there. I'm as big as civilization now: Mr. Doogie. But I miss her. The lights and the black walls, the round stations, the satellites, and the capital of the Moon all disappear: Oh, Tokyo! Oh, New York! Oh, Paris! The cities live inside cubes. The inhabitants are more than civilized, Doogie: they're I-party-you-party, and their food comes from planet Earth. "Mr. Doogie, we don't have to do anything here. It's an off-ground civilization, and we live like gods!"

The woman with a thousand pearls and a hundred jewels laughs and twists her neck. She looks at the Doogie across her glass of champagne. "To your health!" How many women, Doogie, how many times? "Mr. Doogie, would you like to come to my room?" The ladies like the monkey.

Doogie gave lectures. "Would you like a glass of water?" "Watch out for the microphone." "Lady, gentleman, young ladies, dear very dear respect," I would say. How many times, a hundred times, I gave lectures in front of seated humans who applauded. The gentlemen see the ape and shake my hand. They look at my muscle and they offer me a cigar. That is the human. The ladies see the ape, they look at my muscle, and they suggest that I have a headache. "You can come back to my room; my husband is busy." You must be faithful to the human. But Doogie is also polite. Doogie bows like a gentleman, and I end the evening alone in my bed. I try to take off my socks. I don't like champagne with bubbles, and I look at the dial of my watch.

Janet, I'm missing from you.

Then Michael counts the money from the patrons, Sindhu and Naoki prepare the Charles Bigleux, and—ready?—we're off again. Another station, another gentleman, another lady, and always Mr. Doogie. I'm educated, but still a monkey. Circus after circus, do your act and go.

Not without sadness, I look out the big round sparkling window at the black universe. It's the final trip; the voyage home is starting. Count the hours: 4, 3, 2, 1 and you'll be back at the Zoo.

How frightened Doogie is about joining you again, how he trembles after getting up from the purple velour seat to change into his pajamas from his shirt and pants with the gilded buttons and the cross. She's wait . . . she's waiting for me. When I get home, after sleeping, you will land with the money that's been collected in the locked safe, and I'll descend from the ship on the steel landing bridge, I'll fall into her arms, and she'll say: "Oh, Doogie, what a good monkey you are. I've missed you so much!"

And then I'll cry.

In the cabin of the old Charles Bigleux, it's a daylight of stars. I'm so scared that my fear is beating my heart, and the floor and the walls are vibrating. The old Charles Bigleux is shaking like an egg timer.

What time is falling from the calendar?

Doogie, you've been in very high society, in a formal tuxedo if you please, so why this fear? You've met ladies, gentlemen, cigars, champagne, and the best living rooms. Doogie, you did a tap dance on the stage, because the old, civilized people like that. Doogie, you cooked in front of old ladies, because they like that. Doogie, you were a children's clown with your teeth painted with chocolate, and children pulled on your hair. And you didn't say anything, Doogie, because each evening you thought about your Janet. But now there is fear inside you. Doogie has spoken to her on the telephone, but Doogie hasn't seen Janet, not once in two calendars. "Doogie, there's no television between the sky and the Earth," she said.

On this night, fear is ringing your hours, and you can't sleep. Like the surface of the ocean, the reflections on the ceiling are having dreams, but you're not. You're so hot. Doogie takes off his pajama pants. In the almost darkness, the camera of good behavior won't be able to see.

Sitting on the vibrating bed, your heart bumps you. Doogie gets up and walks in your little circle of steps. I open the metal door of the cabin, I step over the bottom of the doorframe—don't bump into it!—and in the corridor of the big Charles Bigleux there's no one and the neon lights are spitting out greenish blinkings.

Oops! Something vibrates and you slip. So much turbulence on the big old ship in the shape of a turtle!

Doogie goes around the little pharmacy cabinet that is painted white and the open door of the old white enamel water reservoir. How tired the Bigleux is, how dusty.

At the end of the corridor, the door of the double-you-see is banging, and the motor is humming, saying *click-clack* and *tick-tock* like an alarm clock, a very mysterious sound. From above me, liquid is dripping and dropping. What compartment is that? There's a silence from the noise. The hours are clicking and clacking, and we'll be arriving soon.

I climb the iron staircase and—*squeak*—I'm on the interior bridge. A pitch and I want to puke. It tosses and turns.

There's a *click-clack*, and I don't hear the noise of the engine coming from down below anymore. I leave the shell and I say hello to the cockpit. Doogie is walking on tiptoes with his pecker in the air. Hee-hee, I'm a real chimpanzee.

I heard, "Sindhu!"

Oh shit, it's Michael.

"What are you doing here? We'll be arriving soon, my boy. You need to get dressed." He throws his eye at my face, and the neon lights make my eyelids blink. "Go put on your outfit. We'll be landing in two or three hours."

Michael seems stressed. "There are some things I need to check on."

"Like what?"

"I'm afraid that something is happening, Doogie."

Doogie doesn't understand. Doogie doesn't understand anything. But Doogie thinks, "I'm coming, Janet!" and Doogie is as happy as a saint.

"Go get dressed, I said. Put on your shirt, your trousers, and . . ." Michael bites his lip. "And good god, put on your underpants!" He snickers. "I've never understood why you wear those big xxl underpants, ape that you are." He shakes his head.

Hey-hey, Doogie jumps down from the chair and walks toward the corridor of his bedroom. I'm just a Doogie, I'm just a monkey. Poor Doogie, poor monkey. So little, so little, and everything is very big.

"You imbecile," I wanted to tell him. "The less hair you have, the more clothes you need."

Yet here I am in the underpants of civilization.

"1, 2, 3, 4 . . . Charles Bigleux, prepare for landing."

"Testing."

Then Doogie started to get dressed, and in my cabin I put on—for what would be a long time, a very long time—the most beautiful white underpants that I had.

But I didn't have the knowledge yet of the very long time that I would have to hold on, or I never would have had the courage to be Doogie until now.

From the Jungle

Rnature is a strange chaos. Everything in the Zoo is in pieces. The animals distrust the white underpants. Naked Doogie is just hair, and the underpants are gone forever, but the skin from his wound remains. Doogie limps as a nudist, his underpants on the ground. Doogie closes an eye that will never open and that hurts me with pain.

Near the swamp at the bottom, in the mud, Doogie survives as an animal among animals. He too squats in the water. When the air rains, the animal gets wet and there's mud. It's gray, it's cold, and it's noisy. The bottom of the hill has collapsed. There are buffalo, seals, and mice. The apes from where there were no trees have roamed off, from night to day and from day to night. Here, at the spring you have to drink from, there is no one but animals. When it's you-have-to-eat time, they bite one another. Doogie nibbles on berries and fruits, but everything here is like after a fire: burned charred dry earth where the trees of Nature were. All these animals want to renature, to prey, hunt, eat, sleep, and screw each other. From the top of the hill, the ruins have crumbled away the past, and the pond is drowned. Without his underpants, Doogie throws your eye on the spectacle. Cats meow, but how their hair is threadbare, dirty, and full of holes from ticks. Horses gallop and then stop, but how ugly is their coat, and the animal is without a master, without pasture, and without hay. Snakes crawl, mice and gerbils run, but each of them is only an actor. How poorly the snake crawls who enjoyed his whole life in the glass of a cage! The little scaly snake from the vivarium has not known freedom, so what will he do with it now? The koala, poor Doogie, is dying of cold, and he's afraid of the woods. It's misery.

Dirty Doogie watches. Watch well. Under the clouds, on what remains of the slave houses of the animals, animals are drifting, poor psychopaths that you are. Lift your wounded muzzle, Doogie, and look up at the pile of sheet metal. That was the roof of the chimpanzee dormitory. The brown teddy bear advances, retreats, and offers his paw. He's gone crazy. I sniffle. Poor teddy bear from the Zoo, without the human master who taught you the show.

He's a poor actor who keeps going, but the spectators aren't there anymore.

In the morning, Doogie sees and goes. Sometimes, naked, he wants to wash-me, but the pond is shit and what is shampoo called? Nature's not a bathroom. When Doogie is washing his dead leg, he hears the dirty animals all around him grunting. The human was bathrooms, the animal is just dirty.

But Doogie scratches himself, standing at the base of the hill. Without the shampoo of civilization, and without the delousing of Nature, what can I do about my skin? Doogie sleeps. In his sleep, Doogie assembles dry leaves into a ball and plunges his sponge into the pond, rubs his arms, rubs his back, and cleans himself. It's cold at night, there's noise all around him, and the only ear of the skull of the ape that I am hears:

"Hu-Man!"

A shadow in the dark. It's one and it's many who growl and scratch. Doogie, you're so clean that they all want to kill you, to lynch you.

Gorilla

—The murder of a cat.—The dog always comes back.—Taken hostage by a gorilla with a silver back.—You must kill to live.

From the Jungle

When the pitiful morning is still little, the sun hits you, but it slugs your two enemies twice, your three enemies three times, and your thousand enemies a thousand times. Breathe, Doogie. If the bastard animals want your hide, show them your face.

On an irrigation pipe lugged between destroyed slabs reigns the big ape king of the assholes. In the silence, he's watching you. A very big gorilla with a silver back and a moist nose who is sizing you up. "Who are you? Grr." Doogie drags his foot, Doogie cleans his nose, Doogie among the apes, tigers, and hyenas. Huge, the gorilla grabs a cracked slab, walks on his fists, and turns in circles. Go back to your Nature, ape that you were! Who are you? In those days, Doogie had a memory of the beautiful animals of the Zoo. He knew the face and the name, he knew the who and he knew the what, all thanks to words. But in the files of what used to be your memory of the gorilla, Doogie, you don't know either who or what.

He's acting aggressive. You stand up, he talks to me, and Doogie prostrates himself. Don't provoke him.

At the end of the silence, under the pipes, a threadbare cat, with hair the color of goose poo with a bit of honey and a bit of pink, meows. The cat with no master is looking for his milk. Back then, Doogie knew how to feed the little cats.

"Hide," I say to the cat, who is wandering around. "They'll come after you, a formerly free servant of the human. You'll end up between the paws of their hands."

The gorilla who has the silver back is not stupider than an animal: he has sniffed out the idea that came from my brain. The cat has a collar of his former faithfulness around its neck, which the gorilla with the silver back violently grabs. There's a weak meow that the cat's throat won't even allow to come out.

Holding the cat in his right hand as he advances, the huge gorilla with the ash-colored back pulls and lifts the heavy square stone with his left hand. He moves left then right, and then suddenly he's standing, rising like the sun. At the edge of the pond there's a smell of shit, and he hits and kills the cat. The gorilla breathes: he's saying, "I kill you." From now on the cat will only be a corpse. You don't exist anymore.

"Now give your eye to me," the gorilla roars, right in front of my face. The gorilla dominates. "Squish yourself down," and I squish myself down. He looks at me, but language is not for him.

From the rusted and twisted grating at the edge of the pond, the cry of the chorus climbs, saying: "Kill! Kill! Kill!"

Three and three Thousand Colors parrots echo the language that the gorilla doesn't have, and they speak.

"Rnimal!"

"Rnature!"

How out of tune is the chorus of parrots! Doogie is nothing but fear. Everything's unclear, and the worst is getting closer.

I look at the three and three parrots. They're the mouthpiece, but who is speaking through them?

On the flank of the sides of the hill, Doogie, are you all alone against all the animals of the former Zoo? The Doogie that I am is dragging his leg as he climbs between the corpses of planks, tiles, holes, and running water. If you retreat, who will advance? The gorilla is walking, and I'm stuck in the broken stairway that once led to the house. It's just a barrier with no steps.

Under the morning sun, Doogie, close your only eye and submit your slave face to the big gorilla who dominates. The Doogie squishes himself down in the mud like a toad, his hair flat, with a smile of weakness. *Crick-crack*, tiles and bricks and stones are rolling. The silverback wants more than slavery from you, Doogie. He raises up his torso and gro-owls. What a number of a number of dirty little mean monkeys with tails around him who make up his court. It's Rnature, Doogie. How far are they expecting you to lose yourself and sink to the bottom? They're waiting until nothing is left of your someone.

"What do you need?" Doogie implores them, alone and cold, filthy and muddy. How far does humiliation descend when it's at its deepest?

Then I hear, behind the crates and the planks and the broken vase, a *woof-woof*. It was him saying, "It's me." Oh woof, oh woof!

And I knew that the departed Faithful was there, having returned.

Oh, save yourself! And save me.

Faithful's gaze asks for the voice of his master. He looks at me like "speak to me." "Doogie," I say to myself, "the Faithful that you have has found you again. He's a he's a dog, he has the goodness of woof-woof, and he has the courage of defend-you." How the mud has dirtied the mustard color of his terrier hair, but he's pure and has a broken leg that drags. *Grr*, his woof says. Standing on three legs, the dog jumps onto a brick, descends the flagstones that are broken into a thousand pieces, and points his tail at the flank of the hill of the former staircases.

"My, my, dog," I say with my big hand. "You came because your master had the need, and you came from far away." I stroked between his tuft and the eye that was blinking, and the dog's tongue licked the hand that was making my poor language. When I'm a master, I'm not so lowly. If a dirty ape has too much closeness to me, Faithful the dog barks his growl and protects the me. I climb myself up the ruins of the stairs, and like a good soldier the dog accompanies me. The dog trots and he never asks, "Where is the master going? Where is the master and where the trail?"

Because it was morning, the heat of mugginess was leaving warmth behind, and hello sweat. Doogie lifts his head and stands up. At the summit of the cadaver of the Zoo, the stairway climbs the memory of banisters. Here, everything is just lizards and the sun that makes you blind.

"Stop, dog," I say, and the hand of my language stops the sound at the door of my eyes. What do I see? In threes and in thousands, there are animals like apes, jaguar, hyena, the one who is panther, and the one who is tapir. They reign over Rnature from on high, and Doogie has brought his dog to the barrier of there's no exit from here.

When the dog growls, I can smell the fear that he doesn't have, because he is only for me. "Good dog," I murmur, while placing the foot of my leg against the sculpture that is just a piece of a hollow pole where the electricity used to run from above like water. The master has no fear, but below me, black and violent with a silver back, the gorilla is raging. He makes the challenge, drumming on his chest. He pounds and pounds, and the chorus of the thousand and the Thousand Colors cries: "Kill!"

"What's going on?" my mouth asks.

"Kill!" And then between his two hands the gorilla grabs and squeezes the dog who was like a poor and feeble soldier to me. What can the sick and skinny dog do when the gorilla is holding his neck, crushing his stomach, and showing the helplessness of Faithful to his master? The one who is protecting you, Doogie, is making you weak because of how much you owe him.

I think that I believed that that animal of a gorilla smiled, with his black eyes of yellow, and held out toward me, Doogie, the dog that was being strangled, the poor distraught woof-woof.

"Kill . . . !" cries the chorus of birds.

". . . me," I thought, and when I stand up, limp, and breathe, I say: "He was my faithful one, just as I'm the faithful one of the human, you pieces of slave ape garbage. Give me back my dog!"

I stand up straight like a human, and I look for the power of the weapon in my hand.

Where's the ape? He's everywhere.

Doogie, standing up straight like a human, threatens the troops of loud-mouths above and around and behind him with his weapon, all around where the house used to be.

The black gorilla grunts, shaking the poor dog with one and with two hands. "Baa-hou!" cries the band of baboon bastards on the ridge of the boulder, on broken walls and upside-down armchairs. Baa-boons! They're overcrowding the feet of the house. How is it that the baaboo animals are friends of the gorilla with the silver back who is kidnapping my dog?

"Hey!" the Doogie yells, and I wave my weapon toward the distance. "What is your Nature, you loudmouths? In the old very old Nature, no species was a friend of the other. It was up to each species to survive. What is this Nature of confederates?"

"Rrrrnature," they grunt. And the squawking Thousand Colors starts to fly up, chattering the chorus of they-don't-speaks.

Walls, cornices, a broken window. I climb, I walk like a slowness, and I point your powerful pistol at their mug. "Give me back my dog. He's faithful to me, and there's only devotion to him!" And as I try to talk, I move the mouth of my head like the one who was human. "Hu-Man!" the chorus of birds says and says again in the summits of the grays and blacks that are ruins.

I puff out my fur coat, mouth my open, and I turn in a circle. I square my shoulders and click your jaws at the thousand baboons. Some are dueling among and between themselves, and then—around the big gorilla who is walks sideways facing me and climbs—they make a line and face forward like the army they are.

On the threshold of the former house, Doogie throws the gaze of his eye: it's a tiger. From time to time a female squeals and the clouds go by.

"Give me my dog!" But Doogie is losing his confidence. Everything is against him; it's Rnature.

And then, for the very first time, Doogie sees the eye of the gaze of the dog who was mine.

How tall, long, thin, and dirty gray he is, the beautiful dog with his tongue hanging out of his mouth, the dog terrier, his eye round like a tear. He sees the Doogie, and he is like thank you. He can't say bark anything, and seeing his master at one two and three steps away is his only joy.

Then the gorilla, awkward in the ungainly animal way, picks up the burned arm of an armchair like a bone of this was the house and he grunts. He lifts it up to the sun, hits the dog, and then looks at the Doogie as if to say: "I'm killing your dog."

"Kill!" hisses the parrot.

But the gorilla, turning his silver back, doesn't kill him. He sniffs and wriggles his that's not a nose. The no-good baboons swarm and press themselves against his butt, without tumult, on the debris, on the legs of tables, the handles of doors, the fringes of curtains, the skull of plaster ceilings, and the earrings of chandeliers. They're waiting.

"Kill!" says the chorus of parrots. They're not flying.

And the gorilla holds out the dog toward it's toward me. He has one broken leg and three straight legs, one still living eye and a pink tongue, and he's breathing very badly. Hi han, it's toward me that he holds him.

They want you to be a nimal. Be it well and kill your dog!

If not, the killed one will be you.

Kill

—Assassin.—The chaos of nature.—The fake color of repainted
animals.—The last memories before nothing.

From the Jungle

Doogie tried to be lordly like a master, I promise. He wanted to make the pistol work and unfold its power, but the pistol doesn't obey the ape, and the monkey is master of nothing. Where do you command it from? The object doesn't know you, my legs hurt from the stand up straight stand up straight, and language can do nothing for you.

Doogie, you're no master, and slave you are nothing. I fall back down on the all-fours of my Nature, I sniff, and I can smell the end. What can I do? The sky is brown, there's shit on the ground, and you're just an example. For a long time, I avoid seeing the dog's eye, because he can see that his master is shit and that there's nothing lower than him. You're a coward, Doogie. I beg for his forgiveness, but who knows if he gives it. The dog doesn't know anything.

Faithful, whom you didn't deserve, kept looking at you. He never abandoned the master that you shat on. "Oh, dog," I said from the bottoms of my lungs that can't breathe out language, "how much more of a master you are than the master!" And do you know what? As I picked up a flat stone, the big pink flagstone from the threshold of the house where I once was and no longer am, he held out his paw to me. The gorilla put him down on the ground, on bricks. He didn't move, his leg bent back. Under his mustache his tongue licked the air, and lying there he looked at me, happy and full of trust.

Dog, o wise one, are you really an animal?

What could I do? He was so happy to have found me again, and he closed his eye because I petted him, and he opened it again just before.

And without language, he said everything: "I am only my faith in you, and I love the master who is mine."

I knew that he knew, because he lowered his head to make it easier for me when I lifted the big rock that is stone. And letting it go onto his head I broke and killed his I am.

Doogie is still breathing, but there's no air alive in *him*. In place of his mouth which was a face, there is the stone, the meat of blood, the death of his brain, the paint from a brick, and the twisted body of the dog, the English terrier, mustard-colored, with one leg bent back.

Doogie, you murdered him to stay alive, but it isn't you living anymore.

Already, the black gorilla turns his back and hobbles back down. He knows that you're not human, assassin animal.

What is this Nature that wants from you that you kill to stay alive?

"A-Ni-Mal!" cries the chorus of the Thousand Colors birds who never fly. The baboons with evil dog heads stampede, they slide on the liquid excrement, and aggressive in the chaos the animals jump and fight, as do I.

In the midst of them, my cheekbones pulled back, I slug, I shit, and I look for my group while going into what used to be the house of my home. Forget the poor dog, you poor nothing. You're just nil, bouncing around. Like everyone else, I'm rnaturing.

Remember and come back to yourself, Doogie. Become me again. No—memories are finished.

Doogie has just one eye, just one. He's afraid, and he screams. One leg is like a stone and one eye is like night. Doogie limps, a half-blind ape, renatured like all of them. He wanders around with nothing to do, tramples on the potted palm trees, breaks columns and shutters, and moves around the ground floor of the house. Sometimes the sun burns between the walls and the holes, then it's dark humid.

Oh, Doogie, what have you done? Don't remind me.

The master is the traitor, and the faithful one ends without mourning. I sniff a leaf, I chew, and I don't remember anything.

I'm a befuddled monkey among the baboons, among the wild animals and the tweeting squawkers, the snakes and the peacocks. Everything is nothing but mayhem. It's a party, it's do whatever. The tiger is trying to nap on the torn-up velour couch, and the macaque is nibbling and squatting. Nobody knows what he is because they were all slaves of the Zoo. All of them were raised by civilized people, and in their rnaturing they're going acutely wrong. The water from the pond of puddles is running beneath our feet in the burned-out hollow of the floor, now black, and the rugs have lint. The sad and skinny cow with no food shits at the entrance of what was the kitchen: pots, glasses, and plates. Bloody animals meow and bellow, and no one has anything to eat.

The whole crowd is delirious.

It's a party for what you want, and that's it. Doogie, sometimes a joyful ape, galops, avoids danger, sniffs, and looks for food. He smells the dusty staircase to the second floor, where vines, planks, clothes, skins, and corpses are hanging. Doogie grabs onto a lynx who is nothing more than meat, splattered under desks and chests of drawers. Doogie climbs, and he sees the spoiled party in the house, the party of rats. There's the hyena, the vulture's on the roof, and in the hollow of the hole bookcases and books have burned. It's a mass grave. It stinks to high heaven. Doogie breaks a stick of bamboo, chews, and crunches. On the second floor, Rnature is only failure: it's lamenting complaints of hunger from animals with nothing to do, with anxiety and no security. Bands of animals—shrews, ouistitis, and jackals—try to plunder, but each one is alone. And then they try again. The animals can't pull it off, no one is having an orgy, and every animal is lying down and moaning.

Sitting on a banana leaf, alone, stoned as if from drugs, on two collapsed beds that are piled up, I recognize silverback, his back rounded. Should I look for an accomplice? I want to kill him.

There's a memory, a vague one. Under the hand of me, the flat stone is heavy, too heavy. In my two hands, it's in the air, and when my hands are no longer there, the stone seeks the ground, and the dog is no longer anything. Doogie saves his own skin, because, gorilla, you wanted to kill me, you wanted to kill the dog, you wanted the animal to be nothing. Avenge yourself, avenge myself! I'm looking for a bastard: a baboon or a couple of the assholes. I'm going to take out the back of your face, I'm going to smash you! Doogie wants blood now.

I grunt and walk in a circle, your hair standing on end, and find a stone. But Doogie, open the only eye that is still yours and hold out your one hand. In the midst of this party of defeat, what would the victory be? What? I move the center of my mouth around. A joker comes out of the chandelier, the budgie whores scream as they bat their wings, a disgusting orangutan catches them, and while all the animals go crazy and ransack the place, Doogie watches, and he notices. I still have a little science, because I can see that the silver of the gray of the gorilla's back is getting dusty like the rusted paint on the grills of what used to be the Zoo. "Hmm," Doogie wonders, "is the color of the gorilla not from nature? What's that all about?" *Quack, crack*: everything is screaming. Doogie protects himself and gives up on taking out the gorilla. I turn around and continue my investigation. For too long, the dirty parrot has been irritating my ear, yelling "Kill!" "Rnature!" and "The A-Ni-Mal!" While he's busy scraping together grains from the edges of awnings, I chop his face and—heh heh—now look who's doing bad things! I sniffle, "Parrot, I would like to eat you," and, *crunch*, I bite his head like an animal and the blood flows. I try to tear off his face. I pull, he squawks, and he toots. It's like plastic: dirty, squishy, hot. I throw away his head, the dirty snitch. Who have you been mooching from? Hmm . . . what's this color on the hand of my palm?

It's paint. This parrot, like Thousand Colors, has been painted and repainted—red and blue, green and yellow—with oil paint.

Frantic, Doogie races over and traps a fluorescent green duck in the bathtub. What's going on? What's this nature of rainbow-colored animals? Nastily, I lick his feathers and his beak. Yuck, it's paint! I spit and I trample the quack-quack.

There's a sky-blue llama, a black fox, and the tiger with red stripes. He rubs himself against a turned-over garbage bin like he's sick. He has ticks, lice, and maybe mange. Well, well. The tiger is scratching at his pink skin, and there's reddish paint that is making the wildcat itch. Look closer, Doogie: the tiger has scars and wounds under the red robe of his paint, and his skin is bare. You're ruined, tiger! And when I bring my eye closer with attention, the old pink and purple baboon has no hair on his back, and he's scarred, so scarred. And repainted. The light gray, mauve, and orange leopard is nothing but marks and crevices beneath the paint. Repainted. Below me, in the pit, the gray elephant has the skin disease, eczema; he's repainted purple.

Old animals of the former Zoo, what happened? You're wounded, tortured. A someone has redesigned you, renatured you.

Fake I discover the colors of each one to be, of each one who parties and wanders, sick, skinny, starving, stricken, who turns and waits, repainted, on the floors of the former home of yesteryear. Because Rnature is just a repainting.

Nor one nor three, Doogie sniffs out the secret, follows the trail, and moves on with the investigation. Hin-hin, I soothe myself at the corner of the door. I steal a piece of bamboo from a koala, I gnaw it ravenously, and on three legs I drag my fourth from the corridor onto the terrace. Is everything just nothing in this Rnature of repainted rooms of faces? Doogie scratches the butts of some of them: it's just cheap paint. The more the animal comes from out there, the more he's repainted. Doogie, since you're a detective: the party is at its height and the day is sunny, so where is the yonder where they paint them? Doogie moves. My body is dirty, my whole is red. I jump onto the door and come back inside, old monkey. No key and no lookout. Beneath the smell of shit I breathe in the old smell: of the floor, the rug, and the sofa-bed. I recognize it. Hey, what do you smell? It's a fragrance from the past, it's a trap, it's deep, it's daddy. It's Father Gardner! The father's desk, Gardner's, is badly maintained, destroyed. I halfway open the eye that blinks: it's a huge round room, or square, who knows? Shit on the ground, shit on the wall. Who shat on you? Here and there, where there are toilets and where pots have been placed, Doogie walks through them—*bang!* Metal of iron and the colors of paint. Cans of paint in the poop, and one three five and a hundred paintbrushes. What is this workshop of someone who's repainting the Nature of animals? I've forgotten, Doogie.

Here's a log half-painted green and blue, with a rooster lying on it. Poor rooster! The paint is drying on the plumage of your wings. You're mired in it. Doogie remembers Thousand Colors who is only gray, just a little bit painted, and who was having such a hard time taking off. Your design is animal, but what is the destiny of the animal? He wades around, cluck-cluck, walks and waddles.

Doogie sniffs the bottom of the desk of ex-Mr. Father Mr. Gardner, and where the darkness is black Doogie roams. When I grope, I can see the model of a farm collapsed on the table. "Calves, cows, the pigs," the voice sang. "Where have you gone?" The past is gone. Who's still here?

The farm is broken, someone has gone poop, everything stinks, and nothing is well painted. The place smells musty.

Doogie hobbles, Doogie moans, and Doogie open the blinds: *squeak.* And when the sun kills my only eye, my two ears hear the noise from the crowds at the bottom of the hill: brouhaha, scream, quack, bleat, yell, yelp, and woof!

Who . . . ?

And the chorus of Thousand Colors birds who couldn't fly because the paint hurts their wings cackles: "The R-Ni-Mal! The R-Ni-Mal!"

What . . . ?

Painfully, through the eye that the sun is hurting, Doogie sees the animals waiting for a show, on the ground floor and at the bottom of the staircase, their faces turned up.

Is it toward me that they're lifting their eyes? Doogie grumbles his anger, and then I see where they're looking. It's higher up. Leaning against the edge of the window made of reclaimed wood, Doogie cranes his neck. Doogie looks up at the roof.

Only sky and a cloud. Blue, and white like salt.

"Haouounh!" Doogie objects. Breathe, Doogie. Do you hear it?

Above me I hear one three five footsteps. The plank squeaks and the wood cracks. Who or what is it? Who are you? You hear the sound of the noise that is coming down without a face. *Crack* and *crack* goes the staircase without steps where there's only a banister, and then something that still doesn't have a face comes tumbling down.

Backed into the window, your hair standing on end, you hear the cry of the crowd, and you turn toward the door facing the banister of the staircase. You can't see anything except the swaying banister, but it's him.

The fear in your back cries: "The Rnimal!"

Memories

What does he remember? Barely a bit more than nothing.

The little ape is sitting in the park, and Mrs. puts the little man down on the ground. The ape puts the big arm of his big hand through the bars and seeks the hand of the human. He tries to pat his stomach, but the little man grabs a fistful of the hair of the chimpanzee and then loses his balance, rolls over, and, lying on his back, he cries.

The ape liked to eat, liked to play. He ate the same porridges as the little man, but when he reached out his hand to add the flowers from the garden to them, the leaves and the bark of plants, the father, the Gardener, and the little girl hit his fingers. "Don't eat that! Do we eat things like that? No!"

He drank a lot of water, the little ape. He was active, and he crawled, following the ants on the ground, never ceasing to watch them. But the little human stayed in his corner. He was hemmed in during his tour of the park, not moving, his mouth open. The ape loved sitting in packing crates, and she was already taking him in her arms to play a game with clothes, or with blankets, or with fabrics or leafy branches.

He took an object and gave it back. But the little human, prostrate in his cage in the park, drooled without answering. He tried. But the ape walked, and the human fell down. The ape threw the ball and the human let it go by him. Sick and silent, the human soon disappeared from the surroundings of the little ape. The little boy who stuttered went away with the mom, and the ape stayed in the arms of the other one.

Who was *she*?

He remembers a fragrance, and something on the fingers of her hands. The little man pushed out his lips toward the cup, while the ape lifted the bowl and drank properly. He took off the napkin before getting down from the table, while the human swung his bib over his head. Frightened, the chimpanzee ran away, ran to her. "Shh! Don't be afraid, monkey," and it was over.

At night, she would open a picture book, because she already knew the meaning of the sounds of words, and under the blanket, under the comforter, she would explain the pictures from the big story to the too little ape.

"Look, monkey!" And he looked.

In miniature, he saw the hairy human of a long time ago come down from the trees, live in caves, and light a fire. "We were apes once," she would say. "And look at what we've become!" Doogie saw: a beautiful red-haired girl with a white nightshirt, the fragrance of shampoo, a ring on her finger, a song in her voice, and the look of a master.

Ounh. "Yes, Doogie, we have become masters."

Doogie dreams. He sees the pictures of how it was.

Man has made progress, man has had a history, but what have you had, chimpanzee?

She opened the end of the picture book. It was by the lamplight of it was night, and there was no sound of the Zoo through the window. The floor creaked and the room smelled fresh.

"Doogie, man has done bad things."

She puts her finger on war, on kill, on the Earth doing badly, the slave, the poor, no more good behavior. "And look! Man isn't here anymore!"

"Why not?"

"Because, Doogie, man is not always faithful to the human. Little Doogie, your brain is too small, and the words only go halfway in. Isn't that right?"

"Doogie," and she takes me in her arms. "We need you. Start again on the first page and promise me that you'll always be faithful to the human."

Little Doogie, a muzzle in the night, I said yes.

And now it's time to sleep in bed.

"Faithful to the human I am, faithful I human to the I am I, human to him I am faithful . . ." repeats the voice at the bottom of my brain.

But I have an urge.

What is it, this urge? It's the poop that urges me. Doogie in his bed turns over once, turns over twice. Oh, my stomach is squeezing my hand. "Doogie, did you go to the bathroom before bed?"

"Yes, yes," he lied. I don't have the courage to go downstairs. Doogie knows that the good behavior camera is punishing you today. There's poop inside you. Push. No, *don't* push!

Doogie walks like carefulness on the floorboards. It's dark. I look for the bathroom and I find the door. It's locked. "Where's the water closet?" I whine, but the poop doesn't knock on the door first, it just goes down through the lock of my butthole.

I squeeze. Quickly. Doogie, where are you going? Across from the bathroom at the corner of the staircase, the door of Mr. Father's study is open. I scratch on it, and I ask: "Is anyone there?" Little Doogie, no one can hear you in the dark. It's just your arm.

There's no light, but the moon makes eyeglasses through the half-blinds for the wandering ape to see. Doogie never enters Mr. Daddy's study. Don't go there! But on this evening, there is poop.

"Be humfull to the faithman," I say to myself. What? What does that even mean? Ouch! My stomach is twisted, and the rocket of poop is opening a hole onto my pajamas. Doogie sees a pot at the foot of his arms. He pulls down his pants, sits, and says goodbye to the poop.

Breathe, Doogie. The moon is soft when you're afraid. The pot is the friend of poop. For a long time Doogie shat in it during his younger years.

He looks around me. The floor creaks. Hello? Inside the darkness I can see a silver platter on the table made of red wood, and on the platter is the miniature of a model. Pull up your pants and take a look. It's an animal farm, very small, as if humans were looking at us from above and they saw the Zoo. Some of the animals are painted, and others are naked.

Who is coloring them?

I walk on paintbrushes on the ground—sorry, paintbrushes!—and some-one has painted on the ground and on the walls, just like on the calves, cows, and pigs of the little farm.

I turn around and I see his painted face.

"Ah! Oh!" I cry, and I tell him: "Shh!" The little old human has covered the front of his beautiful white face with black. It's black and brown, and the palm of his hands is pink. He's on all fours, his weenie hanging down, and he looks at you, his teeth open.

"Droogie!" he says. But what's he doing?

Doogie cries, Doogie screams. It's an alarm!

Suddenly, the light comes on.

What?

Mr. Gardner is there, with his mustache and his bathrobe, a weapon of rifle in his hand. What does he see? He sees me, standing up, frightened, against the wall, wearing pajamas, barefoot, and he sees paintbrushes. Oh, please know that I very much faithful to the human!

And he sees *him*—who is he?—on all fours, his feet painted black and black like the ape, his hands pink and his mouth red. He grunts and tries to talk, but he can speak only grunts.

"Animal," I say in my thought, "you deserve to have your face in the shit that comes out of the hole."

"Donald!" Mr. Daddy exclaims. "My model!" He holds Donald in his arms, he looks at the animal farm sadly, and he murmurs: "Now I'll never finish painting them. Who did this?" He suspects me. Poor Doogie, poor monkey, aren't I proof, standing up and wearing pajamas? Who could be less of an animal than me?

Then Mr. Daddy looks at Donald, my naked brother, shivering with cold and with paint stuck to him. He's catching a sickness. He says: "Diane is right." He's about to get a blanket when he looks at the pot and he screams:

"Damn it! Who took a shit in the paint can?"

Doogie lowers his head.

And when he raises it again, Janet has come into the study. She is walking and explaining: "It's him. He didn't want to go to the bathroom, daddy, he never wants to. He doesn't want to go, and you know that he can't hold it in."

She takes Doogie in her arms, and with her chin she points at Donald. "He really *is* an animal sometimes."

"Poor Doogie," she says. She caresses my neck as if to take off the lice that aren't there.

Mr. Gardner's face is red. He puts Donald down on the ground, he slaps his cheek, and he trembles. "I'm going to see Diane. We need to put an end to this. This little bastard is behaving like an animal! Like an animal!"

And he raises his hand to him. "Stop acting like a dog!"

Wretched Donald, crushed down on the rug, his eyes crusted over because the paint is dripping, whimpers. And with white eyes, protecting himself, he speaks gibberish, he grunts like a hiccup as he crawls:

"R . . ."

"Ni . . ."

"Mal . . ."

"Work on your language!" And the father hits him three times on his head.

When he lifts his head back up it's a maw.

Donald

—*The face of the Animal.*—*The final battle.*—*The head of the father.*—*Victory.*—*The ape is nothing anymore.*

From the Jungle

Crack, the banister cries. It plummets, and in front of me it's him.

"The Animal?" I ask. Dust flies and the planks squeak.

Then the shadows around his still-dark silhouette fall away. On all fours, his mouth open, he grunts, and the light illuminates him.

Oh, memories! From beneath a hundred memories a single memory returns. But who is remembering it?

"Donald," I say.

He doesn't say yes, but every animal that is here cries "Ar-Ni-Mal!" And the person who was my brother turns in circles around me. I open and close my eye: is it really him? He's big, he's white, he's redheaded and handsome like a Donald. But he's been painted and repainted: he's black. "What have you done to the face of your mouth, my brother?" He doesn't say anything, but he didn't say no. His face is like wiped-off coal. His lips are too pink, his nose is broken, and his teeth are crooked. Oh, but when I see the hairs of your hair and your eyes, I know. You're human.

"Donald?" I ask with my hand. Dragging my lame leg, poor chimpanzee that I am, shame and misery, only an ape and only dirty, I retreat the length of the corridor and I placed the big mute hand of my language on the swaying banister.

From around him and me, the beast animals have fled. Through holes in the planks, on the ground floor and everywhere on the hill, they're waiting for the show, but they can't see anything.

"Donald the ghost," I think. "Donald, where did you die?" He didn't say anything. "The father had buried you. As for me, I have the regret of remorse of the heartache of the guilty one."

"And would you please pardon the excuse-me?"

"Excuse-me for what?" I ask myself. Donald so white, so redheaded, painted like an animal, jumps slowly around the Doogie that I am. Did the father lie, with bad behavior? Oh, you were never really dead, Donald! The father lost you in the forest with the animals, and he said you were dead. And you became the Animal. Poor Donald! Mr. Gardner didn't tell the truth, so that he could abandon you.

"Get up," I say. "It's over now, so come and shake hands like two humans, brother. To see you again, how happy I am."

But he shows, he displays his teeth. What I sense is hatred coming from his mouth.

"Donald," I beg.

But when I speak with my hand, he doesn't understand anything.

"What a funny face he has, grimed up like an ape," I think. You have humanness in your face. How regular is the face that is his, how fine his mouth, how lifted his nose like a trumpet, how wide and high his cheekbones, and how soft his neck. But Donald is trying to look ugly.

When the light hits through the window, he comes toward me, and I retreat by climbing onto the banister of the former staircase, the dead staircase. My eye looks all the way up. It's the floor where the bedrooms were back then, and there's no longer a roof over it.

Donald stands up almost straight, and his hair sticks up like a brush on his head. He shows me his canines.

"Brother that you were." I tremble as I climb the banister of former days, which shakes. Beneath me is the void.

Suddenly, violently, he yells and reaches out his painted pink hand. Viciously, his lips pulled back to his gums, Donald jumps and grabs onto the banister, and as I move away, he plants one three teeth from the top of my forehead to my mouth where my blood is flowing. Slashed, opened up and disfigured as I am, the palate of my mouth bleeding into my nostrils, suffocating, I cough up red. I hit the stomach of his balls with my hand, and he crumbles. Where do I flee to? I run, I climb, cursed chimpanzee, I cavalcade and I climb the banister of the staircase with no steps like a vine to the top. With my big hand on the dusty ground of the floor of the second story, I can feel his two hands on my back. It's a rumble.

He yells and he hoots, "I'm going to kill you."

My every brother is murdering me.

With one hand, Doogie rubs the blood from his eye. From above me, the Rnimal that is Donald attacks me and holds the hand of the little chimpanzee down on the ground. Sitting with his butt on my head, which is moaning, he pins Doogie's legs with his elbow, and then he bites bites bites the big hand of my language.

"Aaaaaaaah ouh!" I cry out, Donald, I weep.

It's not a hand anymore.

Who will save the brother of the brother? Oh, she will. Oh, my father will. Bite after bite, it's not like a punch with a fist. It's like being hit with a stone on the hand of me, which is being torn off, with blood on the floor. I can only moan. I can't speak, I can only "hiinh."

As the chimpanzee drags himself toward the door, Donald clicks his teeth and twists the leg that lames me. Then he pins me and blocks my trachea. My lung can't breathe anymore.

Suffocating, I spit blood. I strike out, waving my hands in the air. With a punch to your face, I slam his skull, and he lets go of me and stamps his foot. Doogie, where is the breath that you're getting back? "Language," I whine, "where have you left me?" And I look for my father and sister, but no one's here. Bedrooms of my bedrooms, it's worse than the Jungle. I'm going to die here.

As the trachea of my breath opens, Donald, his head in the blood, flat on his stomach, pulls off one three and five fingernails with his teeth and bites my wounds. I cough, I lift my leg, I roll onto the purple rug, and Donald slips, hinh hinh, monster of a redhead brother. The black paint that has rubbed off his face is running into his blue eyes.

I give my eye to the sky without a roof. Soon it will rain, and there is only wall and no tiles above me. I hold myself against the wall. Where is refuge? I hobble and I get away, but I can't see anything. Nothing remembers me. The chimpanzee looks for the door that was once there, and he lifts his head.

He is there.

Donald is panting, and even with his nose broken, his nose is more of a nose than my muzzle, with his hairless white skin of a redhead. He pounds his chest, he acts crazy, he displays himself like a demon, angry, his arm around my shoulder. He wants to kill you! His scream pierces me, and he flexes the muscles of his back and catches my cheek through my mouth. On the story below us, there are the barkings of animals. They're climbing up now, and they can see us.

And "kill"!

Donald hits the face of me with one and three slaps. I stagger and topple over.

"Oh, father," I would like to say, but when I look at my naked hand it's only a strip of nothing. My language is nothing more than nil.

Now I accept death and defeat, because the true human brother in front of me has the upper hand, and Doogie—the ape that you were and that you're becoming again—you're on the bottom. Everything is resigning me to it. I breathe and I wait for death to come.

"Brother," I would have liked to say, "for a long and far time I have deserved this death by your hand. I was nothing, and I'm returning from there. One day a long time ago I took your place, and now you're taking mine. Hoist me up, human: I only want to be an ape." And I thought: "In the depths of the Jungle where I was born a chimpanzee, I would have liked to live as just a monkey, and for you, as a man, to be the human. Donald, take back my you. I don't know what to say or what to be anymore." I sigh.

And as Donald leans over and strangles me, I gurgle. And oh! Above me, fixed on a branch I can see through the keyhole of the old wooden door, I see my father. It's you.

The former face of Mr. Gardner the daddy, his head cut off, his tongue hanging down, crumpled like an old piece of fruit rotted by flies, was stuck there. He's dead.

And in the hollow of the eye of my brother the murderer I saw only an animal.

"He's not human, this killer of the father!" a voice in my muteness said. "You killed the daddy!"

Oh, Doogie, for as long as you live, be faithful to the human.

And the last of all my rages stirred my only arm.

Faithful to the human of nothing, I fight you like a chimpanzee.

Daddy Gardner's head falls from the branch into the keyhole and smashes the door. It rolls and rolls down the hole in the staircase. "Hooouunh!" I cry. Everything has fallen.

I hand the hurt arm. It limps me, but I get up like the ape. I threaten Donald, yell, and make an assault. Houh houh! Woe to your face, Donald, and prepare a bandage because a bite is going to hurt you! A crack of the door and jump, and the two of them roll on the ground. The bedroom is nothing but rubble. Take that in your cock! And display your incisors. One slap! Three slaps!

Doogie drags his hand along the tables and under the bed, searching for an implement. He picks up a pen and grabs Donald's back, stabs the dirty Donald in the ear, in the cheek, in the balls of his face, and then he lets go.

Come eat my shit!

Dark room, black clouds. Doogie sniffs, expecting rain. A lot of blood is painting your hair, and you have only one hand. The other hand is hanging off dead, it's finished. Oh, anger, anger! I display it. It's I-yelp-at-you, you-yelp-at-me, rat face!

He semlls like fear! "Donald," my tooth grunts, "you feel fear like a human!" For me, it's I'm-an-ape-you're-an-ape. Doogie squeezes his lips and spits out blood. He dances on the foot that can still move, dances on the dead foot, looks for a stick, screams your panic, punches, and fractures Donald's knee. Then I grab him, slam his face against the wall and the plaster goes *crack!*

A hole in the wall and a hole in the weakling.

The bastard's bleeding, and I say "hooouuunh!" I slug your head and you tip over and fall into the next room.

Then Donald, his head covered in blood and plaster dust, holds out his hand for pity and he moans. His face is smashed, his hair is falling out. He begs me.

What?! Not on your life!

Doogie, I stand on it's a limp leg, and puff your chest! I victory! I destroy you! Tell me I dominate! Ha! And as I fall back onto four feet, my hand in the mouth of his dog head, the dirty Nald, his back on the floor, I sense where I am, and I know it.

Then I breathe.

This was *my* bedroom, the bedroom of my younger days!

What do you remember? Father dead, Zoo destroyed, everything gone, and Doogie feels the blood of the dust of the planks under his dead foot. To the right of the rights of the left there's a bed, it's *your* bed. I fall to my knees, I let go of the Nald and I look at myself.

Oh, bed of white pine. I was the child.

The old rug, broken like the window where the it-was-me looked out. Looked at what? I look down below us, and everywhere animals are crowding who are wandering with grunts, still waiting for the battle. Once, all this was the Zoo.

Oh Doogie, I remember that she had a name, and that everything has a name. If you could only remember it, Doogie. Who? The name tickles my big hand, but I look at the bloody stump of my pain and I feel sick. Language has fallen from me, and pain is knocking me out. Doogie, collapsed against the bed, lies down.

In front of the me of him, he crawls flat on his stomach and looks at me. There was silence, then animal noises, the grunt.

To the left of the right, moaning from his mouth, Doogie touches the wooden chest with his fingers, wreckage, and five ten stuffed animals fall out, koalas and pandas.

Under the wounded ass of my balls there's a comforter, and everywhere there's the smell of a very long time ago. It's cold, and there's a drip.

Where are the bathrooms with shampoo of bygone years? Three drips.

Nature's shower is click-clacking from the sky and will soon wash us.

"Hi hi hinh," I say.

But language is not for me anymore. It's finished, going away.

Faithful as I was, I search for the name of what I'm thinking, but I won't find it.

With just my gaze, black chimpanzee, as drip by drop the rain rains, contorting my wounded mouth I implore the he-was-my-brother.

"Who?"

"Who?"

And he, lips twisted, curled up on the big rug under the small rain, shattered, his eyes crusty because paint was dripping, he drones. His eyes white, speaking gibberish like a hiccup as he crawls toward me, he looks for the voice of his humanness.

And he says: "Ja-Net."
Janet.

Oh, poor Doogie, Janet is a thing you remember.

When Janet says, "Doogie, a cuddle," Doogie is only happy.

And I smile.

I try to say "Ja-Net" too, but I don't have my big hand anymore, the other hand hurts, and I don't have a voice.

"Ouh. Aooouuunh!" I murmur.

"Ha-ha," Donald laughs in his teeth. When I see his fair head, as sad as I am, he's my brother, redheaded and handsome and with a voice. He spits out the blood from his veins and he says, "Janet-Sister."

He says, "Sister-Janet."

And since I want to weep, I say "houh-houh, yes." Oh, sister! And my flesh remembers how much it misses the cuddle and the smell of her, alone hurt, alone here, monkey, monkey.

"Ha-ha-ha." Donald grins to himself and rolls over on the rug, turning his back on Doogie.

"Sister . . ." he pushes out of himself as if belching. Moving his throat like a rooster, he says: "Sister-of-me." He touches his chest with his hand, and he pouts. "Bad, bad." He points to the bed, and he points to Doogie.

"No-oo-ot you." He breathes and smiles, shows his teeth, "No."

Oh, I would like I want to speak, to say that I know how to say things. But my hand is dead, and in the voice I have of only an ape I force my brain and I spit out of my throat:

"Aaaa-Ou-Ounh." And I haven't said anything.

Donald crawls. He keeps talking. How hard he works to push out the sound of his language. He smiles, smiles, redheaded, and he laughs.

"I . . ."

He says: "Is."

He repeats: "I-Is."

"I-Is-Man."

And then he stops.

With his pink hand, a human hand, with his thumb and index finger, he makes a zero, and he points at me, at Doogie.

"You."

"You. Ape."

He smiles, and the smile cleaves the hairs on his face. He says, "Kill-Kill-Kill."

I moan. It was *you* who taught them! But I don't say the word. I think: "The chorus of Thousand Colors birds. You made them chant 'Kill!' when you could still speak a little, even if badly."

You trained Jack badly so that he would kill. You commanded all the animals as a master.

I know this. But I can't say the words anymore, and you, my brother, are drooling.

And Donald falls onto his back again, and the rain falls. Wet and wetter, the room is filling with water. Sad, pitiful Doogie, what do you have to say about it? Cold and sick, I have a dead hand that's hanging down, a stump, a hand that is nothing anymore, neither pink nor brown. With the only eye I have left, I look. I know, Doogie: I'm just a monkey.

But since it's raining—Doogie happy, Doogie sitting, Doogie bloody—the rain washes the old guy.

It's just water, rain, water. You hear the animals walking and climbing: tigers, panthers, baboons, and what's-their-name? The animals are watching Doogie and watching Donald.

"Ha-ha," Donald laughs, and it's a cynical laugh.

Doogie smiles. I'm just a Doogie. Nothing speaks inside me, but everything is remembered: hair, feet, hands, and the caress of it's her. I still remember "come have a cuddle, little ape," and I fall into her arms when I was afraid and then I cry. She held me so tight that I trembled. She stroked my neck and looked for lice. "You're a nice, a good, a very good monkey. You're *my* monkey."

"I want you to be happy."

Donald laughs in the rain and then he says: "Ex-Periment!"

What? Wet Doogie opens his eye. Hmm? What's he . . . what's he saying?

"Ex-Periment. You."

Doogie lowers his head, and he thinks: "Janet."

Donald grabs the leg of me and he grins. The rain falls. "You. Ne-Ver. Never Jungle."

No. I shake my leg. Go away. I don't have desire to fight. Doogie is only think of Janet.

Donald laughs. "You."

Me.

And he knows how to show with his fingers. "Experiment."

All around the two of us, the animals are grunting, the tigers and apes and baboons. "Experiment, you. Experiment, me."

Doogie sniffs and, chimpanzee that I am, cheek to cheek, I try to make peace with Donald, to calm us down.

"Ha-ha." Donald pushes me away with his hand. "You. Me. Experiment." And he makes a face. He laughs and he grins. "Dad!"

What *about* dad? You *killed* dad. Doogie is tired, lying back against the old bed, bathed in the drip-drop, in the rain.

"Experiment."

The animals come closer, grunting and growling, asking, "What is this language?"

"Be quiet," I want to say to Donald, my brother. I put my stump over his mouth. But the human always wants to speak. And speak. That's just how it is.

Donald is agitated, he's suffering. When Doogie sees his eyes behind his hair and the beauty of the beauty of his face—because the rain is washing his painted and wounded skin—he knows who the human is. It's him.

"Experiment!"

"Experiment. Him. Us. You. Never Jungle. You. Me. Same experiment."

Doogie hardly understands the language that is moving away from him. All the animals are grumbling. They rage against the human who is showing too many words.

Shut up!

"Experiment. You. Ape."

Ha-hounh. Doogie tired. Rain falls. And he talks and talks.

"You. Ape. Experiment. Me, not educated."

What?

The animals around us, around him, are saying *grrr*.

You're talking too much, human brother.

Then the last word that Doogie wanted to say with all his might by moving his lips and with his gaze, the last word that I thought so strongly that I almost said it under the rain:

"Janet!"

Donald spat and he stood up, hunched over like a man. He looked at me from above. "Janet the whore," he said.

"Janet," he said, and he spoke, and he screamed. "Janet, she, she, she, Janet. Is doing. Experiment."

And standing straight like a man, with his blue eyes, he said: "Janet the whore, Janet, she knows! She knows!"

"Janet. For her you are . . ." And he had a burp, a hiccup. Then he said: "Experiment. For her, you *were* it."

When he stopped talking, a thousand and a hundred animals stopped grunting and they killed him. Animals don't like words. The human's dead, the human who talks too much, Donald standing up, Donald bitten, Donald bloody, Donald naked.

The Nald talked, talked, and talked like his human nature, and his formerly faithful animals understood that he was a man. They killed him to death. Torn apart by claws, bitten by teeth, and struck by hands. Chimps, baboons, tiger, and lynx.

The end of the Nald.

And Doogie?

Doogie sees, and Doogie goes. Rain stops. He's just a corpse. Doogie forgets. A brother who does what?

Doogie who? Donald rain? Nothing more.

Was he brother? Was it you? No brother anymore, no you anymore.

Edge of bed, body in pain, Doogie drags himself and leaves house. The Rnimal dead. The Rnimal a man with too many words. Everything is nothing, and nothing doesn't care.

Doesn't care about who? Doesn't care about what?

One last time, Doogie. Ape looks at the house. He's there, but an ape. One said to be faithful, but faithful to what? Sometimes there's still a name, and the name says:

"Janet."

Janet to who? Janet to what?

The voice says: "Janet no longer exists."

I don't remember anything. Soon everything is just Jungle, and I too will jungle.

•　•　•　•　•　•

From the Jungle

The jungle jungle, the sky sky, the earth earth.

They act themselves. Animal ah, monkey yes. Every bird chatters. *Who's that? Who's that?*

Hand hurts, head hurts, be quiet. Nor nest nor night, warm up high, not your house.

Just an act, macaque. Everything's afraid.

The earth sky, the sky rain, the rain jungle. My head hurts less. You be less quiet.

The nest at night, it's cold. Animal not good, healing everywhere.

Screams that, screams what? Macaque fears him, shuts the mouth, strong monkey, weak monkey.

The night denies him, he has less hand, shows teeth, master murder.

Animal weak, female weak. Strong, strong, strong.

Not-animal, not-me, you act attack. Monkey strong, dominates domain.

Nimal is me, nest high fears night, me master.

No zoo, no warm, no high. All domain, earth jungle, sky jungle, strong dominates.

It's healing. Me animal, me monkey. All roof repels water. Earth sky rain, breaks the soul and dark.

Macaque fears, animals fear, females weak, only strong is master, is me.

Murder one.

Murder one.

All jungle nothing sky, all earth nothing high. Me is master.

Evening black, every nest every branch. Everything's zone, nothing's zoo.

Si-i-ilence.

Flat is morning, get up my wash me, pee-e-pee. Then eat.

Eat skin, bite kernels, everything chirp-chirps. And screams.

Animals weak, animals thin. It's master, it's me, all zone, all yellow, earth very earth where I eat! Hou hou.

Animals search, animals thin. It's jungle, it's eat.

Fru-u-uit! *Gimme gimme* eat. Then scream.

Evening, every bed, everything pale. The zoo jungle, the zone greening. Si-i-ilence.

Mute in the morning, me get up, me wash, peee-pee. And eat. Every animal its own animal. Chimps for chimps. And shut your macaque.

You chimp my chimp-me, me is master. Young weak, weak female.

And screw-him, screw-her.

Down below under water everything is fishes.

Black soot, night evening, who's branching, who's screwing? Then sleep over there.

Silence.

Kiss mouth, cuddle lick, let her, let me.

Screw cock, kiss animal, limp and jerk off. It's night.

Monkey here, monkey there, stiff dead gorilla. Master who screws and master of fights is me.

Who zoo? What I there? Not mine, not me, fight. You chimp, chimp-me, young weak, young strong.

Mate one morning, sometimes a challenge. Females and fake males, fight.

Hit my hit-yourself, kiss your lick, it's daytime.

Murder one. Fight your cock, fight the animal, clobber your head. You death, me life, victory.

Female fake weak, victory, victory! Houh, I scream.

Silence.

Kiss your mouth and screw your cock. It's me so master, you weak, and everything screws me.

Mute one morning, si-i-ilence, challenge from one, challenge from a male, it's fight and beat up the asshole.

Murder one, battered.

Blood mouth, feel nothing, lick it, leave me alone.

All night they all screw, monkey here monkey there, stiff dead young one strong, stiff dead challenge.

Life me, victory, and everything screws me.

It's me that's king. Nothing is better, everything is less.

What zoo? Let it jungle. I king.

Everything comes around. He's getting older, wearing down.

In the morning the hand the stump hurts. In the sky, sixes and fours, four scars slice.

Then you forget.

The sky bird, the earth cat, everything jungles. Nest at night, eat as master and dominate them.

Everything ages, cycles. You forget, all white. Ape black, evening beige. Jungle.

At the sound of chimps, everyone in trees, defiance of males, kisses from girls, it comes around, and gangs.

A slap, macaque, turns green, green yellow, grebe laughs. A gang of macaques, and it goes by.

Then you forget.

Everything greens, nothing speaks, it's cool, it's fake, where zoo was is forest.

Here nothing thinks, nothing here of everything that was, my words, my pouts, the years, nothingness.

Who says, who was? It's a strong fire, forest grows back, earth ends, and the sky swarms.

From the treetops, disorder descends, vermin fall, winds, laughter.

Then you forget.

Who was is the master? He's used up, because of age, because tired. He nest, he night, acts strong, does his screwing. Defeat to the weak, work for the strong, victory.

Everything comes around, strong, weak, chimps and champs. Everything fades out, everything sings, that night.

He dominates, used to dominate. Young one believes the king is used up. Young one plots.

Mouth of the kiss of the females, tired of fights, tired of heights, tired of screwing cocks and limps and eats.

He sleeps over there, the body arm, nothing thinks, nothing deafs, nothing hands.

He dreamed.

Memories

"When was he born, Gardner?"

"I don't know . . . Five million years ago?"

"Gardner, this isn't a joke. When did the female chimpanzee give birth?"

"Yesterday, McVey. I called you right afterward."

"Hmm. And where is she?"

"Somewhere else. Downstairs, in the garage. I discussed it with Diane. There can be no contact, none. Look, he's moving again: he's opening an eye. There's something special about him, I knew it."

"And you put his mother Dinah down below in a cage?"

"This isn't easy, McVey. I know that I can talk to you about it. Payne is more . . . Payne is less . . . He's an animalist and not really an ethologist. I mean, he wouldn't hurt a fly."

"He's a beautiful baby. He can hear you, you know."

"Ah, McVey! Yes, yes, it's true! I'm going to reassure him. Easy, little one."

"What are you going to do with Dinah? You're not even putting her in the reserve? You're putting her in the garage with the apes in formaldehyde that the zoo inherited from . . . ?"

"No contact. As you know, Dinah was our hope, or at least Diane's, but she . . . We have our disagreements about it, but as you've seen, Dinah has her limits. In terms of language, obviously, but not only that. She's a superb female, with a big mind in her own way. Everything she's taught us . . . All those years in the lab, laughing, organizing sets, recomposing images, playing with toys, putting the right head on the right body of plastic animals, understanding the connections in causal chains, forms, colors. But good god, I've had enough of it! Our science will never go beyond that, beyond the tea party and the phrases from a bad conversation manual . . . We already know all of that. We know it. What I want to do is something different."

"So, you're just going to scrap Dinah?"

"No, we'll take care of her down there. I'll need Payne's help with that. She's sick, very sick, and I don't know if she'll make it. I'm afraid we'll have to be prepared to bury her in a few months. Fortunately, *he* is here."

"Him?"

"Yes."

"And who's the father?"

"It was artificial insemination. It was . . . we had samples of Leonard's sperm in the sperm bank. It's illegal, I know."

"Leonard? The actual Leo? Fifty years later?"

"Mm. He's the only ape to have been out there. We know all that, even if we don't dare to talk about it anymore."

"Gardner, you remember the media, everything that happened. 'The ape that could speak.' All the publicity around it, and the rumors of . . . of genetic manipulation in the labs."

"It's true, it's true. We don't know anything about that. Did the Korean team tinker with the genome? I'm not persuaded. Leonard was a chimpanzee that was perhaps the product of a mutation, of an event . . ."

"Gardner . . ."

"We're going to raise this chimpanzee and make him believe that he was born naturally, in the wild, and that he has memories of the jungle."

"And then . . . ?"

"And then, one day, we'll place him back into that condition."

"Into what condition?"

"Into the jungle. We'll let him fend for himself, and we'll observe him."

"And what will *that* prove?"

"We'll see whether he's able to rediscover his nature, or if he remains faithful to his upbringing. He has the genes of apes that have been born in captivity for centuries. They're perfectly capable of playing dominoes, but they're not really built for climbing vines!

"He needs to believe that he's wild. He needs to believe that he can re-discover his reflexes, rediscover habits that he has never had but that he will think he has known. We must give him a synthetic nature, in a way. Can we recreate a nature that we have in fact only imagined? Can we write the memories of another nature, McVey?"

"How would that . . . ?"

"If the ape breaks with his upbringing, if he re-natures, then in a sense we will have reinvented his nature. And if we can transplant a species, renature an ape that has been educated, then we can discuss the re-anthropomorphizing of humans."

"That isn't very clear to me, Gardner. I'm skeptical. Do I have your as-surance that no harm will come to this chimpanzee? That you won't try to play the sorcerer's apprentice?"

"Of course not, McVey. I love him. He's my child. Sincerely. And I need your help at Pointe du Bec."

"And what about your son?"

"Which one?"

"The one Diane is carrying."

"Well, McVey, he'll be a control subject, a tremendous one. We'll see his progress at the same time as that of the chimpanzee, and we'll be able to compare them. That will be the first stage of the project."

"Let's just hope that the ape progresses, and that the boy doesn't deteriorate."

"No, I don't think that will happen. There's no risk of it. He'll be protected. Diane will take care of him, she'll love him. I'll be closer to Janet for my side of things. It's an extraordinary project."

"I hope so, Gardner. You never know what might happen. I hope that you won't leave your wits behind."

"Apes are our only chance to evolve, McVey. No offense to your whales, but . . . We must hold out our hands to them, love them, help them. If we can change them, *we* will change. We need that so badly."

"I . . ."

"Daddy!"

"Oh, Janet, don't open the door. What is it?"

"Come, daddy! Come quickly! Mommy says she's about to give birth."

"Oh! Has the nurse gone up?"

"Yes! Ye-es! Hurry! Oh, daddy, I'm so excited! I'm going to have a little brother, right?"

"Exactly. Come, McVey. No, leave the light on."

_____

From the Jungle

Mist waking, beast waking. You don't belong nor here nor there.

Fog gone, forest black. Not ape not anything. Who?

Every golden cat, eats birds, eats apes, little ones. Hunts and eats snail. They're all animals.

Waking from the dream, things start up. Head mist, lost. Who?

Nest at night, earth in the evening, who screws my cock and eats the fruit.

What dream, which what? Mounts of mountains, clouds of clouds, and who I?

Not me not mine, ape wanders. Not at home, not here, not there.

What animal I? What said dream? What black awakening? Not from here, but where I from?

That's fern, that's wind, that's green. Everything streams, everything fishes, who waters himself?

Every ape wanders, every cat, every bird, and chirps and cries and meows.

Disgust with the ones like me. All chimps, all shit. Who's there? Eye limps. Blind and dominate-them.

Young doesn't know, young challenges, young fights. Who I? I'm olding.

Under wood, under you, wanderings, the water rock, the bird white, foam and dead, branched and rancid.

Dream of sniff, smell the air, smell the water, the orchid and the sleeping water.

Awakening, not hunger nor rut. You don't belong. I sit, I there.

Who-I? Then I leave, I quiet. Si-i-ilence, I don't say or said goodbye.

Never again nest, never again screw, never again jungle. Always jungle.

The ape walks, the foot limps, the ape leaves, the sky damps, he crosses termite stones.

On my hike, I fog, I mist, I clear, cross thickets of parasites.

Never here again, I walked and where-I? To where I'm going.

On hike, that's mushroom, that's butterfly, that's thirst without hunger. I'm sinking.

When night, I kennel, I nest. When morn the morning, I limp, I where I'm going.

Nature a thousand natures, search the skull a thought. I never think but feel.

My head hurts, everything spins and I sick, but I roam.

I beat-me beat-you on monkeys, pitiful enemies, but I walk.

A thousand forests, a thousand days, when it's morning, when it's night. I never think, I dream, I scream, come back to me.

Awakening without dream, I want dream. I have only air, I have only water, I limp dark, I limp light, I but who-I?

Then done, then what. Noise in the woods, someone's hiking.

Sick head, everything worn down, I limp. My foot is dying.

Nature a nature, search the skull a thought, who days what think, never think.

But I walk limp.

That's manioc and that's bush. Everything spins, and at end of forest beginning of horizon, hill, moor and plain.

Where-I? Then I leave jungle. We call it quits.

Barren desert, after lakes dry prairies. Heathland, valley bottom, overcast sky.

I sniff, I hand, but I nothing.

How my leg hurts, how tired of it, how sick, like me. Sometimes fires. I'm afraid! I scream.

But alone.

Dry grasses. After the fruits, bark and leaves. Then nothing.

I wander, I desert, but I remember nothing, it's dead. Neither speak nor dream.

Sans apes, savanna. One zebra stripes, two zebras drank. A little water, not much water.

There are gnu but no impala here. What lion, what jackal?

Stones.

It's going down, it's desert.

Red then night then cold. Poverty of grasses, poor foot. Cross sand, don't sink.

If death, if it's time, why not? It's all the same to me, and everything desert.

Arid desolates, hot land. Leg weak, rest takes effort, rest tires out.

What ape is born for the so hot? What desert loves the ape?

But I wander. When I cry out, my voice changes. When sky, that earth, where the horizon?

Dry skin, heavy head, light I wander.

Under white stone cool, under gray stone warm, and no rest for the step, the sad, the skin.

I lose my foot.

He who is light ends up in the sky.

Oh, sky, whereto I come.

Poor.

Behind the dune, who knows? He'll never know.

I set the sun. Nothing sees anymore. I soft, I lie. I wandered, I walked.

Finished. Foot on the ground, who mirage, nor laugh nor rage, no water, rest.

At the dune, at the duo, behind where the sand of sands horizons, behind what's not, what is?

Nor said nor dreamed at lying down. Hundred nights no nest. Everything alive save me. Save me.

It's dead, it's done. Desert hours, nor end nor beast, I disappear.

Poor who, poor him, finished, sun setting set, parched desert flat, desert me.

Behind the dune, who'll ever know? Not ape, not him.

Who ape? I show hand, I seek watch, I seek human.

Human! I say to the sky: "Human, my life I have spent and spent, and faithful have I remained."

I wait for who, I wait for someone. Hollow of the neck of a nape, hollow of a dune, give me your hand.

Now night, now done. Wait for the cuddle when it's the end.

But I don't know who anymore. Waiting for who, faithful to what, I soft, I lie. I believed, but I'm waning.

"Haouh!" I say.

And poor, I made night.

Memories

That's when he woke up and he started yelling, and I saw him.

When I closed my eyes, a big little chestnut-redhead girl with pigtails held me in her arms. I don't remember the words of that moment, but . . .

"Oh, Donald, be quiet!" And she left the white baby, who yelled when he saw me, in the dark. She closed the door behind us.

"Phooey. Let him cry. He's mommy's baby. He's not really my brother. I like you better. Come on, I'm going to wash you and dress you.

"Come into my arms, monkey, my sweet monkey."

She caresses my skull. I'm not afraid, and she caresses my neck with the skin of her hand that smells like the cleanest fruit.

And I look into the eyes in her eyes.

"Don't worry. I'm the smartest one. I'm going to take care of you. Forever. And ever. And ever."

And she murmured: "I know who you are. I know where you *really* come from. I know everything. I heard it."

She's wearing a perfectly white shirt, and her eyes are shining.

"I'm going to make something out of you."

Softly, without making the floor squeak, she carried me down the dark corridor and she whispered: "I'll love you, and you'll be like my dog, yes, like my little dog. A faithful dog, a little dog. I'll call you Doggy."

She paused, her finger on her lips.

"No. *Doogie*. That's better." She smiled. "Like Douglas, like a movie star."

I blinked my big eyes under the eyebrows of my forehead, she lifted my chin, the palm of her hand so pink against my poor brown muzzle.

"You will always be mine."

A Human Being Always Has the Last Word

1.

"There are no more animals for us. For a long time, we have sensed and known that we human beings, like an island drifting away from a continent, are gradually detaching from other animals, which hardly exist in our minds anymore except in the form of memories, of symbols, of characters in stories, of affectionate names, of images in films, of well-trained pets, or of species to be protected in the abstract.

"Even without humans, there are still animals. For several years now, following the bankruptcy of the Zoo and the unfortunate events that brought it about, many animals have 'renatured,' as we said in those days, rapidly taking back possession of the land: of the forests, oceans, and deserts. At first ineptly and savagely, as you are sadly already aware, and then naturally, like the grass that always grows back, mammals, insects, birds, fish, and all kinds of invertebrates spread out across the environment that had been left fallow by man. Today, there are no longer any human eyes to watch them, to observe them, nor are there any human hands to put on their flanks, for better or for worse. They are where they are and what they are, and that, I believe, is no longer our concern. We did not intend for the last bastion of our species, at the edge of the jungle of the former African continent, to fall, exhausted by war. The circumstances that led us to lose this place, circumstances that are impossible for me to evoke without nostalgia and without pain even though they have become clarified, remain and will continue to remain too dark to be depicted in detail.

"We said farewell to the last zoo, where, for the last time, species other than ours were conserved in living form, studied, and at times educated. And we said hello to the Museum, which we now offer to children as well as adults.

"Built three years ago here at Pointe du Bec—a name that was taken from the name with which we baptized the place during my childhood—the Museum of Natural History, which it is my joy to direct, offers you—thanks to its inexhaustible collection of animal footprints, images, skeletons, and accounts of all kinds as well as sound clips—temporary exhibits that have been reconstituted in three dimensions and in the complete sensory environment of the animals of yesterday. With no further ado, I now invite you to go in search of our close cousins the great primates, moving through a series of environments, of games, and of situations that will allow you to come closest to the experience that we had: that of being able to touch and interact with these brother beings, these last separate fruits that came from a common branch of our evolution.

"As you are aware, I knew the great apes personally, and being around them was so important for me that I sincerely wish for you to be able to imagine what it would have been like for us.

"As far as we know, there are no longer chimpanzees, bonobos, gorillas, or orangutans alive today. The unimaginable violence of the process of 're-naturation,' performed on and by populations that were too fragile and too few in number, left the diverse species of the great apes without offspring, and made them victims of famine, mutilation, infanticide, and massive inter- and intraspecies massacres.

"We speak about them only in the past tense.

"And now I will leave you—far from these thoughts that are making my voice break, since I devoted my entire life and my whole heart to them—to take full advantage of the exhibit, of your brief but intense stay on our old Earth, and of its images, these wistful holograms and artifacts that constitute our only surviving memory of what they, the apes, were to us.

"I thank you."

How many times, with a cold, frozen smile, I've repeated these same forced sentences, hoping that the constantly growing number of visitors would allow our museum to survive and justify its existence in the eyes of the other representatives of the Consortium. How many times I've smoothed down the false pleat of my trousers in front of the screen before botching my final bow and returning to close myself up in my large brown and window-paned office, five meters above the beach where I remember swimming so many times, at the very foot of the laboratory of Payne and McVey.

Leaning on my desk, I look at a photo and I think of him.

I saved what could be saved. I saved myself, first of all, and I allowed the Museum to exist, because I would not have been able to live without at least the image, the idea, and the memory of animals.

And then, as I look in vain—through the reinforced smoked window-pane, beyond the barriers and the barbed wire, toward a spread-out ocean under an overly fat sun—for the shadow of a dolphin, for what had once been Bobbie Beamon, or what was once Feng Po-Po, my brief moment of solitude is abruptly over.

Someone is waiting for me.

2.

I'm in the elevator. I can still hear the whirring of the motors of the ship, and I think about the past.

The crash of the *Charles Beagle*, the antique space shuttle that connected the continent with the very first orbital station, was an accident, the consequences of which still make me weep. How many times do I have to swear to myself that I didn't want it to happen, that I did not orchestrate this event with the goal of forcing Michael's reticent hand and of releasing the subject of the experiment into what we commonly call virgin nature (although that expression hardly satisfies me)? Everyone knew that the *Charles Beagle* was in a pitiable state (the tragic accident involving my mother had unfortunately clearly proven this), but the collapse of our finances did not allow us to replace it or even to repair it. Michael was the victim of this slackness, a fact that I recognize. But I don't believe that there was a bomb on board, as some have absurdly suggested. Nor is it the case that Sindhu and Naoki, who survived the accident, sabotaged the ship on my orders. The fact that people at times insinuated this a few years ago, with no proof, still wears down and corrodes my soul.

Nonetheless, I bear responsibility for the crash and for all the misfortune that resulted from it.

Sindhu and Naoki, who escaped the flames, fled by inflatable boat. It is true that they abandoned the others, but how can we reproach them for it? Like them, I also thought the others were dead. As far as we knew, they had definitively perished in the fire: Michael, and also *him*.

3.

I was still a child the first time I saw Doogie, but I was old enough to know what he could be for me: an ally, someone who would be faithful. In a familial situation in which I was not wanted by my mother because I had interrupted her scientific career, but was idolized by my father, I had become the rival of my very young brother—who was cherished by our mother and was the pretext for a provisionary reconciliation with dad. I, the poor little overly intelligent girl, sometimes mannered and precocious, felt that this being who was brought by my father, Gardner Evans, would always be less than a rival, as my brother was, but more than a pet, as most of the animals of our zoo at Victoria Falls essentially were.

I never knew how to attach the right word to what I came to feel for this baby ape, who was at once my companion, my stuffed animal, my child, and my "plaything."

Since he depended entirely on me, this small fragile being, I became a sovereign, as sure of myself as a queen. Without him, I would probably not be me. He progressed, and he did it with and for me, but that wasn't enough. I pushed him, and from that point on the experimental mindset of my father took me over. I could be strict. I tested him, and obviously I manipulated him. But I would hold him sincerely in my arms like the little lost ape that he was, and, in my eyes, remained. I lied to him bold-facedly when I had to, because he needed my affection in order to become something other than what he was. So I never had a guilty conscience, and I can honestly say that I loved him as the special and quite brilliant animal he was, but not in any other way, and he had neither the need nor the desire for me to behave any differently toward him.

There were happy years, when the family and the zoo operated more or less in harmony. It's sometimes said that my father educated this chimpanzee, Doogie, as if he were my brother. I repeat: I had only one brother, Donald, who was my enemy, and Doogie was never anything more than an animal that was raised in our company.

I knew absolutely nothing about the supposed manipulations carried out by my father, Gardner Evans. If he made mistakes, I don't believe that we can put this one on his account. Clearly, Doogie was a talented ape who wandered freely in the house and who was at first my plaything and then a bit more than that. But he wasn't thought of as a human being; that I can guarantee.

When the sickness of my brother occurred, my mother accused my father's ape, who had become mine, of being the cause of the terrible disease that had left him anemic and partially paralyzed.

The atmosphere in our home—which was gradually abandoned by visitors, lab workers, and service personnel—rapidly deteriorated. Mom left for a station of the Consortium in the hopes of getting medical treatment for Donald, who apparently regained his strength while far away from us. On the return flight, however, during the landing, the old *Charles Beagle*, the big vessel that had at one time been armed for the war of the last century, crashed near our property. People accused my father—(and my mother was not the last to do it)—of sabotage, and my parents indulged in a real little war. Today, I understand what my father must have felt, especially since it was he who went out in search of Donald—who had fled the scene of the crash—and it was he who found Donald savagely killed and buried him. He was the one who told us about it. My brother was probably the victim of an escaped big cat who was wandering in the proximity of the zoo, since the surveillance of the cages and storage bays had been considerably reduced. In any case, the death of my brother remains a mystery.

It was starting on that date, so fraught with consequences, that the Animal appeared, a disquieting, menacing figure who destroyed our lives, haunting the jungle and the zoo right up to the home of Payne—who was accidentally killed during one of the experiments at the beach—and that of McVey. I believe today that the Animal was probably only the fruit of the imagination of my father, who was disturbed or even rendered half-crazy by the loss of his son, himself nearly the murderous beast of the legend. It seemed that an enormous, intelligent animal allowed various animals to escape from the zoo and then organized them, gradually encircling our home at night before attacking it.

This was the tragic era of all the conspiracies. I learned by accident that it was my father who had implemented the "replacement" of quite a few animals, which were processed, manipulated, and then abandoned into a kind of false freedom and forced to invent new forms of survival.

The pressure from the animals around the zoo increased, and Doogie lost a bit of his role as Michael became my principal support and my boyfriend.

Poor Doogie. What was he feeling at that time?

My mother died during a night of panic, and I thought that the zoo, having been invaded by our enemies, was lost. It was at this precise moment that Doogie was able to be of service to me. I ordered, in effect, that he be sent, the poor savant ape, as a kind of circus animal, to the orbital stations of the high society that lived up above, with the purpose of offering him to them as a spectacle that would stir up excitement and raise the funds that would allow us to expediently transfer our activities at the zoo to Pointe du Bec, on the seaside, in greater security, in the former house of the now defunct Payne and McVey. The two friends of my father, both idealists and specialists on marine mammals, especially dolphins, had finally become victims of their own protégés, which had become aggressive.

It was on the return flight of the *Charles Beagle* that an unexpected and terrible accident occurred. I had, with some difficulty, completed the first part of our move when I learned of it.

Father, who had gone crazy, had remained on the hilltop of the zoo among the animals, waiting for his Animal as if for death, and I had left in the most complete panic for the barricaded laboratories of Pointe du Bec, where, exhausted and hopeless, I was present for the events that followed.

Doogie, in fact, always wore what I used to call his "watch" on his wrist. Before his departure, I gave him a watchband with a camera inside so that I could follow his actions and gestures, even if only partially and without any possibility of communicating with him. It was a frustrating device, and for a long time I was angry with myself for not having chosen something better.

4.

While I lacked the power to change what happened next, I was at least able to observe it with my own eyes.

At first incredulous, sitting with a cup of bad coffee, my knees under a threadbare checkered blanket, I was seated in front of the old video monitor in the control room at the moment when the little chimpanzee Doogie woke up, and I felt a bit more pride than sadness at seeing him agilely pull himself from the grounded *Charles Beagle* onto an unidentified beach which I supposed was somewhere in the western part of the African continent.

Gradually, the signal became uneven and unclear. At one point, communication seemed to be cut off, and then the watch was recuperated by our former orangutan, who wisely brought it to Doogie, just as in the past he had brought me shiny objects that I threw into the garden to amuse him.

I thus found my little Doogie, after several days of anxiety, not far from the colony of bonobos that my parents had patiently studied. As I was expecting, I was able to observe the gradual animalization he underwent after he had been welcomed into the society of bonobos. It was with a pinching of my heart—perhaps like that of a bad mother—that I felt, in fragments, that what I had given him was eroding, and that what had always been inside him but had taken on a new meaning through the contact with his distant relatives was reappearing.

His departure from the colony of bonobos, and his violent fights with chimpanzees of his own species, completed the process. Alone, and left to his own survival instincts, Doogie rediscovered violence, as well as the use of the sounds, signs, postures, and attitudes that had been flowing through his blood without ever having taken form in his brain, his mind, and his representations.

The ethologist in me was intellectually satisfied by the logic of these facts, but the educator that I also was felt devastated.

Badly dressed, then completely undressed and walking on all fours, a rogue chimpanzee, Doogie found himself absorbed by the jungle that was rising to the surface of his being, and I was certain that he had completely forgotten me.

Stupid person that I am, I began to cry. I had lost! I saw him intermittently falling into unconsciousness, and out of necessity using only the gestures that are specific to chimpanzees when they are in the presence of other chimpanzees and feeling angry and nervous. I remembered the first time we met. I was a little girl, and he was just a little stuffed animal.

I don't know if there was an accident or a sudden brawl, or if the watch simply broke down, but the signal ended. The screen stayed black, and I remained in darkness, the notebook filled with notes between my hands, and exhausted from having experienced, as if along with him, what I had at no moment actually shared with him, horrible voyeur that I was.

By forcing him to climb higher than himself on a ladder that was actually mine, I had condemned him to plummet lower than himself.

He had lost everything that he had previously gained. What, in my view, remained inside Doogie in the end? Was it the depths of his natural being? Perhaps. There was not much there, and certainly less than what he really was, or what he should have been.

Would I say that I was unhappy with the results, or that he had disappointed me? No, poor Doogie. It was *my* fault, and I know what he truly was: a being who was tricked, educated, and then abandoned, and who had fallen.

I put the cassettes and the notebook in the wooden chest, which I carefully locked. I grieved for this experiment, and then I forgot all about it.

5.

Several years later, after having met my husband, and after the birth of my two daughters, I was inspecting the state of our building site at Pointe du Bec.

It's a country of gray and pink stones, a place of strong winds, and only a tiny boat with a triangular sail, which was putting markers and mines on the underwater barrier with the help of divers, was slicing across the blue-and-white horizon. I was happy, holding my older daughter in my arms while the younger one remained asleep in her stroller. At the moment—I remember it well—when a young engineer was explaining to me where and how to reinforce the foundations of the house so that it could support the extra floor that would connect it to the main building, my husband, at the other end of the property, suddenly became agitated and began making large gestures with his arms, like a crazy, incomprehensible semaphore. Anxiously, I left my nervous daughter in the care of the amazed engineer in his yellow helmet, and then, wearing pirate pants and holding against my neck the little red scarf that had been given to me by a patron of my husband, I crossed the dune that was covered with tufts of dry, gray and green vegetation, like bandages on a skin disease, under the blast of the ocean breeze, advancing gradually toward the bulge that surrounded and very fortunately protected the site during its reconstruction. On the other side of the pink and then lemon-yellow dune, at the edge of the flat and dreary desert, I saw my husband and a soldier, who it appeared didn't know what to do with their hands over a black spot that seemed to be embedded in sand that appeared from a distance to be dirty.

Because the overly white and overly round sun was blinding me, despite my sunglasses, I wondered for a minute what this sack with a slumped black back was, and what it contained. I even thought it might be a bomb . . . At last, I could see, at the feet of my dear husband, who was crying out several repeated and incomprehensible words, and those of the soldier, who was tapping the inert object with the end of his bayonet, a mass of unkempt hair.

An intuition, a premonition, took hold of me. I knew that it was him. I yelled to the soldier with all the strength of my lungs to move away and leave the body of this ape, this body of Doogie, in peace.

I said a few words to my husband, who brushed my shoulder and went back to reassure the soldier. I squatted down and touched the immobile, thin, unrecognizable, scarred body of Doogie, and then I cautiously pulled back. I bit my bottom lip when I discovered, curled beneath him, an arm that no longer had a hand, a gray and pinkish stump, and another no doubt amputated limb with its bruised flesh.

And when I saw his face . . .

My God, I will not describe it. Clearly sick, tortured, and destroyed, he no longer *had* a face.

I put my hands on him, and I recognized him. I was about to say something to this body when, gently feeling the base of his neck with my three fingers, I felt the slight outflow of his blood, and I knew that he was alive.

I immediately asked for the doctor to be brought, and I demanded that he be taken into the house.

My husband looked at the ape, then at my bewildered face, and he agreed, even though I don't think he understood.

6.

On certain evenings, when my husband is away and my daughters are with him, I turn off the lamp on the desk in my bedroom, I close my notebooks, I put the cap on my pen, and I take the staircase down from floor to floor to the bottom level, the "garage."

After having entered the secret code, which I now easily remember, on the numeric keypad to the right of the shuttered door, and without ever turning on the ceiling lights, I enter the large, deserted storage area, with walls whose color I guess to be light gray with an oily, glossy appearance, as my slippers squeak on the concrete that is covered with a badly glued linoleum that sometimes comes off. The vague glow of the corridor no longer allows me to adjust my eyes to the space of the subterranean storage area, with no moving crates or vintage cars, and to the small shelter, behind the silent pipes, where, in the semi-darkness, a cage stands.

He cannot tolerate light anymore—either daylight or artificial light—and he lives, or rather subsists, curled up, his bottom half on a banana leaf that I change regularly and his top half on a little, old, dusty pillow. His lower back remains glued to the concrete wall at the far end of the cage, the three other sides of which were grilled on the insistence of my husband and with my reluctant agreement. Hours and days go by, and he never sees them. There is a soldier who is sworn to secrecy and who brings him, as discreetly as possible, his food and his medicine—dozens of painkillers and tranquilizers—passing them through the opening, like a cat-door with metal lattices, in the front of the cage, facing which I am now squatting. Is he asleep, and does he dream? How would I know? He breathes, with difficulty, through his blocked nostrils and his destroyed mouth, and I watch him. My God, I watch him for a long time.

At first, he stays where he is, without opening his only eye, its eyelid traversed by a terrible scar, the scar of another age, and I can make out under his threadbare hair the shape of the broken body of the old chimpanzee.

Then I whisper. I start to speak, and I say the words to him like before. Softly, I speak the words of his childhood, and of mine. I laugh, I smile, and I talk about his games, his pine bed, his bedroom, and our walks. I adopt the tone of the schoolteacher I once was, and I describe his cubes, the classroom, and all those years.

I know that he never reacts. But I like to speak, without saying much of anything, to let the voice of my past and his past resonate in the dark and cool garage, where even the echo seems to be suffocated.

I know that despite the words and the sentences he had learned and repeated, Doogie had never really *spoken*, and I never completely understood him. He spoke gibberish, he signed, he became agitated. He liked me: I'm sure of that. What did he have in his head, the poor chimpanzee? If I could open his skull, his heart, and his memories, what would I find there? Probably nothing, or what for me would be only the hollow appearance of something. But for him . . . ?

I contemplate his ravaged face, which is distant and almost invisible. I look at his hands, which are no longer there, and I hold out mine while murmuring with an infinite sympathy: "Hey, little monkey!" He never liked it when I called him *ape*. His first childhood language was made up of simple words, so I still sign when I greet him.

Sometimes, I recall, I used to be unsettled by spending time with him, to the point of wondering whether he believed that he could really speak and that I understood him perfectly, while in fact there were never more than fragments of proto-syntax and ready-made expressions, which were designed for his computer screen and could be presented to the rich suckers—the people from up above—as the instantaneous translation of what he was thinking. It was obvious to us that aside from the profound interactions that connected us there was no real and specific language that he had mastered and could fully express. But it seemed to me, holding him close, seeing him constantly gesticulating with his hand, that despite his mutism and his simian deafness to humanity he was convinced that he was really communicating.

I understand the nature of the illusion I was prey to, and it still sometimes blinds me today when I see him. It's as if I read in him a story that he could not tell me and that never existed, but that I nevertheless persuade myself of vaguely glimpsing when I observe him for too long. He was a little bit my baby, and to a large extent my plaything. Did I perhaps do him an injury? How can I know, and how can I forgive myself? It's stupid. I know that I'm an idiot to tell myself stories while holding out my arms to him.

Because those stories don't exist. The jungle definitively swallowed my ape, and the jungle has no memory.

I wait another moment—I know that he has no one other than me—and then I retie my braid while biting my lip. I think that I'm an imbecile, but I do it nonetheless: through the bars, I sign to this poor, black, half-crazed mass, who doesn't move, his shoulders pulled in, his head lowered. I make the sign of the tickle and the cuddle, and I tell him, "come."

Then, cautiously, I open the door of the cage, slowly turning the key in the rusted keyhole, and I advance toward him on all fours. I hold out the palm of my hand, I twist my neck to see if I can find his gaze below me, and since I don't see anything, I speak without stopping, in a very low voice. "Poor little monkey, what a good ape you were. Janet loves you, you know." I don't know why, but it seems that I owe him at least that.

And slowly, rubbing his buttocks against the pillow and the banana leaf, a muffled, rough sound coming from his breath as if his throat was closed, he barely pushes his chest forward and lightly rocks, his stumps still glued to the hollow of his stomach, leaning forward and backward like a strange child. Then he lowers the nape of his neck and offers it to me, along with his upper back, which is clean, having been washed by the personnel of the certified service, and slightly perfumed.

Then I hold out my fingers, I bury them in what is left of his hair, and for a long time, for a very long time, I stroke him while he rocks insensibly. And when I do it again while massaging his warm skin, which never shivers but which relaxes and becomes peaceful, I sense it. "Oh, my poor Doogie, my poor monkey. You're just a Doogie, you're just a monkey. Everything is too big for you, you've done everything right, and Janet loves you so very much, little ape. Shh, be calm, be peaceful, Janet is here." And he barely grunts, neither asleep nor awake. He's like a faithful old dog, I tell myself while tearing up. "Shh!" I whisper again. "Poor ape, good ape that you are, in the dark forever, I'm here. Everything's all right, and everything will be all right."

At times, perhaps, he barely opens his one eye while letting himself be stroked, and who knows what he's thinking about if he still can think. Today, squatting down near him in almost total darkness, I have no idea what might still resonate from our language, from my language, in the soon-to-be-condemned room of his brain, just as in the closed-off minds of all our animals.

I rub his neck as if searching for the lice that the shampoo has always kept from his fur, and, without knowing exactly how, as he moans imperceptibly, I am very fleetingly sure that he is happy in my hands, that his whole life is being pacified in this way, and that, through my palm, my fingers, his skin, and my mouth, he hears me and is restful and content.

"You have nothing more to prove," I tell him. "The experiment is over."

With complete trust, he offers—he who has always served me and by whom I have always been served—he unreservedly offers me his neck while moaning weakly, and I hold him tightly in my arms while giving him the only recompense that his little and too uncertain life could ever find: the never-ending embrace of my two arms.

THE END

www.ingramcontent.com/pod-product-compliance
Lightning Source LLC
Chambersburg PA
CBHW030235250325
24024CB00002B/102